W9-BZQ-301

UNWELCOME VISITORS

"Relax, Eugenio," the seated man said in a soft voice. "Your wife and daughter are fine. For now."

Eugene started to move forward but two guns appeared, Glock A-17's, one in the right hand of each man leaning against his counter. Eugene stopped. "Where is my wife?" His words were like acid.

"Sit down, Eugenio. Threatening me isn't going to help your situation."

Eugene glanced at the guns, and sat at the table, opposite the man. "Who are you?" he asked.

The man smiled. "Now that's a question I *can* answer. My name is Javier Rastano. I'm from Medellín. It's a city in southern Colombia, in case you're not familiar with it."

"I know where Medellín is," Eugene said. "But I don't understand why you're here."

"You are related to the Escobar clan, who, at one time, lived in Medellín. One of your cousins was Pablo Escobar."

"Pablo is dead. He died a violent death years ago."

"Did he?" Javier asked, amused. "We have reason to believe that your cousin isn't as dead as he would like the world to believe. In fact, we're sure he's alive…"

BLOODLINE

JEFF BUICK

LEISURE BOOKS NEW YORK CITY

To Teresa Buick.
My love. My angel. Forever in my heart.

A LEISURE BOOK®

February 2005

Published by

Dorchester Publishing Co., Inc.
200 Madison Avenue
New York, NY 10016

If you purchased this book without a cover you should be aware that this book is stolen property. It was reported as "unsold and destroyed" to the publisher and neither the author nor the publisher has received any payment for this "stripped book."

Copyright © 2005 by Jeff Buick

All rights reserved. No part of this book may be reproduced or transmitted in any form or by any electronic or mechanical means, including photocopying, recording or by any information storage and retrieval system, without the written permission of the publisher, except where permitted by law.

ISBN 0-8439-5515-5

The name "Leisure Books" and the stylized "L" with design are trademarks of Dorchester Publishing Co., Inc.

Printed in the United States of America.

Visit us on the web at www.dorchesterpub.com.

BLOODLINE

Prologue

December 1993

It was a quiet street, with rows of two-story stucco houses lining the narrow strip of pitted asphalt. A thin sidewalk, chipped and gouged from the impact of thousands of tire rims and undercarriages, bordered one side. On the other was a narrow strip of grass with a handful of short, sickly palm trees. The buildings were in disrepair, and in many places chunks of mortar and stucco had fallen to the street below. A handful of decrepit cars were parked at uneven intervals. A group of young boys played marbles on cracked concrete.

A white panel van pulled onto the street and cruised slowly past the kids. A pregnant woman glanced at the darkened windows as the van rolled by. The passenger window was open a crack and she saw a pair of eyes scanning the buildings. Dark eyes. Dangerous eyes. She looked away in fear. Even quiet streets in the Colombian

city of Medellín were not to be trusted. The van continued, pausing only once for a brief second as it passed one
of the houses, then disappeared around the corner. Inside the vehicle, one man was talking in rapid Spanish.

"It was him," he said, unable to control his excitement.
"I know it was him."

"Are you sure?" the driver asked. "You only saw him for
a split second."

The passenger grabbed a cell phone from the seat and
nodded vigorously as he dialed. "It's Escobar. Even with
the beard, I know that face." The line connected and he
spoke quickly into the phone. "We've spotted Pablo Escobar. We have a precise location on him."

"Give us the location," said the strong voice on the
other end of the line. It belonged to Col. Hugo Martinez,
the head of Search Bloc, the often covert arm of the
Colombian government put in place to remove the drug
lords from Medellín and Cali. "Our ETA is ten minutes.
Don't lose him." The line went dead.

"Pull up here," the passenger said, pointing to an opening against the curb. He slipped a revolver from his waistband and snapped off the safety. "Let's go."

The two men leapt from the car and jogged back to the
corner, slowing as they approached the intersection. The
passenger said, "He's on the second floor, fourth house
on the opposite side of the street." His name was Manuel
Sanchez, and for the past sixteen months he had searched
the dirty and dangerous streets of Medellín for the richest
and most ruthless drug lord in the world. Now they had
him. Pablo Escobar was less than fifty yards from where
they stood. Sanchez ran his finger down the gun barrel
and gave his partner a knowing look. "This is it, Enrico.
This is the moment we've been waiting for. We cannot let
him escape." He paused for a second, planning the attack. "I'll take the back of the house. You wait here and
cover the front. No one leaves that house alive."

"They're dead men, Manuel." The words were tough, but the voice was scared.

Sanchez patted his partner on the shoulder and was gone. He walked across the intersection, holding the gun at his side in his left hand. He kept his gait as normal as possible, out of view of the second floor window where Escobar had been only minutes before. Was it Escobar? Was it really the elusive drug dealer? Yes, he was sure. It was him. Manuel's pulse was lightning quick, his breathing shallow. He felt exposed, and thought that if Pablo glanced out that window, the *narco* would instinctively know he was a cop. And then he would be dead. But running was out of the question; it would give away the advantage of surprise. He had to walk at a normal pace across the intersection. And risk his life yet again.

Manuel reached the building on the far side and ducked in behind the wall. The stucco felt rough on his back, even through his shirt. He looked down and took another deep breath. He had forgotten to strap on his Kevlar vest. Christ, of all the times to screw up. If he lived through this it would be a miracle. A couple of cleansing breaths to slow his pulse and he moved to the narrow walkway behind the row of buildings. A dirty street urchin in a ripped T-shirt watched him with disinterested eyes as he took a quick glance around the corner. He could see the back of the house, but the midday sun glinting off the second-floor windows made it impossible to know whether anyone was looking his way from behind the glass. He checked his revolver again, saw the bullets in the cylinder and felt a surge of confidence. One more deep breath and he moved into harm's way, crouching low and driving hard with his legs. It didn't matter if Escobar saw him walking or running now; he knew the drug lord would be firing at him.

Nothing.

Manuel reached the stone wall between the target house and the walkway and hugged it for safety. He was breathing hard now, his adrenaline pumping through his veins like never before in his life. So close. So long to find him, now so close. How many men had died chasing false leads? How many millions of dollars had been spent in the pursuit of this one man? He had lost track, but the figures were staggering. He slipped his cell phone from his pocket and hit redial. Martinez answered.

"How long until you get here?" Manuel whispered.

"Two, maybe three minutes."

"No sirens, come in quiet," Manuel said. "There's no sign he knows we're onto him."

"Roger that. Good work, Manuel. Hang on, we're almost there."

Manuel closed the phone and powered it off. An incoming call could alert Escobar. He stayed low against the wall, the afternoon sun baking the narrow alley and turning it into a furnace. Sweat trickled down his forehead and he wiped it away with his free hand. He was shaking almost uncontrollably. He breathed deeply, trying to calm himself and bring his heartbeat down so he could shoot accurately. He checked his watch. Martinez was a minute, maybe two, out. He decided to risk a quick look over the wall.

He raised his head above the rounded stucco edge. Nothing but silence greeted him. The building was a two-story adobe, attached on both sides to the adjoining buildings. The main floor was slightly larger than the upper, and a sloping tiled roof ran under a large second-floor window. There was no balcony or verandah. If Escobar came out the back, it would be through the window. From his vantage point Manuel knew he had a shot; not a great one, but he'd have to work with what he had.

Then it happened. Manuel heard a series of loud thuds as Martinez and his men used a battering ram on the heavy metal door at the front of the house. No more stealth now. He raised his head and shoulders above the wall and took aim on the window with his revolver. Seconds later the glass shattered and a chair flew into the yard. A figure kicked at the remaining shards of glass, then leapt from the window onto the tiled roof directly below. Manuel recognized him. It was Limón Alvero de Jesus, Escobar's personal bodyguard. He resisted the urge to fire and waited for the next figure. The man himself.

Escobar appeared in the window for a brief second, then jumped to the tiles below. Manuel waited until Escobar landed, then squeezed the trigger. The Smith & Wesson barked and sharp pieces of stucco flew about only an inch or two from Escobar's head. He fired again, but Escobar was already moving and the bullets smacked harmlessly into the pale stucco behind him.

Manuel briefly caught a glimpse of Limón sighting on him, then the wall in front of his face exploded and slivers of stucco slammed into his forehead and scalp. The pain was excruciating. Blood poured from the wounds, but he jumped up and lowered his gun at the running figures.

He pumped round after round at them, but they were moving too quickly and the shots missed. The hammer clicked on an empty chamber. He swore as he reached for his belt and another cylinder of live cartridges. Then, when it looked like the two men might escape, Limón jerked violently and fell face first to the ground, unmoving. A few seconds later, Escobar took three slugs in quick succession. The first one shattered his femur, the second cut through his chest cavity and the third smashed squarely into his skull. He dropped straight down, his body falling hard on a pile of cinder blocks and tiles. Blood pooled under the body and small rivulets ran off the broken tiles onto the parched earth.

Manuel glanced quickly around. He saw movement on the roof behind him, then the figure was gone. But the image stayed. American. CIA. He knew the face. Christ, the Americans had been monitoring the Search Bloc cell phones and had moved in and covered the rear of the house before Martinez could get his men in place. Thank God they had been in position.

He jumped from behind the wall, wiping the blood from his eyes as he ran to the prone figures. With his revolver pointed directly at Limón's head, he kicked the corpse. Nothing. He lodged his toe under Limón's shoulder and lifted. The body rolled over, dead eyes staring at the midday sun. Manuel glanced up at the window where police and Search Bloc members, guns in hand, watched his progress. He approached the second body with caution, the Smith & Wesson leveled and his finger on the trigger. Just as he reached the body, a sound from behind startled him. He turned and saw Col. Martinez entering the yard from the alley. The crunching of broken tiles underfoot was the only sound as Martinez walked quickly to where Manuel hovered over the body. Together, with their guns at the ready, they rolled over the corpse.

It was Pablo Escobar.

Martinez stared at the dead man for a few seconds, then turned to Sanchez and quietly said, "You did it, Manuel. You found our needle in the haystack. You are a true Colombian hero."

He swiveled about and raised his arms above his head, smiling to the men staring down from the second-floor window.

"Pablo Escobar is dead," he yelled.

The men erupted into cheers, slapped each other on the shoulders and shook hands. Each wore a smile. The devil was dead. The nightmare of looking for one man among millions while suffering daily reprisals from Escobar's death squads was over. Some semblance of normalcy could now return to the streets of Medellín. The men dispersed as the coroner arrived to remove the bodies and transport them to the morgue. Martinez and his crew headed to their office to fill out the paperwork, but today they didn't mind. They would stop at the local tavern later and drink beer. This was a great day.

Unnoticed amid the commotion, an older Mercedes with tinted rear windows was parked a block to the north. From there the two occupants had an unobstructed view of the house where Escobar had hidden. The two men watched the bodies being removed. The coroner slammed the rear doors shut and left the street, followed by a bevy of police and army vehicles. Only then did the man in the rear of the Mercedes tap the driver on the shoulder. The car pulled away from the curb and turned the corner, disappearing into the congestion and chaos of Medellín.

The figure in the back seat bore a striking resemblance to Pablo Escobar.

Chapter One

The Present

The fishing boats began arriving in port just before dawn. The night sky was clear, and the fish were running shallow. Most of the small wooden craft were awash in fresh catch. A six-kilo tuna sat next to a dark-skinned, weather-beaten fisherman, and he held it aloft as his partner threw out the anchor. The first tuna of the season. Soon there would be more. The wives and children who waited for the return of the boats cheered when they saw the steel-colored fish. Tuna meant money, and when the big fish were running the nets were full.

Eugene Escobar watched the scene from the deck of his dive boat, a scene that played out every day of the year. He knew many of the fishermen by name. His children had played with their children years ago, before they reached their teens and stopped playing the simple games of young children. Now it was girlfriends and boyfriends.

Eugene didn't like them fishing the waters off Los Frailles, it depleted the coves and inlets of the fish his diving clients paid money to see, but without the fish the simple Venezuelan men of Isla de Margarita would have no income. And men without money were dangerous. In South America, if you couldn't buy food and clothes for your family you stole them. Or robbed someone with a fat wallet.

He watched the men anchor the time-worn boats and ferry their catch ashore in ratty wicker baskets. A fuss was made over the tuna, but soon it would be commonplace. The fisherman who had netted the tuna held his prize out for all to see and admire. Eugene wished the fish were still alive and free, cutting through the Caribbean waters between Margarita and the Venezuelan mainland. But it wasn't so. He glanced toward the row of pasty stucco buildings bordering the beach as a red Nissan truck pulled off the road and bounced down the steep incline to the hard sand. Eduardo, the dive company owner, was here with the divers and air tanks. He hoisted himself off the gunwale and jumped overboard, the salt water cool on his legs. The top of the sun crested the eastern horizon as Eduardo stopped the Nissan and stepped onto the beach.

"*Buenos dias,* Eugene," he said, walking to the box of the truck and lifting out the first of many compressed air tanks.

"Eduardo," Eugene said, then turned and spoke in rapid Spanish to an overweight man leaning against a post watching the sun rise from the gently rolling water. The man rose, hooked his fingers under the valves atop two of the tanks and headed for the boat. A moment later, a young man of perhaps twenty appeared and asked Eugene if he could help load the boat. "Five hundred bolivars," Eugene said. "And that includes helping the divers with their gear."

"*Sí, señor.*" He grabbed two tanks and headed for the boat.

Eduardo returned from dropping the tanks at the water's edge and Eugene asked, "Who am I taking out today?"

"Three Germans," Eduardo said. "Two dives, then home. You'll be back just after noon."

"They speak any Spanish?"

Eduardo shook his head. "English."

"They all certified divers?" Eugene asked and Eduardo nodded.

"Yeah, but double-check their C-cards before you gear up," the owner of the dive company said. "I had a quick look this morning, but it was dark."

"Okay." Eugene smiled at the two men and one woman as they passed him, headed for the boat.

The sun was well above the horizon when Larry, the overweight boat pilot, started the engines and signaled to Eugene to pull up the anchor. They weaved through the fishing boats, now bobbing on their anchors in the harbor, and headed for open water. The ocean was relatively calm, and the sky was still clear. It promised to be a good day. Eugene waited until they were clear of the harbor, then introduced himself to the Germans.

"I'm Eugenio, but everybody calls me Eugene," he said in English. "Welcome to Venezuela and Isla de Margarita. Your first time to our island?"

He got to know the group a bit as the converted fishing boat rolled up one side of the waves, then slid down into the troughs. Even four-foot seas could be unsettling in a small wooden boat, but the Germans seemed okay with the motion. The trip to Los Frailles, a group of seven uninhabited islands off Margarita's east coast, was about forty-five minutes. Eugene took the time to explain the different sites they would be diving.

"We'll dive Penâ first. It's a deep dive, about a hundred and ten feet. Visibility today should be forty to fifty feet.

There's a bit of a drift, so keep with me. Remember, when I knock my index fingers together like this," he said, holding out his hands with his two index fingers extended and touching them together a few times, "I want you to stay close to your buddy. Visibility and currents can change quite quickly down there. This is a good dive to see big stuff, like groupers, and maybe even barracuda. But keep in mind that barracuda are dangerous. They won't think twice about attacking you if they feel threatened. Don't approach them, let them come to you. If they open their mouths as they swim past, think of that as the same as a rattlesnake shaking its tail. They're warning you. Barracuda are far more dangerous than sharks."

They neared the dive site and Eugene watched the divers ready themselves and their gear. Two of the three were proficient with their regulators and slid their buoyancy control devices over the air tanks and easily attached their first stages to the tanks. The third diver, a tall blond man named Hans, was all thumbs. He set his tank in the BCD backwards and fit his second stage so it was coming over his left shoulder. Eugene moved up in the swaying boat and stopped the man.

"Scuba is a right-hand sport," he said, removing the straps on the tank and spinning it around so the mouthpiece was accessible over the right side of the BCD. He checked the pressure on the first stage and opened the valve. The pressure was dead on at 3000 psi. "Okay, guys, I have to check your certification cards before we dive. Standard procedure."

All three dug out their cards. Eugene glanced at the two belonging to the competent divers, but looked closely at Hans's. The picture matched. He handed it back. "I'll buddy up with you, Hans," he said, still wary of the man's abilities. Larry had the boat in position, and they finished suiting up. They rolled gently in the protected waters just off Los Frailles, perhaps two hundred yards from shore.

One by one they dropped backwards off the edge of the boat into the water, Eugene going in last. Hans was already descending when Eugene entered the water. The German seemed more under control now, equalizing the pressure in his ears every few feet as he floated down through the light green water. *Maybe I was wrong,* Eugene thought.

They reached the bottom and checked their depth gauges. One hundred and twelve feet. Eugene gave the okay sign. All three returned it. He pointed to the north, and they started kicking their fins and moving slowly in that direction. The sea life was abundant even beneath a hundred feet of water. A few grunts swam past, then a couple of creole and some yellowhead snappers. An occasional sea snake slithered across the ocean floor and Eugene caught one, holding it for the other divers to feel. He released it and moved on toward a sheer wall to their left. It rose at least seventy feet from the seabed, the entire wall a living reef of urchins and coral. The colors were slightly muted at this depth; the sunlight had trouble penetrating through a hundred feet of water. Eugene found an eel and all four divers hovered near the tiny hole in the wall staring at the eel's open mouth as it protected its home. When they turned back to the open ocean, they saw the barracuda.

An entire school of the deadly fish was only feet from them, trapping them against the wall. Eugene motioned to the Germans to stay calm, that the fish would swim past and leave them alone if they didn't panic. Too late. Hans was sucking air too fast and that gave him positive buoyancy. He started to rise, then made a crucial mistake. He pumped air into his buoyancy control device. The air entering the bladder made him even more buoyant, and he began to rise quickly. Eugene had a split second to react. He motioned to the other two divers to stay together and to surface. Then he pumped air into his own BCD, and shot up at an alarming pace, passing eighty feet, then seventy, then sixty. Hans was just ahead of him, but Eugene could see no bubbles. The man was holding his breath. Eugene had only a couple more seconds before Hans would be critically injured. Or dead.

Eugene knew that air at one hundred feet is compressed to one quarter its volume at the surface, and that when a diver rises, the air expands. The shallower the diver gets, the faster it expands. The air in Hans's BCD was expanding, and the German was going to the surface fast. Too fast. Without a slow ascent and a safety stop at fifteen feet to release the nitrogen in his body, he would get the bends. And the nearest decompression chamber was in Guatemala. Total disaster. But worse, if the German was holding his breath, the air in his lungs would expand until his lungs burst. Worse than disaster. Death.

Eugene had one shot at the German. If he missed, he'd have to break off and stop his ascent, or pay the price of decompression sickness himself. He grabbed Hans's ankle, his grip a vise on the man's leg. Then he released the air from his own BCD and grabbed a handhold in the wall. It stopped their ascent. But the air in the German's BCD was pulling toward the surface and Eugene was losing his grip on the coral. Hans was no help. He was panicking, thrashing about like a trapped fish. Eugene kicked off his left flipper and rammed his foot in another break in the reef. Then he released his handhold, pulled his knife from its sheath and rammed the blade into the German's BCD. The air poured out and Eugene felt the upward tug subside as their buoyancy returned to neutral. He tried to pull the man down to his level, but a sudden surge of pain shot through his body. He'd felt it before and he knew the cause. Grabbing the diver's leg and stopping their ascent had dislocated his shoulder.

Without releasing the panicked diver, he made a controlled ascent, stopped for the safety break at fifteen feet, then broke the surface. Larry leaned over the gunwale the second they appeared and helped pull them out of the water. They flopped into the boat and Eugene sat gingerly against the gunwale. He spoke to Larry in Spanish, and then the pilot took Eugene's arm and lifted it over top of the motor. Eugene steadied his ribcage against the side of the motor and nodded. Larry gave his arm a sharp tug and the bone popped back into its socket.

"Mother of God," Eugene screamed as it popped. He slowly rotated his arm, then let it drop to his side. "What the hell were you doing down there?" he said to Hans. The German didn't answer him and Eugene leaned forward. "I've never met a certified diver who would do something that stupid. No one fills their BCD, then holds his breath on the way up. Where did you get that C-card?"

Hans took a couple of deep breaths, then said, "It's not mine. It's my twin brother's."

"And you've never dived before?" Eugene asked.

"No."

"Christ Almighty," Eugene said. He ran his hand across his forehead and pushed his hair back out of his eyes. "Larry, get us back to Margarita. We're finished for today."

Julie Escobar heard the Vespa and glanced out the window of her modest bungalow. Her husband was home. She leaned on the kitchen sink and watched him hoist his scuba gear from the box over the rear tire, the muscles in his arms and chest rippling from the exertion. His shoulders were broad and well defined, his hands calloused and rough. He was brown, but from the sun, not his heritage. She knew his parents well. His father had enjoyed a long and auspicious career as a plastic surgeon in Caracas, and his mother dedicated her life to the children. They were of European descent and tended to fair skin and light-colored hair. Eugene had inherited their genes and was often mistaken for a *gringo* rather than a native Colombian. He had also inherited his father's handsome facial features and curly hair. He finished unloading the gear and entered the house.

"You're home early," she said, wrapping her slender arms about his waist. Julie Escobar was an attractive woman, with fair skin and brown hair that fell past her slight shoulders. Her nose and cheeks were dotted with a few freckles, and her eyes sparkled with mischief. She was tall for a woman and he only of average height, so they looked eye to eye. He smiled and she saw his even white teeth appear from behind lips dried from salt water.

"Slight problem with one of the divers; he wasn't certified. We headed back for Margarita after the first dive." He kissed her on the lips, then broke away and pulled open the fridge, removing a bottle of water and spinning off the cap. "Idiot almost got himself killed." He tipped his head back and drank from the bottle.

"What happened?" she asked. He steered her to the couch and told her the story. She gingerly rubbed his shoulder when he came to the part where Larry had pulled his bone back into the socket. "That must have hurt," she said.

"Oh, yeah. It hurt like a son-of-a-bitch. But Larry did a good job yanking on it."

They both glanced up as the door opened and a teenage girl entered. She was dressed in tight jeans and a short top. Her skin was light, like her parents', and her hair between blond and light brunette. She had inherited her dad's blue eyes and warm smile. Her straight, white teeth had never needed braces. She grinned when she saw her parents sitting close to each other on the couch.

"You guys look like a couple of teenagers getting ready to kiss."

"And how would *you* know about that?" her mother asked.

"Get a grip, Mother," the daughter said, one hand on her hip. "I'm almost sixteen."

"How was school, Shiara?" Eugene asked, changing the subject before mother and daughter got going on what was acceptable for a mature fifteen-year-old.

"Good, Dad," she said, leaning over and giving both her parents a kiss on the cheek. "We're studying American history in social studies class. It's interesting." She opened the fridge and pulled out a mango. "A lot of people died in their civil war."

Eugene's smile faded. "People die in wars, honey. All wars, not just the American ones."

"I know, Dad," she said lightly, then scampered back out the front door. Eugene caught a glimpse of a teenage boy on a bicycle near the fence, and then the door slammed behind his daughter.

He relaxed back into the couch. "How was your day? Kids behave themselves?" It was Friday just before Carnival was to start and classes were over at noon. An early day for the kids and the teachers.

Julie laughed. "They're young, Eugene. They're too full of energy to behave themselves. Remember back to when you were ten years old. Were you good all day long in school?"

"No. But I never had such a beautiful teacher as you," he said.

"They're too young to think of me as beautiful or ugly. They just see me as nice or mean."

"And today you were . . . ?"

"Nice."

Eugene grinned. "Are you still nice?"

It was Julie's turn to grin. "I think so. Want to find out?"

"Oh, yeah." He followed her from the living room, a smile on his parched lips.

Chapter Two

A bank of clouds skirted the cordillera and slid down the Cauca valley, bringing cooler temperatures and the threat of rain to Medellín. Pedestrians walked a little quicker, wanting to be indoors before the weather turned brisk. Palms swayed as the breeze ruffled their fronds, and the air was charged with static electricity. A storm was brewing.

A black 740i BMW pulled up to the curb on Calle 52 and a well-dressed man in his mid-twenties jumped from the passenger seat and strode quickly through the gates of the Joaquín Antonio Uribe gardens. He branched off the main path and headed for the far side of the lake, where water lilies punctuated the crystal waters and rare orchids lined the pathway. He approached a man sitting on a bench beside the lake. Few people were in the park, and the setting was tranquil.

"Javier?" the young man said quietly, as if simply speaking could incur the man's wrath.

The seated man turned and glanced at the newcomer. Javier Rastano was casually dressed in designer jeans and a Polo golf shirt. He wore sandals with no socks and no jewelry save a thin gold chain with a tiny pendant around his neck. He was thirty-six, but looked closer to thirty. He kept himself in excellent physical condition and his tanned skin still stretched tight over his facial bones. His eyes were deep brown, his hair jet-black and swept back from his face, falling halfway down his neck. When he spoke, his voice was deep, but soft.

"Yes? What is it?"

"Your father has requested a visit," the young man said.

"Now?"

"Yes, sir. Now. I have a car waiting."

"Very well," Javier said, reluctantly lifting himself off the park bench. "Bad timing, Julian. It's always the most beautiful here just before it rains."

Javier followed the messenger to the exit and slid in the back seat of the car. Julian got in the front passenger seat, and the driver pulled away from the curb. Javier knew where they were going—his father's house in the upscale subdivision of El Poblado along the southern edge of the city. Morro El Salvador, the southernmost of the three hills inside the Aburrá valley, rose above the congestion of small houses and busy streets, its crest obscured by the increasingly thick clouds. The first few drops of rain splattered on the windshield. Javier turned his gaze from the window and let his mind drift to what his father might want.

Mario Rastano was a successful businessman in Medellín, one of the new breed of entrepreneurs who had invested heavily in the city after the downfall of the notorious *narcos* of the eighties and early nineties. Javier managed three of his father's nightclubs and oversaw day-to-day operations of the six fitness centers in and about Medellín. He liked horses, and spent considerable time at the equestrian facility his father had built some five kilometers south of El Poblado. Javier's handsome face was well known in the city's best restaurants and clubs, and he was often touted as the most eligible bachelor in Medellín. Being his father's son was not a great burden.

But shadows obscured the origins of the money that had built the nightclubs, the fitness centers and the other thriving business ventures that were part of the Rastano business empire. Prior to establishing themselves as one of Medellín's premier families, Mario Rastano had often been linked to the drug cartel and, most notably, to Pablo Escobar and Carlos Lehder. Mario Rastano's association with the kingpins of the Medellín drug cartel was common knowledge, but time had eroded the ties, and with his new image as a major benefactor to the prosperous city, the government turned a blind eye to his past. As did his neighbors, many of whom were judges and politicians. Mario Rastano and his son were legitimate business leaders who paid taxes and donated their money and time to charity. And that was the way things were.

Javier returned his gaze to the passing scenery as they entered El Poblado. Shiny glass and steel buildings towered over parking lots filled with Mercedes and Jaguar convertibles. Rows of royal palms lined the access roads to the buildings that housed the South American headquarters of many global companies, and shaded the pedestrians that sported Armani and Gucci outfits and accessories. The BMW passed an embossed sign that read *Century Capitol*, the flagship of the Rastano financial empire. The four-story building was surrounded by palms and water and tucked back from the main road. The parking lot out front was filled with employees' cars. People hired to administer the Rastano fortune. Javier couldn't resist a slight smile as the building disappeared behind a bend in the road. He liked being his father's son.

The building complexes dwindled, and residential

apartments and condos took over. Main Street brimmed with restaurants, trendy shops and pretty Latina women, their arms full of shopping bags. The driver veered right at a fork in the road and the scenery changed again. Gone now were the shops and condos, and in their place were walled estates with expansive, manicured grounds and monolithic houses set back from the winding road. Towering palms lined the cobblestone road; the grass and shrubs were impeccably cut and trimmed. The road gently rose as they neared the east side of the cordillera, and when the mountainside seemed almost upon them, the driver steered into the final driveway. He entered a code in the keypad and the iron gates slowly swung open. They cruised up the meandering driveway, past a duck pond and acres of lush lawns. A few gardeners were busy working, but none of them glanced up as the car drove past. They rounded a final curve, and the main house came into view. It was a two-story white colonial home, with sixteen evenly spaced pillars and a second-floor balcony that ran the entire length of the house. A tennis court and swimming pool were set off to the right of the main house, and three small cabanas were tucked in the trees on the left. Guest houses for Mario Rastano's overnight visitors. The BMW pulled up in front of the main doors. The driver jumped out and opened Javier's door.

The young millionaire eased himself off the leather seat and let himself in the house. He angled through the massive foyer, his sandals clacking on the Italian tile, past the main hall and into his father's study. The room was a man's room, with dark paneling and heavy draperies over thick, beveled glass. Bookshelves covered three of the four walls, with texts in Spanish, English and French. Thick carpets covered the floor and the chandeliers provided precious little light. Mario Rastano sat at his desk, a lamp casting light on the letter he read. He glanced up as Javier entered and motioned for his son to take a seat.

Mario's piercing brown eyes finished reading the letter, and he gently set it on the desk. His hair was receding, but still dark with only an occasional hint of gray. His broad shoulders and powerful arms were evident under the thin silk shirt and his hands dwarfed the page he held. Rastano's face was aging now that he was in his late sixties, but his features still held an authoritative look. There was nothing old or feeble about his presence. He looked up and addressed his son.

"How were the gardens?"

"Wonderful. As always."

"What is it about the Uribe gardens that entice you so? We have a beautiful estate, Javier. I don't understand why you insist on visiting a public garden."

Javier shrugged. "I like it. It's peaceful. It's that simple, really."

The clan elder shrugged. "So be it." He reached across the desk and picked up another piece of paper. "I received this about an hour ago." He handed it across to his son and waited as Javier read it.

"How is this possible?" Javier asked, a questioning look in his eyes. "These Swiss accounts are impenetrable."

"Yes, that's true. Only one man has access to them."

"And he's been dead since early December 1993."

"Almost twelve years," the elder Rastano said. "Imagine that."

Javier rechecked the figures on the page. "Eight million American dollars withdrawn fifty days ago, and another six million yesterday. Why did it take our contact in the bank almost two months to get this to us?"

"I think he just missed the first withdrawal. But he caught the second one. I can live with that."

"Then so can he," Javier said, smiling. It was a different smile, evil and cold.

Mario nodded. "He's important to us right now. I can overlook the mistake. Anyway, we have a problem.

Money that is rightfully ours is being withdrawn from that account."

"What can we do?" Javier asked. "Can we track the wire transfers once the money leaves Zurich?"

Mario shook his head. "Not a chance. Our banker friend tried, but whoever is behind the withdrawal bounced the money electronically off a handful of satellites going in and out of thirty international banks. It's impossible to trace."

"There's almost a billion dollars in that account," Javier said, his jaw clenched. "We've waited years to get our hands on that money. We can't just sit back and watch it disappear."

"Over a billion," his father corrected him. "Interest on nine hundred and forty million dollars, compounded semi-annually over twelve years, is substantial. And no, we're not just going to sit around and let him take it from under our noses."

"Again, I ask: What can we do?"

"Find him."

"You think he's alive?"

Mario Rastano slammed a huge fist down on his desk. The sound echoed through the room. "I *know* Pablo Escobar is alive, Javier. I feel it. He's been living in obscurity for the better part of twelve years and now he needs the money from the Swiss account to keep him afloat. He will continue to take that money until there is nothing left. He's alive and we're going to find him."

"How?" Javier asked.

"Pablo Escobar has a cousin. I'd like you to pay him a visit."

Chapter Three

Larry cut the engines and Eugene heaved the anchor into the calm waters of the bay. It caught in the mixture of sand and rocks, and the small craft slowly eased to a halt, just short of the beach. A skinny teenager grabbed the second mooring line and waded ashore, fastening it to one of many wooden pegs driven into the sand. The divers disembarked, and Eugene and his crew ferried their gear to shore. They tipped Eugene, thanked him for a great day of diving, piled into Eduardo's truck and were gone. Eugene sat on a log and waved Larry over.

"Here," he said, splitting the tip in half. "Twenty for you, twenty for me. Not bad for a Friday, my friend."

Larry took the American dollars and grinned. "Happy clients, happy pilot." He trotted off toward his house, a few short blocks from the playa. Eugene rocked his head back and forth, stretching his neck muscles and working out the knots. He raised his right arm and rotated it, wincing at the pain. It had been more than a week since the incident with the Germans, and his shoulder was still sore. He leaned against the log and looked skyward. The moon was a sliver, the sky cloudless. He and Larry had put in a long day, with two dives during the daylight hours and one more after the sun had disappeared behind the mountainous outline of Margarita. He was tired, and lifting himself off the log and walking to the Vespa seemed almost too much. Somehow, he managed.

Once he had the scooter moving, the breeze invigorated him and gave him a second wind. Larry was right; it had been a very good day. Night dives paid well, and the twenty-dollar tip was gravy. He weaved around the potholes, his headlight dancing on the road and the shrubs that bordered the asphalt. The football stadium loomed up on his left, eerie in the blackness that enveloped Playa El Tirano. His turn came up quickly and he braked, then steered onto his dirt drive. A solitary light burned in the kitchen. He locked the steering on the scooter, lifted his gear and trudged across the mixture of saw-grass and rock chips, his running shoes making a strange crunching noise.

"Hello," he called, entering the bungalow and dumping his gear on the floor next to the front door. "I'm home. Sorry I'm late." He kicked off his shoes and rounded the corner into the kitchen. "We had six divers who wanted to try a night—"

He stopped in mid-sentence, his mouth open. Julie and Shiara were nowhere to be seen. Three men were in his kitchen, one of them at the table and two leaning against the counter. All three were Latinos, with dark hair and brown skin, but it was the figure sitting at his table that immediately caught his attention. The man was in his mid-thirties with longer hair swept back behind his ears, and deep brown eyes like ice. His manicured hands rested on the table.

"Who the hell are you, and where is my wife?" Eugene asked.

"Relax, Eugenio," the seated man said in a soft voice. "Your wife and daughter are fine. For now."

Eugene started to move forward, but two guns appeared, Glock A-17s, one in the right hand of each man leaning against his counter. Eugene stopped. "Where is my wife?" His words were like acid.

"Sit down, Eugenio. Threatening me isn't going to help your situation."

Eugene glanced at the guns, and sat at the table opposite the man. "Who are you?" he asked.

The man smiled. "Now that's a question I *can* answer. My name is Javier Rastano. I'm from Medellín. It's a city in southern Colombia, in case you're not familiar with it."

"I know where Medellín is," Eugene said. "But I don't understand why you're here."

"You are related to the Escobar clan, who at one time lived in Medellín. One of your cousins was Pablo Escobar."

"Pablo is dead. He died violently years ago."

"Did he?" Javier asked, amused. "What makes you so sure?"

Eugene looked puzzled. "The entire planet knows that Pablo Escobar died during a shootout in Medellín sometime in December of 1993. You should read the newspapers."

Javier's smile disappeared. He leaned forward. "Don't get sarcastic with me, Eugenio. Remember, we have two people very dear to you." He held up his hand as Eugene began to ask again where his wife and daughter were. "Don't keep asking about them or I'll make a phone call and they *won't* be okay."

Eugene settled back into his chair. "Okay. Okay. Everything's cool here." He swallowed, his throat dry. "What do you want from me?"

Javier also reclined back into his chair. "We have reason to believe that your cousin isn't as dead as he would like the world to believe. In fact, we're sure he's alive."

"That's impossible. The Colombian government ran all kinds of tests on his body. They proved beyond any doubt that it was Pablo. They verified his fingerprints and ran DNA samples of his blood and skin."

Javier laughed. "The Colombian government. The same men who were terrified of Pablo Escobar. The politicians and police either accepted Pablo's bribes or he killed them. *Plata o plomo,* silver or lead. And these are the people who authenticated his death. Fingerprints can be changed with lasers and DNA samples can be switched. Especially in a country like Colombia."

"The American DEA and CIA were involved."

"At a distance. They weren't allowed to be in direct contact with the body or any aspect of the verification. The Colombians saw the American influence as meddling in their affairs, and since Escobar was dead, they didn't have to worry about reprisals. So the DEA and CIA had to stand back and let the Medellín police prepare the forensics reports." He waved his arms in the air. "So many opportunities for deception."

"All right. Even if Pablo is alive, what does that have to do with me?"

"You're his cousin. Maybe you know where he is."

"You haven't been listening. Until five minutes ago, I thought he was dead."

"I wouldn't be here if I wasn't positive he was alive," Javier said, his tone ominous. "He's alive, Eugenio. Take my word for it." He lit a cigarette, then continued. "My father and I want you to find him."

"What?" Eugene said. "Are you crazy? How can I find Pablo Escobar if he doesn't want to be found."

"You're his cousin."

"I've only met the man three times in my entire life. I

hardly know him. He's a black mark on our family tree."
He made a sweeping motion with his hands. "Look
around. I'm not exactly living in opulence here."

"I didn't say you knew him well, all I said was that you're
his cousin. That alone can open doors."

"How? And where? I don't understand."

"Someone walks into the DEA and tells the agent in
charge that he's Pablo Escobar's cousin and that he thinks
Pablo is alive. Do you think they're going to listen? I do.
At the very least, they'll interrogate the hell out of him.
And once they're finished, they'll want to know if the per-
son is correct. And that could start an investigation."

"You want me to involve the DEA? Are you nuts? Why
don't you just go and talk to Pablo's son, Juan? He's living
in the Caymans, from what I hear."

Javier's face clouded over. "Juan Pablo is off limits. Any
of Pablo's immediate family is strictly off limits. If Pablo
found out we had approached his mother, his daughter
or his son, he would go on a rampage. He wouldn't rest
until we were dead."

"Jesus Christ, you're scared of someone who is probably
dead."

"Anyone who isn't scared of Pablo Escobar, dead or
alive, is a fool," Javier said. "I respect his abilities."

"You never answered my question about the DEA."

"I'd rather you found a different way to locate Pablo,
but if you have to approach the DEA, so be it. Just keep
my name out of things."

"Or my wife and daughter get hurt."

"No, they die."

"You bastard," Eugene fumed. "You heartless, fucking
bastard."

Javier shrugged and a slow smile spread across his face.
"I've been called worse. And by a lot tougher people."

"Why don't you just find him yourself?"

"Oh, that would be smart," Javier said sarcastically. "A

respected businessman from Medellín asking about Pablo
Escobar. Talk about painting yourself with the same brush
as Pablo. Maybe I could just turn myself into the police as
a *narco*. I don't think so, Eugenio. My father and I will try
to find him in our own way, but you have more options
than we do."

"None of them very palatable."

Javier shrugged again. "You can pick your friends, but
you can't pick your relatives. Unfortunately for you, Pablo
Escobar is part of your family tree, a nasty little part of
your bloodline." Javier snapped his fingers and one of his
goons moved forward and dropped a small package on
the table. The contents were encased in brown paper and
wrapped tight with packing tape. "There's a hundred
thousand American dollars in the package. It's for your
expenses."

Eugene stared at the package but made no move to
pick it up. "Say I find him. What then?"

"You let us know where he is."

"That's it? You want me to give up Pablo so you can
kill him?"

"I don't want to kill Pablo. I want a number from him.
A ten-digit number. In fact, get me that number and I
don't care if you tell me where Pablo is hiding. Your
choice."

Eugene was silent for a minute. "It's a number to access
a bank account," he said. "Pablo has money in a foreign
bank, and you want it."

Javier leaned forward again. His eyes were burning em-
bers. "The money in that account is rightfully ours. Pablo
and my father had an agreement. They jointly ran a number of cocaine pipelines through Central America into
the United States. Most of the drugs were moving
through the Caribbean to either Bimini or Norman's Cay
in the Bahamas, but the DEA was watching, and it was
dangerous to move large shipments along those routes.

So we improvised. We began ferrying the drugs through northern Colombia into Panama, and from there the cocaine went north to California. The DEA never knew of the secondary route. We banked hundreds of millions of dollars with no one the wiser."

"And that money is in some bank, waiting for you to withdraw it. Except you don't have the number to access the account."

Javier nodded. "Pablo is the only one who knows the number. When he disappeared from La Catedral prison in July of '92, with the number, he was a fugitive from that day on."

"Surely you talked with him at some point."

"Many times between then and December of '93. But he wasn't stupid. Pablo knew that if he was the only one with the number to access the bank account, my father and I would do everything in our power to keep him alive. Otherwise, he was expendable. In the last few months, someone has begun making withdrawals. A few million in January, a few million earlier this month, nothing major. Except that Pablo is only person who can withdraw the money. It's not difficult to add two plus two, Eugenio."

Eugene swallowed hard. "I'll do what you want. Just release my wife and daughter."

Javier gave Eugene one of his patented cruel smiles. "Yes, Eugenio, you'll do exactly what we want. Or your family will be returned to you in pieces."

"You hurt them, and I'll . . ."

Javier appeared amused. "You'll what? Kill me? I don't think so. And by the way, we're on a timetable here. You've got two weeks. Not a day longer."

"That's insane," Eugene protested. "Two weeks? Why two weeks?"

"Why two weeks, Eugenio? Because I said so. Because I have your wife and daughter and if I wanted to, I could kill them tomorrow. It's that simple. Without some sort of deadline, you might take your time trying to find him. And that's unacceptable. We're playing by my rules now, Eugenio, and my decision is that you have two weeks, starting tomorrow morning. From the twelfth to the twenty-sixth. Not a moment longer."

Javier rose from the table. A small piece of paper floated from his hand to the table. On it was a handwritten phone number, no name. "When you have Pablo or the number, call me." He started toward the door, then paused. "Oh, I almost forgot." He slid his hand inside his jacket pocket and withdrew a small plastic container, like the ones that contain playing cards, in convenience stores. He set it on the table. "Ciao, Eugenio. Don't let us down."

Eugene stared down at the clear plastic case, his mind processing what his eyes were seeing. It took a few moments for the image to register. He drew in a sharp breath and picked up the container, then dropped it back on the table and spun around, ready to leap from his chair and go for Javier Rastano's neck. He stopped. He was staring into a gun barrel, only inches from his face, a finger tight on the trigger. Rastano had already left the house, and now his man slowly backed to the door, the gun unwavering.

"You walk outside that door, you die," the man said, letting the door close quietly behind him.

Red liquid was smeared on the plastic, but the contents were readily visible. Two severed fingers, one slightly larger than the other, laid side-by-side, like sardines in a tin. Traces of blue nail polish covered the nail of the smaller finger, the same shade of polish his daughter liked to wear. With shaking hands he lifted the container from the table and gently stroked the smooth plastic.

"I'll get you back," he said quietly, tears forming in the corners of his eyes. "As God is my witness, I'll find you and bring you safely home."

Chapter Four

Eugene couldn't sleep. His mind was alive with the horror of what had happened. His wife and daughter were being held by vicious drug dealers who had once been involved with Pablo Escobar—the most dangerous man on the planet in the eighties. And Eugene knew that people who had been involved with his cousin, and had survived, were either equally as ruthless or lucky. From the steely coldness of Javier Rastano's eyes, he didn't think it was luck.

His wife and daughter, gone, abducted. It was unbelievable.

His son was safe in Caracas. He had phoned his parents and checked after Rastano and his goons had left. *Why the concern?* his mother had asked. *No concern, Mom, but can you keep Miguel for another week or two? Julie and I are heading to Bolivia for a bit to visit some friends. Shiara is staying in Margarita. Carnival is on, and school is out anyway.* She had pressed for details, but he had been tight-lipped. Finally, she had agreed to keep the boy until he and Julie returned from the mainland. He hated lying to his parents, but the alternative was to tell them the truth, and that would devastate them. His father hated that his brother's son had been—and maybe still was—a notorious gangster, and finding out that the family connection was threatening the life of his daughter-in-law and granddaughter might kill him. No, the truth was out of the question.

In a zombie-like mode he readied himself for bed. The outer doors had yet to be secured, and he latched them as he always did. But tonight the action seemed wasted. Everything worthy of stealing had already been spirited away. The toothpaste tasted foul and he spit in the basin, then rinsed with cool water. He splashed some on his face and neck and let it drip back into the sink and onto the tile floor in the cramped bathroom. A bottle of toilet water sat near the spigots, and he touched it, his finger gently tracing the graceful curves. Inside the glass was an aroma that seemed to have been made for Julie. Somehow the tiny bottle now embodied her; not of great culture, but irreplaceable in design. He lifted the bottle—it seemed so light—and unscrewed the cap, touching his finger to the mouth and tilting it slightly. He closed the lid and carefully set the bottle back on the vanity. Their bedroom was next to the bathroom and he moved around the bed to Julie's side, touching his finger to her pillow. For a full minute he stood unmoving, his eyes closed, just breathing.

He slipped under the covers and stared at the ceiling above their bed. It occurred to him that since their marriage he'd never slept without her beside him. They always talked about the day before making love or drifting off in easy sleep. The bed was strange without her and sleep wouldn't come. Eventually he rose and dressed, then drove into Porlamar, the island's largest city. It was after two in the morning, but he knew someone who would be awake. The streets were quiet, but not deserted. Avenue 4 de Mayo, dimly lit now that the shops were closed, was home to an occasional prostitute, and groups of various sizes and ages moved between the nightclubs that punctuated the street with music and flashing lights. Eugene cut off the main drag onto a dark side street and found a parking spot for his Vespa. He locked the steering and wrapped a chain through the front spokes and anchored it to a metal railing. *Lock it or lose it* took on a very real meaning in South America.

The building that housed his friend's apartment was set back from the road behind a commercial store that sold auto parts. He walked through the darkness to a flight of stairs and took the risers two at a time. The door at the top was thick and heavy, and he rapped the knocker hard against the wood. A second later an eye appeared in the peep hole, and the door opened. A man in his late fifties with a substantial potbelly stood in the doorway. His hair was long and uncombed and two or three days' growth of beard went unchecked on his heavily lined face. He smiled, revealing uneven yellow teeth, and motioned for Eugene to enter.

"Hey, *amigo*, what brings you down to Porlamar at this time? Julie kick you out for being a good husband?"

"I need to talk with you, Fidel," Eugene said, closing the door behind him. "You okay to talk?" The odor of marijuana hung in the air.

"Sure, Eugene," his friend said as they moved into the sparsely furnished living room. The television was on, but no one else was present. Fidel picked up the remote control and hit the mute button. The room was quiet but for the distant whine of an air-conditioning unit. Fidel pointed to one of the two threadbare couches and sat in the other one. Numerous beer bottles littered the coffee table and the ashtray was piled high with cigarette butts. "What's up, my friend?"

"I've got a problem, Fidel. A serious problem." He spent the next five minutes telling him what had happened at his house earlier in the evening. Fidel sipped on a beer and listened as Eugene relayed the visit from Javier Rastano. Then he thought for a minute.

"Javier Rastano," he said. "You're sure about that?"

"Positive. Why?"

"His father is Mario Rastano. As Javier already told you, he was a major player in the Medellín cartel back when Pablo was involved." Fidel wasn't much to look at, but he was intelligent and connected. He knew more about the illegal drug industry in South America than the DEA. On rare occasions, he would drink too much and tell Eugene stories about when he had worked with the cartels in both Medellín and Cali, scary stories that always involved violence, and often death. "Javier was only about twenty-two or twenty-three when Search Bloc nailed Pablo, but his father had started him young. He'd been dealing with Pablo and the Ochoa family for two or three years. But it was old man Rastano who was the driving force behind the business partnership with Escobar."

"So they moved a lot of cocaine out of Colombia?"

"A shit load. Most of it through Norman's Cay until Carlos Lehder was out of the picture. After that they used Bimini. But that wasn't the only corridor. They had another route."

"Through Panama?"

He shook his head. "Not really. Sure, it went overland from Colombia to Panama, but that wasn't where it left for the United States. Noriega was an absolute bastard to deal with and he screwed the *narcos* more times than you can imagine. How he survived Pablo's wrath has always amazed me. Anyway, the Americans were watching Panama and Noriega was a problem, so your cousin and the Rastanos moved the stuff overland to El Salvador before mixing it in with coffee shipments and loading it on boats for California. Not many people knew about the route."

"How did you find out?" Eugene asked.

"My ties were with José Rodríguez Gacha . . ."

"The Mexican," Eugene interrupted.

"Yes. The Mexican. Anyway, Gacha needed someone to watch the books in South America. For some reason, he trusted me. Not that I didn't earn the trust. I never stole from him, and I forwarded more money to Efraim Roa for laundering than I can remember. Roa was the key man in the Cali cartel, and he was more than happy to get some of the Medellín cartel's business. So I knew how much money was coming in and where it was coming from."

"Sounds like you knew a lot of details about how the cartels operated. You're lucky to be alive."

Fidel grinned and his teeth protruded from beneath thin lips. "I was never a threat. I didn't dress nice and flash wads of cash around at hip discos. I kept my mouth shut and my nose in the books. Gacha made a ton of money, and I was merely an efficient cog in the wheel."

"What happened when the Colombian government killed Gacha in '89?" Eugene asked.

Fidel disappeared into the kitchen for a minute, then returned with two beers. He handed one to Eugene and sat down. "I got out. Gacha was my contact to the cartels. With him gone I was like the guy without a chair when the music stops. I knew your cousin and Carlos Lehder and the Ochoa clan, but it wasn't the same. I had Gacha's trust, but that never extended through to the higher levels. If I'd stayed, I would have died."

"You left with nothing?" Eugene asked.

Fidel motioned to the decrepit surroundings. "It's not so bad, Eugene. I've got enough money stashed away to keep me in beer and pot until I die. It's not the Taj Mahal, but this place is paid for. And I got out with my life. That's more than a shit load of others."

Eugene took a sip of beer, and nodded. "What can you tell me about Mario and Javier Rastano that might help me find Julie and Shiara? Anything at all, Fidel."

Fidel grinned. Again, the ugly teeth. "I might be able to help you there, my friend. So long as you forget where you heard this."

"Of course."

"There's no way the Rastano clan would risk taking hostages back into Colombia. They're respected businessmen in Medellín, and the last thing they want is problems that could tie them to the cocaine trade."

"They're not still active, are they?" Eugene asked.

Fidel gave him a disbelieving look. "You've got to be fucking kidding me. You think that these guys just closed up shop on a two or three hundred-million-a-year operation? Not a fucking chance. They're still moving product. None through Bimini though. So what does that tell you?"

"The pipeline through Panama into El Salvador is still intact?"

Fidel held his beer up in a mock toast. "You got it."

"And you think my wife and daughter might be in El Salvador?"

Fidel just shrugged. "Maybe. I don't know."

Eugene pursed his lips and gave Fidel a long, hard stare. "I've got a question for you, Fidel."

"Ask away."

"You've been out of the business for almost seventeen years. How come you know so much about what's going on?"

Fidel finished his beer, and found a small space on the messy coffee table to set the empty. He lit a cigarette and breathed in the smoke. "Think about our conversation, Eugene. Everything we just talked about, with the exception of the El Salvador route still being open, is history. Read a book on the cocaine trade in the eighties and you'll get the same story. Except without the personal touch. So, in fact, I don't really know what's going on these days."

"But the El Salvador connection. You're sure it's still active."

"Positive." There was a twinkle in his eyes. "I'm out of the business, but a couple of guys I met while I was involved are still running drugs. One is a boat captain and the other is a port coordinator for the shipments. They stop by on occasion. Isla de Margarita is a wonderful vacation spot, and I make sure they're well taken care of while they're here. In return, a couple of packages of prime marijuana buds show up at my doorstep every few months. And while they're here, they like to talk."

Eugene nodded. "So Mario and Javier Rastano are still drug smugglers."

"Yup."

Eugene held up his empty beer and Fidel lurched off the couch and grabbed two more from the fridge. He opened them and handed one to Eugene.

"Thanks." Eugene drank thirstily, then said, "Pablo Escobar, what did you know about his death?"

"Oh, that's one very convoluted mess, Eugene. He wasn't your average drug smuggler. He was rich, powerful and very ruthless—common traits among Colombian drug lords. But there was something about Pablo that set him apart from the Ochoa family or Giselda Blanco de Trujillo, or any of the other major players back in the eighties. Pablo thought he was a hero to the Colombian people, an icon of success and generosity. The football stadiums and housing developments he built in Medellín gave him a degree of legitimacy. He *was* well liked by hundreds of thousands of people who saw him as a benefactor and a humanitarian. He liked that image, and he began to believe it was the truth. Christ, he was elected as an alternate to El Congreso, a legitimate political position within the Colombian government. But then he made a couple of grave mistakes."

"He killed the justice minister, Rodrigo Lara," Eugene said.

"Yes. He had him killed because Lara publicly accused him of being a drug dealer. Lara had powerful friends. There was nothing Pablo could do once Lara opened Pandora's Box. From the second Pablo Escobar took his seat in El Congreso in 1983, he was a marked man. Everyone knew he was a drug trafficker, but until then they'd swept it under the carpet. Pablo blamed Lara for destroying his reputation. And Lara also opened the door to American involvement in Colombia. He allowed the U.S. State Department to dump herbicides on the coca and he authorized the raid on Tranquilandia that netted fourteen labs and over ten tons of cocaine. Pablo was some kind of pissed off. So he had Lara killed."

"That didn't go over well with the Colombian people."

"Nope. Pablo could get away with murder at street level. But not this. Not the murder of a justice minister. The people turned against him, and the politicians drafted an extradition treaty with the United States. Extradition was Pablo's greatest fear."

"I remember him talking about it on one of the few times I met him. He was livid. I thought he was going to grab a gun and start shooting."

Fidel ground out his cigarette in the overflowing ashtray. "Pablo was Colombian, and he wanted no part of the American justice system. He could control his own destiny to some degree while sheltered inside the Colombian borders, but dealing with the Americans was something else. They couldn't be bought off as easily as Colombian politicians. And they were powerful. So Pablo faced extradition to the States if he stayed in Colombia. He and the Ochoa brothers hightailed it to Panama, where Carlos

Lehder and my boss were already hiding. Imagine that, the entire Medellín cartel ousted from Colombia because of the extradition treaty."

"So the movers and shakers of the Medellín cartel were in Panama. What then?"

"Pablo drafted a six-page proposal to Belisario Betancur, the president of Colombia. He offered to shut down his entire cocaine operation and sell the planes and boats he used to ferry the product to the United States. The cocaine industry would cease to exist if he could return to Medellín and live in peace. No extradition."

"I remember the offer. They came back with a 'no deal'," Eugene said. "Killing Lara was too much. And downing that Avianca airliner with 107 people aboard in '89 was way too much."

"Yeah. That was a stupid thing to do. The Colombian government thought Pablo Escobar was completely out of control. And many of the people saw it that way too. Not that he was completely ostracized. He still had a following in Medellín and the people in Envigado, his hometown, thought he was being persecuted. Anyway, that was the beginning of Pablo's downfall. He eventually returned to Colombia, but he was a fugitive from that point on."

"That doesn't explain his death," Eugene said.

"No. But it lays an interesting foundation. You have certain factions that want him dead, others that revere him and others who want him extradited. It all adds up to, as I said, a very convoluted mess."

"So what actually happened?"

Fidel shrugged. "I don't know. But I don't think Pablo's death was as straightforward as the Colombian government would have us think. Whether he's alive or not is another story."

"Javier Rastano thinks he is."

"And his reasoning is that someone is withdrawing

money from a numbered account that only Pablo had access to?"

"Yes."

Fidel was thoughtful. Finally, he said, "Well, from my experience with banks and laundered money, they won't open the vault without absolute proof that the person wanting in is the legitimate owner. So from that end, it could be possible that your cousin is alive."

"Where would he be?" Eugene asked. "Any ideas?"

"He could be anywhere, Eugene. He has the money and connections to disappear and never surface. In fact, *if* he's alive, the only people who know are those close to him, the Rastanos and you and I."

"Puts us in a dangerous position," Eugene said.

Fidel grinned. "You don't trust Pablo?"

Eugene shook his head. "Not if my poking around threatens his situation. He's a survivor, Fidel. I sure wouldn't be the first family member he had killed."

"True enough."

"Javier Rastano suggested I involve the DEA. What do you think?"

"If any agency in the world could help you find Pablo, it would be them. Strange that Rastano would say that."

"I thought so too. But he had his reasons. And what other options do I have?"

"What about his son, Juan Pablo?"

Eugene shook his head. "Javier said that if anyone approached Pablo's son or daughter, they were as good as dead. Pablo would kill them. I believe him. And there's no way his son or daughter will give him up. That's a dangerous dead end."

"Yeah. I suppose so."

Both men were lost in thought for a minute. Eugene thought of Julie and Shiara. Fidel went down memory lane: his connections to the Cali and Medellín cartels now vivid pictures in his mind. Rooms filled with stacks of

American tens and twenties, and rows of money counting machines continually spitting out the bills into hundred thousand dollar piles. Cocaine, kilos and kilos of the white powder that America fell in love with. Bodies of suspected informers or bit players who skimmed a little too much off the top and got caught. Heads with bullet holes and throats sliced open, their tongues pulled out, slit and dangling down past their shoulders like neckties. Men without their genitals. Women with their breasts carved off. Children with their throats slit. The pictures kept coming, like a bad slide show that wouldn't end. He jerked out of the trancelike state when he realized Eugene was speaking to him.

"What about Julie and Shiara? Where do you think they are? Give me your best guess."

"Well, if they're not in Colombia, then probably El Salvador. Mario Rastano has an extensive collection and distribution network set up there, and that would be the safest place for him to keep hostages. You asked for a guess, you got one."

"El Salvador," Eugene said quietly, his mind already working on the problem. "You suggested that earlier too. And that may be a good thing, Fidel."

"How's that?"

"I know someone from San Salvador. A good guy, and very capable. He's working in Caracas right now. I don't know if he'll help me, but I can always ask."

"You don't want to be going into San Salvador blind," Fidel agreed. "It's a dangerous place."

Eugene slowly turned to face the decrepit figure who was far more than he looked. "When you're dealing with these guys, everywhere is dangerous."

"Amen," Fidel said, raising his beer bottle. They clinked bottles, and drank.

Chapter Five

Dawn was just breaking over Porlamar when Eugene closed the door to Fidel's apartment. The street looked depressing in the pale morning light. Garbage and empty bottles were strewn about, and an old car without a motor leaked transmission fluid onto the stained pavement. Laundry fluttered from a line strung between two buildings, and the only life in sight was a thin cat scrounging through a trash bin. Eugene unlocked his Vespa and wrapped the chain around the seat. He started the motor and pulled onto the deserted streets.

Fidel was a gold mine. He knew the ex-smuggler would be helpful, but his knowledge of the cartels, and Javier Rastano in particular, was much greater than he'd imagined. Eugene knew he was not much closer to finding his wife and daughter, but now he had a ray of hope. And hope had to count for something. Out of nowhere his life had changed, reduced from quiet, ordered normalcy to deadly survival. The prize for winning was a return to where things had been less than twenty-four hours earlier. Losing was unthinkable.

Julie and Shiara. Snatched from him and held by violent men who would murder them and not lose a moment of sleep over it. Colombian drug lords and their sycophants. The nightmare he had lived with all his adult life had finally come to pass. For decades he had played the ostrich, stuck his head in the sand, tried to ignore the genetics that tied him to the greatest cocaine dealer in history. He had ignored it, but always had lived with the nagging fear that someone with a grudge against Pablo would appear and level reprisal at him and his family. He had played his cards the safest way possible by staying out of the picture and ignoring his connection to that side of his father's family. But it hadn't worked. He finally had been targeted and retribution had been swift.

His wife and daughter kidnapped.

And now he had two weeks to do what had taken thousands of police and DEA officials sixteen months. Find Pablo Escobar. But this time it would be harder. Colombia was too hot for Pablo. Despite aging and altering his appearance, someone there eventually would have identified him. But that hadn't happened, and it had been almost twelve years since his supposed death. No. He was not in Colombia. He was elsewhere on the planet. But where? The possibilities were endless. A tiny Caribbean island? Continental Europe? An estate tucked away in the remote mountains of Montana or the Canadian wilderness? He needed information that would point him in the right direction. But right now he didn't have any idea where to start.

He pulled up to his single-story brick and cinder-block house in Playa El Tirano. Inside it was cool. The night air was trapped, and the morning sun had yet to heat the tile roof. A worn suitcase was stuffed under his bed, and he pulled it out and dusted it off. He packed a few pairs of

shorts and long pants, a couple of shirts and socks and un-
derwear. The suitcase was small, and he was limited to
how much he could take, but that suited him fine. The
lighter the better; he was going to be on the move.

As he could see it, his problem was two-pronged. Finding Pablo Escobar was his priority, but that didn't guarantee his wife and daughter would live through the ordeal.
He needed to locate them and be ready to move on their
captors in case he couldn't find Pablo. And failing to find
the drug lord inside a two-week window was a distinct possibility. Twelve years had passed since Pablo's death in
Medellín; twelve years for him to blend into his new environment and twelve years of the natural aging process to
further disguise his appearance. Nothing was certain
about finding Pablo.

Then another thought flashed through his mind. What
if he *did* find Pablo? What would Pablo's response be? His
name was synonymous with violence and death. Would he
simply kill him if and when they came face to face? Jesus,
this was a no-win situation. If he failed to find Pablo, his
wife and daughter would be killed. But if he did find him,
chances are Pablo would lash out with a vengeance. And
if Eugene were to die before giving Javier Rastano Pablo's
location or the ten-digit code, then Julie and Shiara
would be brutally murdered, despite his success.

The odds of success were incredibly small. But he had
no choice. Javier Rastano was a Colombian drug dealer
and a murderer. He would not hesitate to kill a woman
and a teenage girl. Eugene's path was clear. He needed
someone he could trust to search for Julie and Shiara
while he tried to unearth Pablo. He hoped his friend in
San Salvador would help him. But what could he offer
him for risking his life? Eugene wasn't sure if he held anything of value that would entice his friend to help. All he
had was friendship. Well, friendship and cash. He glanced
down at the table, to the wad of bills sitting where Shiara

usually ate her breakfast. Drug money, but necessary to fund his search. He reached out and fingered the top bill. It felt like any other American twenty, but he knew it wasn't the same. It was dirty money. Money that had reached the palms of the Rastano clan through violence and oppression. He closed his eyes and replayed the events of the day when he had lost his innocence.

Pablo Escobar had invited Eugene's parents to his Nápoles estate, an oasis of decadence in the Colombian jungle. And when Pablo Escobar invited you, you attended. Eugene had made the trip, a lad of sixteen who barely knew his cousin, but even then he was aware Pablo was a wealthy and influential man. His school friends often referred to Pablo as a *narco*, but his father always dismissed the allegations with a wave of his hand. *Pablo works hard for his money, Eugenio.* But the trip to Nápoles had forever changed his perception of his cousin.

Pablo met them at the main house when they arrived, a short, plump man with his thick hair swept off to one side and an anemic mustache. He grinned like a school kid when Eugene asked about the bullet-riddled car parked atop a knoll of grass outside the front entrance.

"That is the car Bonnie and Clyde were driving when they were surrounded by police and tried to shoot their way to freedom."

"Did they get away?" Eugene asked.

Pablo laughed. "No, Eugenio. They died in the car. Both of them. That's what makes this car so valuable." He wrapped his arm around Eugene and steered the family toward the house. "Come in, my cousin. My house is your house."

Eugene wandered around Escobar's jungle escape, alternately trying his skill at the pinball machines and pool tables. He changed into his trunks and swam a few laps in one of the six swimming pools set among the manicured gardens touching the house, then returned to the main house and looked out over the thousands of unfenced acres where Pablo's exotic animals roamed. He spotted a few ostriches and gazelles moving across the grasslands, but even with the binoculars one of the servants had given him, they were mere specks. He searched out his cousin, who was sipping tea on a verandah talking with his parents. He asked if he could go and look at some of the animals.

"Certainly, Eugenio," Pablo said, grinning. He called to one of the servants and a few moments later a young man, perhaps eighteen, came jogging onto the verandah. "Miguel, take Eugenio to the hippo ponds and show him some of the trails."

"Sí, Señor Escobar," the young man replied. He gave Eugene a wide grin. "Let's go have some fun and leave these guys to their tea."

Eugene followed Miguel to a modern outbuilding on the perimeter of the landscaped grounds. Inside was a fleet of ATVs and trail bikes, all washed and sitting in rows, ready for back-country action. Eugene was an expert trail-bike rider and chose a 360cc Yamaha, lots of power and stylish to boot. They roared off from the house and into the wilds of the adjoining rainforest. The path was narrow, bordered with thick trunks of giant emergent ceiba and eucalyptus trees, and fraught with danger. The path opened in places to sudden and unexpected cliffs dropping hundreds of feet to the valley floor. Toucans and horned screamers flitted about the dark enclaves under the jungle canopy, and when the path cut close to the river, Eugene sometimes spotted a jaguar lounging on the exposed sand banks.

He stayed immediately behind his guide, alternately laying on the throttle and the brakes. A couple of times, Miguel glanced back and gave Eugene a nod for keeping up with him. Eventually they reached a pond with muddy banks and dense vegetation to the water's edge. Miguel stopped the bike and switched off the ignition, and Eugene followed suit. A strange quiet descended on the tiny clearing next to the pond.

"Watch," Miguel said, pointing to the glassy surface of the pond. A few moments later the water stirred slightly. Then a large, round snout with two large nostrils appeared above the water. Two humps with huge eyeballs followed. For a few seconds, only the one hippo was in view, then another surfaced, and another, until the water was dotted with nostrils and eyes. "They like to swim here," Miguel said, glancing over at Eugene. "They've got another pond a few hundred meters through the jungle that has huge mud pits. They use that one more for sunbathing."

"Holy shit," Eugene said. "Hippos in Colombia."

"Yeah. Señor Escobar had them shipped in from Africa. Along with a bunch of other exotic animals. What Pablo wants, Pablo gets."

Eugene turned to his guide. "How well do you know my cousin?" he asked.

"I just work for him. Why?"

Eugene shrugged and lifted his leg off the motorcycle. He walked slowly to the water and watched the closest hippo watch him. "I don't really know Pablo. My father only gets together with Pablo when he calls." Eugene was silent for a minute, then turned and asked Miguel, "Is he a *narco*? That's what a lot of kids in my school say. And all the men who work for him have guns, including you."

Miguel didn't answer for a while. Then he said, "Your cousin is a very rich man. There are many people who would take his money if they were given a chance. As for me, I work for Senor Escobar and he treats me very well. I wouldn't know about these things your classmates speak of. We should be getting back." He switched on the ignition and pumped the kick-start with his right foot. The motor coughed, then caught, spewing blue smoke into the humid jungle air.

Eugene straddled his bike and started the engine. He pushed the gear shift down with his left foot, gave it some gas and popped out the clutch. But instead of heading back toward the house—just for the hell of it—he darted off down the path they had been traveling on, moving deeper into the jungle. He could hear Miguel screaming at him, but he ignored the shouts and increased his speed until he was sure Miguel could not attempt to pass or stop him on the narrow trail. He glanced back and saw the other bike fifty feet back and following him. Miguel waved at him, but he ignored the plea to stop and kept on the gas. For twenty minutes the two riders twisted along the dark floor of the rainforest, Eugene using all his skills to stay ahead of his cousin's employee. Then, without warning, they rounded a bend and entered a clearing. Eugene stopped and cut the motor. Facing him were a handful of rugged looking men, each holding a gun. And to a man, they were pointing the guns at him. Miguel pulled up beside him and switched off his bike.

"Put the guns away," Miguel said. "He's with me."

The men lowered their weapons and turned their backs on the two riders. They filtered back into a series of six wooden huts that took up most of the clearing. Smoke spiraled up from tin chimneys, and a gentle breeze blew it in Eugene and Miguel's direction. The smell was foul and Eugene's eyes burned. He recognized the odors from his science labs in school; a mixture of hydrochloric acid, acetone and ether. Eugene got off his bike and walked slowly toward one of the huts where a few barefoot men stomped about in a huge vat filled with leaves and some form of liquid. To a man they all looked stoned.

"This is a cocaine lab, isn't it?" he said to Miguel. It wasn't really a question. "So Pablo is a *narco*." Eugene shook his head in disgust and started the bike. He turned a stern face to his guide. "Don't worry, I won't say anything to Pablo. I don't want to get you in any trouble." He started back for the main house, Miguel on his tail.

Eugene opened his eyes and Pablo Escobar's Nápoles estate was gone. The opulence was replaced with his small, clean kitchen, the stack of dirty money on the table. Twenty-six years had passed since that fateful day, and over that time he had built himself a wonderful life, with a loving wife and two children. Somehow, through all the misery and shame that went with the Escobar legacy, he had kept his ethics intact. He worked for his money and held his head high, even when Pablo's name surfaced. He had risen above the abyss into which his cousin had dragged the family name. But now everything had changed; the scum had resurfaced. And they were threatening to take his life apart, seam by seam.

That would only happen over his dead body.

Chapter Six

Eugene watched the outline of Isla de Margarita disappear into the afternoon mist rising off the Caribbean until it became a fuzzy haze on the distant horizon. Everything was out of focus: his island, his life, his wife and daughter. What had happened? He felt the bile rising as the plane touched down on the Venezuelan mainland. Caracas airport, dull, gray and ugly between the coastline and the slum-covered hills to the west. One question weighed on his mind: Would his friend help him find Julie and Shiara? Only a face-to-face meeting would give him the answer.

He deplaned at Maiquetía, the domestic terminal, and was saved from the madness of Simón Bolívar terminal, which serviced international air traffic in and out of Caracas. A queue of taxis waited at the curb and he checked three sets of ID before settling on a driver. Taking the wrong cab from the airport was akin to wearing a "Please Rob and Beat Me Senseless" sign on your back.

The cab entered the city of five million and moved with the frenzied flow of traffic, much like the men of Pamplona with the bulls at their heels. The once sleepy town of Santiago de León de Caracas, its red-tiled roofs glinting in the equatorial sun, was long gone. The discovery of rich oil reserves in Venezuela brought unprecedented growth to the city as workers flooded in from the rural areas; slums and wealthy enclaves sprang up along the strip of habitable land between the ocean and the mountains. The *ranchitos* were nothing more than hovels that provided some protection from the elements, and no protection from the high levels of crime and violence. But people kept coming, and Caracas kept growing. Now the city spread like a cancer over the steep hills, the roads slicing across the sharp ridges and the houses multiplying and filling every gorge and canyon. Eugene directed the driver to an industrial section of town where even the *ranchitos* refused to take root.

The tile factory was a dreary building in a cluster of similar windowless concrete buildings. Nothing grew here without a monumental struggle against the pollution and the onslaught of poorly finished cement. Trucks and factories belched dark, sooty smoke into the air and Eugene's nostrils and eyes stung from the acrid smog. He considered rolling up the windows, but the taxi lacked air-conditioning and the heat would be unbearable in less than a minute. The cab came to rest in front of a nondescript set of doors with a small sign hanging askew above the upper jamb. Stenciled onto the weather beaten wood was *Cerámico Cuidad.* City Ceramic. Eugene slipped two twenty U.S. dollars from his pocket and ripped them in half. He handed one half from each bill to the driver and re-pocketed the other two halves.

"Wait for me," he said, turning and heading for the entrance.

"Sí, señor," the driver said, clutching the two twenties.

Forty dollars for this fare was excellent pay. He would wait however long his client was in the building.

Inside, Eugene found himself in an administrative bullpen with numerous employees, mostly younger women, at their desks, filling out forms or talking on the phone. One of the women at a desk off to one side, attractive with long hair and piercing brown eyes, glanced up and smiled.

"Can I help you?"

He weaved through a couple of desks to where she sat. "Yes, please. I'd like to speak with Pedro Parada."

Again, the smile. "Sure. I think he's on the floor. You want to follow me?"

"Thanks." Eugene fell in behind the woman as she moved through the tangle of desks to a door against the back wall. A wall of sound hit them as she opened the door and entered the shop area. It was a cavernous room, perhaps two hundred square feet with a thirty-foot ceiling, and filled with machinery and conveyors for forming and packaging ceramic tiles. The antiquated equipment was labor intensive, and workers were plentiful, watching the machines, adding oil and adjusting relief valves to keep the internal pressure constant. One corner of the room, where the tiles were formed and kiln dried, produced enough heat to keep the entire room sweltering. The woman rounded a large conveyor that bound the finished tiles in cardboard and rolled them down to waiting pallets. She pointed to a group of men working on one of the machines.

"Pedro is the crew leader for maintenance," she said. "They're working on one of the hydraulic units."

Eugene nodded and smiled. "Thank you." He walked the last few yards to the group of men and waited until one of the four noticed his presence. He pointed to Pedro, who had his head down and was tightening a new hydraulic line with a wrench. The man tapped Pedro on the leg and he looked up. A broad grin spread across his face as he recognized Eugene. He dropped the wrench and stuck out a greasy hand.

"Eugene, my friend," he said, rising to his full height of five feet eight inches. He wore a short sleeve shirt and his muscles bulged against the material as he shook hands. His forearms were thick and well defined, his skin dark brown from the sun and his mestizo heritage. He wore his dark hair short and neatly combed back from a broad forehead and prominent cheek bones. His smile was glistening white against the soft brown of his skin.

"Hello, Pedro," Eugene said, ignoring the grease and accepting his friend's hand. Both men had strong grips.

Pedro motioned to his crew to finish the repair and steered Eugene toward the coffee room where they could escape the noise and pollution of the main factory. "What brings you to the mainland?" Pedro asked, fixing two coffees and sitting with Eugene at a corner table. The room was about half full of workers on their break and many voices vied to be heard over the din. "You finally tire of living the good life on Margarita?"

Eugene knew Pedro too well to dance about. "I'm in trouble, Pedro. I need your help."

Pedro's eyes narrowed and he leaned forward on his elbows, closing the distance between the two men to keep their conversation private. "What's wrong, Eugene?"

"Julie and Shiara have been kidnapped."

Pedro's face remained impassive for a few moments, and then a tiny vein appeared in his forehead and his lips turned slightly down. The friendly face had turned nasty, almost vicious. The warmth in his eyes evaporated, replaced with steely resolve. "How did it happen?" His voice was ice.

"Javier Rastano and some of his goons took them. He's a drug dealer from Medellín. Sort of a continuation of what Pablo was into a few years ago." Eugene explained the visit from Rastano to his house on Margarita and finished with the small plastic container with two severed fingers. Pedro was silent for a minute, then he nodded.

"I think I understand. You're going after your cousin. You think Julie and Shiara are in El Salvador and you need me to find them."

"I wouldn't ask if I wasn't desperate, Pedro." Beads of sweat dripped from Eugene's forehead onto his cheeks. He wiped them away and dabbed at his face with a napkin. "It's Julie and Shiara, Pedro."

"Jesus, Eugene. One wrong move with these guys and I'm a dead man." They were both quiet for a minute, then Pedro said, "What do you know about their setup in El Salvador?"

"Nothing," Eugene answered. "I'm not even sure they took Julie and Shiara to Central America. But one thing's for certain: They aren't in Colombia. The Rastano clan has spent too much time and effort to appear legitimate to blow it all by keeping kidnap victims in their back yard. They've got Julie and Shiara somewhere away from Medellín. And since their strongest presence outside Colombia is in San Salvador, I think that's where they took my wife and daughter."

"Where's Miguel?" Pedro asked.

"Safe in Caracas with his grandparents," Eugene said. "Thank God for small miracles. But time is limited, Pedro. Javier Rastano has given me two weeks to find Pablo."

Pedro was quiet for another minute. Street-smart and tough, he knew the consequences of his answer were huge. If he chose to shy away from danger, he would be abandoning his friend in a time of dire need, and possibly sentencing Julie and Shiara to death. But accepting the challenge held the very real possibility of another early death. His. The people Eugene was asking him to go against were Colombian drug dealers. Ruthless men. He closed his eyes and for a few seconds he was fourteen years old, in San Salvador, walking home from school on that hot, humid afternoon.

School had gone well and he had the results of a social studies test in his book, ready to show his grandmother. Ninety-four percent. She would be so proud. He took his usual route, passing near the zoo on his way to the small adobe house on Colonia America where he lived with his grandmother. The neighborhood was never really safe, but the walk home from his classes was usually uneventful; most of the thugs who prowled the streets were looking for better targets than a fourteen-year-old schoolboy. But not that day.

Pedro passed a house with an open front and a couple of soda machines set against an inside wall. Two tables sat in the shade, one occupied by three young men in their late teens. Pedro caught some sort of a motion as he cruised past, but never gave it a second thought. A moment later he heard a voice behind him.

"Where you going so fast, *chiquillo*?" One of the teens had lurched outside the hole in the wall and was trailing Pedro down the road.

Pedro glanced back. The youth was covered with gang tattoos, on his arms, his neck and ears. His face was criss-crossed with scars from knife fights. He yelled at Pedro again, this time accusing him of being from a different gang. Pedro began to run, his legs pumping quickly, his eyes on the ground, watching where each footstep landed on the broken pavement. He reached a clear spot and risked a look behind him. Another four gang members had joined the first and they were only a few steps behind him.

Pedro knew if the gang caught him he was dead. He started screaming for help. The streets were alive with people and cars and buses, but no one stepped forward. They just watched as he ran for his life, knowing that getting involved would only make them targets. Pedro rounded a corner, his legs and lungs burning and his breath coming in short gasps. He had nothing left. A church loomed up at the end of the block, but his muscles were too tired to make it. Just as the gang seemed to be on top of him, a strong arm grabbed him by his shirt and yanked him off his feet. His feet swung back to earth and his head and shoulders smacked into the man's back. The hand let go and he dropped to the pavement, staring at the gang through the man's legs.

"You want the boy, come and get him," the man yelled at the group. They pulled up short, brandishing knives and waving them wildly about. The man's right hand was behind him, close to the small of his back. "I've got a gun, and I've got enough bullets for each one of you. You want him, you go through me."

"Get out of the way, asshole," one of the gang yelled. "We want the kid."

"You get the kid when you get past me," the man yelled back. "And if you try, I'll kill all of you. No fucking survivors to tell the story."

Lives hung in the balance. Witnesses to the standoff crawled into doorways and behind buildings, wary of stray gunfire or of being slaughtered because they'd seen too much. There were no police, and even if they were near, this wasn't their fight. This was one man against a gang.

"You fucking guy," one of the gang yelled. He snapped his blade shut and rammed it in his pocket. "I ever see you around here again, I'll kill you."

"You do that," the man said as the rest of the gang followed suit and retreated. A minute later they were gone, swallowed by the grimy labyrinth of streets and alleys. The man finally looked down to where Pedro was huddled on the cement. "You okay?" he asked.

"Yeah," Pedro said, standing and dusting off his school clothes. "I'm fine. Thank you."

"Not a problem, but we got a bit lucky if you ask me."

"How's that?" Pedro asked.

The man lifted up his shirt to reveal the small of his back. "I forgot my gun today."

"Holy shit," Pedro said. His knees buckled and he collapsed back to the ground. "It was all a bluff."

The man nodded. "I'm Eugene Escobar," he said, wiping a few beads of sweat from his brow. "Just visiting from Venezuela. Is it always this exciting around here?"

Despite the seventeen-year difference in their age, the two became friends. At first, it was more of a father-son relationship, but as Pedro matured and entered his twenties, the friendship blossomed into one of mutual respect. They stayed in touch, Pedro often traveling to Venezuela and to Eugene's island to visit and help on the dive boat. Eugene made a couple of trips to El Salvador, but it was more difficult after Shiara was born. Still, despite distance and time, the friendship endured.

Now Pedro sat at the rickety table in the lunch room of Cerámico Cuidad, already knowing what his answer would be. He adored Julie; she was like a sister to him. And Shiara had turned into a wonderful young woman. She and Miguel always called him Uncle Pedro. It was the family he had been denied as a young boy surviving the rough-and-tumble streets of San Salvador. He took a sip of coffee and cupped the warm mug in his hands.

"I'll need some expense money, Eugene. I'm kind of tapped out right now."

Eugene finally let out his breath and nodded. "Money's not a problem. I can give you twenty thousand American dollars. That should pay for your plane flights, hotels and food."

"Where did you get . . . ?" Pedro let the question die, not really wanting to know the answer. "What should I do? How do I get close to Javier Rastano and his father?"

Eugene shrugged. "I don't know. You're a resourceful kind of guy. You'll think of something."

Pedro finished his coffee. "And if I find your wife and daughter? Then what?"

"That's your call. Get them out if you can. Call me. Call the police. Do whatever you have to."

"Are they in El Salvador right now?"

Eugene shrugged. "A friend of mine thinks so. He was tied into the drug business a few years ago and he's still in the loop. You're going to have to wing it, Pedro. Make it up as you go."

"How do we stay in touch?" Pedro asked.

"I'll get two cell phones from a dealer in Caracas this afternoon. I'll be the only person with your number, and vice versa."

"I'm assuming you'd like me to leave for El Salvador right away," Pedro said, and Eugene nodded. "All right, I'll have to settle up a few things here before I leave. I don't want to burn any bridges. I like working here. I'll just tell them I've got a family emergency."

"Thanks, Pedro."

"Not a problem, my friend." He rose to finish his shift. "Where are you staying?"

Eugene shrugged. "Hadn't thought about it."

"Try the Plaza Catedral, on Boulevard Plaza Bolívar. It's in the colonial section of Caracas. Nice rooms, great restaurant on the roof."

"I know it," Eugene said. "You want me to check in and wait for you?"

"Sure. I'll need a few hours here to wrap things up. Give me another hour to pop by my apartment and have a shower and change. I'll see you then."

"Ciao, amigo," Eugene said, shaking Pedro's hand.

Their eyes met. "It's going to be okay," Pedro said, seeing the agony in his friend's eyes. "We'll find them."

Eugene nodded and they split. Pedro headed back to the problem with the hydraulic system, and Eugene cut back through the office to the parking lot. He thought about Pedro's words as he slid into the cab and gave the driver the name of the hotel. *We'll find them.* The words were hollow, just spoken to appease his suffering, both men knew that. But somehow, just hearing someone else say what he wanted to believe was encouraging. And one huge weight had been lifted from his shoulders now that he had Pedro helping him. Without Pedro he was dead in the water. He closed his eyes and the vision of Julie and Shiara, captive with blood-soaked bandages wrapped about the stumps of their severed fingers, came to him.

Despite his eyes being tightly closed, his cheeks burned as the tears slowly rolled down.

Chapter Seven

They met in Les Grisons at seven in the evening, the sun just setting on the rugged horizon. Splashes of color streaked across the evening sky, and then a muted gray washed across the palette and dusk descended. The lights of Caracas flickered and then glowed dimly against the stark darkness of the towering hills to the west. Beneath the rooftop restaurant, the city pulsed with energy and readied itself for another night of pounding music in crowded nightclubs.

Pedro ordered a lite beer as he stared out over the spires of the cathedral toward Plaza Venezuela and the adjacent Jardín Botánico. The gardens were poorly lit and appeared as a black blotch against a sea of oscillating streetlights. He took a sip of cold beer and wiped a drop of condensation from the bottle. It fell on his dark denim jeans and he absently rubbed it into the material with his index finger.

"Rastano give you the money?" Pedro asked. He didn't know why, but he had to know.

Eugene took a long pull on his beer and nodded. "Yeah, it's drug money. Rastano gave me a hundred large for expenses. If you need more than twenty . . ."

Pedro shook his head. "Twenty is fine. Hell, my job at Cerámico Cuidad only pays thirty-five U.S. a year and I survive on that. I think I can get through two weeks with twenty. Anyway, I don't want to appear in San Salvador throwing cash around. That attracts a lot of unnecessary attention. I'd rather stay at a hotel that's cheaper than the Hilton."

"Any ideas on how to find Rastano?" Eugene asked.

Pedro grinned. "Finding Rastano will be easy. Rich people aren't all that common in San Salvador, and they all tend to stick to one area: Escalón. Getting to meet him will be the tough part."

"Escalón? Is it a subdivision or a neighboring town?"

"It's a subdivision," Pedro said. "Huge estates with walls and gates. Armed guards everywhere. And I'm not talking your average rent-a-cop idiots. These guys are ex-military types, and they're well paid. Kill you in a second if you give them a reason."

"Rastano's type of people," Eugene said.

Pedro ordered another beer, and asked Eugene, "What do you know about Javier Rastano? From what you've told me, he seems to be the front man for the family these days."

"That's only my take on it, because he's the only one I've met. I wouldn't be able to pick out his father in a crowd of three. Then again, Javier didn't seem to need his father's approval to kidnap my wife and daughter. But I don't know that for sure."

Pedro looked thoughtful for a few moments. Then he said, "Rich young man in a foreign country. He's got to have some vices that need satisfying. Drugs, booze and women; he can certainly take care of those necessities himself, but rich guys usually need something else."

"Like what?"

"Gambling, fast cars, cock fights. Who knows. When you've got more money than you can hope to spend, you've got to find new and exciting ways to get rid of it. I've known a few high-level drug dealers, and they were all fucked up. I'm sure Javier Rastano is no different."

"Where does that get you?" Eugene asked, his voice tinged with skepticism.

"Get Javier on his home turf with nothing to do but take a good hard look at me, and chances are he'll be suspicious. But put him in another environment, one where common sense is diverted and pure adrenaline takes over, and I might stand a chance."

"A chance for what?"

"To get inside his gardens, his house, his world. That's the way to find Julie and Shiara. Busting down the front door with guns in hand isn't going to work. And standing outside his mansion gates won't get me anywhere. I've got to meet him and get in his life."

Eugene ran his fingers through his curly hair and nodded. Pedro was right. Javier Rastano may be rich and pampered, but with his position in the drug underworld came street smarts and hands-on experience in treachery and deception. The man was no fool. He would be alert for the wrong people trying to infiltrate his inner circle. Getting close to him would be difficult. But men were often most vulnerable about activities they considered pleasurable. Sex with younger women, motorcycle or car racing, extreme sports. Whatever the man's button was, Pedro needed to find it. And then exploit it. Not easy, but Pedro was already thinking on the right track. Eugene slipped an envelope from the inside pocket of his windbreaker.

"Here's your cash," he said. "American dollars."

"Universal currency," Pedro said, taking the package and tucking it in his pocket without glancing inside. "You traveling with the other eighty in cash?"

"No chance," Eugene said. "I've got about ten on me. I stopped at a bank earlier today and put the rest on my credit card. They won't be asking for a payment for a few months."

Pedro laughed. "They'll probably up your credit limit."

"Just what I need."

The waiter, young with shoulder-length hair, came around, pad in hand, and took their orders. He thanked them, and was gone.

"How are you going to find Pablo?" Pedro asked. "If he is alive."

"There's a family member I can try before I resort to the DEA or the CIA. Raphael Ramirez. He's a cousin, once or twice removed, I can't remember. Anyway, he's a shady kind of guy. Always looked up to Pablo, but Pablo wouldn't give the guy the time of day."

"I thought Pablo liked sycophants."

"He did. But Raphael borrowed some money once to open a business in Medellín, which he never got around to doing. Spent the money, then came nosing about for more. He's lucky Pablo didn't get one of his guys to whack him."

"You think this Raphael might know something?"

Eugene shrugged. "I don't know. But it'll only take a day to check it out. I booked an early flight for Medellín tomorrow morning." Eugene slid his hand inside his jacket and withdrew a cell phone. It was the latest model Motorola, tiny with an extra capacity Li-Ion battery. "Your number flashes across the screen when you turn it on. Here's mine," he said, jotting down the number for his new cell phone on a match pack and sliding it across the linen tablecloth.

"Thanks. You said no one else will know these numbers. Is that still on?"

"Yes. Just us. And they've got call display, so we'll know when a call comes in if it's a wrong number."

"Excellent."

Eugene leaned forward slightly. "You have a gun?"

"In Caracas, yes. But I'm going to leave it here. Easier to travel without one. I'll pick up another one in San Salvador. I've got lots of connections in the city."

"Okay."

The food arrived, Creole cuisine with hearty sides of fresh vegetables and rice. They ordered fresh beers and dug in. They talked about other things; Pedro's job and where he was living in Caracas. But the small talk was forced and it quickly came back to the matter at hand.

Pedro said seriously, "Eugene, you've got to do me one favor."

"Of course, my friend. Just name it."

"If for some reason I don't make it through this alive, I want you to visit my grandmother and tell her I died trying to do something good. She may not see it that way if I end up getting shot or knifed, but I'd hate for her to think I was some street punk. That would break her heart."

"She still lives on Colonia America?"

"Yeah, she's still there."

"I'll tell her, Pedro. But *you* have to do *me* a favor."

"What's that?"

"Don't get killed."

"I'll try, *amigo*. I'll try."

Chapter Eight

Eugene flew Aeropostal, Venezuela's national airline, directly from Caracas to Medellín. The spiny backbone of the Cordillera Central, engulfing the city on all sides, dwarfed the José María Córdova International Airport and created dangerous up- and downdrafts for incoming flights. Eugene recognized a few landmarks as the landing gear unfolded and the plane thundered through the unsettled air pockets. A football match was underway at Atanasia Girardot stadium and the stands looked full despite it being a Monday afternoon. The plane banked hard right and crossed the beacons, alternately dropping and lifting with the wind shear. The landing was surprisingly smooth, given the rough approach, and the pilot came over the intercom and made a comment about how much better his landings would be once he got his commercial license.

Medellín's airport had undergone a major facelift, as had much of the city since its release from the violent grip of the drug cartels in the early 1990s. Eugene nodded his approval at the upgraded facility as he carried his solitary bag through the wide, tiled corridors. The taxi queue was non-existent and he hopped in the back seat of the first in line. He gave the man Raphael's address and sat back for the ride.

It irked Eugene that Medellín's reputation on the world stage was, first and foremost, associated with Pablo Escobar's cocaine cartel. Few knew that the city and the surrounding countryside were the country's premier suppliers of coffee, bananas, cut flowers and energy. The creative pulse of the city revealed itself in a multitude of museums housed in buildings of stunning beauty and grand architecture. Almost every major hotel had a resident art gallery, many displaying the works of local artists. Two hundred and seventy-one *barrios* melded together to form the municipal structure that crept up the Aburrá valley between spines of the central cordillera. The weather was temperate, the flora without peer, the people friendly and educated. Yet, mention Medellín and people thought drugs. Eugene directed the driver to a working-class suburb, one of Medellín's rougher edges.

Raphael's street was typical for the area: narrow, with dilapidated houses whose façades were cracked and crumbling. Dirty curtains hung in grimy windows, and small children in ragged clothes threw the taxi suspicious looks as it cruised up and came to a halt in front of number 35. Eugene showed the driver a hundred U.S. bill, then tucked it back in his pocket.

"If my friend is home, I'm going to speak with him for a while. You wait, you get the hundred."

"*Sí, amigo,*" the driver said, all smiles and hoping his passenger's friend was in.

Eugene slid out of the cab, ignored the street urchins begging for coins and knocked on the door. At one time it had obviously been bright red, but the heat and humidity had reduced it to a slab of raw wood with an occasional patch of flaking paint. Dry rot had eaten through in places, and even a half-hearted kick would reduce it to a pile of splinters. Eugene heard the sound of a latch moving the bolt back. The door opened an inch or two and a bloodshot eyeball peered out from the darkness.

"What do you want?" a gruff voice asked.

"Raphael, it's your cousin, Eugene. Eugene Escobar."

The door cracked open another two inches, enough to reveal a wizened face with three or four days' stubble. The lips split into a grin, revealing irregularly spaced teeth, rotting and yellow. Then the door opened completely, and Raphael waved him in. The house was exceptionally dark for midday; all the curtains were pulled tight to the window jambs. Illumination came from a solitary lamp with a bare bulb sitting on a coffee table piled high with magazines. The unmistakable odor of mold and mildew was strong, mixed with a fishy smell emanating from the kitchen. Raphael shut the front door behind Eugene and the house was plunged into almost total darkness.

"You turned into a vampire?" Eugene asked, his eyes slowly adjusting to the low light levels.

Raphael burst out laughing, his foul breath almost knocking Eugene over. "That's funny, cousin. Am I a vampire? No, I don't think so. I just like it dark. Too much sunlight makes me feel sick to my stomach. You want a beer?"

Eugene didn't, but acquiesced, knowing that to do otherwise would insult Raphael. "Sure, a beer would be great. But only one. I drink more than one and the sun almost knocks me over."

"See," Raphael said, heading down the hallway to the kitchen. "We're the same, you and I. It runs in the family."

Eugene took in the room while Raphael got two beers from the fridge. A couch, so stained that it was difficult to tell that the original fabric had been a paisley design, sat against the wall that fronted onto the street. A spring had broken and actually protruded through the fabric. Eugene ignored the couch and sat in one of two stuffed chairs. It smelled of body odor and stale cigarette smoke, but it was better than a thick, sharp wire up the ass. The floor was completely coated with dirt and grime and Eugene couldn't tell if it had originally been tile or wood. A small color television, turned to one of the daytime soap operas, occupied a far corner.

"Nice and cold," Raphael said, entering the room and handing Eugene one of the beers. He sat on the end of the couch without the protruding spring.

"You really should fix that," Eugene said, taking a sip of his beer and pointing the neck of the bottle toward the couch. "If a guy sat on that he could become a woman."

Again, the raucous laughter. "I'd fix it if I had something to cut it with. But I don't. So fuck it." He took a long swig, and said, "What brings you to Medellín, Eugenio?"

"Been away a long time," Eugene said. "Thought it would be nice to visit."

"You still living in Venezuela?"

He nodded. "On Isla de Margarita. I like it there. I take people scuba diving."

"Good money in that?"

Eugene shook his head. "Not really. Maybe if you owned your own live-aboard, but just taking customers out for the day isn't all that profitable. How about you? What are you doing these days?"

Raphael waved his skinny arms about the room. "Living well. Government pays me to survive in such splendor."

"Really. The Colombian government pays for this. Why?"

"Our cousin, Pablo Escobar, kind of tarnished my reputation. I couldn't get a job because I was related to him."

"But you're related on his mother's side. Your surname isn't Escobar. How could anyone know?"

His eyes took on a darkness that shocked Eugene. "You

have no idea, Eugenio, what it was like to be related to Pablo Escobar. You didn't live in Colombia. Your father was wise enough to get his family out of this place and into a different country. Pablo Escobar ruined my life."

"We still had contact with him, Raphael. He didn't ruin us."

Raphael dismissed Eugene's comment with a wave of one hand and hammered back the beer with the other. When he set the empty bottle on the table, Eugene noticed Raphael's hands were shaking almost uncontrollably. The man disappeared into the kitchen and returned with a fresh beer. Eugene was relieved to see he brought only one.

"The man was a tyrant, Eugene. What he wanted, he took. No one stood in his way. If they did, they died. And they died in horrible ways: Colombian neckties, disembowelment, castration. Christ, Eugene, Pablo's goons stuffed these poor bastard's nuts in their mouths, then slit their throats. And if you managed to survive Pablo, Search Bloc and Los Pepes were just around the corner."

"Search Bloc was Col. Martinez's team, right?"

"Yeah. They were the arm of the government that worked with the American DEA and CIA. Fuckers those guys were. They were almost as bad as Pablo's killers."

"The vigilantes were worse," Eugene said. He may not have lived in Colombia while the world was looking for Pablo, but he knew some of the stories that went along with the manhunt.

Raphael ran a shaking hand through his thinning hair and finished the second beer. "Los Pepes were the worst. They felt justified murdering anyone they thought was in cahoots with Pablo or the Ochoa family. And they were arrogant bastards. They even left notes on the corpses that said, *Another victim of Los Pepes.*"

"So now the government gives you a monthly stipend to live on. Something for your suffering."

"Yeah, for my suffering. Nicely put."

"When was the last time you saw Pablo?"

"What the fuck do you care?" Raphael asked, his eyes narrowing. "He's been dead almost twelve years."

"Relax, Raphael. I'm just visiting, remember."

Raphael lit a cigarette and gave a curt nod. "Yeah. Just visiting."

"I've got to use your washroom," Eugene said, rising from the dirt-encrusted chair.

"First door on the right."

"Thanks." He wove his way down the cluttered hall, where stacks of old magazines and piles of dirty clothes lay strewn about. He doubted Raphael had many guests, and if they came over more than once, they shared the bottom of the barrel with the owner. He closed the door and lifted the toilet seat. It was newer, not really new, but definitely in better condition than any other part of the house. In fact, as he glanced about while his stream hit the water, the overall condition of the room struck him as odd. The tub area and the floor had been retiled, and all the fixtures, not just the toilet, were in reasonable condition. The paint was in poor condition, but without upkeep it would begin peeling inside five years. It was the fixtures that intrigued him. And he thought he knew why.

Eugene flushed the toilet and rejoined his cousin. Raphael had opened another beer in his absence. "So how's your family?" Eugene asked as he ambled about the room. Raphael chirped away. Eugene nodded and grunted on occasion to keep the man talking. He couldn't care less about the man's family; they were so distant to his they were veritable strangers. Then he saw it: a small plastic container with a single item in it, tucked back on a crowded shelf amid bric-a-brac and garbage that hadn't made it out to the street. Inside the container was a battery, like the ones used in flashlights.

"That's interesting," Eugene said when Raphael finally quieted down.

"What?"

"That battery in the case." He turned slightly and focused on Raphael. "Almost like it's a trophy of some sort."

Raphael's hands were going again. "Naw, just a battery is all."

"But it reminds me of an interesting story. I think it was early to mid-October of 1993, just a couple of months before Pablo was killed in the shootout. He was holed up in a *finca* on a hillside in Aguas Frías. You know the place? It's just outside Medellín."

"I know the place," Raphael was quiet, almost mouse-like, as he listened.

"Anyway, Martinez was sure Pablo was in the house on top of the mountain, and he had the place surrounded by over seven hundred police officers and soldiers. They watched the place for three or four days before they got the signal they needed to be sure he was there: Pablo placed a call to his son from the *finca*. Immediately the police swooped in. They were all over the place, pumping in tear gas and ripping the place apart. When they didn't find Pablo, they brought in the dogs. Still, nothing. He escaped. You know how?"

Raphael just shrugged and Eugene continued. "He concealed himself in the forest until it was safe to head down to lower ground. And to make the trip down the mountainside, he used a flashlight. And flashlights need batteries. Two batteries. Pablo sent one of those batteries to his wife, but he kept the other. It reminded him of how close he had come to being captured or killed."

"So where is this going?" Raphael asked.

Eugene was quiet for a moment, then calmly asked, "When was he here, Raphael?"

The man was sweating now, and shaking even more than before. "I don't know what you're talking about, Eugenio."

"Don't play games with me, Raphael. I doubt you've seen him in years, but I know he was here."

"Of course I haven't seen him in years. He's dead."

Eugene ignored Raphael's remark. "Before Pablo was gunned down, he was on the run. The police knew he spent some of that time here in Medellín. He drifted from place to place, never staying in one location too long. But before he moved into new digs, he always had the bathroom renovated. New toilet, new sink, new bathtub. The whole nine yards." He glanced down the hall. "That bathroom looks a lot newer than anything else in this house, Raphael. Maybe twelve years old, give or take. And the battery. No one frames a battery. Unless you're Pablo Escobar. I'll put money on it that Pablo forgot to take the battery with him when he left."

Raphael was silent, save for a sucking sound as he inhaled on a cigarette. Finally he ground out the butt in the ashtray and leaned back in his chair. "He stayed for about two weeks in October '93. Less than two months before Martinez and his men found him and killed him. He swore me to secrecy, Eugenio. To this day, I've never told another soul."

"Thanks for the honesty, Raphael. I need to know what he said to you while he was here."

Raphael looked stunned. "Why, Eugenio? He's dead. He's been dead for years. Why all of a sudden are you in my living room asking questions about a dead man? What's going on?"

Eugene shook his head. "I can't tell you, Raphael. And trust me, you don't want to know. Suffice to say that I'm looking for something."

Raphael leaned forward, his dark eyes eager with anticipation. "You think he stashed some money?"

"I'm not saying."

"But you want me to help you."

"Yes, I do. I need to know what happened while he was here. What he did, what he said, who he called on the phone."

Raphael rose from the couch, slightly unsteady on his legs. The beer was starting to hit him. He shuffled into the kitchen and reappeared with a beer in both hands. He offered one to Eugene, who reluctantly accepted. He dropped back into his chair and said, "Pablo used to talk a lot on his cell phone. He spoke to his wife and son mostly, seldom to his daughter. Limón, his bodyguard, lived here with him, so Pablo didn't call him unless he was out on an errand." He took a long drink of beer. "He liked talking with Juan Pablo and from what I could judge of the conversation, Juan Pablo liked being the son of a *narco*. He kept Pablo up to date on what the government forces were doing. From what I could tell, Juan Pablo had an inside connection somewhere in Col. Martinez's Search Bloc."

"Surprise, surprise," Eugene said sarcastically. "How come Martinez couldn't locate him using some sort of electronic device? He had access to CIA technology."

"Pablo used to talk about that all the time. He had a telephone that used a higher range than normal; 120 to 140 MHz, I think. Martinez couldn't trace the calls."

"Smart fellow, our deceased cousin." Eugene took a small sip of beer.

"Yeah. It really pissed off Martinez. They talked about the colonel a lot. I could tell whether Martinez was closing in or completely lost by what Pablo said to his son. One time, he said, *We all know what Martinez wants. I should just give it to him.*"

"Now that's an interesting thing to say." Eugene pondered the statement. Then asked, "When did Pablo start growing a beard?"

Raphael looked puzzled. "He never grew a beard. Just

that shitty little mustache that never seemed to fill in. He shaved every day."

Eugene's mind was racing, but he pushed the issue no further. "He stayed here for two weeks. What the hell did he do all day? This place isn't very big."

Raphael showed no signs of being insulted by the remark. "I don't know. He slept every day until after noon, got up and showered, drank some coffee and smoked a bit of weed. He stayed out of the sun; almost like he didn't want to tan. He liked to watch movies and just before dinner he rode on his bicycle."

"What?" Eugene said, sitting up. "What bicycle?"

"One of those stationary ones. You peddle like a crazy asshole for half an hour and don't move an inch. He'd be sweating like a pig when he was finished. Always took another shower, then had dinner."

"Pizza?" Eugene asked, knowing it had been Pablo's favorite food.

Raphael shook his head. "Never. He ate chicken, vegetables, brown bread and lots of fruit."

Eugene polished off his beer over the course of the next hour, pumping Raphael for anything else he could remember about Pablo's stay. Mostly it was useless information, but the trip yielded more than he thought it would. He shook Raphael's hand at the front door, waved and slid into the backseat of the taxi. It was late afternoon and cooking odors wafted out from the neighboring houses into the street. He gave the man an address on Carrera 51 and sat back, watching the residents of one of the world's most infamous cities go about their daily routines. Things had changed in Medellín with the demise of the drug cartels, at least on the surface. Pablo Escobar, Carlos Lehder and the Ochoa brothers were gone, but in their place were Mario and Javier Rastano, and God knew who else. The drug trade wasn't dead, just legitimized. Javier Rastano had achieved what Pablo Escobar had dreamed of doing: living the life of a respected Colombian businessman while amassing hundreds of millions of *narco* dollars in foreign accounts. At least there was one positive spin to the whole affair. The level of violence was down, and the citizens of Medellín weren't walking about looking over their shoulders.

They arrived at the address and Eugene reminded the driver of his reward for being patient. Again, the man smiled and settled in to wait. Eugene walked across the sidewalk and into the grassy expanse of Cementerio San Pedro. He walked on the winding path until he reached a gravesite adjacent to a large expanse of unused field. Small bushes ringed the site and wrought-iron bars curved over the slightly raised earth. The headstone was average for the cemetery, and above it was a picture of Pablo Escobar in a suit and tie. A few visitors were at the grave, and Eugene waited until they had gone before he stood next to the carefully tended tourist attraction.

He was silent for a couple of minutes, then he said, "You're not in there, are you?" He stared at the picture, a good one of Pablo that didn't show much of his double chin or heavy jowls. He looked like an average Colombian citizen who died at an early age. Eugene was alone at the graveside and he spoke aloud to the testament to his cousin.

"When you were killed, you had a beard. Yet less than two months before you died, you were shaving every day. Look at that mustache, Pablo. It's pitiful. It would take you the better part of three or four months to grow a beard. And you stopped eating pizza. You never ate healthy or worked out in your life. You know what I think? You had some poor bastard altered surgically to look exactly like you, fattened him up and probably even burnt your fingerprints onto his with a laser. Then you set up him and Limón by giving them a phone Martinez could trace. You had the imposter grow a beard to disguise the exact shape of his face. And then you left Colombia, with a smaller waistline and countless millions in banks around the world. Your own words, Pablo: *We all know what Martinez wants. I should just give it to him.* Martinez wanted you dead, and you gave him that. Except you didn't die, you just disappeared. Somewhere."

A couple paused, hand-in-hand, by the grave, and spoke about the good things Pablo Escobar had done for the city of Medellín, then moved on. Eugene couldn't help shaking his head at the lunacy. Sure, the man had built some soccer stadiums and constructed homes in some of the most squalid slums, but his legacy was one of brutality and conquest, not diplomacy and kindness. He glanced at the grave one last time before leaving the cemetery.

"Where are you, Pablo Escobar?" he asked in a hushed tone. The life of his wife and daughter hung on him finding the answer.

Chapter Nine

Pedro Parada was home.

Home in El Salvador, the country whose government's response to civil unrest was to create death squads that killed indiscriminately and tortured innocent citizens.

Home to the smallest Central American country, but one that bore the dubious honor of being the most dangerous country in the world. A fact backed by statistics that showed a homicide rate almost twice that of Colombia.

Home to a country finally at peace after a horrific twelve-year civil war that threatened to rid the country of any sanity or civility it had achieved since the Mayans ruled the virgin rainforests.

And home to some of the friendliest, most peace-loving, simple people God had ever placed on the planet. It was an ugly irony.

He walked through the San Salvador terminal, his step light and purposeful. The building was similar to many American airports, with wide halls and high ceilings.

Restaurants and colorful kiosks stocked with brand-name products were plentiful, and Salvadorians in Armani and Versace strolled the tiled corridors, their arms laden with bags of duty-free merchandise. He passed the open-air patio, an oasis of palms and ornate benches where travelers sat and watched the incoming and outgoing flights.

Outside the terminal was the usual line of taxis vying for business. He chose a brightly painted yellow cab whose driver was young and eager. The driver quoted a price to drop Pedro off in central San Salvador, but Pedro just smiled and shook his head. He turned toward the next driver in the queue and was rewarded with a price almost half the first driver's. Pedro slid into the back seat, a warm sensation running down his spine. It was good to be home.

He had the driver stop at the market midway between the airport and San Salvador, a popular spot for grabbing a traditional meal before hitting the congestion of the city. Pedro searched out his favorite stand and found it still operating, the stooped and aging vendor serving the same pupusas as when he was a child. She gave him a toothless grin when he ordered, and he wondered if she remembered him. He paid for two, but when he picked up his order, three of the cornmeal and refried bean staples were on the plate, with a side of *curtido*. He sat at a picnic bench off to one side, topped the pupusas with the pickled cabbage and a touch of hot sauce and watched and listened to the crowd bartering back and forth over prices and discussing the latest football match. He finished his meal and stopped by the booth, dropping an American twenty on the counter before heading back for the taxi. He gave the old lady a wave as she shouted *"Gracias, gracias."* The flies were thick, the air was oppressively hot and humid and the roads congested with smoke-belching beaters. God, it was good to be back.

San Salvador hadn't changed one iota in the year he

had spent working in Venezuela. When they reached El Centro, he paid the driver and continued along Avenue Independencia on foot. He dodged the buses as they roared down the streets, passengers clinging to whatever handhold they could find, reminded that his father had been killed by a micro-bus that had failed to stop after running him over. Pedro briefly wondered if more people were murdered in San Salvador or run over by buses. Whatever the count, both were high. A couple of gang members approaching him on the crowded sidewalk veered slightly into his path. He looked away and crossed to the other side. Confrontation with anyone who had gang tattoos was stupid at the best of times, but without a gun in your waistband it was suicide. They passed him with some remark about his mother and sister, but Pedro just ignored them and kept moving. He didn't look back, knowing any eye contact at this point would result in a fight. He turned at the next corner and slipped into one of the many bars along the strip. He sat at a table in the back. He could see the street, but it would be difficult for anyone in the bright sun to make out his face. A few moments later the two gang members sauntered past. They glanced in, but kept moving.

Welcome home. He needed a gun.

The bar was one of the nicer ones in El Centro, moderately busy for midafternoon, its clientele a mixture of office workers and unemployed men with a few dollars to spend. Pedro knew that within walking distance were a hundred bars that would make this one look like a lounge in the Ritz. He ordered a beer and nursed it for twenty minutes, time enough for his friends to get their mind on mugging someone else. He paid the tab and walked quickly back to the main drag, his eyes searching out a specific address. He found it halfway down a block a few hundred yards farther to the west. The tiny numbers were nailed above a door squeezed between an electronics shop and a deli that served fresh *frijoles* and *panes*. He knocked on the door and waited. A tiny peephole in the thick wood flipped open, and a moment later the door creaked back on its hinges.

"Pedro?" the woman asked. She was about fifty, with a round face and sagging cheeks. The rest of her body was an extension of her face, flabby with little form. She held out her arms, and Pedro gave her a hug.

"Minerva," he said, holding her at arm's length. "You look great."

"Shush, you," the woman chastised him. "I've grown fat since you left."

"More of you to love," Pedro said, giving her a disarming smile. "Is Alfredo in?"

She nodded and pointed to the narrow flight of stairs leading to the apartment above the retail shop fronting onto the boulevard. Pedro climbed the stairs and she followed, puffing by the time she reached the top riser. The interior of the apartment was in stark contrast to the simple entrance. The floors were gleaming hardwood, inlaid with ebony designs of ancient Mayan symbols, and the walls were painted in soft colors and decorated with masks that pre-dated the arrival of the Spaniards. A solitary south-facing window flooded the room with natural light. An overweight man in his late fifties entered the main room from a hallway. He broke into a wide grin when he recognized his guest.

"Pedro Parada," he said, extending his hand. "You're finally back from Venezuela."

"Just visiting," Pedro said, shaking the man's hand.

Alfredo Augustino, a close friend of Pedro's father, shook his head. The rest of him seemed to shake with the same motion as his head, just out of phase. The result was a large, jiggling mass that reminded Pedro of Jabba the Hut. Alfredo ran his chubby fingers through his thinning hair and scowled. "Pedro, this city is crowded with gangs and drug smokers. Those people I would like to see leave. But you, you are a good man, honest and hard-working. It would be nice if you moved back. I would hire you and pay you well."

Pedro smiled tiredly, a smile he reserved almost exclusively for Alfredo. How many times had the man begged him to move back to the dangerous streets of San Salvador with the promise of good pay and a nice place to live? Pedro had perfected that smile while saying no, although the offer was attractive. Alfredo ran an auto parts store in El Centro, supplying used parts that helped keep thousands of wrecks on the already congested streets. He also had a monopoly providing new parts to the city's Mercedes owners, at jacked-up prices that would make even Bill Gates blush. On the surface he appeared to be completely legitimate. But everyone needs a hobby, and Alfredo was no exception. His hobby was peddling guns.

Guns in El Salvador, especially San Salvador, were as common as cell phones in New York. But the guns Alfredo sold went one step beyond what the average dealer could lay his hands on. Light submachine guns and RPGs were the norm, with heavy caliber fully automatic tripod-mounted weapons on the upper end. He was careful whom he sold to, and a direct result of his discretion was that he was still alive. And very wealthy. He kept a few on hand in his home, but most were in a secure warehouse in an industrial sector of the city. As someone who referred business, and whom Alfredo explicitly trusted, Pedro had visited the storage facility numerous times. But what he needed now was most likely close by, in the house.

"What brings you back to El Salvador?" Alfredo asked as they sat on comfortable brogue furniture. Minerva disappeared into the kitchen.

"A friend lost something. I'm helping him find it and get it back."

Alfredo adjusted his girth in the seat until he was comfortable. His eyes narrowed and he cocked his head slightly to one side. "Really."

Pedro drummed his fingers on the arm of the chair. "Really."

"What sort of item did your friend lose?"

Pedro shrugged. "Something very valuable to him." He paused as Minerva entered with two trays loaded with bits of fish and freshly cut vegetables. Cold beer accompanied the food. He thanked her and she took a seat next to her husband.

"No games, Pedro. What's going on?"

"His wife and daughter were kidnapped."

Alfredo nodded. "He's a rich man, this friend of yours?"

Pedro shook his head. "No, not at all. The people who kidnapped his family want information, not money."

"And this friend of yours, he lives in Venezuela?"

"Yes."

"Then why are you back in San Salvador?" Alfredo asked.

"Javier Rastano was the man who met with my friend. He and his father, Mario, are behind the abduction."

Alfredo nodded, both his chins moving in unison. "The Colombians. I know these people. They've had a considerable presence in El Salvador for a number of years now. I think they have a house here in the city, in Escalón."

"Have you ever met them?"

"No. Nor do I wish to," Alfredo said, popping a bit of shellfish in his mouth and chewing. "I have no desire to do business with Colombians. I don't trust them."

"My friend thinks Javier Rastano may have brought his wife and daughter to El Salvador rather than keep them in Venezuela or risk being caught holding them in Colombia. From what I understand, they're respected businessmen in Medellín."

Alfredo laughed. "Respected businessmen from Medellín. Now there's an oxymoron."

"Eugene is sure they're running cocaine through Panama and into El Salvador. That would explain why they keep a house here."

"I suppose it would. What do you want me to do? Ask some questions?"

Pedro was hesitant. "Perhaps. But you've got to be discreet. I don't want them to know that Eugene has someone helping him."

"What kind of info do you need?"

"Without raising any red flags, I need to know something about Javier Rastano. His likes and dislikes. His vices. Things you can find out without Rastano being aware that we're nosing around."

"I know a few people I could talk to on the sly. Not a problem. When do you need to know?"

"The clock's ticking. Rastano gave my friend two weeks to get him access to a numbered account, or his wife and daughter die. That was Saturday, two days ago."

"So you want to try to get close to Javier Rastano and see if you can find the two women."

"That's the plan."

"Risky," Alfredo said quietly. "You're dealing with Colombian drug dealers, Pedro."

"Yeah. I know." He crunched on a cracker topped with a prawn. "I need one more thing."

"Let me guess. A gun or two."

Pedro smiled. "Maybe two or three. And I'd like one to be fully automatic."

"Okay," the big man said, rising from the couch. "I'll see what I can find out without causing any ripples on the pond. In the meantime, let's get you a gun."

Pedro followed Alfredo down the hall and out of Minerva's line of sight. Her eyes were worried for him and it was unsettling. He knew she thought of him as a son, and seeing him in harm's way was difficult for her. They reached a room Alfredo used for his home office and he triggered a hidden switch. A trophy case filled with loving cups and medals from Alfredo's equestrian days swung out, revealing a shallow gap between the false wall and the exterior brick. Alfredo pulled on the glass case and the door opened completely. In the enclosed space were an assortment of guns, mostly pistols and revolvers, with a few automatics and semi-automatics. Alfredo waved his arm at the arsenal.

"Your choice, Pedro."

Pedro walked slowly to the ensemble, spent thirty seconds looking over the merchandise, then plucked two handguns from where they hung on the wall. Both were Smith & Wesson, one a 9mm carbon steel model 910 with a ten-shot clip, the other a classic .44 Magnum revolver. He set them on Alfredo's desk, then returned to the wall, taking more time in choosing an automatic weapon. The selection was impressive: various Yugos, a couple of Thompsons, a Heckler & Koch and two Brownings. He fingered one of the Yugos, an M-70AB-2 AK, similar to the ones used by the Viet Cong in the Vietnam War. He replaced it and pulled the H & K MP5A3 from its moorings, testing the weight and feel. He nodded and set it on the desk beside the two handguns.

"How much?" he asked Alfredo.

"At cost," Alfredo said, retrieving a small, orange book from a drawer in a desk in the secret room. He totaled the damage on a calculator. "Two thousand, one hundred. And I'll throw in the ammunition."

"Hell of a deal," Pedro said, knowing the same buy on the street would have been at least three times that much. He peeled off the correct number of bills and laid them on the desk.

"How much ammo do you need? Fifty rounds enough?"

"A thousand," Pedro said. "Nine hundred for the sub-machine gun. Fifty each for the handguns."

"What?" Alfredo said. "That's ridiculous."

"No," Pedro said. "That's thinking ahead. Remember, they're Colombian drug dealers."

Chapter Ten

"Where is he?" Mario Rastano asked.

"About ten minutes from your house. We had a man tail him to the Caracas airport. He took a flight to Medellín and we picked him up again once he landed." Javier's voice sounded distant over the phone line.

"What? He's in Medellín? What the hell is he doing here?"

"He visited a fellow named Raphael Ramirez. He's a cousin of sorts, on his mother's side. He stayed in the house a couple of hours, then took a cab to Cementerio San Pedro. Spent some quality time at Pablo's graveside."

"What did you get from the meeting with this Raphael character?"

"Not much. The street was really narrow and there was no place for us to set up surveillance equipment without being seen. We picked up a few scraps from down at the end of the block, but nothing of any importance. They talked about him renovating his bathroom and a battery must have worn out in some device, because they were talking about a battery. We only got pieces of the conversation so we really don't know much."

"All right. At least he's on the move, checking things out. Maybe this Raphael knew Pablo before the Search Bloc supposedly killed him. I'll check it out from here. How are things in El Salvador?"

"Fine. Weather's nice, women are behaving themselves. Couldn't be better."

"Talk to you soon, Javier."

"Bye, Dad."

Javier Rastano dropped the phone back in its cradle, interlocked his fingers and stretched his arms above his head. A calm surrounded him on the expansive patio that stretched the full length of the rear of his Escalón mansion. Potted palms and ferns ringed the carefully inlaid bricks that formed the patio and lined a wide path that wound downhill to a kidney-shaped swimming pool surrounded by mature mango and eucalyptus trees. Interspersed in all the shrub and tree beds were thousands of perennials, most of them orchids in various stages of flowering. The gardens stretched for acres, and the twelve-foot stone wall, which delineated the Rastano estate from the main street and their neighbors, was barely visible through the foliage. Javier rose from his chair and strolled slowly down the path toward the pool, admiring the plants in full blossom. He stopped in front of an *Encyclia vitellina*, an orangey-red flower with five distinctive petals and a bright yellow stamen. The flower, native to Mexico but doing well in its new habitat, was exquisite. Immediately adjacent to it was one of the *Restrepia* genus, brought from his Colombian homeland some ten years ago. It was a far more delicate flower, and it resembled a small tongue sitting on a larger tongue, both vibrant red, mottled with brownish spots. Next to the flower was a long bare stem. He scowled at the broken plant and glanced at the bricks under his feet. A light brown stain covered an area a few feet in diameter, blood residue from the gardener who had accidentally snapped the flower off its stem. As a simple, very effective message to the other gardeners, he had slit the man's throat on the spot when he learned of the carnage. He made a mental note to remind one of his staff to pull up the stained bricks and replace them. The reminder of the man's incompetence irritated him. He continued down the path until he reached the pool. He dipped a toe in the water, then slipped off his shirt and dived in. The water was a cool and refreshing break from the incessant humidity. He floated on his back, staring at the cloudless sky and thinking about the day's business.

Fifty-eight kilos of pure cocaine were due to arrive at their warehouse in the coastal town of Puerto Avalós later in the afternoon. The settlement, a quiet fishing and farming community, was well protected from the ocean by a long, narrow entrance through the Bahia de Jaquiisco, and his warehouse was well protected from the government authorities by a long list of bribed officials. No one looked twice at the freighters that docked at Pier 26, loaded up with coffee, and left the port under the cover of darkness. No one cared, so long as the envelopes with American dollars continued to arrive on time. Once the fifty-eight kilos arrived from its overland journey through Panama, Costa Rica, Nicaragua and Honduras, it would join eighteen truckloads of product already mixed in with the coffee on the freighter. The sea lanes from El Salvador to the United States were heavily patrolled by the U.S. Coast Guard, but vessels were seldom boarded. They reserved that special service for the Colombian freighters, especially those departing from the port city of Buenaventura, close to Cali. No drug smuggler with a hint of intelligence tried to slip a shipment past the U.S. Coast

Guard on those sea lanes. But a small freighter registered in El Salvador, no problem.

Javier pulled himself out of the pool and toweled off before making a quick call to see if the truck had arrived in Puerto Avalós. He was informed that it had and the final preparations for sailing were underway. Fifteen hundred kilos of cocaine was a small shipment, but that was how his father ran this pipeline to the United States. It netted the family about three million dollars per shipment, and they had yet to lose any product to the Coast Guard or Customs. All the coffee boats were equipped with an underwater hatch which could be opened, dumping the cocaine in the ocean. And the powder was weighted, as cocaine tended to float. But to date, they had only had to dump one shipment, and that was in open waters when their freighter had been forced to call for help after being disabled in a violent squall. The route was profitable and was working fine. It didn't need fixing, and Javier realized that his father's reasoning was sound. Thirty successful shipments of fifteen hundred kilos with no loss was far better than five shipments of five thousand kilos with one or two of them ending up with the DEA.

He finished drying and donned his shirt before heading back up to the house. The front of the mansion was colonial, with pillars and a massive portico overhanging the main entrance, but the rear was almost all windows. They were thermal glass, with UV protection and heavily tinted to keep prying eyes out. Not that anyone could see the house from the rear, as it was completely protected by the wall and the lush foliage inside the grounds. He reached the rear entrance and padded through the entertainment room, complete with pool and ping pong tables, pinball machines and even a row of slot machines. He headed down a set of curved stairs to the basement. The lower level was fully developed, with a media room and numerous bedrooms where his security staff slept. He walked past the giant plasma screen television and down a long hallway lined with doors to the staff quarters. An armed guard sat in a chair beside a metal door at the far end of the hall. He rose as Javier approached.

"Everything okay?" Javier asked.

"Yes, sir. Would you like to see them?"

"Yes."

The guard let his M-16 drop to his side and worked the key in the lock. The heavy metal door groaned as it opened. Javier followed the man into the room. It was a self-contained suite, with a small kitchen and a private bathroom, flanked by two separate bedrooms. The main living area was well appointed, with couches and a television. Two women sat close to each other on one of the couches and watched warily as he approached.

"Hello, ladies," Javier said, sitting on the edge of another couch. "How are you?"

Neither one spoke. They just sat and stared at him, holding hands. Both women had bloodstained bandages on their hands.

"Your husband is doing as we wish," Javier continued. "If he's successful, we'll release you."

"And if he isn't?" Julie Escobar asked. "What then?"

Javier shrugged. "Don't be such a pessimist. Have some faith in him. He seems like quite a resourceful man."

"How long are you going to keep us here?" Shiara asked, her voice barely a whisper.

Javier smiled. "As I said, if your father gets us the information we require, you'll be free to leave. We're reasonable men and we realize this could take some time, so you may be here for a while. If I were you, I'd get comfortable and try to enjoy yourselves. Have you gone through the DVD selection we prepared for you?"

"Yes, thank you," Julie said. "Could you arrange for a

doctor to check Shiara's hand? I think it's beginning to get infected."

"Yes, of course. I'll see to it." He rose. "Anything else you need?"

"How about a telephone?"

He grinned and retreated through the door. He heard the guard sliding the bolt back in place as he walked the length of the hallway. The women were his prisoners, and for a moment he wished his father would back off and let him have some fun. But the old man had been adamant that neither woman should be harmed or mistreated until Eugene Escobar had located Pablo or retrieved the number to the account. They may need the women to reassure Eugene at some point that they were alive and well cared for. But once the two weeks was up or Eugene came through with the goods, the prisoners were expendable. And at that time he knew his father would relinquish control. Then he could have his way with them before slitting their throats.

The only decision he had to make was which one to rape first.

Chapter Eleven

The Drug Enforcement Administration had twenty-nine offices across the United States and another twenty-two in foreign countries. Its mandate was to reduce drug usage inside U.S. borders and to halt the drugs entering the country. Faced with having to choose one location to approach the DEA, Eugene opted for the El Paso, Texas, office. His choice was not made without careful thought.

The El Paso Intelligence Center, or EPIC as it was often called, was second in importance only to the main office on Army-Navy Drive in Arlington, Virginia. EPIC was the center for worldwide intelligence gathering and dissemination by eleven different federal agencies, and much of that information concerned activity in and around Colombia. Operation Selva Verde, a joint effort involving the Colombian National Police and the DEA's office in Bogotá, was run from El Paso. And El Paso had been the American office for the senior agents who had been working the Escobar case in 1993, like Joe Toft, the senior DEA official during the years they scoured the underbelly of Colombia for the drug kingpin. Eugene was convinced El Paso was the key if he was to involve the DEA in the search for Pablo Escobar.

There was no direct flight from Medellín to any city in the United States, and the best Eugene could do was to hub through Mexico City and fly into Dallas-Fort Worth. He had a six-hour layover in Mexico and another three in Dallas for connecting flights. Those delays, plus flying time, and he had lost the better part of a day in transit. It was late Tuesday, almost midnight, when he arrived in the border city of El Paso. He grabbed a cab and had the driver pick a reasonable hotel that offered suites rather than just rooms, in case agents from the EPIC center wanted to meet with him at his hotel. His cabbie, a cheerful Mexican who loved to talk, dropped him at the Comfort Suites El Paso, on Sunland Park Drive. He checked in and paid a bit extra for a room on the third floor overlooking the pool. Once in the room, he unpacked his toiletries and lay back on the bed, his body spent but his mind on overdrive.

What was he doing here? Contacting the DEA wasn't his idea, it was Javier Rastano's. And here he was in El Paso, running to do exactly what his wife's kidnapper had suggested. How stupid was that? He tried to clear his mind, to think independently, but nothing would come. The thought passages of his brain were focused on his current course of action, and nothing was going to change that. The DEA had been one of two choices, the other being the Central Intelligence Agency. Both departments of the U.S. government had been extremely active in tracking down Pablo Escobar, and both agencies would have extensive files of that search stored in their computers. It was sheer lunacy to think he could track down his cousin in two weeks without some sort of help. Pablo Escobar had incredible resources at his fingertips. Back in the early '90s, for the better part of three years, the Americans and Colombians had pooled their resources in an all-out search for Escobar, knowing he was somewhere inside Colombia. And it was either a stroke of luck, or Escobar's decision to let them find and kill an imposter, that finally brought the manhunt to an end. How could he hope to find this man now that eleven plus years had passed and the world was Pablo's stage? The odds against success were astronomical.

Yet the consequences of failing to find Pablo were unthinkable. Julie and Shiara were his life. If they were to die at the hands of Javier Rastano because he was unable to find Pablo, his life would be over. He thought of his son, safe with his grandparents in Caracas, and he realized that giving up on life would be impossible. Miguel was another innocent victim in this travesty, and Eugene knew that no matter what happened, he would have to continue. Some shell of his former self would have to guide his son through the loss. Then another thought hit him, one that left his guts churning.

What if the DEA just brushed him off? What if they had no interest in his predicament and simply laughed off the possibility that Pablo Escobar might be alive?

Eugene closed his eyes and clenched his fists. Seething anger mixed with futility and his emotions boiled over. His breathing quickened and his chest constricted as he fought to control the rage fueled by his hatred for Javier Rastano. He leapt from the bed and shot his right foot out in a karate style kick, the sole of his shoe hitting the television screen and smashing the picture tube. The impact sent the ruined television careening off the bureau onto the floor. The plastic housing cracked open, spilling its electronic innards across the tile. Eugene just stared at the mess, his eyes unblinking. In his mind, Javier Rastano lay on the floor, broken and dying. Somehow, that calmed him. He flopped back on the bed and closed his eyes, his breathing back to normal and his mind relaxed as one thought kept synapsing through his brain.

He was going to kill Javier Rastano.

Eugene awoke on top of the covers, still dressed in his street clothes. He glanced at the alarm clock sitting on the night table next to the bed. Almost seven in the morning. He got up and walked unsteadily into the washroom, taking time to shower and shave before heading downstairs for breakfast. He leafed half-heartedly through the current *USA Today* before asking the desk clerk for the address to the DEA center.

"First time I been asked that," she said. "Carlsbad Caverns, that's a different story. Everyone wants to see the caves." She was Mexican, a little on the high side of thirty-five and still quite attractive. Her long dark hair looked like something out of a shampoo commercial and she had a nice smile. "You talk good Spanish," she said, smiling as she thumbed through the government pages of the El Paso phone book.

"I'm Venezuelan," Eugene said. "Spanish is my native language."

She gave him an inquisitive glance. "From Venezuela, look like an American and wanting the address for the Drug Enforcement people. You're an interesting person Señor . . ." she took a quick look at his name on the room manifest, "Escobar." She looked at him again.

"No relation," he lied. Under normal circumstances the reaction to his surname was predictable, but in this case, with him asking for the DEA's address, he knew she'd ask.

"Okay," she said, then added. "Here it is. El Paso Intelligence Center." She jotted down the address and slid it across the desk. "How long are you staying?" she asked.

"A couple of days," he answered, ignoring the flirtatious tone in her voice. "Thanks."

On the cab ride to the DEA center, he alternated between watching the brilliant red and ochre hills that surrounded the city and thinking of what to say when he arrived. When the cab pulled up in front of the long, squat building, Eugene still hadn't thought of a really good way to entice the DEA to get involved. The bottom line was, he was going to sound like a lunatic. He entered the building and approached the receptionist.

"Can I help you?" she asked pleasantly.

"I hope so. I'd like to speak with an agent who has ties to the drug problems in Colombia."

"What is this concerning, sir?"

"It's confidential," Eugene said. "No offense, but I'd like to speak privately with an agent."

She didn't look at all miffed by his comment. She picked up the phone and dialed an extension, then turned slightly so Eugene couldn't hear the conversation. A few moments later a young man in a blue suit entered the lobby through a security door. He was early twenties, with slicked back black hair and deep brown eyes. His skin was dark brown and Eugene suspected he was Mexican on at least one side of the family. He spoke to Eugene in English, but Eugene answered back in Spanish. The DEA agent continued in Spanish and introduced himself as Eduardo Garcia.

"What can I do for you, sir?" Garcia asked politely.

"I'd like to speak with you in private," Eugene said.

"Certainly. This way, please." He steered Eugene down a short hall with a metal detector at the end. They both took all metal objects from their pockets and passed through. Three closed metal doors led in different directions and Garcia picked the one on the left, entered a code in the security mechanism on the handle and pushed open the door. "Down here. There's a conference room we can use. I think it's vacant right now."

Garcia was correct and they settled in at a table with twelve executive chairs, Garcia at the head of the table and Eugene in the first chair to the right. The room was painted the same off-white as the rest of the complex and the carpet was an inoffensive brown. It was the blandest building Eugene had ever been in. "What can I do for you, Señor . . . ?"

"Escobar. Eugenio Escobar. But everyone calls me Eugene."

"Okay, Eugene. I'm okay with Eduardo if you are."

"That's fine. And you're one of the agents working Colombia?"

Eduardo laughed. It was an easy-going, soft laugh. "Sort of. I wouldn't say that I'm exclusive to Colombia, but I do work that sector quite a bit. I know my way around the Bogotá field office."

"All right. I guess I'll get right to the point. I'm Pablo Escobar's cousin."

Eduardo steepled his fingers and leaned back in the leather chair. "That's interesting. Especially to us at the DEA."

"I'm sure it is," Eugene said. "Anyway, if I had to sum things up in one sentence, I would say this: I think Pablo is still alive."

There was absolute silence in the room for the better part of thirty seconds. The room was so quiet that Eugene could hear the low hum of the ballast in the fluorescent light. Garcia focused on him for a few seconds, then on the table. He made a quick note in the leather-bound book he'd brought with him into the interview, although Eugene didn't think he really needed to write that down. It wasn't something a DEA agent would easily forget. Finally, Eduardo said, "That's quite a statement, Eugene. Do you have any proof to back it up?"

"Yes, and no. My wife and daughter have been kidnapped by someone who is sure Pablo is alive. They've given me two weeks to find him, or they'll kill my family."

"Who?"

Eugene shook his head. "Sorry, their names are off limits. Part of the deal."

"Why do they suspect Pablo is alive?"

"They've been watching a numbered bank account for years now. Supposedly at least part of the money in that account is theirs. There was no action for years, but in the last few months there have been a couple of withdrawals. A few million in January and another few million earlier this month."

Eduardo made a few more notes. "If they have access to this account, why didn't they just empty it years ago? Why wait for Pablo to start withdrawing money?"

"Pablo is the only person with the ten-digit account number. Without that, no one gets in. The money has been sitting, collecting interest, for the better part of thirteen years."

"How much money are you talking about?"

Eugene shrugged. "I don't really know. Hundreds of millions of dollars. Minimum. Could be a lot more than that now. For these guys to want the account number, it's got to be substantial."

"Why did you come to the DEA?"

"Believe it or not, the drug traffickers who have my family suggested it."

"Now that's rather unusual."

"Not really, when you think about it. Who knew more about Pablo Escobar than the DEA and the CIA? Maybe the Colombian National Police, but I doubt it. You guys, and the administration in power in Washington, D.C. at the time, were the driving force behind the push to kill Escobar. So who would have better files on the manhunt than you?"

"So what is it you want from us, Eugene?"

"I want a couple of agents, as many as you can spare, to help me find Pablo. I want access to your files. Maybe there's something in them that will tell us where he is."

"If he's alive."

"Oh, trust me, Eduardo, he's alive." Eugene stood up and walked the length of the table, lightly touching each of the chairs as he passed. "He's alive and well, somewhere on this tiny planet of ours. Pablo was always a runner, not a fighter. He wouldn't have let himself get trapped on the second floor of a ramshackle house in the heart of Medellín with no means of escape except the front door and a window overlooking the rear courtyard. My father once told me that Pablo was crafty beyond measure. Despite the efforts of your organization, Eduardo, he's alive."

The young DEA agent scanned his notes. "You have no idea where this account with all the money is located? Cayman Islands, Bahamas, Switzerland?"

"No idea."

"And you won't tell me who has your wife and daughter?"

"If I do, he'll kill them."

"This isn't much to work with," Eduardo said. "Let's go over it once more. Maybe we missed something the first time. When exactly did this man tell you he had your wife and daughter?"

The interview continued for about twenty minutes before Eduardo wrapped it up, telling Eugene that someone from the El Paso office would be in touch with him at his hotel within twenty-four hours. They needed time to pull files from the archives and cross-correlate the data they had stored on their computer's hard drive with this new information. They shook hands and Eugene left the cool building for the dry heat that engulfs El Paso almost daily. Eduardo Garcia retreated for his office with his notebook.

"What was that about?" a fellow worker asked as Garcia passed her in the hall.

Eduardo shook his head and grinned. "Maybe a nutcase. He thinks Pablo Escobar is alive."

The woman laughed. "Now that's a good one."

Garcia grabbed a coffee and stirred in some cream and sugar. He walked carefully to his windowless office and dropped his notebook on his desk. A small stack of paperwork, ready for inputting into the mainframe, sat on the edge of his desk. He ignored it and opened a new file, turning to the notes he had jotted down during the forty minutes with Eugene Escobar. He filled in all the necessary blanks, then typed the gist of the meeting in his own words, being accurate and refraining from peppering the interview with his own feelings or emotions. As silly as the whole meeting probably was, his superiors would eventually cast an eye over the report, and the last thing they wanted to see was his opinion of whether this was important or not. Stick to the facts and you got promoted. Get emotional or opinionated and you rot in your cubicle. It was kind of an unwritten rule at EPIC. He finished the report, inserted his DEA number at the bottom of the page, his electronic signature, and hit the enter button. Then he drained the last of his coffee and dug into the pile of paper on the edge of his desk.

Agent Eduardo Garcia had no idea what wheels he had just set in motion.

Chapter Twelve

When Eduardo Garcia hit the enter button on his computer, two things happened. His report was saved to the hard drive on EPIC's mainframe computer, and the file was scrutinized by ghost programs from every agency with ties to the El Paso center. Red flags immediately went up in two of those agencies. One was at DEA Headquarters in Arlington, Virginia. The other was in Langley, home of the Central Intelligence Agency. Within nanoseconds of each other, the report was downloaded and sent to specific personnel at each agency. It was almost lunch time on the eastern seaboard, but both agents who had flagged reports that included Pablo Escobar's name were in.

Alexander Landry was chairing a meeting with the divisional section chiefs from Atlanta and Chicago when Garcia's report was electronically transferred through the system and into his mailbox at the DEA headquarters in Arlington. Landry's executive assistant, Gwen Allen, read the report and immediately walked a paper copy of it into his office, cleared his desk and placed it front and center. She returned to her private office, just outside his, placed a call to their corporate travel agent and booked a seat on the first available flight to El Paso. When Landry passed her office after concluding the meeting, she flagged him down.

"Something very interesting in from EPIC," she said. "It's on your desk. I've already booked your flight and I'm in the middle of clearing your calendar for the next two days."

"Better be good, Gwen," he said gruffly.

Alexander Landry was a bear of a man, six-four with a sturdy frame that carried two-hundred and fifty-five pounds of muscle and precious little fat. He had a barrel chest, and the rest of his body was in proportion. Long arms, coursed with thick tendons over well-toned muscles, ended with hands the size of baseball gloves. His waist tapered to a size thirty-six, and he usually wore loose-fitting khakis or suit pants that hid his thick legs. Since his five-year stint with the marines, Landry had always worn his blond hair short and kept his rugged face clean-shaven. His eyes were cool blue and intelligent. He had spent the last twenty-three years with the DEA, eleven of those years in Colombia. From all the years in South America, Spanish was his preferred language, although English was his native tongue.

Landry retreated to his office and picked up the two-page report. His face remained impassive as he read Garcia's account of Eugene Escobar's visit. Once he was finished, he switched off his computer, grabbed his briefcase and locked his office door behind him. Gwen was on the phone when he stuck his head into her office. She quickly put the other party on hold.

"One thirty-six departure," she said. "Had to book you business class. Sorry. That's all they had."

He nodded. "Thanks. I'll be on my cell phone if you

need me." Despite his size, Landry disliked flying business class. The DEA didn't blow its budget on expensive airline tickets or three hundred dollar lunches. At least, Alexander Landry didn't.

His Lexus ES300 was underground, on the fifth level close to the elevator, and he thumbed the key fob as he pushed through the fire door into the parkade. The beep was loud in the enclosed space, and he disliked using the automatic opener for that reason. Today he didn't even notice it. A packed suitcase was in the trunk, a precaution he now made standard practice after flying out on short notice with nothing but his choice of clothes for the day. It included three outfits, a fresh set of toiletries and a new pair of black Nunn Bush shoes. He slipped the key in the ignition and gunned the motor. Forty-three seconds later he swiped his card key at the exit, then swung out into traffic, heading for Washington National Airport. The fifty-three-year-old section chief placed a quick call to his wife at their upscale Forest Hills home, and gave her the news. She took it well, considering tomorrow was their son's twenty-first birthday and dinner plans were already in place. He hung up feeling a pang of guilt. Maybe retirement wasn't so far off, he thought.

Alexander Landry was section chief of the Bogotá field office during the wild ride that was the late '80s and early '90s, reporting directly to Joe Toft, who ran the entire DEA operation in Colombia. Despite their efforts, cocaine was flowing out of Medellín and Cali unimpeded. Between Carlos Lehder, the Ochoa brothers, Pablo Escobar and José Rodríguez Gacha, the flow was staggering, and seemingly unstoppable. Colombian police forces and the army were intimidated by the cartel's use of *plata o plomo*, and most opted to accept the bribes rather than the bullet. Justice was sheared off at the knees as judges and other officers of the court were murdered. Car bombs exploded in the streets and the murder rate went through the roof. And amid all this carnage were the DEA and the CIA. Their mandate was to stop the flow of cocaine into the United States. Easier said than done.

Landry pulled into the parking lot at Washington National, his mind on Pablo Escobar. Of all the cartel leaders, Escobar was by far the most violent. In reality, he was probably a psychopath, incapable of feeling the pain his victims suffered as he executed them. His word was law, and in a country careening out of control as Colombia was in the '80s, the law was ruthless. There was no known estimate of how many people Pablo Escobar had ordered killed. His hit men, or *sicarios* as they were known, went about their job with complete impunity from the law. Murder was not only acceptable, it was expected. If you crossed the drug lords, you died. This was the insanity he had lived through for eleven long years.

Landry reached his gate and scanned the crowd for his CIA counterpart. He knew she would be en route to El Paso, just as he was. He didn't see her, but that meant nothing. She was coming, he knew it. He wasn't sure how he felt about that; they had knocked heads so many times in the past, yet he had great respect for her intelligence and ability.

The boarding crew announced his flight, and he joined the short line of business-class passengers. Eugenio Escobar. Pablo's cousin. The past was rearing its ugly head.

Cathy Maxwell, thirty-eight and one of the highest ranking women in the CIA covert ops sector, was at her desk at CIA headquarters in Langley, Virginia, when the communiqué arrived from El Paso. It took three minutes and twenty-one seconds for the two-page report to leave the printer and reach her office. She scanned the contents of Garcia's report and glanced up at Donald Adams, her assistant.

"Get me on the next flight to El Paso," she said. He nodded and was gone. Maxwell re-read the report, then pulled open her bottom desk drawer and dug through a slew of files. She reached for the one with labeled "International Accounts." She scanned down the long list of individual accounts at different world banks, watching the left column for small check marks, then scrutinizing the account opposite the mark. The ninth one was the account she was searching for. She dragged her index finger across the page to the latest activity on the account. One withdrawal of eight million dollars on January 19 and another for six million on March 9. The dates were within the time frames provided by Eugene Escobar. She leaned back in her chair and ran her hands through her shoulder-length hair, thick, wavy and chestnut brown with red highlights. The hair suited her fine, as did the soft facial lines—both belied her inner strength. More than one person had found out in other ways how cunning and persuasive she could be. The smarter ones took one look at her deep brown eyes and instinctively knew better. She withdrew the sheet of paper from the file, copied it and replaced the original just as Donald appeared at her door.

"One thirty-six out of Washington National or two forty-seven from Dulles?"

She did the math. A trip to her house was an absolute necessity, as her daughter Elsie had a half day at school and was bringing home her report card. She'd promised to be home in the afternoon so they could go over it together. "Dulles," she said, grabbing her car keys and heading out the door.

"I'll arrange for your ticket to be at the Delta counter," Donald said as she banged through the outer doors and was gone.

Cathy Maxwell was a woman to both fear and respect. Her academic background was a Master's in Science, majoring in chemistry at MIT, and her physical qualifications were 'best of class' at Quantico in her tenure as a student with aspirations to become a field operative. She joined the DEA nine days after her twenty-fourth birthday and, partly because she was fluent in Spanish, she was immediately shipped out to the Bogotá field office. It was July of 1991 and *narco* activity in Colombia was rampant. The Ochoa brothers ruled northern Colombia, with Rancho Ochoa spreading over thirty-five thousand acres between Cartagena and Barranquilla. Pablo Escobar was just settling into his new digs at La Catedral prison on a hill overlooking his home town of Envigado. She'd visited the drug lord in his lavish 'cell' and came away realizing that Pablo's incarceration was a joke. In fact, Escobar had pissed off so many groups and individuals that the only place he was safe from retaliation was inside the grounds of La Catedral. Inside six months, Cathy Maxwell was a jaded agent, working what she knew to be a losing battle. The drug lords were simply too powerful. So she targeted them in her field of expertise: the supply of chemicals necessary to process the raw coca leaf into cocaine.

And that put her head to head with the cartel kingpins, especially Pablo Escobar. While both Pablo and the Ochoa brothers moved thousands of kilos of processed cocaine into the United States, it was Pablo who bribed government officials and procured the chemicals the labs needed to cook the coca leaves. Without acetone, ether and potassium permanganate there was no product. And the Americans knew it. So rather than concentrating entirely on stemming the flow from Colombia, they allocated some resources to keeping the most important chemical—potassium permanganate—out of Pablo's hands. Cathy Maxwell was promoted and put in charge of the chemical aspect of the CIA's covert battle against the Colombians. She did her job well, perhaps too well, as the cartels targeted her and her family for death. They missed her, but they didn't miss her parents. Cartel *sicarios* paid her parents a visit at their Boston home, slicing both of them into unrecognizable pieces. The Bogotá station chief had walked into her office, closed the door behind him, and told her the grim facts about her parents. Cathy Maxwell was a changed woman. Bringing down Pablo Escobar became the focus of her life. It was common knowledge around DEA offices that two days after her parents' funeral she had stormed into La Catedral and confronted Pablo Escobar. He had been surrounded by bodyguards.

She had stood two feet in front of him, and said, "I'm going to surgically remove your nuts and stuff them up your nostrils, you sick, fat little fuck."

That elicited a stream of laughter from the guards and one of them grabbed her from behind. She spun around, pulled down on the man's arm and wrapped her elbow around his neck as his body doubled over. She twisted and a sickening snap cracked through the room. His body crumpled to the floor at Pablo's feet. The guards pulled guns and moved toward her, but Pablo held up his hand.

"We've got quite the little tiger here," he said. "Unfortunately for you, I'm a guest of the Colombian government at this time, and it would create quite the headlines if you were to kill me while in custody. I think my nuts are safe while I'm here." He walked back to one of the many soft couches in the living room that formed part of his jail cell. He waved his arm and the guards escorted Cathy Maxwell from the room. Not a word was ever mentioned about the guard.

She steered off the Dolley Madison Boulevard onto Route 695, driving more from memory than actually watching the road. McLean, Virginia was a heavily wooded and very secluded bedroom city within throwing distance of Langley, and a reasonable drive to downtown D.C. A few of the agency's top brass lived in the exclusive subdivision, but not many could afford it. Cathy and her husband had paid just shy of a million for their ten-year-old colonial style home on Sugarstone Court. She pulled into the driveway and killed the engine of her BMW 540i.

No minivans in her driveway, she vowed, grabbing her briefcase and hoofing it into the house.

"Hi, sweetie," Darren Maxwell said as she pushed open the front door. He met her and they embraced. "Missed you this morning."

"Missed you too," she said. "You writers have the life. Up at noon, tap away on the keyboard for a couple of hours, and then spend the rest of the day telling everyone how difficult writing is. I wish."

"It's true," he said, trying to look hurt. Darren Maxwell was forty-one, three years her senior, in excellent physical condition, and an attractive man whose hair just beginning to gray at the temples. At six-one, he was four inches taller than she, but knew that size meant nothing when dealing with a wolverine. Truth was, ever since they met in Colombia, her with the CIA and he on assignment for *Time* magazine, they had been madly in love. Three kids had failed to douse the fires. Their oldest, Elsie, was in grade two, and the twins were in pre-school. Darren wrote his articles from home, giving the kids one full-time parent.

"I have to fly out today," she said, her arms still encircling his waist.

"Where?"

"El Paso. Some guy walked into EPIC this morning, told the DEA agent he was Pablo Escobar's cousin and that the son-of-a-bitch is still alive. The report was fielded by Langley about forty minutes ago."

Darren pushed back from her slightly.

"You know how it works. When Escobar's name pops up, especially when someone says he's alive, I have to check it out."

"Hi, Mommy." A smiling little girl in jeans and a yellow top came racing around the corner. Her hair was in pigtails and both front teeth were missing. The tooth fairy had been in a very generous mood when she visited and had coughed up big bucks for the 'prime chiclets' as her father called them. Elsie had stashed the money in a jar and was saving for a new bike.

"Hi, Elsie," Cathy said, dropping to her knees and giving the little girl a hug. "Is this your report card?" she asked, taking the offered paper.

"Yes, and I did really, really well."

Cathy went over the report card with her daughter line by line, reading the teacher's comments and showing great pleasure at the series of 'excellent' marks issued for understanding, effort and work habits. They agreed that a deposit of five dollars to the bike jar was appropriate for such a stellar performance, but Cathy reminded her daughter that the real reward wasn't the money, but achieving the marks. She spent another half hour with Elsie and her two younger sisters, quickly packed and headed out the front door for the airport.

"How long will you be gone?" Darren asked, leaning on the hood of her car as she dropped her suitcase in the trunk.

"A couple of days tops. I'll call you once I've met with Escobar's cousin."

"Okay, take care." Darren kissed her and watched as her car rounded the curve and disappeared behind the thick stand of trees that sheltered their home from the road.

Pablo Escobar alive. Not good news.

Chapter Thirteen

Eduardo Garcia looked up from the pile of paperwork on his desk. A huge man was framed in the doorway, blocking any light from the hallway. Garcia dropped his pen on the papers and leaned back in his chair, irritated at the interruption. The man was dressed in khakis and a golf shirt, but the white skin had Garcia thinking that the man spent little time on the links.

"Can I help you?" he asked, allowing irritation to creep into his voice.

"Eduardo Garcia?"

"Yeah. That's me."

"Alexander Landry," the man said, letting a business card slip from his fingers. It dropped on Garcia's desk, face up. Landry watched as the young agent leaned forward and read the fine print under Landry's name. *Deputy Administrator, United States Division.*

Garcia hit the front of his knees on the desk as he

jumped to his feet. He ignored the pain, and said, "Mr. Landry. Welcome to El Paso."

"Thank you," Landry said wryly. "Eugenio Escobar, where is he?"

Garcia swallowed hard. "I'm not sure, sir. At his hotel, I think."

Landry leaned forward, his huge hands on Garcia's desk, his face close to the young agent. "Want to find out, Agent Garcia? I'd really like to speak with the man."

"Yes, sir," Garcia said, reaching for Escobar's file.

"Comfort Suites El Paso," Landry said before Garcia could open the file, reciting the phone number without taking his eyes off Garcia.

Garcia dialed the number, sweat stains beginning to grow under his arms. Christ, what if Escobar wasn't at the hotel? What if he had left town, made a run for it? His career was over. A moment later the ringing stopped and a man's voice answered. "Mr. Escobar?" Garcia asked.

"Yes."

Garcia tried not to let his relief show, but he knew Landry was more than aware that Escobar had been cut loose without any sort of surveillance, and that Garcia was lucky the man hadn't decided contacting the DEA was a bad idea and left town. "Mr. Escobar, I'd like to send a car over to pick you up. Could you be ready in ten minutes?"

"Yes, ten minutes is fine."

"I'll have my driver meet you in the lobby."

"Fine." The line went dead.

Landry leaned even closer to Garcia. "Don't ever do something that stupid again, Agent Garcia, or you'll be enjoying the Russian winters as part of our hand-selected team in Siberia." He glared at Garcia for a few seconds, then added, "I want you to sit in on the meeting when Escobar arrives. Let me know if there are any changes in his story."

"Yes, sir." Garcia called the front desk and ordered a car to the Comfort Suites to pick up a Mr. Eugenio Escobar in the lobby. ASAP. Landry waited until Garcia had finished the call, then disappeared into the hallway. Garcia grabbed his head in his hands and squeezed. One of the top ten ranking DEA chiefs in the world had just visited his office, and he'd completely blown it. So much for his career. He picked up the Escobar report with shaking hands and gave it a quick glance. At least he'd prepared a decent report, given the low priority he had felt it deserved. Obviously, he had been greatly mistaken about what sort of status the DEA was attaching to Eugene Escobar. He pulled open his bottom drawer and withdrew a neatly folded shirt and quickly changed. If nothing else, he wouldn't have on a sweaty shirt for his second meeting with Alexander Landry.

Cathy Maxwell cabbed it straight to EPIC from the El Paso airport, presented her creds at the front reception and was ushered directly into the interview room with the boardroom table and leather chairs, where Eugene Escobar was talking with Alexander Landry and Eduardo Garcia. Landry had left a note with the receptionist that if Maxwell showed up to bring her straight in. They all glanced at the door as she entered.

"Hello, Cathy," Landry said, not bothering to get up. Both other men did.

"Alexander," she said, her eyes resting on him for a second, then taking in the rest of the room. A young Hispanic man with his badge on his belt, she figured him for Eduardo Garcia, and a fair-haired, light-skinned man in his late thirties or early forties. Eugenio Escobar, Pablo's cousin.

"I'm Cathy Maxwell," she said, extending her hand first to Garcia, then to Escobar. "You must be Eugenio Escobar." They shook.

"Most people call me Eugene," he said, amazed at the viselike strength in her grip.

"Eugene, then," she said. "Has Alexander filled you in on who I am?" Both men shook their heads. "Alexander and I worked together quite closely in Colombia thirteen or fourteen years ago when Pablo Escobar was on the run. We worked with our respective teams, Alexander was with the DEA and I was with the Central Intelligence Agency. I'm still with them, Deputy Director of HUMINT. Human Intelligence," she added when she saw a puzzled look cross Eugene's face. She turned to Alexander. "What did I miss?"

"Not much," Landry said. "Eugene was just filling us in on what he did after his wife was kidnapped."

"Please continue," Cathy Maxwell said, sitting and motioning to Eugene. "I'll get what I need from the transcripts."

Eugene ran his hands through his curly hair. He'd hoped for some response to his request for help, but hadn't expected top level agents from Washington to fly in on a moment's notice. "I visited a friend of mine in Porlamar. That's the largest city on Isla de Margarita. He was involved with the cartels back in the '80s, taking care of the books for José Rodríguez Gacha until Gacha was killed in '89. During his time in the business he met Pablo, the Ochoa brothers, Carlos Lehder, and many others. But when The Mexican was killed, he got out."

"Lucky man," Landry said quietly.

"He admits that," Eugene agreed. "When I mentioned the name of the man who's holding Julie and Shiara captive, he knew him. My friend told me that this man still runs a ton of cocaine overland from Colombia to El Salvador, where it's put onto boats and shipped up the coast to the States. And the man with my wife and daughter was quite tight with Pablo at one time. That told us three things: that the money really does exist, that my wife and daughter are probably in El Salvador, and that Pablo is probably alive."

"How does that tie your wife and daughter to El Salvador?" Cathy asked.

"The kidnappers are prominent businessmen in Colombia," Eugene said, turning slightly to face her. "My friend was adamant that they wouldn't drag hostages back to their own country, and that since they had such a strong presence in El Salvador, they'd most likely take them there."

"I see."

"I left Isla de Margarita and flew to the mainland. I have a friend working in Caracas who is originally from El Salvador. I asked him to check it out for me and see if he could find any trace of them in San Salvador. He said yes. He left Caracas two days ago."

"How will you know if he has any success finding them?" Landry asked.

Eugene held up his cell phone. "We both have new ones. No one else knows the numbers."

"Excellent idea, Eugene," Landry said. "Have you heard from him yet?"

"No."

Landry nodded and shifted slightly in his chair. "Go on."

"I flew south from Caracas and visited a cousin in Medellín. His name's Raphael." He recited his cousin's address off for them and all three agents made notes in their respective books. "We talked for a while, then he admitted that Pablo had stayed with him in October '93, less than two months before he was killed. But here's the strange thing. While he was staying with Raphael, Pablo ate healthy food, exercised regularly and shaved every day. Yet when he was shot, he was still grossly overweight and had a beard."

The room was silent for a moment. Eugene was shocked by the expression on Cathy Maxwell's face. She looked like a volcano ready to blow. Her teeth were clamped together so hard her jaw was turning white, and pure hatred glowed in her eyes. Then she seemed to relax, to bring her body back under control. Her brown eyes returned to normal: inquisitive and penetrating. She handed Alexander Landry a sheet of paper. On it were two highlighted entries.

"These two withdrawals coincide with the time frame Eugene gave to Agent Garcia during their first interview."

Landry scanned the list, his gaze lingering on the two horizontal lines. "Banque Suisse de Zurich. One of the cartel's favorite banking institutions a few years back. CIA has been watching this whole page of accounts for all these years?"

"That's one page out of thirty. But let's not be coy, Alexander. You guys have sixty pages," she answered. "The dates jibing like that give some credence to Mr. Escobar's story."

"Agreed," Landry said.

Eugene sat back in the soft leather chair and watched the two key players as they discussed Swiss banking: the ten-digit codes used by Banque Suisse de Zurich, who had access to them and how they triggered the electronic safeguards to open the account for withdrawals. Landry and Maxwell, high-ranking officials in their organizations, had immediately dropped what they were doing to personally visit the El Paso office. They hadn't sent flunkies to gather information and report back. They had made the trip personally. And quickly. It was certainly more than he had expected.

When there was a lull in the conversation, Eugene said, "I know what Col. Martinez and his Search Bloc team were up to, but what was the American DEA and CIA involvement in searching for Pablo?"

Landry weighed the comment, then said, "What is said in this room, remains in this room, Eugene. You okay with that?" Eugene nodded and Landry reached over and switched off the recorder before continuing. "The situation in Colombia during the '80s was so convoluted it was almost impossible to keep tabs on what was happening. People involved in the drug trade were being murdered in record numbers, but no one knew who was killing whom. Each time a body surfaced, the list of suspects was pages long. If someone inside Pablo's organization was killed, we had to consider whether the victim had pissed off Pablo and it was an inside job by the drug lord himself, or if maybe another cartel had taken him out. The guerrillas were notorious for killing the *narcos*, as both the Medellín and Cali cartels had an ongoing war with Ejército de Liberación Nacional and Fuerzas Armadas Revolucionaries de Colombia. But FARC and ELN stayed mostly in the mountains; they didn't venture into the cities too often. Then there were our guys: CIA, DEA, Delta Force and Centra Spike, and we all had our own agendas. The Colombian police and army had units that operated under the radar and circumvented the court system. But they were totally cowed by the cartels. And after Los Pepes was formed, they killed record numbers of Pablo's men every day. Add to this that it's Colombia we're talking about, and that random murder is a great possibility. It all led to one thing: When a cartel member died, no one looked very closely at who killed him."

"Delta Force commandos are top-level U.S. soldiers, but what's Centra Spike?" Eugene asked.

Cathy Maxwell answered his question. "The CIA and the National Security Agency were the primary watchdogs during the Cold War. But when hostilities ended between our country and Russia, and the Cold War died a lingering death, both agencies were too cumbersome to perform the covert surveillance needed to stay on top of things globally. Centra Spike was formed to fill the gap. These guys were the best of the best, hand-picked from the SEALs and Delta Force, each with special skills. Communications was the essence of the team; each member was able to operate the most modern tracking and surveillance equipment the military had. Locating and tracking targets was their priority. And once they found the target, they moved in. I'll give you an example. If the President of the United States happened to be speaking to the right person at a dinner party, and told them that our international position would be much better if so-and-so were to be assassinated, Centra Spike were the guys who went in, performed the sanction, and get out, without anyone being the wiser. They were, and still are, ghosts. It's not hard to understand why we used them to help us find Pablo Escobar."

"Did they find him?" Eugene asked.

"Several times, yes. But Pablo was a runner, not a fighter. Pinpointing him was difficult, but getting a team in place in time to corner him, even Delta Force or Centra Spike, was next to impossible. We just couldn't move quickly enough. He slipped through our fingers more times than I can remember."

"Did Centra Spike isolate him on the mountaintop at Aguas Frías?"

"Yes. And I think we could have had him if Col. Martinez hadn't insisted on bringing in the Colombian army and surrounding the place. He thought large numbers of men were the answer. Turns out he was wrong."

"It would appear," Eugene said.

"Pablo was damned elusive," Landry interjected. "Cathy and I had a few good scraps over who was responsible for Pablo slipping past the nets we drew around him. But in the end we had to admit that he was one very lucky guy."

"And now?" Eugene said, turning to look at both Landry and Maxwell. "What do you think now? Is Pablo alive?"

Both agents were silent for a minute, then Cathy said,

"Eugene, I know this is difficult for you. You're emotional, and well you should be. But we have to look at the facts and only the facts. And as of right now, we haven't had enough time to answer that question. We need more time and more information before we can proceed. Give us a day or two so we can review the 1993 files. The Colombian police could have tampered with the evidence that proved the body was Pablo Escobar. We need to know if there's a possibility they altered the DNA samples they provided us. We had Pablo's DNA on file, and we based our conclusions almost entirely on the positive match to the DNA provided by the Colombian police."

"I don't have time to waste," Eugene said. "It's already Wednesday. I've only got ten days to find Pablo or get the access code to the bank." He paused for a moment, then pointed at the page with the two highlighted entries. "You already know what bank the money is deposited in. Can you get the ten-digit number from the bank?"

Cathy Maxwell shook her head. "Absolutely no chance. The banks recognize the CIA as a legitimate arm of the American government, but we've tried to use our position in the past to free up information like that and have never even come close. They stonewall us the instant we try to circumvent their privacy laws. Sorry, Eugene."

He nodded. "Okay. But at least we have some proof that backs up what I've told you."

"That's true. The existence of the account adds credibility to your story. Now let's go back over the time you spent with your cousin Raphael. We may have missed something there the first time through."

Two hours later the group broke up. Eduardo Garcia was assigned to drive Eugene back to his hotel and to stay in the adjoining room. Cathy Maxwell and Alexander Landry left EPIC about ten minutes after Eugene and Garcia, and drove to a nearby restaurant. It was just after six, and they both ordered a drink and dinner.

"What do you think?" Landry asked as his beer and her rum and cola arrived at the table.

"I don't know what to think, Alexander," she said, stirring the drink with her swizzle stick and taking a small sip. "You've got to remember that this is pretty personal for me."

"None of us have forgotten the price you paid, Cathy," he said. "Maybe we weren't sympathetic enough at the time and I'm sorry. But soon after Escobar sent his *sicarios* to Boston for your parents, he also killed the Galeano and Moncada brothers. From that moment he was on the run; La Catedral was no longer a refuge, and he fled the prison. Every level of the Colombian government was after him, and our entire focus was finding him, nothing else."

Cathy pushed her hair behind her ears, and slowly turned the glass on the coaster. Finally, she said, "He killed my parents, Alexander. He had them tortured and cut into pieces. I thought I had some closure when we got him, but there was always this nagging thought that maybe the Colombian forensics experts had been bought off, that the corpse wasn't actually Escobar. Now his cousin shows up and pretty well confirms my worst nightmare."

Landry nodded. "Who do you think has his wife and kid?"

"Good question. There are quite a few Colombians with strong ties to Central America. The Alzate family has used Costa Rica and El Salvador as transition points for their cocaine for years now. So has Rubin Tapias, but he's located more in Nicaragua than El Salvador. Probably Mario and Javier Rastano. They're the only Colombians I know with strong ties to El Salvador."

"Anything the CIA can do to get them back?"

She shook her head. "Not without indisputable proof. And even then I'd be calling in too many favors. I'd need to know exactly where they are and every detail about the security forces holding them before I could get clearance for a covert op. Even then the director would probably dump it off on Delta Force or Centra Spike. And then we're back to the same problem we had thirteen years ago."

"The leak," Alexander said.

"The leak."

The server arrived with their entrées and both were quiet as the meals were placed in front of them. Both agents alone with their thoughts. And both thinking the same thing. Back in 1992, when the Colombian government had finally swallowed its pride and asked for American assistance in finding Pablo, there was an informant somewhere inside one of the agencies. Someone working for DEA, Delta Force, CIA or Centra Spike was dirty. They were feeding Pablo Escobar the information he needed to stay one step ahead of the covert forces tracking him. And that was the real reason Centra Spike had never been able to nail him. The voice whispering in Escobar's ear was never found. The voice was still out there. Somewhere.

"Probably retired by now," Cathy said, picking up her fork and knife. She sliced off a thin piece of steak and popped it in her mouth. "But then again, you never know."

Landry was digging into his food with a vengeance. Neither agent had eaten since breakfast. "If we're going to pursue this, we should keep it contained."

"How do you mean, contained?"

"Just you and I and Garcia. No sense trying to cut him out; he's already in the loop. We can still access whatever resources we need from our home offices. The last thing we need is for the rat to find out we're actively searching for Escobar. And if you want my opinion, I think Eugene Escobar may be right about Pablo being alive."

"You think we should look into this?" she asked.

He shrugged. "I thought your mind was already made up," he answered.

"It is now."

Alexander Landry lifted his glass. "To finding Pablo," he said.

Cathy Maxwell clinked her glass against his. "To *killing* Pablo," she replied.

Chapter Fourteen

With the darkness came danger.

Pedro Parada was no stranger to the nocturnal world of San Salvador. He moved through the rough and tumble district of El Centro with confidence, his body language telling those watching from the shadows that this was not a man to fool with. The suit jacket he had purchased earlier in the day fit him well, and if he buttoned it, the unmistakable bulge of a handgun was visible under his left arm. He had bought it to fit for specifically that reason. What the average thug lurking in the shadows couldn't see was the second gun tucked into his waistband in the small of his back. Both guns were loaded.

Pedro's eyes moved between the street and the alleys with a fluidity that came from a lifetime of practice. He saw every movement and smelled every odor, be it machismo or fear. A rustling noise caught his attention and he turned slightly to the vicinity of the sound. A drugged-out street person crawled out from under a pile of garbage, his hand outstretched for coins. A setup. Pedro's right hand instantly found the gun butt under his arm and he spun the opposite direction from the guy on the ground. Three men, in their early twenties and armed with knives, appeared from a crack in the wall a few yards behind him. Pedro pulled the gun from its holster and flipped off the safety. He pointed it at the thieves.

"No easy target here, *amigos*," he said, his hand steady, the Smith & Wesson targeted on the closest man's forehead. "Go find some other mark or your night's going to get real messy."

The men quietly disappeared back into the shadows between the two buildings, and Pedro kept moving. Once he was a hundred feet along the street, he reactivated the safety and holstered the gun. El Centro. Nice part of town to visit at night. He'd have to have a chat with Alfredo about his choice of meeting spots. Pedro finally found the bar where Alfredo had suggested they meet and saw the big man in a booth near the back. The establishment was typical of El Centro, run down and dark, with enough shady, tough-looking characters to cast an entire Quentin Tarrantino movie without leaving the place.

"I almost got mugged," he said, sitting down opposite Alfredo Augustino. He ordered a beer when the waitress came by.

"You leave San Salvador, you get soft," Alfredo said lightly. He didn't seem at all put off by Pedro's close call. "Even in Caracas you can forget how to take care of yourself."

"That's not such a bad thing, Alfredo," he said. "I hardly need a knife in me to keep me on my toes. I'll take a nice quiet street where families walk their dogs anytime."

Alfredo waved his hand in deference. "I'm not worried about you, Pedro. You can take care of yourself. Always could."

The beer arrived and Pedro found himself drinking it

faster than usual. His pulse was still higher than normal; he was still on the downside of the adrenaline rush. "You said you had some information about Javier Rastano."

The big man nodded. His double chins wobbled about as he moved his head. "I do. In two days of asking around, I found out the three things that turn Javier Rastano's crank. His buttons, so to speak."

"What are they?" Pedro asked, finishing the beer and motioning for another one. The waitress, watching Pedro as she made her rounds, caught the motion and nodded.

"Orchids. The man absolutely adores orchids. He spends time in a public park in Medellín just to stare at the orchids. And his estate here in Escalón is packed with them. Along with the indigenous ones from Costa Rica and the other Central American countries, he's imported them from Mexico, Colombia, Thailand and Cambodia. Rumor has it he recently killed a gardener for breaking a flower off its stem while in the orchid was in bloom."

"That doesn't help me," Pedro said. "What else does the guy like?"

"Believe it or not, snow skiing. He travels to Switzerland and Canada to ski at least three times a year. From what I hear, he's quite good."

"Again, Alfredo, not much help."

"This might be." Augustino shifted his considerable bulk slightly to get comfortable. "He likes boxing."

Pedro was silent for a moment, then said, "Really? How *much* does he like it?"

"A lot. He hangs around some of the better gyms while he's in San Salvador scouting out new talent. He doesn't go for the heavyweights; he likes welterweight and flyweight. What weight division did you used to fight in?"

"Welterweight, but that was a few years ago. I'm out of practice."

Alfredo just laughed. "Look at you, Pedro. You work

out, keep yourself in great physical shape; how hard can it be to slip on some gloves and trade punches?"

"You'd be surprised," Pedro said, smiling at the server as she placed his second beer on the table. It was frosty cold and went down easy, a little too easy, perhaps. "It's not hard to get your face smashed in if you're out of shape or forget to duck."

"It's your way in, Pedro," Alfredo said. "You asked me to find you a way inside Javier Rastano's life, and I found one. Plus, I went one step further. I found someone who might be able to get you into one of the boxing clubs that Javier likes to visit."

Pedro leaned forward. "Really?" He knew how difficult it could be to cross the socio-economic boundaries in San Salvador. The rich people liked to hobnob with their own kind. "How can I meet this person?"

"He's at La Luna Casa y Arte tonight. You know it?"

Pedro nodded. "Sure. It's probably the best club in San Salvador. I doubt I can even get in."

"He's left your name with the doorman. His name is Oscar Bernardo and he's expecting you."

"What time?"

Alfredo glanced at his watch. It was eleven o'clock. "Anytime after ten, so you can head over whenever you want. Just for your knowledge, this Bernardo has a real hate-on for Javier Rastano. I'll let him explain things to you."

Pedro just nodded and finished his beer.

"Take care, my young friend. Javier Rastano is an evil man. Everyone I spoke with was very worried that their name may come up in a future conversation. I assured them that no names would be mentioned."

"What about Oscar Bernardo," Pedro said. "He doesn't seem to mind."

"He has his reasons for helping you, but I'm sure you'll find that he would prefer his name stay out of this."

"Okay. Good night, Alfredo. And thanks."

"Good night, Pedro."

Pedro left the bar, waved down a taxi and gave him the club name. Every driver in town knew exactly where it was, although it was doubtful even one of them had been through the front doors. While San Salvador's rich and pampered played at La Luna Casa y Arte, the uninvited survived another night on the dangerous city streets. No one objected, they just accepted it as part of life. You were either born into it, or you weren't.

The taxi left El Centro behind and wove through a labyrinth of backstreets, staying off the congested main thoroughfares at Pedro's request. Pedro had always preferred the scenic route through the city in lieu of the major arteries; the back roads offered a kaleidoscope of El Salvador's people as they went about their daily lives. Folding card tables were set up on the narrow walks between the adobe houses and the streets, and men played cards and women talked about their day. The mosquito hours would soon be over for the evening, and the people could then venture back into their houses. In El Salvador, only the rich, with air-conditioned homes, could stay inside as dusk approached and the mosquito population searched for windless places to roost. The hot little adobe houses were mosquito magnets and Pedro couldn't count the number of evenings he had spent outside, unable to sit in his house for fear of being eaten alive. They drove on toward the Ciudad Universitaria, the city landscape changing, mutating into the more upscale shops and houses of the small Salvadorian middle-class. The driver turned onto Boulevard de Los Héroes and pulled up in front of a nightclub, its chrome and glass frontage vibrating from the Latino rock music. A line of hopefuls waited along the curb, but the doors were closed and the bouncers in place.

Pedro slipped the driver the fare and a decent tip and

walked to the front of the line. Those waiting didn't complain; they knew so much as a whimper and they were out of the line. Two body-builder types stood on each side of the door with their arms crossed over their chests. Pedro approached them tentatively. He had always been the one in the line, never the *hombre* with the connections.

"Good evening," he said. "I'm Pedro Parada. Oscar Bernardo is expecting me."

One of the goons picked up a clipboard and ran his finger down the short list of names. Even upside down, Pedro could see his name. "Don't see you here," he said. "But my eyesight is always better once the cover charge is paid."

Pedro slipped an American twenty from his pocket. "How's your eyesight now?"

"Much better, thank you," he said, pocketing the twenty. "Oscar has a regular table. I'll show you where it is." He glanced at Pedro's jacket, just under his left arm. "I'll check the gun first," he said.

Pedro un-holstered the gun and handed it across, butt first. The bouncer looped a tag through the trigger guard and ripped off the bottom half of the stub. He checked to make sure the safety was on, handed Pedro his claim check and deposited the gun in a locked cabinet just inside the doors.

"Okay, let's go," he said.

"Thanks." He followed the man into the club. The music was extremely loud, to the point of causing pain in his eardrums. They skirted the dance floor, covered with gyrating bodies dressed in Guess and Versace. Pedro drew a few admiring looks and smiles from the women. He smiled back, his even white teeth reflecting the bright strobe lights that throbbed with the music. As they cleared the dance floor, the music from the speakers subsided, and when they reached the tables in the rear of the club, the noise level was not at all irritating. The bouncer pointed at a man seated with two women on either side of him. Both were eager looking and young, probably in the club only at Oscar's invitation.

"That's Oscar," he said, then turned back to the front of the club.

Pedro walked the last few paces alone, Oscar's eyes watching him as he approached. Bernardo was in his late thirties, with slicked-back hair that just touched his shoulders, and very suspicious eyes. His face and shoulders were lean and Pedro knew the man kept himself in excellent physical condition. He was tanned and his fingernails manicured.

Pedro reached the table, covered with a crisp white tablecloth that reached the tile floor. "I'm Pedro Parada," he said.

"Oscar Bernardo," the man replied. They both leaned forward and shook hands. "Sit down, Pedro," Bernardo said, his voice a smooth baritone. "The girls are Savanna, Carmela and Felisa."

Pedro cocked his head slightly and gave Oscar a puzzled look. "There are only two girls, Oscar."

A moment later, a head popped up from under the tablecloth. She gave Pedro a wicked smile and disappeared back under the table. "That one is Felisa."

Pedro slid onto the curved leather bench, careful where he put his feet. "Thanks for meeting with me."

"Not a problem."

The waitress happened by, and Oscar asked what Pedro wanted, then ordered for the table. There was a repeated banging sound as Felisa's head kept hitting the underside of the table, then Oscar made a bit of a face and groaned slightly. The banging stopped. A few moments later, Felisa appeared, sliding up onto her seat and taking a long drink of beer.

"Why don't you gals go dance or something for a few minutes," Oscar said, handing one of the girls two crisp hundred dollar bills. They left quickly, knowing he wanted time alone with Pedro.

"She's got a good attitude," Pedro said, nodding his head slightly toward Felisa.

Oscar grinned. "They all do." He finished the drink in front of him and asked, "What do you want with Javier Rastano?"

"That's kind of confidential," Pedro said.

"Then leave," Oscar said, setting the drink on the table-cloth. "We either trust each other, or we don't."

"Okay," Pedro said, leaning back into the leather seat. He could feel the impression of his second gun hard against the small of his back. "Rastano kidnapped the wife and daughter of a friend. I'm trying to find them and get them back. I think Rastano might have them somewhere in San Salvador."

"Really? Why doesn't your friend come looking for his wife and daughter himself? He's a coward?"

"He's being squeezed from more than one direction. They want something else from him and he's concentrating on finding it. That's why he can't search for his family himself."

The drinks arrived and not a word was spoken until the server had left the table. Bernardo finally said, "Alfredo tells me you are a boxer."

Pedro shrugged. "I spent some time in the ring a few years ago, but nothing much lately."

"Javier Rastano likes boxers. He scours the local gyms looking for diamonds in the rough. He likes to discover new talent. You good enough to be noticed?"

"Maybe," Pedro said. "It depends who I'm up against."

"How about if I arrange for a bout between you and another guy with average skills? I'll have someone put the word out that you're worth watching, try to entice Rastano to show up and check you out. But that's all I can do. Once you're in the ring, you've got to hold your own."

"I'll try," Pedro said. "When and where can you set this up?"

"He belongs to an exclusive club in Colonia Escalón. I'll try for the day after tomorrow. Friday. That work for you?"

"Yeah, that works fine. What do I do?"

"Show up at the gym by ten in the morning. We'll try to have you and your sparring partner in the ring by noon."

Pedro sipped on his beer and eyed Oscar Bernardo. "You know why I want to get near Javier Rastano, but why are you so willing to help? What's in it for you?"

Bernardo's steel-gray eyes bore into Pedro's for the better part of thirty seconds before he answered. "Rastano is a prick. He's an arrogant, ruthless, Colombian bastard."

"True. But that doesn't answer the question. What's your motive?"

Bernardo spread out both his arms on the back of the couch. "Three years ago, my little brother was fifteen. He was in Escalón selling raffle tickets for his football team. They were at the gate to the Rastano estate, trying to get the guards to let them in when Javier drove up in his Ferrari. My brother leaned on his car and held up the tickets so Rastano could see what he was trying to sell. Rastano went ape-shit. He jumped out of the car, raced around to the passenger's side and threw my brother to the ground. Then he started screaming that my brother had scratched his car with the rivets on his jeans. He grabbed an M-16 from one of his guards and pumped six bullets into my brother. Murdered him right in the street."

"But there were witnesses," Pedro said. "Even in San Salvador some things are too brutal to ignore. There should have been a trial."

Bernardo laughed. But it was cynical, not joyous. "The police were going to file charges, until the witnesses either had accidents or couldn't remember exactly what happened. Then I got pulled aside and told in very simple terms that if I ever even looked sideways at Javier Rastano, my entire family would be killed. Every brother, sister, cousin, in-law, and my parents. I can't move against Javier Rastano myself. But you can."

Pedro nodded. "Okay, you set up the bout, I'll be there."

"I won't be there," Oscar said. "And whatever you do, don't mention my name."

"Never," Pedro said, shaking Bernardo's hand.

"By the way, good luck getting into Rastano's estate. Word on the street is that he's holding a couple of women somewhere inside the house. Could be your friend's wife and daughter."

Pedro nodded. He thanked Bernardo again, then claimed his gun and left the club. He returned to the street, quiet in comparison to the lively nightclub, and hailed a cab. He gave the driver the address to his hotel and sat back. The cab smelled of incense and a tiny statue of the Virgin Mary dangled from the rear view mirror. Julie and Shiara were probably in Javier's house. That was good news; Eugene would be pleased. But now he had to think about boxing. He hadn't set foot in a ring for almost two years. True, he had been an excellent fighter back when he made his run at the Olympic boxing team, but never quite good enough. And two years was a long time without lacing up the gloves. Still . . .

He dialed Eugene's number on the cell phone, and when his friend answered he asked the driver to stop at a small park and jumped out of the cab. The last thing he needed was some cabbie going to Javier Rastano with a story of what he overheard in the back seat of his hack. He strolled across a stretch of grass to a bench and sat down, watching the cab and the street traffic as he said hello.

Eugene's first words were, "Do you have any information on Julie and Shiara?"

"Not for sure, but the word on the street is that Rastano has a couple of women at his estate. Might be Julie and

Shiara, but no guarantees. And I may get a chance to meet personally with Javier on Friday."

"That's excellent news," Eugene exclaimed. "Let's hope the word on the street is right." He paused for a second, then asked, "How could you meet him? Rastano, I mean."

Pedro explained the meeting with Oscar Bernardo at the club, minus the young woman with the sore head. "This Bernardo guy absolutely hates Javier Rastano, but he can't do a thing or his entire family gets whacked. Pretty sick stuff."

"Typical for Colombians. What are your chances of turning Rastano's head at the bout?"

"I don't know," Pedro said, his voice now uncertain. "I haven't been in the ring in two years, and I have no idea whether the guy I'll be facing is a good fighter or a bum. I won't know until I'm face to face with him."

"Well, don't get your head pounded in," Eugene said.

"I'll try not to. This is going to be my only shot at getting a look at how Rastano lives."

"Beat him senseless, Pedro. Impress Rastano."

"Yeah, okay, Eugene. But how are you? How are things in El Paso?"

"Oh, man, you won't believe what's happening here. One of the top DEA guys in the United States flew in from Washington, and a high-ranking CIA agent is here as well. They worked together in Colombia back when the U.S. was helping the Colombian army find Pablo. They seem to be taking my situation pretty seriously."

"That's great news," Pedro said. "Have they got any ideas?"

"Well, they knew about the bank account the Rastano's insist is theirs. They were monitoring it and saw the debits."

"More good news, Eugene. Anything else?"

"Nothing right now."

"I'll call again on Friday. Maybe later in the day. I'm not sure."

"Okay, talk to you then."

The line died, and Pedro snapped the phone shut and slipped it back into his suit pocket. Things were moving ahead for both of them. Now all he had to do was keep from getting his ass kicked on Friday, and maybe he'd get an inside look at Javier Rastano. That or one hell of a headache.

Chapter Fifteen

Julie Escobar slowly turned up the volume on the television. It helped cover the sounds of her scraping metal against metal. A slight noise at the door caused both her and Shiara to jerk around and stare at the door handle. It didn't move and Julie returned to the task at hand.

"We'll never get it to fit the screw head," her daughter said quietly. "It's too thick."

"It'll fit," Julie said, taking a moment from rubbing the two pieces of metal together to stroke her daughter's hair. "And when we get it to fit, we'll find a way out of here."

The basement room in which they were imprisoned was well designed, most likely for exactly its current use. It had no windows and only one door, which was constructed of steel. The interior walls were cinder block covered with drywall, the exterior was solid concrete. There were no telephone jacks or cable connections, just a DVD hooked up to the solitary television. A convection microwave substituted for a stove, and although there was a fully stocked fridge, not one container was glass and all utensils were plastic. The mirrors were stainless steel. But even with such foresight, their prison still had one weakness: the heating and air-conditioning system.

To supply the five-room suite with enough fresh oxygen, and to keep that air at the correct temperature, required a larger than normal duct. That duct was positioned about six inches from the ceiling in the main room, and covered by a heavy metal screen. The opening was less than two feet across and eighteen inches high. It was too small for a man to navigate, but just big enough for a small woman, or a fifteen year-old girl. The grate covering the duct was tightly affixed by eight heavy screws, and fashioning a tool to twist those screws out of their housings was what Julie Escobar was working on. Her screwdriver was a metal clip off the back of the fridge and she was using the rough, rear edge of the DVD player to shape the end of the clip to fit the screw heads. It was slow going, but after four days, it was close to becoming usable.

"What's going to happen to us, Mom?" Shiara asked. "Why are we here?" It wasn't the first time she'd asked the questions.

Julie set the clip on the carpet and pulled her daughter close. Involuntarily, her hand went to her daughter's bandage and lightly touched it. Both women's hands were healing now that the doctor had visited and left them salve and clean bandages. "Whatever it is your father is doing for these thugs, he'll be successful. He won't fail us, Shiara. He never has, and he won't start now."

"I want to believe that, Mom, but we're completely at their mercy. And we're a long way from home. We flew on that plane for hours. How will Dad ever find us?"

"Have faith, Shiara. And don't forget we've got a shot at freeing ourselves." She tilted her head slightly toward the air-conditioning duct. "That has to go somewhere."

"Yeah. To an air-conditioner."

"Every cooling and heating system needs fresh air, Shiara. There's a vent to the outside somewhere along the line. We'll find it."

"I'm so scared." She grabbed Julie and held her tight. "I don't want to die, Mom." Tears flowed and Julie dabbed at them with a tissue.

"Have faith in your father, Shiara," she said softly. "He's a resourceful man." She didn't tell her daughter that her father could also be more dangerous than a cornered wolverine. Could be something to do with the Escobar blood that ran through his veins.

Chapter Sixteen

They occupied a room especially designed for research by a small team. Six computers sat on the polished oak desks, all tied into EPIC's mainframe, and capable of accessing restricted databases at Langley and ten other agencies. All six had dedicated ADSL lines and color laser printers and scanners. To highlight the urgency of the situation, they set up a calendar on Landry's desk and X'd off each day with a red pencil. A large whiteboard covered one wall, a twelve-by-twelve cork board another wall, and the final two walls were home to hundreds of research books and catalogs. Every subject, from serial killers to the chemical composition of illicit drugs, was there for the asking. A few of the texts, those concerning the Medellín and Cali drug cartels, were spread over the central table, but most of the research data was coming from DEA and CIA databases.

Cathy Maxwell was working the case files from 1981 to 1993, both DEA and CIA, while Alexander Landry pieced together where Pablo Escobar's immediate, and not so immediate, family were living. Eugene was working with Landry, identifying the huge assortment of uncles, aunts, cousins and so on, while Eduardo Garcia was the gofer. He was enjoying the role, which gave him the opportunity to rub shoulders with the brass from two of the country's premier spy agencies.

After a few hours, Eugene and Alexander Landry had split the family into two distinct divisions on the white board. On the left side were the relatives who had shown disdain for Pablo's career choice. On the right side was a much smaller collection of names: those who found the money and power that emanated from Pablo too much to resist. Pablo's immediate family—his wife, Maria Victoria; his son, Juan Pablo; and his daughter, Manuela—were all on the right, as was his brother Roberto. His sister, Luz Maria, and another brother, Argemiro, were firmly planted on the left.

"Argemiro and my father would have nothing to do with Pablo's lifestyle. When he called and asked us to visit him at Nápoles, you didn't refuse. But my father hated the violence. So did Argemiro. In fact, Argemiro and Luz Maria fled Colombia to Costa Rica. But the Colombian government found them and complained to the Costa Rican government, and had them deported. The government thought immediate family would provide good leverage for bringing Pablo out of hiding. They liked to keep us close by."

"But your family lived in Venezuela," Landry pointed out.

"My mother was a Venezuelan citizen, so they couldn't deport us. My parents were much happier in Venezuela than in Colombia. We were almost totally removed from the *narco* violence."

"Okay," Landry said to Eduardo Garcia, looking over the eleven different names on the right side of the whiteboard. "I want telephone logs from everyone who supported Pablo's drug business. Land lines, cell phones, the whole enchilada. I want to know who called them, when and how long they stayed on the phone. I'm really interested in any calls coming in from South or Central America."

"Yes, sir," Garcia said, pleased to have a specific task assigned to him. "It's going to take a day or two at least. Each person is going to have a different telephone provider."

"Get it done as quickly as you can," Landry replied.

"If Pablo is alive, do you think he'd risk talking to his family?" Eugene asked Landry.

Landry shrugged. "Maybe. I think Juan Pablo is the most obvious. When Pablo was on the run in the early '90s, he found ways to speak with Juan Pablo despite our efforts to pinpoint him. He drove Centra Spike crazy with his technology. Whatever money could buy, Pablo had it. And even though the Centra Spike guys had the newest gear from the U.S. military, they still couldn't catch him. So if he took the risk of talking with Juan Pablo back when he knew we were listening, he could well be talking with his son now."

"The risk is probably greater now," Cathy Maxwell interjected. "Back then we knew he was alive. Until two days ago, we thought he was dead. He's got a lot more to lose now that he's living a secret life somewhere."

Landry gave her an inquisitive look. "You sound convinced he's alive."

Maxwell's face flushed. "It wouldn't surprise me."

Landry chewed on the end of his pen for a minute, then said, "Why don't we look closely at Pablo's supporters at the time he was supposedly killed. Who was still on good terms with him?"

Cathy shook her head and her hair whipped about her shoulders. "I can hardly think of one person of any importance who wanted Pablo alive. The Ochoa brothers were his partners until the bitter end, but I think they stayed with him out of fear rather than loyalty."

"You're kidding," Eugene said. "Are you talking about Jorge, Fabio and Juan David?"

"Yes, the Ochoa brothers. That surprises you?"

"That the Ochoa family was scared of Pablo, yes. Christ, they were billionaires and all three of them were equally as ruthless as my cousin."

"Don't bet on it," Landry said, leaning on the central table. "Nobody, not even The Mexican was in the same league with Pablo when it came to terrorizing people. I don't think there was a soul on the planet who didn't take Escobar seriously. One word from him and you were a dead man. No exceptions, no exclusions. He liked killing people, Eugene. Do you know what his favorite way was of disposing with those he disliked?"

"Can't say I do," Eugene replied, not really wanting to know.

"He liked to hang them upside down and set them on fire."

The room was silent. Then Cathy said, "Suffice it to say he was, or is, a heartless creature. If he's alive, we need to find him and kill him."

Eugene's face suddenly flushed. He said, "That's why you don't want to pull in any more agents. You don't want your hands tied when you finally track him down. You want to dole out your own justice on the spot."

Maxwell looked like she was going to erupt. "He's not getting away again, Eugene."

Eugene held his hands up. "Okay. But let's not forget what the objective is here. We need that ten-digit code. Without it, or Pablo alive and kicking, my wife and daughter are dead."

"It's a big world out there, and he could be anywhere. You need us to find him. And when we do, we'll get your ten-digit code. But after that, I suggest you turn your back or leave the room."

Eugene, Eduardo and Alexander stared at the woman. Her veneer of civility was gone. Her hands were clenched in tight fists, the single sheet of paper she held was crushed beyond smoothing. Slowly, she relaxed and set the crumpled ball on the desk next to the printer. Then she calmly maneuvered the mouse to the print button and reprinted the page.

"I may want him dead, Eugene," she said, her voice smooth and steady. "But there is another reason why Alexander and I want this operation to stay completely covert. During the time we were tracking your cousin through Medellín and across the Colombian countryside, we had a leak. Someone inside one of our organizations was dirty. They were feeding Escobar information that allowed him to stay ahead of us. And I'm not willing to have that happen again. The fewer people who know about this, the better."

"I understand," Eugene said, glad for the explanation.

Landry brought the conversation back on topic. "While Agent Garcia looks over the phone logs, I'll be checking with Customs and Immigration to see which of Pablo's relatives have been using their passports in the past few years. But that only gives us the international flights."

"Check their frequent flyer miles," Cathy Maxwell said. "They may have used frequent flyer miles from their credit card or one of the airlines to take a domestic flight."

"Excellent idea," Landry said, making a note in his book. He swiveled around in his chair and directed his next question at Eugene. "Have you heard from your friend in San Salvador? The one trying to track down your wife and daughter."

Eugene had given this a fair amount of thought and knew exactly how to answer. Pedro was *his* ace in the hole, and he wasn't about to hand over control of his inside man to the task force. He could sense by now that it was in Maxwell and Landry's nature to take charge of situations, and that wasn't going to happen with Pedro. "No, I haven't," he replied evenly. "I thought he might have called by now, but we agreed that if there was nothing to talk about, we wouldn't call."

"You should try calling him," Landry said. "You never know."

Eugene shook his head. "No. He may be in a compromised situation, and a phone call could raise suspicions. I'll just wait for him."

"Okay," Landry said, irritated at Eugene's firm stance. "Whatever you say."

A knock on the door interrupted them, and one of the junior agents stuck her head in. She held a page off a memo pad in her hand.

"Mr. Landry, this gentleman called for you a few minutes ago. I thought you'd like to know."

Alexander Landry took the paper, thanked the woman, and glanced at the name. His lips turned down, and frown lines appeared on his forehead. He swallowed and said, "It appears our little group just got bigger." He handed the paper to Cathy Maxwell. She looked at the name and shook her head.

"What's wrong?" Eugene asked.

"It's a summons from one of our old colleagues. He wants us to fly up to Kentucky and meet with him concerning our sudden interest in Pablo Escobar."

"You don't like him for some reason?" Eugene asked.

"He's just not someone you trifle with," Alexander said. "We've just lost control of our investigation."

He handed the scrap of paper across to Eugene. On it were three words and a telephone number.

Senator Irwin Crandle.

Chapter Seventeen

Irwin Crandle, Republican representative to the U.S. Senate for the State of Kentucky, was a king-maker of the highest echelon. Although his state represented only eight electoral votes, the president, when asked to name his most cherished supporter, always included Irwin Crandle on the short list. His influence in D.C. was legendary, and those who crossed him were political roadkill in a very short time. Mess with Crandle and you better start contemplating retirement.

His tenure in the international arm of the National Security Agency during the tumultuous years when the Colombian cartels were pumping cocaine into the U.S. at an unprecedented rate gave him firm footing in the espionage community. His NSA posting in Bogotá stuck him squarely in the middle of the action. And since Centra Spike was run jointly between the NSA and Delta, Crandle had his fingers in both the military and political pies. That coveted position gave him free rein as to methods in the clandestine fight against the *narcos*, and he yielded that power with malice. Some observers commented that they were glad Crandle was American, not Colombian, or he would have been their fiercest foe. Crandle didn't fight the war to eradicate drugs, he fought it to look good and get promoted.

He took the same approach to politics as he did the Colombian assignment. He used his connections in Delta and NSA to dig up dirt on his opponents. And once he had it, he didn't just sit on it. He used the dirt to pummel opponents into submission. His tenacious behavior allowed him to achieve a position of immense power in D.C. *Show me a good loser and I'll show you a loser*, was his unofficial motto.

Irwin Crandle was well known to both Cathy Maxwell and Alexander Landry, and they recognized him the moment they stepped through the French doors and onto the paving-stone patio behind the senator's stately mansion on the outskirts of Frankfort, Kentucky. He was now in his early sixties, well tanned with silver hair and a fashionable matching goatee. At five-ten and one-seventy he was not a physically intimidating man, but his intensity more than made up for his average physique. His teeth were too perfect, and screamed caps. He stretched his hand out, and a large diamond set in eighteen-carat gold glittered in the afternoon sunlight.

"Hello, Cathy," he said, wincing slightly from the strength of her grip. "How's the family?"

"Fine, Senator," she replied. "And yours?"

"Very well, thank you." He withdrew his hand and turned to Alexander Landry. "Alexander, it's been a few years." Again, the hand and the smile.

"Six years, Senator. The last time was at The Willard Inter-Continental in Washington. You were the keynote speaker at an anti-drugs convention."

"You've done well at the DEA, Alexander," he said warmly. "And you with the agency," he added, glancing back at Cathy Maxwell. "Look at us, a handful of jungle-rats who tracked *narcos* fifteen years ago. Who would have thought we'd all do so well?"

Landry motioned to the remaining two men. "Senator Crandle, this is Agent Eduardo Garcia from the El Paso office, and Eugene Escobar, Pablo's cousin."

Crandle shook Garcia's hand first, then grasped Eugene's. "My thoughts are with you at this difficult time, Eugene," he said, steering his guest to a set of patio furniture beside a large pond covered with water lilies. A plate of cheese and crackers and a large pitcher of lemonade sat on the wrought-iron table. It was a practiced habit of Crandle's to always use given names when first meeting someone. "I understand your wife and daughter have been kidnapped."

"Yes, sir."

The politician's face took on a look of grave concern. He spoke directly to Eugene when the group of five was seated. "This is a serious situation, Eugene. Cathy called me from the jet while you were en route from El Paso and brought me up to speed. I understand you're reluctant to reveal exactly who has your family."

"They were specific, sir. Mention their names and my wife and daughter die."

Crandle pursed his lips and remained thoughtful. "It would help to know, but we can work around it. But if you ever feel it's time to let us know, we'll use the information however we can to help our investigation." He leaned forward, his gaze intense. "Eugene, we've been here before, Alexander and Cathy and I. These are not uncharted waters. We worked under the most arduous conditions during our time in Colombia, and we got results. And we'll get results again. I promise you."

Eugene swallowed and nodded. Sitting in the research room in El Paso, he had been overwhelmed by the response to his predicament, but this was on another scale altogether. During the flight from Texas on Crandle's personal Learjet, Alexander Landry had taken the time to enlighten him on just how powerful the Kentucky senator was. He had direct access to the President of the United States, could empower the considerable resources of the NSA with a single phone call, and was a wealthy man, with access to millions of dollars. His personal fortune was a direct result of his time in Colombia, chasing Pablo Escobar. While jointly running Centra Spike he had employed every form of electronic tracking device in existence, most of them not yet on the open market. When Escobar died, Crandle's job was done and he had returned home to the United States. But he brought with him an arsenal of knowledge of surveillance hardware and software. Crandle created a public company, floated an IPO on the New York Stock Exchange, raised one hundred and forty million dollars, and never looked back. He provided state-of-the-art surveillance equipment to America's largest and most paranoid corporations. He charged a fortune for his expertise and the companies paid gladly. When he moved into the political ring, he was barely challenged in his run for the senate. For whatever reasons, his competition melted away at just the right times, and Crandle slid into his seat in Congress unopposed. And now, this well-connected and powerful man sat across the table, assuring Eugene that they would get results.

Eugene managed a slight smile. "I'm feeling much more confident, sir, with you on board."

Crandle returned the smile, then broke into a low chuckle. "Pablo Escobar. Who would have dreamed the man would still be alive? It's almost incomprehensible."

The French doors leading to the great room opened

and a man walked onto the deck. He was in his early fifties with a thin horseshoe of hair encircling an otherwise bald head. He wore aviator glasses, which hid his eyes and didn't suit his narrow face. He kept a neatly trimmed mustache, just touching the top of his upper lip, and sideburns, which he allowed to creep down past the bottom of his earlobes. His clothes were golf casual with slip-on loafers, no socks. He broke into a grin when he saw Cathy and Alexander.

"Bud," Cathy said with a wide smile, rising and giving him a handshake and a hug. "My God, it's really you."

"Hi, Bud," Alexander said, shaking the man's hand and pulling up an extra chair. "You look great."

"Irwin told me I'd recognize a couple of old faces, but I never dreamed it would be you two," he said, sitting in the proffered seat. "Who are the new guys?"

Irwin Crandle did the introductions. "Agent Eduardo Garcia, El Paso DEA, and Eugene Escobar, this is Arthur Reid. But no one ever calls him Arthur. I bet he doesn't even remember that it's his real name. Call him Bud." The three men shook hands. Bud Reid poured a glass of lemonade from the pitcher and took a sip.

"What's this all about, Irwin, that I have to jet in from Seattle on a moment's notice?" He looked at Cathy and Alexander. "And what's with the spooks? We back in the *narco* business?"

In 1993, Bud Reid was a key player in the search for Pablo. He coordinated the field operations for both Centra Spike and Delta Force. Only Irwin Crandle, and General William F. Garrison of Joint Special Operations Command, had greater authority over the clandestine movements of American troops on Colombian soil. But it was Bud Reid who made the decisions that continued to bring the men safely home. He was revered for his ability to predict the cartel's moves, and numerous major busts, including airfields and jungle laboratories, were attributed directly to his cunning. In the world of counter-*narco*-terrorism, Bud Reid was a legend.

"We're back," Alexander said quietly. "And guess who the target is?"

Bud Reid shrugged. "No idea."

"Pablo Escobar."

Reid cocked his head slightly, as though one ear was full of water. A smile began to creep over his face, then disappeared. He reached up and slowly removed his sunglasses. His eyes were those of a man who has seen too much for one lifetime. "You're not kidding," he said.

"No, we're not kidding," Cathy said. "It's starting to look like we missed him." She and Alexander took turns filling in the ex-special ops coordinator, including the kidnapping, the numbered Swiss account and their progress to date.

At the end of the quick briefing, Bud turned to Senator Crandle and asked, "How did you learn about this, Irwin?"

"I still have my fingers in more pies than Little Jack Horner," the senator said with a grin. "Actually, this one was easy. It isn't often that high-ranking agents from DEA and CIA book flights to El Paso within a few minutes of each other. It was simple to look back over the reports EPIC filed that morning and see what they'd latched on to."

Cathy looked puzzled. "Then you knew about Eugene's report to Agent Garcia at the same time we did. Why wait almost two days before contacting us?"

"I figured twenty-four to forty-eight hours and you'd either be back in D.C. or set up in El Paso. When you didn't buy tickets to return home, I knew you were on to something."

"Christ, Irwin, you don't miss a thing," Alexander said.

"It's Senator now, Alexander," Crandle said, but there was levity in his voice and Landry knew he was kidding.

"But back to the point at hand. It seems we have a problem. If Pablo Escobar is indeed alive, we're going to look like complete fools on the world stage. Not to mention the fact that this is one very dangerous man."

"He must have cooled his jets a bit," Bud said. "He's not running around killing people like he used to or we'd know about it."

"If he decided to disappear," Alexander said, pouring lemonade into his glass, "he would disappear. Pablo Escobar was never the type to do anything half-assed. And even though we were tearing his drug empire apart, piece by piece, he still had incredible financial assets at his disposal. From what Eugene saw when Pablo was staying with his cousin Raphael in Medellín, he was planning his disappearance long in advance. He lost weight, started eating healthy and exercising and stayed out of the sun. And he must have had the look-alike who was killed surgically altered months beforehand. He knew what he was doing, all right."

"Then let's look at where he was diverting money just before he died," Crandle said. "Cathy, look back over any known accounts Escobar was using at the time and see where the money was going. Maybe there's something out of the ordinary."

"Senator, there's one thing we should discuss," Cathy Maxwell said. "I think I speak for Alexander when I say we don't mind Bud Reid coming on board, but this little task force is beginning to grow. And we all know what can happen when you involve too many people."

"Ah, yes. The leak we never plugged. Keeping the group small is an excellent idea, Cathy. Agent Garcia and Eugene had no involvement in tracking Pablo in the early '90s, so that just leaves the four of us. Surely to God it wasn't one of us who kept Pablo one step ahead of a firing squad."

Alexander Landry nodded his approval. "We'll be fine

if we keep it in-house and do our own research. No support staff. We've got everything we need at our fingertips at EPIC down in El Paso."

"I'm sorry I couldn't come down to see you in Texas," Crandle cut in. "But the president is in Kentucky today and I have to meet him in about two hours. I couldn't possibly have made EPIC and back in the allotted time. I'd like to thank all of you, especially you Eugene, for flying up for this meeting. Now, I still have an hour before I have to dress. Let's formulate our action plan and delegate the work. Cathy, how do you think we should approach this?"

"CIA database is a wealth of information, sir. We have ongoing records of many of Escobar's associates from the time we allegedly killed him until present day. We can go back over those records and . . ."

Eugene waited until Cathy had finished talking and then excused himself. He strolled down the path past the lily pond and into the neighboring woodlands. The talk was technical, and specific to the programs on the CIA and DEA computers—and Egyptian hieroglyphics to him. If any questions came up that only he could answer, they could wait and ask him on the flight back to El Paso. He wondered briefly if Crandle still had top-secret clearance to the National Security Agency database; rumor had it that the information stored on NSA's computers was second to none, worldwide. That would certainly help.

He had been in the gardens for about half an hour when his phone rang. He answered it on the third ring. "What's new in San Salvador?" Eugene asked.

"Nothing. I'm trying to get in shape for the bout tomorrow, but I'm rusty as hell. I'll be lucky to make it through five rounds."

"You'll do fine," Eugene said. "Things are really coming together on this end. We've got another heavy-hitter interested in helping us find Pablo." He explained the appearance of Senator Irwin Crandle on the scene. "This guy is connected."

"No grass growing under your feet," Pedro said. "Maybe you guys will actually find Pablo in time. You've certainly got one hell of a team put together on short notice."

"I've been lucky," Eugene agreed with his friend. They spoke for another minute or two, then terminated the call. Neither man wanted to be overheard and the shorter the calls, the less the risk.

Eugene branched off the main path into a grove of white pine and mature tulip poplar. He craned his neck and stared up the towering trunks. At eighty feet the top branches swayed gently in the afternoon heat, and beyond them was luminescent blue sky. It reminded him of the rainforest canopy near Angel Falls where he had spent eight years of his life with the most wonderful woman on the planet. For some reason, thinking of Julie didn't depress him as it had for the past few days, but gave him strength and optimism. Tomorrow was Saturday and once it rolled past, one week of his time allotment was gone. But he had made monumental strides over the past six days; far more than he could ever have hoped. And now the group of DEA and CIA agents, coupled with Irwin Crandle and Bud Reid, were poised to begin the search in earnest. The resources of the United States's three premier agencies were at their disposal. If Pablo Escobar was out there, living life on the lam, the net would soon begin to close in.

Eugene stopped beside a Kentucky coffee tree and ran his hand across its rough bark. The sound of running water crept through the trees, and somewhere in the forest a starling trilled. And for a moment he was home again, in his beloved Angel Falls, with his wife in his arms and his children running through the trees. The virgin forest, thick with ferns and dripping with moisture, closed in on him like a warm blanket. He pulled Julie close to him and kissed her on the lips. She mouthed *I love you* and returned the kiss. They had lived the simple life, yet wanted for nothing. He was a happy man.

Then reality returned and he was alone in the Kentucky hills.

But for the first time in a week he felt invigorated, hopeful even.

Chapter Eighteen

Pedro closed the phone and smiled. The news from Eugene was good. He didn't know Senator Irwin Crandle, but someone of that stature had to be a good addition to the team searching for Pablo. He slipped the phone in his jacket pocket and looked around.

The taxi was just passing San Salvador's Galerías shopping mall, a flashy monument to the wealth of Colonia Escalón. But it didn't interest Pedro, and he stared out the other window as they drew deeper and deeper into the most exclusive enclave of the mountainous city. The houses bordering the street were set back, their expansive front lawns decorated with beds of bright orchids and ornamental shrubs. A strip mall, similar to millions of malls in the continental U.S., appeared, tucked between a football field and a school. A fitness center occupied almost half the mall, and the parking lot adjacent to the gym was filled with Mercedeses and other high-end cars. Two women dressed in spandex exited the club, as Pedro paid the driver and grabbed his bag from the rear seat. They both smiled as he passed, and he grinned back. Being noticed by attractive women was one part of his life where he'd never had problems. He entered the club and crossed the tile floor to the reception.

"Hi. I'm Pedro Parada. I have an appointment in the gym at ten o'clock."

She glanced down at her schedule sheet where visitors were listed alphabetically on the right side. His name was on the list. "Could you sign in, Señor Parada?" she asked, indicating a guest book just off to the right. After he had signed, she said, "The gym is toward the back of the facility, but you'll want to change first. Men's lockers are around the corner immediately behind me, first door on the left. The locker attendant will find you a locker and supply you with a combination or a key lock. Enjoy your visit."

He thanked her and found the locker room. He was given a quick tour, so he'd know how to find the showers and sauna baths after his workout, and then assigned a locker. He tipped the attendant and quickly slipped into his shorts and T-shirt. It was just before ten when he entered the vacant and quiet gym. Pedro had been in a slew of gyms and boxing facilities, but never anything like this. The floor was a regulation-size hardwood basketball court with a temporary boxing ring set up in the center. A moveable rack sat against one wall, covered with skipping ropes, boxing gloves and head protectors. Next to the gear was a freestanding punching pillar with a heavy bar and two smaller punching bags. Although it wasn't a permanent fixture, the ring was of better quality than Pedro had ever set foot in. The sprung floor was lively, the ropes taut but forgiving. The lighting was excellent; there would be no fooling an opponent by working bad lighting in this ring. He bounced about the ring for a minute, just getting the feel, then hopped off the canvas to the hard-wood, picked up one of the skipping ropes hanging on the wall and went to work.

It had been a couple of years since he laced on the gloves, but he had worked out almost every one of those seven hundred and some-odd days, and kept himself in prime physical condition. His routine was brutal: cardio, weights and agility training that lasted almost two hours. And he took few breaks. Couple that dedication to staying fit with a careful diet, and Pedro Parada was still the deadly machine he had been a few years back as an Olympic hopeful. He just needed a tune-up.

He was sweating from the rope when a couple of men entered the gym. The wall clock read 10:20. Both men were dressed in street clothes and stayed just inside the door, watching him. From the description Eugene had given him, neither man was Javier Rastano. He finished with the rope and hung it on the wall before selecting a set of gloves from the eclectic collection of bag and spar-ring gloves. Before donning the gloves, he removed two long tensor bandages with Velcro ends from his bag and wrapped his hands. He put a few turns on his wrist, then covered the knuckles, spread his fingers, loosely wrapped them and then snugly wrapped his thumb. He made a fist and the wrap felt perfect. He affixed the Velcro and slipped on the gloves. When he looked up, there were four more people in the gym, all standing close to the first two men. Again, Rastano did not seem to be present. As he watched the six men watch him, his opponent entered the room.

The man was dressed in boxing trunks and wore no shirt. His gloves were already in place, which struck Pedro as ridiculous. The man wasn't sweating so he hadn't worked out at all before donning the sparring gloves. That meant he had no intention of skipping prior to the bout. To Pedro, that categorized the man as either so far his superior that he didn't need to warm up, or a complete idiot. He knew he would find out soon enough.

As the other fighter walked closer, a casually dressed man in his early to mid-thirties walked in and stood just inside the door. He was tall and tanned with long hair almost to his shoulders, slicked back behind his ears. The look suited him. And from the description Eugene had given him, Javier Rastano had just arrived. The six men, who had previously been milling around or just leaning against the walls, came to life. They gathered about Rastano, talking and gesturing. This continued for a minute and then Rastano came forward.

"I've been told you're not a bad fighter," he said when he was a few feet from Pedro. "Do you feel up to a sparring match?"

"Sure," Pedro said. "Who am I sparring with?"

Rastano motioned to the other fighter, who had entered the ring and was dancing about, bouncing off the ropes and hammering out a few jabs and truncated undercuts. "His name is Sal. He's not great, but he's not bad either. If you're any good you should be able to beat him."

Pedro nodded. "And who exactly are you?" he asked.

"Javier Rastano." He glanced at Pedro's hands, encased in the sparring gloves. "I'd shake your hand, but . . ."

Pedro grinned. "After," he said.

Rastano returned the grin. "Sure. After. You ready to get going?"

"Not really. But I don't think Sal's had much of a warm-up either, so fair's fair."

"Then let's go," Javier said.

Pedro slid under the ropes, inserted his mouth protector and knocked gloves with Sal. A referee, complete with a striped jersey, entered the ring and had them meet in the middle. "Five rounds, three minutes each, with a one-minute break between each round," he said. "No low blows, break when I tell you and if I call the fight you stop punching. Does each of you understand these rules?"

"Fuck, yes," Sal said, salivating. "Let's get going."

"Sure," Pedro answered, wondering what the hell he was doing in the ring with this rabid dog.

They split and went to their corners. A small man in his late fifties was in Pedro's corner, with towels, water and a stool. His face was creased with wrinkles and he was dressed in faded jeans and a simple T-shirt. "I'm José," he said as Pedro approached. "Your corner man."

Pedro shook his head. "Rich people," he said. "Best ring I've ever fought in, a carded referee and now my own corner man. Where's the ESPN film crew?"

José laughed and Pedro knew from the look on his face that they were from the same side of the tracks.

The bell rang, signaling the start of the fight. Sal waded right in, throwing a few jabs and even a quick left hook. Pedro danced lightly on his feet, staying in a classic basic boxer's stance, one foot ahead and one back, and easily avoided the first few punches. He traded a couple of punches, but let Sal come to him for most of the first round. Pedro counted the attempts and when the bell rang to end the first round, Sal had thrown forty-one jabs, seven left hooks and twelve straight rights. Of the sixty punches, not one had landed. And Pedro had learned the answer to whether the man was a technically superior boxer or an idiot. He was an idiot.

While dancing about and avoiding the ill-timed and lame punches, Pedro had noticed glaring flaws in the man's style. Straight off, Sal was watching his eyes, and that in itself was a fatal flaw for a boxer. An opponent's eyes tell you nothing; his chest, shoulders and feet tell you everything. A boxer who concentrates on his opponent's eyes is not going to remain vertical for very long. In addition to this most crucial mistake, Sal's left hook was a sweeping roundhouse with little to no power. He didn't transfer any weight to his left side and left himself completely open every time he threw the punch; he could stun Sal every time the man threw a left hook. Sal's footwork was non-existent and he was consistently off balance. The only question Pedro had when the bell rang to start the second round, was how long to toy with this guy before knocking him out.

Sal came at him again, jabbing ineffectively and trying a right-left-right power combination. Pedro blocked the rights and ducked the left, then started with his jabs. His left hand shot out from his chin in a lightning fast motion, smacked Sal in the face, and was back protecting his chin before Sal even saw the punch. Again, the jab, and again, no response. Again, and again, Pedro hammered the man in the face with jab after jab that inflicted minimal damage but angered his opponent. Sal countered back with a flat-footed straight right that earned him his first uppercut of the fight. He staggered back, stunned from the glancing blow to his chin. Then his eyes lit up and he charged in.

Pedro had one rule he lived by. Never charge your opponent in the ring when you're mad and off balance. You'll only get your ass kicked. And Sal was in for an asskicking. Pedro started his combinations, throwing a quick couple of jabs, then smashing into the man's face with straight rights and left hooks before stunning him with a lightning-quick uppercut. When the bell rang to end the second round, Pedro had landed sixteen of twenty punches and had yet to take one. He returned to his corner, and José offered him some water.

"I get the feeling you're going to kill this guy," José said, squeezing water into Pedro's mouth.

Pedro pulled out his mouth protector. "This Sal guy, he a regular around here? A friend of Señor Rastano's?"

"Shit, no. He's some punk from down in the barrio.

Rastano doesn't know him from a street turd. But then again, he doesn't know you either."

Pedro laughed. He liked José. "So should I take him down now, or just fuck with him for a bit?"

"Oh, fuck with him, boy. Give Javier a show. Go to the fifth then annihilate him. That'll get Javier's attention, if that's what you're hoping."

"Wouldn't mind. I hear he promotes good fighters."

"Good ones, yeah. But you gotta show him."

The bell rang, Pedro slipped his mouth protector back in place, smacked his gloves together and went back to work. He toyed with Sal, letting the man get close with a few jabs but always staying ahead of any of his power punches. What little footwork Sal had was easy to read; the cross-over right was his most dangerous punch, but it was always preceded by his right foot dropping back. Sal was so easy to read it was child's play. By the start of the fifth, Sal's breathing was labored and he was bleeding from above his right eye and from a cut on his left cheek. As Pedro entered the ring for the fifth and final round, he crossed himself and apologized to God for what he was about to do.

Round five was nothing short of a mugging. Pedro's feet were everywhere, his body bobbing, weaving and bowing, then firing power punches that stunned Sal and sent him crashing into the ropes time and time again. Pedro lit into the man with combinations, holding back on the uppercut until there was about a minute left in the round. Then he danced over to where he could look directly into Rastano's eyes, pointed down with his gloves, and shrugged. Rastano nodded. He wanted to see Pedro put the man to the canvas. And that was exactly what Pedro did. He let loose with everything he had, pummeling Sal's head with a flurry of right-left combinations followed by a crushing uppercut that sent him sprawling to

the canvas, unconscious before he hit the mat. Pedro
stood over his downed opponent for a second, then retreated to his corner.

"Now that's fighting," his corner man said. "You fucking killed him."

"Naw," Pedro said. "I looked. He's still breathing."

When José finished unlacing Pedro's gloves and washing Sal's blood off his arms, Rastano was gone. The fight
had drawn a crowd, swelling to over a hundred people,
many of them attractive female members of the club. And
more than one of them was giving Pedro the eye. He swallowed back some water and asked his corner man, "You
do this a lot? Work corners for fighters you don't know?"

"Whenever they have a fight, they call me," José said.
"They like to keep these sparring matches as official looking as possible. It amuses them. I ran a gym down in El
Centro for years and trained a lot of fighters, so I know
the ropes, so to speak. In fact, you look a little familiar."

Pedro patted the older man on the shoulder. "El Centro is more my turf than this place, my friend. I may have
gone a few rounds in your gym at one time or another."
They finished unwrapping Pedro's hands, and he
thanked José for his help. It took a few minutes to get
through the remnants of the crowd, as a few people
wanted to pat him on the back and thank him for winning. Pedro couldn't believe these assholes; they were
betting on a sparring match. He finally managed to wade
through the last of the spectators and out the front door
into the parking lot. Javier Rastano was sitting behind the
wheel of a red Ferrari F-50, and he waved Pedro over. Pedro jogged the hundred feet or so to Rastano's sports car,
and as he neared the million-dollar car he wondered how
this man could kill a young boy over a paint scratch.

"That was impressive," Javier said. His lean, tanned face
and long, black hair fit the image of the car.

Pedro shrugged. "The guy wasn't much of a fighter. He would do better in an alley fight than in a boxing ring."

"Quite right, Pedro," Javier said, taking a long slow drag off his cigarette. "If you're up to it, I've got another opponent who may be a bit more of a challenge."

"You're not going to pull some Olympic gold medal contender out of nowhere are you?"

"No. He's good, but not that good. In fact, you and he would be an even fight. Nothing like that blowout we all just watched."

"When?" Pedro asked.

"In a week or two?"

Pedro shook his head. "I'm just visiting. I don't know if I'll be in San Salvador in a week."

Javier looked thoughtful. "Tomorrow's too soon and next week's out. Too bad."

"Tomorrow's not too soon for me," Pedro said. "That was just a warm-up."

A smile crept over Javier's face, but it made Pedro's whole body chill. There was nothing warm about that smile. "Tomorrow, then. Same time."

"Ten o'clock is fine. One thing, though. I'd like José in my corner again. He knows what he's doing."

"He'll be there, *amigo*." He gave Pedro a rippling of his fingers. "See you tomorrow."

The Ferrari crept out of the parking lot and Pedro turned and headed back to the club to hail a cab. Tomorrow was the test. Javier Rastano now knew that Pedro could fight. He wouldn't be bringing some punching bag this time. Pedro rolled his shoulders forward and back a few times, feeling the muscles beginning to stiffen. He'd been through this enough times to know he was going to be hurting tomorrow. Sal hadn't penetrated his defenses even once, but blocking over two hundred punches with his gloves and arms had taken its toll. When he thought about it, Rastano was right, tomorrow *was* too soon. But he didn't have the luxury of waiting. Tomorrow was Sunday and that was the start of week two in the hunt for Julie and Shiara. He had no choice.

A solitary cab was waiting in the taxi queue. He threw his bag in the back and climbed in the front seat with the driver. One thing he was not, and would never be, was above his fellow man. He patted the astonished driver on the shoulder and gave him the address of his hotel. They chatted idly as the cabbie navigated the congested streets, but Pedro's mind was elsewhere.

He was already in the ring facing his next opponent. And the man was kicking his ass.

Chapter Nineteen

Senator Irwin Crandle, grounded in Kentucky while entertaining the president for a couple of days, had little need of his Learjet and loaned it to the two intelligence experts, and Eduardo and Eugene, for their flight back to El Paso. It was almost noon on Saturday when they arrived at EPIC, having over-nighted in Frankfort. A second meeting with the senator, after his day with the president, had gone late into the night and produced tangible results. Each member of the team was re-focused on his or her individual task.

Cathy Maxwell was still working on sorting through the DEA files from the early '90s, but with a twist. The addition of Senator Irwin Crandle to the team opened a back door into the Department of Justice files that would have otherwise remained sealed. Members of Congress and their immediate staff could circumvent section 5 U.S.C 552 of the Privacy Act, and that added an entirely new angle to their investigation. Informants who had worked with the DOJ back when Pablo was all-powerful were identified, and a network link to the Witness Protection Plan allowed access to their files. Names and addresses were blacked out, but that information was available on a need-to-know basis. She started the arduous task of sorting through Pablo's past contacts and deciding which ones were priorities.

Crandle had agreed that Alexander Landry and Eugene continue working together targeting family members and close friends who may have stayed in touch with Pablo after his "death" in Medellín. Narrowing down the number of names would make Eduardo Garcia's job of monitoring phone calls a lot easier. The sheer volume of calls was astronomical; well into the hundreds of thousands, and every person Alexander and Eugene could eliminate reduced the volume substantially. Nonetheless, Garcia was attacking the problem with zeal. Phone logs were strewn all over his desk and he had developed a color-coded system to quickly identify calls from sources he knew were not Pablo. Alexander Landry watched for a few minutes and nodded his approval. Garcia's stock in DEA had just risen appreciatively.

Bud Reid did not return to El Paso with the rest of the crew. He flew to Dulles from Louisville and caught a direct flight to Zurich. If the bank account at the Banque Suisse de Zurich was tied to Pablo Escobar, then they wanted to locate Pablo's contact and speak with that person. Narrowing it down shouldn't be too difficult. Bud Reid intended to find out which employee controlled the suspect account, and have a chat with him. Including time changes, flying time and layovers, he was due to arrive in Zurich at eight o'clock Sunday morning. Bad timing for visiting a bank, but it was the best he could do.

Despite his commitments to the president, Senator Crandle was busy opening doors for the team. He invoked senatorial right to bypass section 5 U.S.C 552 of the

Privacy Act and left his personal phone number with the appropriate staff at the DOJ; when Cathy Maxwell needed access to a file she got clearance in minutes rather than hours. Their research room buzzed with activity, and the mood was upbeat, despite the staggering odds against their success. Especially given the tight time frame.

Eduardo Garcia leaned back in his chair and rubbed his eyes. The printouts were starting to blur, and he needed a break. "Crandle is a pretty visible figure these days," he said to Alexander Landry. "What was he like when you guys were working together in Colombia?"

Landry smiled. "Are you asking whether he was the same then as now?" When Garcia nodded, he continued. "Nothing has changed with Irwin Crandle. Fifteen years ago, he was a self-righteous, arrogant, pig-headed son-of-a-bitch who had no idea what the word failure meant. And he still is. His idea of the subtle approach was to kick in the back door as opposed to breaking down the front door. Diplomacy was making sure there were no marks on the *narcos* after we interrogated them. I'm surprised it took him as long as it did to track down Pablo."

"It sounds like the *narcos* weren't the only ones operating outside the law," Garcia said.

"Agent Garcia, you want to bring these guys down, you fight at their level," Landry said sharply. "That was the way things were a decade and a half ago, and that's the way things are now. You'll do well with the DEA if you keep that in mind."

"Yes, sir. Creative field work gets recognized."

Landry cooled his jets. "Yeah, exactly, Eduardo. Creative field work. I like that."

Garcia returned to his work, wondering just how creative Landry, Maxwell and Crandle had been while looking for Pablo. It had never occurred to him until now, but the three agents who had moved to the upper echelons of their chosen fields had probably taken out a few street-level dealers to achieve their goals. He knew rules were stretched, even broken, under arduous field conditions, and he was sure the woman and men he was working with were guilty of enough infractions to fill a two-inch binder. But working elbow to elbow with this level of agent was intimidating enough, and he kept his views of right and wrong mostly to himself. He just wondered if they would resurrect their previous field tactics to find Pablo. Murder and torture might have worked in Colombia, but this was America.

It was a chilling thought.

Chapter Twenty

The air had a slight chill despite the sun hanging almost directly overhead. That was something the man could never understand. How the sun could be out and shining, yet there was little to no heat. He touched the white railing that encircled the deck; it felt cool on his fingertips. Spread across the expanse of land between the house and the lake were thousands of deciduous trees, all barren of leaves like stark twigs rising from the ashes of a fire. It was depressing, the lack of lush green forests. But at least the snow was gone.

Pablo Escobar detested the snow.

He buttoned his coat against the cool spring air and sipped his coffee. Most of the warmth had dissipated and even the mug now felt cool. He left the mug on the railing and padded across the massive cedar deck and into the house. The river rock fireplace was at work, the fire licking at a few generous birch logs. An occasional crackle from the fireplace split the silence, but otherwise the house was quiet. Somewhere in another part of the house the muffled sound of a ringing phone came to him, but it was quickly answered. He sat in one of the chairs opposite the fireplace and stared alternately at the flames and through the picture window at the valley that lay far below the house. It was beautiful. But he missed his home.

A thin man, late thirties with pale skin and a bushy mustache, quietly entered the room. In his right hand was a cordless phone. He handed it to Pablo, closing the door behind him.

"Hello," Pablo said, his English without an accent.

"We have a problem," a distant voice said.

"It is safe to speak on this line. Please continue."

"Your Zurich connection is in jeopardy."

"How long do we have?"

"Monday morning, at the latest."

"You're sure?"

"Trust me," the voice said, "I know exactly when your man in Zurich will be compromised. He's working both sides. For you and for the Rastanos. Take care of him or our little team will be all over it. It's inevitable."

"So. Herr Shweisser is a man who likes to take risks. I've suspected for some time now that he was also in bed with Mario and Javier Rastano. Unfortunately for him, that was a fatal mistake. Do you have anything else for me right now?"

"No."

"The team is still five members, plus Eugenio Escobar?"

"Yes."

"Thank you." Pablo hung up, waited a minute, then dialed a number prefixed by an international area code. The phone rang a few times and a woman's voice, soft and enticing, answered.

"I have a job for you. It must be handled immediately." He spoke for a couple of minutes, giving the woman all the necessary details, then hung up. The fireplace was generating a great deal of warmth and he unbuttoned his coat, slipped it off and laid it on the arm of the chair. He stood and walked to the window, again looking out over the valley that stretched far to the south. A solitary cloud drifted toward the sun, and he watched the shadow move up the valley. It engulfed the house; the strong sunlight dissipated and the room instantly darkened. He could see the fire reflected in the window, the flames slowly and methodically devouring the wood.

And now with the sunlight just a ghost of its former brilliance, he could also see his own reflection. His face was somewhat oval, his eyes deep brown and watchful. His cheeks were full, but not yet drooping. He jowls and chin were firm, belying his age. He sported a full head of curly hair, parted in the middle and allowed to grow about halfway down his ears. His face was clean-shaven and well proportioned. Although he was not a handsome man, neither was he ugly. His shoulders were slightly rounded, but his chest was full and his waist narrowed to a respectable thirty-four inches. He looked younger than his fifty-six years, a fact he credited to the many hours he spent in his basement gym. He turned from the window at the sound of a door opening. The same man who had brought him the phone was standing in the doorway.

"Lunch is served, sir."

"Thank you."

The servant bowed his head a fraction and was gone.

Pablo Escobar took one last out the window and smoothed the lapels on his shirt before attending the midday meal.

Chapter Twenty-one

Pedro Parada was glistening with sweat, the skipping rope a blur as he warmed up for his second fight at Javier Rastano's private club. His opponent was working the heavy bag and after watching him for a couple of minutes, Pedro knew he was in for a punch-fest. Luis, the man's name, was in his mid-twenties and probably a few pounds over the welterweight division. He was in excellent condition, toned and very light on his feet. This guy was no street fighter; he was a boxer. He even had the typical boxer's face; flat nose, cauliflower ears, and he kept his hair cropped close to his head. His skin was badly scarred with pock marks from a severe case of adolescent acne. Pedro continued skipping as Javier, surrounded by an entourage, entered the gym. Most of the club members were also there. News of the fight had traveled fast, and interest was high.

Javier nodded to both fighters, then took his seat at ringside. Someone had taken the time to arrange a couple of hundred chairs on the floor and they were filling up fast. Money was flowing and the excitement level was rising as the clock approached noon. At five minutes before the hour each fighter was escorted to his corner. Pedro grinned at José.

"This guy any good?" he asked the grizzled old pugilist.

"I've only seen him once before, in one of the *barrio* gyms. And yeah, he's good. In fact, he's really good. But he's new around the club. I think Senor Rastano just met him a few days ago."

"Looks a little heavy for welterweight."

"No shit," José said. "Probably about ten or fifteen pounds."

"So no walk in the park this afternoon."

"Nope."

"Got any words of advice?"

José didn't waste a second replying. "Hit him more than he hits you."

Pedro shook his head. "Thanks a lot."

The bell rang and the fighters moved to the center of the ring, listened to the rules, banged gloves and returned to their corners. A second later the bell rang and the fight was on. Both Pedro and Luis had a degree of mutual respect, and they spent the first two rounds bouncing about the ring, throwing jabs and taking an occasional punch to see what kind of power the other man had to offer. In the third round they both got serious. Pedro could see few flaws in Luis's style and he tried to collect. Pedro waited until Luis threw a left jab and pulled his right foot a bit too close to his left. That left Luis slightly off balance and Pedro drove in with a vicious right-left-right combination. All three punches landed, but the following uppercut missed. The flurry stunned Luis, and brought an appreciative cheer from the onlookers with money on Pedro. The referee waded in and backed Pedro off for a few seconds. When the fight resumed, Luis came straight back at Pedro and nailed him with straight right and a left hook. Pedro bounced off the ropes and right into another straight right. He almost went down, his legs like jelly for a few seconds, his hands up around his face fending off a solid rain of punches. Nothing else was getting through and Pedro had a few seconds to recover. He took a risk, dropped his right and fired a stunning blow into Luis's solar plexus. The boxer doubled over and backed off, hurting big-time from the body blow. Pedro let him go and took the time to shake off the thrashing. The bell rang, and he returned to his corner.

"You asked me for advice before the fight started," José said, pouring water over Pedro's head and shooting a stream into his mouth. "What part of hit him more than he hits you didn't you understand?"

"Sorry, chief. I'll try to do better this round."

"You do that, boy. Because if you don't, you're going down."

Pedro just grinned. "You like that shot to the solar plexus?"

"Yeah, that was real nice. Now hit the fucking guy in the head."

"Okay, boss," Pedro said, opening his mouth for his mouth guard as the bell rang. Round four.

Pedro took a beating through most of the fourth round, unable to counter-attack the series of combinations Luis threw at him. He still had strength and his legs were okay, but he couldn't react fast enough to the speed of his opponent's punches. After the round he plunked down on the chair in his corner and spit out his mouth guard.

"Okay, José, I'm all ears. What can I do to get at this guy?"

"I've got an idea. I want you to jab, jab, jab at him and keep them coming. When you've got the jab working he doesn't like to open himself to your right so he backs off on the offense. No offense, no combinations. Keep jabbing at him. Jab, jab, jab. Got it?"

"I'm getting smacked around out there, but I'm not deaf. You want me to jab. Right?"

"Right. And then when you get him off balance, wade in. You've still got lots of power left."

The bell went for the fifth and final round. Pedro came out jabbing. His left arm shot out with clockwork regularity, tagging Luis's gloves and occasionally making it through to his head. By a minute into the round, Pedro saw another benefit to José's strategy. Luis wanted to come at him, but kept holding back because of the steady barrage of jabs. And the longer he waited, the more his frustration showed in his footwork. He was cheating, bringing his right foot forward, ready to unleash with a left-right-left combination. But Pedro kept coming at him, snapping hard jabs that hurt when they hit, and even when they failed to penetrate Luis's gloves, they threw him off balance. Then, at the two-minute mark, Pedro saw his opening.

Luis was dragging his right foot now, itching to counterattack the endless series of jabs, and that made him vulnerable. Without losing his rhythm, Pedro changed from the quick jab to a straight right, catching Luis on the chin and stunning him. The right was followed by a six-punch combination that ended with a blockbuster uppercut. Luis staggered back, fell against the ropes and hit the canvas. He stood up immediately, but the ref kept Pedro away until he checked Luis to see if he could continue. With thirty-three seconds left in the round he backed off and Pedro waded in. There were no more jabs. Every punch had power behind it, driving Luis back across the ring into the ropes, where Pedro let loose with a flurry of body blows. Then, when the trapped fighter dropped his gloves to protect his abs, Pedro shot out a straight right that ended the fight. The punch caught Luis in the chin and snapped his head back so hard and fast his mouth protector flew into the crowd. He crumpled on the ropes and fell unconscious to the canvas. The half of the crowd that had bet on Pedro was in a frenzy, the other half dug into their pockets for cash. Pedro returned to his corner, where José wiped him down and slipped off his gloves.

"See. Jab, jab, jab. You bored him to death. Good work."

Pedro couldn't help laughing. The old man had won the fight for him and he cared nothing about taking any credit. "I think he's going to have a headache. I caught him pretty good with that last punch."

"You did, boy. You hit him good."

Javier Rastano slipped between the ropes and into the ring. He had a wireless microphone with him and addressed the crowd over the PA system. "Thank you, ladies and gentlemen, for attending our Saturday main event. The winner, by knock out, Pedro Parada." He waved his arm toward Pedro's corner. Pedro jumped up and bounced about with his arms above his head, giving the crowd a show. They loved it and even some of the bettors who had gone against him were clapping. Pedro danced to the middle of the ring, where Javier handed him an envelope. "Open it," he said.

Pedro ripped open the envelope and pulled out a wad of cash. American hundreds. Even without counting Pedro knew he was holding at least five thousand dollars. He held it up like a trophy, and the yells from the crowd grew even louder. Eventually the din died down and the audience moved toward the exits in small groups, discussing the fight and complimenting Javier Rastano on bringing together two such evenly matched and talented fighters. Pedro and Luis had showered and were getting dressed when Rastano poked his head into the locker room.

"You two busy this afternoon?" he asked. Both men just

shrugged. "Good. I'll have a driver wait for you. When you're finished dressing come up to the house. We'll have a late lunch and I'll show you around."

"Sure, Mr. Rastano," Luis said.

"Sounds okay," Pedro said nonchalantly. But under the calm veneer his heart was pumping.

He was in.

Chapter Twenty-two

The air-conditioning unit supplying cold air to the west wing at EPIC went down at two on Sunday afternoon. The team worked in the heat for another hour, then called it quits until the maintenance staff could fix the problem. Eduardo Garcia headed home to spend time with his wife and two young children, while Eugene and the senior members of the team found an air-conditioned Mexican restaurant. They settled into a booth directly beneath a ceiling fan. Sombreros hung on the walls, one per booth, and pictures of Pancho Villa in full Mexican garb, with pistols in each hand, were plentiful. The tables were rough-hewn oak, and the seats stitched hemp.

"When do they think the air-conditioning will be working?" Eugene asked Alexander as the waitress, a fifty-something Mexican woman in authentic garb, dropped off their drinks.

"Around eight this evening," Landry said. "That's why I can order a *cerveza*. The working day is done."

Cathy Maxwell had stuck to a tall glass of water and a Coke. She drained half the water, than asked, "You guys come up with a family member you think might be working with Pablo?"

"The best bet so far is a distant cousin, Mario Correa," Landry said. "He's living in Miami, has been for almost eight years now. Owns a Renault dealership near Miami Beach. Eduardo is concentrating on his phone logs from the dealership and his house. I'm checking his credit cards, frequent flyer miles and passport to see where Señor Correa has been traveling lately."

"This Mario fellow in tight with Pablo at any point?"

"Sort of. Mario knew Pablo's first cousin Gustavo Gaviria Rivero really well. And Rivero was one of the cartel leaders. We're looking for a recent link between Mario and Gustavo first, and if we find one, conversations with Pablo could be next."

"Excellent work," Cathy said. She sipped her Coke and looked thoughtful. "How does the cousin of a scumbag drug dealer get U.S. citizenship? That doesn't make sense to me."

Eugene's eyes narrowed slightly. "I'm one of Pablo's cousins," he said. "And I think if the U.S. government ever looked closely at my life, they wouldn't have a problem issuing a green card."

Maxwell's face flushed. "I'm sorry, Eugene," she said hastily. "I wasn't thinking. It's just that some of your relatives were in the gutter with Pablo."

"It's easy to paint us all with the same brush," Eugene said. "I've had to deal with my family tree all my life. My friends know I'm related to Pablo, and they love to talk about it. It's a great ice-breaker at a party. *Hey, that guy over there, he's Pablo Escobar's cousin.* And people I've never met take one look at my last name and ask me if I'm related. There's no getting away from it. It sucks. But you learn to live with it."

The waitress stopped by and asked them in Spanish if they were ready to order. Eugene ordered a quesadilla with refried beans and handed their server the menu. The others ordered the same. Then Cathy Maxwell asked, "Are you two heading for Miami?"

Alexander shrugged. "That depends on what Eduardo digs up. If there's a connection, we'll be on the next flight. If not, we're back looking at the rest of the family. And that's no easy feat. There are brothers and cousins and uncles and aunts in more countries than you could ever imagine. Even dealing with only the family is a haystack."

Cathy nodded. "I remember, Alexander. It wasn't much different thirteen years ago."

Eugene finished his water and asked, "Why did you guys do it? Why did you leave your families back in the United States and travel to Colombia to track down Pablo? I can't think of a more dangerous assignment. You put your lives on the line every day to bring him down. What I don't understand is why."

Neither the DEA man nor his CIA counterpart spoke for the better part of a minute. When one of them did, it was Cathy Maxwell, and she spoke distantly. "At first you take the assignment the agency hands you and you don't ask questions. Green agents, eager to fight crime, leave D.C. with bright eyes and their ethics intact. But once you're in the jungle, thrown into the insane world of the Colombian drug lords, you change. The metamorphosis is quick; it has to be, or you won't survive. You begin to think on their level, your vision of humanity and the value of a human life are downgraded. What you would have viewed as atrocities when you first arrived becomes normal. Heads on spikes by the side of the road, gutted children, men with their testicles stuffed in their mouths; it forms a veil over normalcy. You track down one of their labs, burn it to the ground and destroy the equipment, and another one springs up a few miles away. They have too much money; you can't stop them. And once you realize that, you start to fight a limited war, like the U.S. did in Vietnam. Hit them hard and fast and get out before they get you. Catch them while they're sleeping and arrest them? Why bother. The Colombian court system is so corrupt that trying to imprison anyone worthwhile is impossible. So you level the gun at them and pull the trigger. You kill them in cold blood, just as they'd kill you, given the chance. And then you head back to Medellín in the choppers, talking excitedly about what a great day you had. A lab, an airstrip, and sixty of Pablo's thugs and cocaine cooks. You give each other high fives and drink beer. Then you head to bed and sleep well."

She stopped for a minute, and rotated her empty glass on the table a few times. It left a series of wet rings on the wood. "So why did *I* do it, Eugene? Because when I first arrived I thought I could make a difference. I had good intentions and high ideals. But all that changed. I think we all left a bit of our humanity on the doorstep when we entered Colombia. And once you've seen what we've seen you don't just forget it and get on with life. It stays with you. And after a while you don't sleep very well. You remember all the times you kicked in a door, and pulled the trigger because you thought you saw a gun. And you get to hate the *narcos* with such passion that you lose touch with what's right and what's wrong; the boundaries get hazy, and sometimes they disappear. So you fight them on their own terms, in the gutter with guns and knives. And in the end, you aren't much different from those you hunt."

No one spoke for a couple of minutes, then Alexander Landry said, "Maybe I should have answered your question, Eugene. I did it because I liked Colombian beer."

They all chuckled at that, Cathy Maxwell included. She snapped out of her introspective mood, and grinned. "Alexander's right. We all liked Colombian beer."

Despite the laughter, Eugene sensed that Cathy Maxwell had bared a piece of her soul, and that working with the CIA in Colombia had had a traumatic effect on her life. Yet once Pablo was eliminated, she had moved back to the States, married and started a family. From her ramblings with Alexander Landry, he knew she had three young girls back in a Washington, D.C. suburb with their father. Three little girls she absolutely adored. In contrast, Landry's kids were grown and out of the house. He talked little of them, other than to complain about the cost of college tuitions. Eugene wasn't sure, but he thought Landry had four kids, all college age or older.

But whatever had motivated these two U.S. agents to leave their homes and live in Colombia fifteen years ago, and whatever motivated them now, Eugene believed he owed them a debt of gratitude.

He watched each of them as they ate their food and washed it down with Coke and beer, and he sensed that a camaraderie between the two *narco* hunters that had existed during their *narco* days was making a comeback. He believed they respected and admired each other. But it was more than that. They trusted each other. Maybe it had been born out of necessity, when the world they had known was left behind and the replacement was too crazy to be real. Maybe it was just a natural chemistry.

He tuned in again as Landry cracked the punch-line to a joke, and he joined in the laughter. But looking at the two experienced *narco* hunters, Eugene felt empowered. And he could only think of one thing:

Hang in there, sweetheart, we're coming to get you.

Chapter Twenty-three

Javier Rastano's home in Colonia Escalón was stunning. Never in his life had Pedro seen anything that even came close to the opulence hidden behind the massive front gates. The grounds were impeccable, acres of cut grass beneath mature mango trees, and clusters of towering bamboo. Eucalyptus trees bordered the twisting cobblestone road leading to the main house. Immediately in front of the colonial two-story were twelve evenly spaced Royal palms, their bases painted brilliant white.

A second-floor balcony stretched across the front façade of the house, its ornately twisted iron railings painted stark white. A massive portico jutted through the balcony, and dominated the front elevation. Empty wicker furniture sat in groups and overhead fans circled sluggishly, moving the still afternoon air. The driveway curved around an island of grass and flowers with a small duck pond in the center. Rastano's Ferrari was parked in front of the main doors to the house, and Pedro and Luis's driver pulled the Mercedes in behind the Italian sports car. He ushered them into the house and toward the back garden.

The main foyer was forty square feet with eighteen-foot ceilings, flanked on two sides by mirror-image curved staircases and an open hall directly ahead. Pictures by little-known renaissance artists lined the walls. Their heels clicked sharply on the Italian marble floors. They passed a fully stocked library, the books reaching to the ceiling, and a parlor with games tables and a professional roulette wheel. A formal dining room with a teak table and eighteen chairs was located just inside the rear of the house, and the view from the table was acres of perfectly landscaped grounds. Javier Rastano sat at a small glass table on the deck just outside the dining room.

"Ah, my boxers are here," he said as Pedro and Luis exited the rear of the house into the harsh afternoon sunshine. The heat was oppressive, but Javier didn't seem to notice. He waved them over to the table. "Sit down. What would you like to drink?"

"Beer, please," Luis said, and Pedro nodded.

"Thanks for the purse," Pedro said as they settled in. "I never expected anything like that. It was most generous."

"Not a problem. But five thousand dollars is just the start." He waved to one of the men dressed in black. The man was by his side in an instant. "Find Alfonso and get ten thousand dollars in fifties and twenties. Bring it here."

"Yes, sir." The man was gone as quickly as he arrived. That he carried a Thompson sub-machine gun and six extra clips on his belt was not lost on Pedro.

Javier sipped his iced tea and ran his fingers through his long hair. It fell into place, like every strand had its own spot and knew exactly where to go. He cupped his hands behind his neck, and said, "I'm thinking about taking on a few fighters, promoting them on a fairly high level. I'm not sure what sort of fights I could arrange, but I'm thinking Las Vegas, Atlantic City, that sort of thing.

I'm not Don King, but I've got a few connections. I might be able to get you on a championship card as one of the opening bouts. Anyone interested?"

"Yeah," Luis said, leaning forward. "I'd fight for you, Mr. Rastano."

"Sure," Pedro said. "But I need time to get in shape. A twelve- or fifteen-round match is a far cry from five."

Javier nodded appreciatively. "Good point. It'll take me a few months to set this up, so that should give you two enough time to tone up. Luis, you're definitely not a welterweight are you?"

"No, I'm over by about fifteen pounds."

"Good, then I've got two different weight divisions. I like that." He turned his shoulder as the guard returned to the patio from the house. "Ahh. Here comes your first payday." He took the money, split it in half and handed one pile to each fighter. "Go buy yourselves some nice clothes, maybe a gold chain or two, and give some to your families." He addressed Pedro. "Where are you staying?"

"Hotel Villa Florencia," Pedro said.

"You like the action of El Centro, do you?" Rastano said. "Well, it's a little quieter here, but there's no mold in the bathrooms. You're both welcome to stay on the estate if you wish. It's entirely up to you." Both men nodded, and Javier smiled. "Then it's settled. I'll have one of the men show you your rooms and the gym. There's a few cars here if you want to drive to Galerías to shop, but don't touch the Ferrari." He stood up. "I'll see you later," he said, and disappeared into the house.

Luis thumbed the stack of bills and let out a low whistle. "Holy shit, *amigo*. We hit the big time."

"Yeah," Pedro said, his eyes roaming across the patio to the grounds, then back to the house. "I think we got what we wanted."

An hour later Pedro was driving through the congestion of El Centro, more than shopping for new clothes on his mind. He needed to get his guns onto Rastano's estate. The Mercedes SL 500 attracted some attention and, in retrospect, he wished he had chosen a slightly less conspicuous car. He parked in front of his hotel and ran up to his room. He gathered his meager belongings and tucked them into his gym bag. He wrapped the three guns in with the clothes, shouldered the bag and checked out.

There were a few decent shops just outside the central region of San Salvador and he stopped in, looking through the racks and buying something in each shop, to help the shop owners more than anything else. He paid cash and didn't barter. Eventually he ended up at the sterile Galerías shopping mall where he dropped a substantial wad of cash on more clothes, and jewelry that he felt Javier Rastano would approve of. It would raise suspicions if a *barrio* rat came into a ton of money and didn't spend it foolishly. Almost four hours had passed when he returned to the estate and pulled up to the front gate.

"What's all that?" the guards asked, pointing at the stack of bags in the passenger's seat.

"Shopping," Pedro said. "Javier told me to get some new clothes."

"Okay," one guard said, opening the gate and waving him through. The other looked like he wanted to poke through the bags, but Pedro was long gone, up the driveway and out of sight. He parked the Mercedes and hustled upstairs with his purchases and his gym bag. Once in his room he dumped the new clothes on the bed, grabbed a couple of beach towels from one of the El Centro vendors and wrapped the guns in the towels. He stuffed the towels in the gym bag. Then he changed into his bathing suit and headed for the pool, gym bag in hand.

He passed a couple of guards making their rounds, but they hardly looked his way. The two boxers were Javier's personal guests and that carried a lot of weight. He bypassed the pool and took the series of winding paths through groves of mango and eucalyptus trees until he arrived at the far reaches of the Rastano estate. A shed, perhaps twenty feet wide by forty feet long was tucked up against the walls that delineated the Rastano estate from the neighbors. Pedro glanced up, noticing the cameras mounted on top of the wall. They were on swivel bases, and could monitor the grounds and the wall. But the shed itself blocked the camera as he approached, and he entered the hut without being photographed.

It was a gardener's shed. Inside were all the implements necessary to maintain acres of perfectly manicured grounds. Two riding tractors and numerous gas powered hand mowers were lined up against one wall, edgers and trimmers as well. Bags of fertilizer were piled near the back, along with equipment that was in pieces and in the process of being fixed. The shed had a strong odor of freshly cut grass and potassium fertilizers.

Pedro quickly found a place to stash the guns, behind and under some equipment that appeared to have been sitting in one place for a substantial length of time. He stood back and had a good look. It was impossible to tell where he had stashed the guns. Then he noticed a phone on the workbench, half hidden beneath a pile of rags used to clean garden equipment. It was an old model, one of the first with push buttons, bulky and covered with dust and grime. He picked up the receiver, not expecting it to work. A dial tone hummed through the line, and he replaced the handset thoughtfully. He covered the phone with rags, thinking it might come in handy at some point. He retreated from the shed and walked leisurely down to the pool. The water looked inviting, and he dove in and swam a few laps. Occasionally, a guard sauntered past, but it was business as usual. He had managed to get the guns inside the estate—and though he hoped he wouldn't have to use them, having the weapons close by felt good.

Now he just needed to find the women.

Chapter Twenty-four

Jorge Shweisser crossed the Bahnhofstrasse with his shopping bags, wary of the heavy Sunday morning traffic. A Renault darted around him and he resisted the urge to give the driver the finger. Now on the east side of Zurich's main shopping artery, he had his choice of many medieval alleyways, most of which led to the Limmat River and ultimately to Zurichsee. He wandered into one of the narrower alleys, which opened, after two blocks, into a small square encompassing St. Peters Kirche. The clock face on the parish church showed eight minutes after eleven. He felt relaxed as he entered Thermengasse, one of his favorite streets in all of Zurich, with the excavated ruins of ancient Roman baths underfoot. He was a romantic, and he liked to imagine himself in that period.

Shcweisser wasn't a strong man, nor was he vibrant or charismatic. He was a mouse in man's clothing, only five-seven and one hundred and forty-six pounds. And he only weighed himself while clothed. He wore glasses, and that

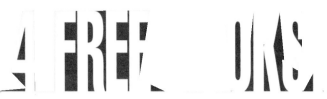

You can have the best fiction delivered to your door for less than what you'd pay in a bookstore or online—only $4.25 a book! Sign up for our book clubs today, and we'll send you FREE* BOOKS just for trying it out...with no obligation to buy, ever!

With more award-winning horror authors than any other publisher, it's easy to see why CNN.com says "Leisure Books has been leading the way in paperback horror novels." Your shipments will include authors such as RICHARD LAYMON, DOUGLAS CLEGG, JACK KETCHUM, MARY ANN MITCHELL, and many more.

If you love fast-paced page-turners, you won't want to miss any of the books in Leisure's thriller line. Filled with gripping tension and edge-of-your-seat excitement, these titles feature everything from psychological suspense to legal thrillers to police procedurals and more!

As a book club member you also receive the following special benefits:
- **30% OFF all orders through our website & telecenter!**
- **Exclusive access to special discounts!**
- **Convenient home delivery and 10 days to return any books you don't want to keep.**

There is no minimum number of books to buy, and you may cancel membership at any time. See back to sign up!

*Please include $2.00 for shipping and handling.

YES! ☐

Sign me up for the Leisure Horror Book Club and send my TWO FREE BOOKS! If I choose to stay in the club, I will pay only $8.50* each month, a savings of $5.48!

YES! ☐

Sign me up for the Leisure Thriller Book Club and send my TWO FREE BOOKS! If I choose to stay in the club, I will pay only $8.50* each month, a savings of $5.48!

NAME: _____

ADDRESS: _____

_____

TELEPHONE: _____

E-MAIL: _____

☐ **I WANT TO PAY BY CREDIT CARD.**

☐ VISA   ☐ MasterCard   ☐ DISCOVER

ACCOUNT #: _____

EXPIRATION DATE: _____

SIGNATURE: _____

Send this card along with $2.00 shipping & handling for each club you wish to join, to:

Horror/Thriller Book Clubs
1 Mechanic Street
Norwalk, CT 06850-3431

Or fax (must include credit card information!) to: 610.995.9274.
You can also sign up online at www.dorchesterpub.com.

*Plus $2.00 for shipping. Offer open to residents of the U.S. and Canada only.
Canadian residents please call 1.800.481.9191 for pricing information.
If under 18, a parent or guardian must sign. Terms, prices and conditions subject to change. Subscription subject
to acceptance. Dorchester Publishing reserves the right to reject any order or cancel any subscription.

alone probably would have meant an early death had he lived long ago. He couldn't see ten feet without his spectacles. In modern times, there were glasses or, if he'd wanted to go that route, contact lenses or laser surgery, to compensate for this inadequacy. But what did the nearsighted do in medieval times? It was a thought that plagued him every time he walked over the baths and thought of ancient Rome. He brushed a wispy strand of hair from his face and continued past the guildhalls toward the lake.

But these were modern times. And he was well educated and very well paid, and thus had status in Zurich society. Shweisser liked hiring large tradesmen to work on his luxurious three-story home in the Altstadt. Once he had them on-site, he berated them, finding fault with the smallest error in the woodwork or the tile, demanding it be fixed before he'd pay the invoice. Money was the master. And he had money.

His position at Banque Suisse de Zurich was cushy and covered the expenses, but his gravy money came from the unknown owner of the billion-dollar account, as he liked to call it. For twelve years he had been receiving regular payments to watch the account for the owner. And although he wasn't one hundred percent positive of the owner's name, he suspected it was one of the Colombian drug lords. And he suspected he knew which one, although it hardly seemed possible. But recently he had been double dipping. A second client, one he knew to be Mario Rastano from Medellín, had come to him a few years back and offered him a great deal of money to report any activity on the account. And although the account had remained dormant, collecting interest for the better part of twelve years, there was now activity. Twice this year electronic withdrawals had been processed and the cash shipped via satellite to some offshore Caribbean bank. He had done his job and reported the withdrawals to Mario

Rastano. And in return he had found five hundred thousand euros in a briefcase in his car one afternoon. He liked working for the Rastanos. Risky, but lucrative. And what the owner didn't know wouldn't hurt him.

Schweisser strolled down Stadthausquai until he reached Zurichsee, the beautiful lake that borders the southern portion of Zurich. The boat docks were busy with locals and tourists queuing up for rides on the tranquil waters. To the south were the Alps, still encrusted with winter snow, their peaks rising above the lake like a postcard. Jorge Shweisser sat on a bench and set his shopping bags next to him. He loved Zurich in the spring.

A woman passed him on the path and took a second glance. She was younger than he by a few years, perhaps in her mid-thirties, and reasonably attractive. Her short hair was dark, almost black, and she wore little or no makeup. Her skin was pale from the long winter and she wore a baggy sweater that covered her top and hung down to mid-thigh. She stopped and backed up, pointing at the bags next to him.

"I'm sorry to bother you," she said, her voice even and smooth. It seemed to match her appearance perfectly. "But I've always wondered about that store." She was now quite close to him and he could tell she was interested in the bag from En Soie. "I think it's maybe too expensive for me, so I've never gone inside."

He smiled at her and nodded. "It is expensive. I don't shop there very often. Usually just for gifts."

She smiled back. It was a nice smile, although a couple of teeth were slightly crooked. "Your wife is a lucky woman," she said, and waved as she moved on.

"It's for my mother," he said.

She stopped again. "A man who shops for his mother. My God, I thought those were all dead centuries ago." She was a few feet away, but facing him. "What did you buy her?"

Jorge dug in the bag and pulled out a scarf woven from raw-textured silk. The colors were muted, but it shimmered in the spring sunlight. "A scarf."

"It's beautiful," she said, moving back to him and touching the material. "And it's silk." She glanced away from the scarf to his eyes. "You have excellent taste. Your mother will be very pleased."

He grinned like a schoolboy who just got the highest grade in a surprise exam. "Thanks. It was tough picking it out. I think it would be easier to shop if I had a woman to help me."

"Take your wife when you go shopping," she said.

"I'm single."

The woman eyed him for a second, then said, "This may seem a little forward, but nice guys are tough to meet, and I'd like to have a coffee with you. Do you have some time?"

"Actually, if you're hungry, we could have lunch."

"That would be nice," she said. "I'm Elsa."

"Jorge."

They passed Bahnhofstrasse then cut north and strolled along Talstrasse for two blocks until they reached Baur au Lac Rive Gauche, a gastronomic jewel set in the heart of Altstadt. Fifty euros convinced the maitre d' that reservations were not really necessary, but a nice touch for those who liked planning ahead. He rewarded Jorge's generosity with a table next to the window that had a great view of the neo-gothic street. They settled in, ordered and quite enjoyed themselves for the next hour. When the check arrived, Jorge paid and left a substantial tip for the attentive waiter. They walked out together into the cool spring air.

"That was wonderful," Elsa said. "Thank you very much for lunch."

"You're welcome. Which way are you heading?"

"I live between the river and Bahnhofstrasse, close to St. Peters Kirche. It's not so far from here."

"I know exactly where it is. I love that part of Old Town. In fact, my favorite part of Altstadt is the Roman baths. I find the history fascinating." He paused and wet his lips with his tongue. "I'm walking that way. Would you mind if I joined you?"

"I'd be delighted," she said, slipping her arm through his and pushing against him lightly. "Now who would have guessed I'd meet such a nice man while out for a walk."

They moved up Fraumünster, just another couple out enjoying a spring walk in one of Europe's most romantic cities. When they reached Münsterhof, just south of the church, she pointed to one of the many narrow alleys dating back to medieval times. They moved into the narrow cobblestone street, the buildings shielding them from the sun and throwing a chill into the air. It was darker here, and deserted. She pressed up against him a little harder, then stopped walking. It took him a fraction of a second to respond and he spun slightly on his heels and ended up face to face with her. They were very close.

"Do you mind if I kiss you?" she asked. Her voice was intoxicating, her lips perfectly formed and moist.

"No," Jorge said. "Not at all."

She touched her lips to his ever so lightly, then pushed harder as he responded. Her left hand encircled his waist and her right hand caressed his neck. He felt a prick on his neck and jerked back, his hand instinctively moving to the spot where his nerve endings relayed pain to his brain. His hand came away sticky and red. Blood.

Elsa shoved off him and moved away quickly to her left. He staggered from the strength of her push, spinning away from her. He saw a trail of blood on the cobblestones and wondered where it had come from. Then another trail and another, and he realized the blood trails were coming from his neck, spurting across the dirty cobblestones. He looked back at Elsa, but she was already twenty feet away and moving quickly toward the main street. He tried to stop the bleeding but the blood just kept pumping out. He felt cold. His vision was going fuzzy and for a second he wondered what was wrong. Then, in an instant, he knew. He was dying. He had been murdered. The woman had cut his carotid artery, and he was quickly bleeding to death in an alley. He tried to call out, but his strength was gone. The blood flow was slowing, but he knew that was only because there wasn't enough blood left in his body to create pressure at the break. He fell to the ground, one hand clutching his neck, the other still holding his parcels.

Slowly his eyes closed, the last vision in his life that of an old woman leaning over asking him what had happened.

Chapter Twenty-five

Julie Escobar worked the metal clip she had removed from the back of the fridge into the screw head and turned. Hours of relentlessly reshaping the piece of metal on the rough backing of the DVD player paid off as the clip fit into the screw head perfectly. The screw groaned for the first quarter-turn, then spun almost effortlessly. Julie left it and started working on another of the eight screws holding the face plate that covered the air conditioning duct. Shiara, at the door listening for the sounds of anyone coming, whispered to her mom.

"Did you get it?"

Julie nodded, then added quietly, "Yes. I'll loosen all eight screws now, and then we'll have a look inside the duct later, when everyone's asleep."

Standing on a sturdily built teak dresser, she worked on the other seven screws for the better part of an hour before she finally got all of them turning. What would have been a relatively easy job with a proper screwdriver and a can of WD-40 was an arduous task, and her hands were cramped and sore when she finished. She hid the impromptu screwdriver and settled onto the couch with her daughter for the nightly check. Promptly at ten o'clock the door opened and two guards, dressed as always in black with sub-machine guns dangling on straps over their shoulders, entered and poked about. They were polite but businesslike and gave the series of rooms a close look before exiting and locking the door behind them. Julie waited ten minutes then got to work.

She popped the grill off once all the screws were completely out, revealing a rectangular hole in the wall about fourteen inches high by twenty inches wide. Julie and Shiara piled a couple of cushions from the couch on top of the wall unit and Julie stuck her head and shoulders into the hole. It was an extremely tight fit and she backed out, shaking her head.

"I don't think I can do it," she said. "It's too tight. I won't be able to move forward very easily and I certainly won't be able to back up. Unless there's some place in the system that's big enough for me to turn around, I'll be stuck."

Shiara glanced at the hole and said, "Let me try, Mom. I'm smaller than you."

Julie shook her head. "No way. I'm not letting you go in there without knowing it's safe."

Shiara grasped her mother by the arm. "Mom, we don't have a lot of options here. We're not getting out through the door, and that's the only way out except for this duct. We need to try. I think I'm small enough to fit."

"It's getting back I'm worried about," Julie said.

"I'll go a few feet into the duct, then see if I can back up. Okay?"

Julie thought about it for a moment, then said, "All right, but you stay in the main shaft. No branching off into smaller ones. Understand?"

Shiara nodded and stepped up on the cushions. She pulled herself into the duct headfirst, her arms in front of her. Once inside, she pulled with her forearms and pushed with her toes and made good progress for about twenty feet. Then she reversed and pushed with her arms, using her toes to keep her centered in the shaft. Moving backward was actually easier than moving forward and she dropped back to the cushions, the front of her jeans and shirt a bit dusty, but otherwise, she was fine.

"It's not that bad," she said. "I can feel the air moving through the shaft. It was cold and it was blowing in my face"

"That makes sense," Julie said. "That vent is for the fresh air to enter the room." She pointed to a much smaller grill just above the tile floor on the opposing wall. "That's the return air. You have to find a return air shaft, Shiara. One where there is no cold air and the flow is away from the room toward the outside of the house."

Shiara shook her head. "I don't think so. The two systems will be independent of each other. The only place they'll meet is at or near the air conditioning unit."

"How do you know that?" her mother asked.

Shiara grinned. "That boy you saw on a bike at the house the other day, his father has an air-conditioning servicing business. He showed me a few things."

"About air-conditioning, I hope," Julie said.

"Don't be silly. Of course. Can I try again?"

Julie glanced at her watch. "Fine, but keep it to about a half hour tops. And when you're in the shaft you can't make any noise. These ducts go through the entire house and the sound will carry."

"I understand," Shiara said, gulping back some water, then hoisting herself into the shaft for a second time.

"Be careful," Julie said as her daughter disappeared into the darkness.

Shiara carefully slid her hands along the metal surface,

aware that any sharp piece of tin would slice her hand open before she could react. She used the bandage over her severed finger, which was also wrapped around much of her hand, to her advantage. Leading with it, but still using caution. She kept her weight to the edges of the duct as best she could, to keep from depressing the tin and having it pop back.

After crawling for a number of minutes, she wasn't sure how long, she came to a junction in the duct. The shaft split off in three separate directions, each one identical in size. The air was swirling about and she couldn't tell the direction of the flow. Shiara stayed at there for a minute or two, thinking. If she were to try one of the other shafts, the problem would be finding the correct one on the way back. Unless she somehow marked her conduit.

She ripped a small piece of cloth from the bandage on her hand and tucked it into one of the joints, then picked a shaft and kept moving. Maneuvering around the corner was difficult, but her back was quite flexible and she managed to drag herself around the corner. She could feel the air flow coming from behind her now, which meant she was heading toward another room that needed cold air, and not toward the source. She was intrigued to see which room, and crawled for another three or four minutes before arriving at the grate.

The results were less than she had hoped, as the lights were off in the room and she could see nothing. Shiara returned to the junction and tried to discern which of the other two shafts fed the cold air. But it was impossible to be sure and she picked another shaft. Again, once well into the shaft she felt the air pushing from behind her. This time she stopped immediately and retreated. It was getting difficult to breathe; the movement of her body had stirred up some dust and she could feel it stinging her throat and lungs, aggravating her asthma. She pushed back to the last shaft and, once inside and moving, felt the air gently pushing in her face. This was the conduit to the air-conditioning unit.

She reversed directions and slowly crawled back through the narrow passage to the junction. She felt around until she found her bit of cloth, then moved cautiously back down the shaft toward where she knew her mother was anxiously waiting. When she arrived, her mother helped her out of the opening. She swallowed back half a glass of water, realizing now how thirsty she was.

"What took you so long?" her mother asked. "You were in there over an hour."

Shiara was shocked. "It didn't seem like that long. Sorry. But there's a junction in the ducts about fifteen minutes from here that splits into three other shafts. I found the one leading to the air conditioning unit, but the dust was getting thick and I came back without going all the way."

"That's okay. You can try it another night. Let's get you cleaned up and put the grate back on."

They fixed the cover back in place, and Shiara had a quick shower, washing away the dust. They sat and talked for a while, then Shiara yawned and headed off to bed. Julie sat up in the darkness, looking at the walls of her prison and wondering if Eugene was making any progress.

She knew he was a resourceful man. And that he loved his family beyond anything else on the planet. But was that enough? Whatever he had to do, she was sure it was against almost incalculable odds. She felt depressed and alone. She and Shiara had been counting the days and she knew today was Sunday, six days from the deadline for Eugene to come through with whatever it was their captors wanted. A shiver ran down her spine as she thought of the consequences. Not for her, but for her daughter. She hadn't missed the looks from the guards, their eyes glancing over her young body. They were eager and wanting.

Finally she rose and headed to her bedroom. Aside from having a finger cut off they were being well treated, and now there was the possibility of escaping if the air-conditioning duct led somewhere useful. Things could be worse. They still had six days.

But then what?

Chapter Twenty-six

The main branch of Banque Suisse de Zurich was located six blocks from the northern tip of Zurichsee, in a baroque-era building on Bahnhofstrasse. The structure was an ornate box with nine evenly spaced windows that had fluted sashes on each of the three floors. The cottage roof had three dormers on the north and south sides, but just dark slate on the other sides of the steeply pitched roof. The stone itself was a drab gray. The Swiss flag flying outside the main door provided the only color.

At precisely nine o'clock Monday morning a bank employee dressed in a conservative pinstriped suit opened the doors to the public. Since Banque Suisse de Zurich was primarily a corporate bank, no customers were waiting as the bank opened for business. But at three minutes past nine, a taxi pulled up and a solitary man exited and hustled up the stairs and through the main doors.

Bud Reid walked up to the young man at the information desk. "Excuse me. I need some information on who is handling one of your accounts. Who could help me with that?"

The blond man, in his late twenties with round spectacles, checked a list and said, "That would be Greta, but she's not in this morning."

"Is there anyone else?"

He shook his head. "This is not a good day, sir. One of our employees had an accident yesterday and quite a few staff members were called on to volunteer information to the police this morning."

"An accident? What sort of accident?" Reid said, his mind already racing to the worst possible scenario: that the person he wanted to contact was dead.

"The police didn't say. They were here at seven this morning and asked anyone who worked with Jorge on a daily basis to accompany them to the precinct."

"Jorge?"

"Jorge Shweisser. He's the man who died."

"I see. What exactly did Herr Shweisser do for the bank?"

"He was an account manager. He handled our private clients."

"As opposed to corporate?"

"Yes, sir."

"Thank you," he said. He left the bank and found the nearest phone booth. He checked the residential listings for Shweisser, and found a listing for Jorge on a side street a coupe of blocks off Bahnhofstrasse. He checked his map and flagged a cab, reciting the address to the driver. It was a short drive, less than five minutes, and when they arrived he told the driver to keep moving. The front door had a band of yellow tape stretched across it and a police squad car with two constables sat at the curb. It was no accident that had killed Jorge Shweisser.

Bud Reid's job in Zurich had just radically changed. Jorge Shweisser was probably Escobar's contact inside the bank, and now he needed proof. In his line of business, Bud Reid didn't believe in coincidences. A banker dying the day before he arrived to ask questions was incredibly coincidental. He needed access to the man's house, his computer and his personal files. And he needed it quickly. That would mean breaking and entering, theft, and hacking into secure computer files. Bud checked his watch and mentally calculated the time difference to El Paso. He had about six hours before daybreak in Texas. Six hours to secure results, so he could phone them in to Landry and Maxwell. He felt the adrenaline start to flow, just as it had when he was in the Colombian jungle with the boys from Delta and Centra Spike. To most people, the thought of breaking into a house in broad daylight that was being guarded by police would be daunting. To Bud Reid it was simply a problem that needed a solution.

And if there was one thing his tenure with the United States government had taught him, it was how to solve this kind of problem.

Chapter Twenty-seven

Pedro awoke at five-thirty, showered and dressed in sweats and a loose-fitting T-shirt. He laced his Nikes, grabbed a bottle of water from the kitchen fridge and quietly let himself out the back door. He moved around Javier Rastano's house at an easy jog, then down the driveway toward the main gates. The two guards working the early morning shift saw him approaching and swung the gates open. He passed through with a perfunctory nod and hit the asphalt.

This was a new world to him, the decadence of wealth and power. He had never even driven into Colonia Escalón before now, let alone lived in one of the houses. Now he had his own room inside Rastano's mansion, the run of the grounds and a new set of clothes from yesterday afternoon's trip to the upscale Galerías shopping mall. He still wore no jewelry. In San Salvador that was simply an open invitation for a bullet in the head. His baggy sweats covered the new Nikes as he pounded the pavement outside the massive walled estates. He increased his pace as he approached a driveway manned by two guards dressed fully in black. Their hands were on the stocks of their M-16s as he passed. But the look they gave him was cold and condescending. It was the look a lesser man on the financial totem pole gives the man on the top. And then Pedro realized: for this slice of time, he was one of them, the privileged with money. For a brief moment he stood atop a pedestal looking down at El Salvador's poor. And for that moment it felt good. Then the image tarnished and he saw the rich for what they really were: Hoarders. They were the keepers of the money that could transform his country into one of haves, rather than have-nots. The rich had the power to enact great change, but they would never dream of opening the vaults and letting their wealth trickle into the gutters. They were happy and insulated in their mansions, behind gates and high walls. They lived a world apart from the good people of San Salvador who struggled every day to survive the harsh streets of the city. Pedro felt a surge of hate for the rich and increased his pace.

He was past a cardio workout now, and pushing his heart rate into the extreme range. The roads were hilly and the uphill climbs were leaving him gasping for air. His heart was pounding so hard his temples pulsed and his head throbbed with the surging blood. He slowed slightly, realizing that even with his athletic body he was pushing the limits. The road forked and he took the branch that curved back toward Rastano's house. Three hundred yards along the tree-lined street he placed a call on his cell phone. He slowed to a walk as Eugene answered it.

"You're up early," Eugene said cheerfully.

"Getting in shape," Pedro said. "Rastano thinks I'm some sort of prize fighter and I don't want to damage that image."

"How'd the fight go on Saturday?"

"Good. I beat the guy, but not by much. Rastano asked both of us back to his house. He wants to promote us and from what I can gather, he's got some pretty good connections in the U.S. He's talking getting us on the same card as a title bout. That's big-time."

"So you considering his offer?" Eugene asked.

"Of course not. The guy's a pig. He's a rich schmuck who needs to be taught a lesson."

"And you're the guy."

"I'm the guy." Pedro was breathing normally now.

"What about his house? Did you see anything suspicious while you were there?" There was a pause, then Eugene asked anxiously, "Any sign of Julie or Shiara?"

"Haven't had a chance to look yet. But I'm staying inside the house. I've got a room on the second floor that looks out over the backyard. The size of this place is unbelievable. And security is tight everywhere. I'd say at any given time Rastano's got twelve guys with automatic weapons patrolling the grounds and watching the front gate."

"Are the guards professionals or rent-a-cops?"

"Strictly professional. I've seen guys like this before, Eugene. They're ex-army, well trained and well paid. They'll kill you without even thinking if Rastano gives the order. And they're not going to let me just walk around the grounds poking my head in anywhere I please. I've got to be careful or I'm a dead man."

"Well, my friend, you've certainly delivered on your end. You're inside his house. Be careful and don't get hurt."

"How are things with you?" Pedro asked.

"Excellent. Landry and I are flying out to Florida today. We're going to see one of my distant cousins. Eduardo Garcia uncovered a few suspicious calls and trips that don't jibe for someone who owns a Florida car dealership.

There's a chance Pablo's been in touch with him as recently as a few months ago."

"So the DEA and CIA guys are convinced Pablo's alive?" Pedro asked.

"I'm not so sure they're convinced as they are scared. They are absolutely petrified that Pablo may be alive, and as more and more evidence points that way there's this controlled panic starting to surface. It's really interesting watching them work. They analyze everything, leave no physical evidence untouched. But at the same time, they have gut feelings that are amazing."

"How's that?" Pedro asked.

"Like when Landry and I were poking through the list of my family members. He was the one who singled out Mario Correa, not me. He said there was something about the guy, and the more we dug, the more we found."

"Like what?"

"He lives in Florida, imports his Renaults from Europe, yet three of his trips last year were to Detroit. And two of those times were in the dead of winter."

"Why would a Colombian living in Florida travel to Detroit in the winter?" Pedro asked.

"That's what we're wondering."

"You think Pablo's in one of the northern states?"

"No idea. I doubt finding him will be that easy, but talking with Mario is a good starting point. And there's something else. Remember that Bud Reid guy I was telling you about when we talked on Friday? Well, Crandle sent him over to Switzerland. He's going to track down Pablo's contact inside the bank and have a chat. He should be calling in anytime now."

"All pieces in the puzzle," Pedro said. "And those pieces are starting to fit together."

"A bit, but we're a long way from knocking on Pablo's front door."

Pedro rounded a corner and the edge of the wall surrounding the Rastano estate came into sight. "Yeah. Hey, listen Eugene, I've got to go. I'm back at the house."

"This a good time for you to call?"

"The best. I'll go for my morning run at this time every day. That way I can talk without anyone around."

"Give me a call tomorrow."

"Tomorrow." Pedro flipped the phone shut and slipped it into his pocket. He increased his pace slightly, jogging the final quarter mile to the front entrance. He was barely breathing hard when he arrived and the guards hit the switch and the massive gates swung open. He thanked them and sprinted the final two hundred yards from the road to the house. His pulse was up slightly as he entered the rear foyer. He was surprised to see a barefooted Javier Rastano in the kitchen, wearing a silk dressing gown. He was slicing a grapefruit as Pedro entered.

"You can use the front door, Pedro," Javier said. "You're not part of the staff."

Pedro shrugged. "This door's closer to the kitchen."

Javier laughed. "You hungry?"

"Famished. I just had a run around the neighborhood."

"You like it?"

"Of course I like it. It's beautiful. I don't think I've ever seen a nicer place to live in my life."

"You can have whatever you want, Pedro," Javier said, leaning on the counter and scooping out a small bit of grapefruit. "You just have to want it badly enough."

"You mean in the ring?"

"I mean in life," Rastano said, his smile turning dark. "But specifically in your case, yes, in the ring. You've got excellent skills. I like the way you fight."

"Thanks," Pedro said, opening the fridge and taking out a couple of fresh oranges. "Okay if I have these?"

Rastano waved his hand. "You don't have to ask. Whatever you want, you take. I want you to make yourself at home."

"I'll do that," Pedro said, sliding a knife from the butcher block and carving up the oranges. He was hungry and gulped them down. "You have an exercise routine set up for Luis and me, or do we just do our own thing?"

"You and Luis can do as you wish. You're already in excellent shape. You know what you're doing."

Pedro finished the last of the second orange and set the plate and the knife in the sink. "The swimming pool open?" he asked.

Javier motioned toward the grounds. "As I said, it's all yours."

"I wish," Pedro said, grinning. "I'm going to change and do some laps. See you in a while."

"You bet," Rastano said, watching Pedro as he left the kitchen.

Pedro could feel Rastano's eyes on his back as he padded lightly across the cool tile floor. He reached the hall entrance and turned the corner, glad to be away from the man's penetrating eyes. Pedro hated Rastano's stare, it seemed to pierce his defenses and look directly into his deepest thoughts. But as quickly as that occurred to him, he knew it couldn't be true. Because his innermost thoughts centered almost entirely on how much he hated Javier Rastano, and how to find Julie and Shiara. And if Rastano could indeed read his thoughts, then he'd be dead. And so far, Rastano seemed to like his new welterweight boxer.

But Pedro knew one thing. When the time came, and it would, one of them was going down.

Chapter Twenty-eight

Alexander Landry cradled the phone between his ear and his shoulder as he jotted a quick note on a loose piece of paper. By the look on his face, he was not a happy man. It was early Monday morning and the team, minus Irwin Crandle, was gathered around a central table in their command center at EPIC in El Paso.

"Yeah, we're off to Florida," Landry said, as he and Bud Reid wrapped up their international call. How did you know?"

"Crandle told me," Bud said. "I've already spoken with him this morning concerning this situation."

"What did he say?"

"Enough. And I'm sure you're thinking the same thing he was."

"It doesn't take a neurosurgeon to realize we have a problem," Landry said. "Are you heading back now?"

"My flight's in an hour."

"See you soon."

Alexander Landry turned to the room, where all eyes were on him. "Bud Reid located Pablo's banker," Landry said, his voice monotone. "Someone sliced his carotid artery open in a dark alley Sunday afternoon."

"Any suspects?" Cathy Maxwell didn't bother asking if Shweisser had survived the attack. People didn't survive a severed carotid artery.

"No witnesses to the murder, but Jorge Shweisser, that was his name, was seen dining with a woman a half hour before he bled out in a nearby alley. She could be our killer."

"You were quite specific a moment ago, Alexander," Cathy said. "You said *Pablo's* banker. What did Bud get?"

"He broke into Shweisser's townhouse and hacked into his computer. According to Bud, the man was fastidious in his record keeping. There were a number of secure files showing just over five years of regular deposits. Bud thinks Shweisser had been using that particular computer for that length of time. The deposits all had the same transit number, so they came from the same source, which is, as of right now, unidentified. Bud copied a bunch of floppy disks but didn't have time to look on them and see what he was downloading. Hopefully one of them will be a backup from whatever computer he used prior to this one. But the bottom line is that Jorge Shweisser looks dirty."

"So we've got our connection to the numbered account," Eugene said. "Do you think the access code may be on one of the disks Bud copied?"

"Not a chance," Cathy Maxwell said. "The banks use a completely different set of numbers for their staff to access the accounts than the clients. That way if there's any cash missing, they can trace back to who withdrew it—the client or the banker."

Eugene looked despondent, but managed a smile. "That makes sense. So we're not much further ahead."

"We don't know that, Eugene," Cathy Maxwell said encouragingly. "Bud has the transit codes for the transfers and if we can decrypt them that should allow us to trace where the regular deposits into Shweisser's personal account originated."

Eugene brightened. "And that will give us Pablo's location?"

Cathy shook her head. "I doubt it will be that simple. If Pablo was sending that money, and right now that's a big if, he probably routed it through a Caribbean country, like the Bahamas or the Caymans. If he was smart enough to do that, then the trail will end abruptly. And the banks have some of the toughest encryption software in the business to mask the account number and the transit codes. It's not easy identifying where the transfer originated. Plus, the offshore banks in the Caribbean are tight-lipped at the best of times, and if Pablo is sitting on money in a Cayman account, it's a well-established account and the bank is going to shut the door in our face when we come poking about. New money, just deposited, is a different story. The banks don't want to be accused of laundering drug money, so they open their books a little quicker if the DEA asks about a recent deposit."

Eugene ran his hand through his thick, curly hair and let out an exasperated sigh. "This is unbelievable. Banks protecting drug dealers."

"Why do you think it took us so long to find Pablo back in the early '90s?" Landry said. "We weren't up against just banks, but entire governments that didn't want to give him up. Nicaragua and Panama were the worst. They stonewalled us for years, pretending to cooperate, while everything they were feeding us was a crock of shit. Christ, Noriega was a pain in the ass. We never knew what to believe when he opened his mouth. And Noriega didn't just dump on us. He pissed off the drug lords by appropriating the money they had on deposit. Nobody was happy with that prick."

"He got what he deserved," Cathy said.

"There are a few *narcos* would disagree. They think a bullet would have been more in line than prison time." Landry checked his watch and pointed at the door. "We have to go, Eugene, or we'll miss our flight to Florida."

They collected their bags from the small table near the door and hustled to the front doors. Their cab was waiting and traffic was light, putting them at the airport in plenty of time for their flight. They hubbed through Dallas-Fort Worth and arrived in Miami just after three in the afternoon. Mario Correa's Renault dealership was in Miami Beach, on the busy south stretch of Collins Avenue. They grabbed a rental at the Hertz counter and arrived unannounced at the dealership at four o'clock, five hours before the nine o'clock closing time posted on the main doors. The showroom was quiet; only one salesman was on the floor speaking with a customer. The middle-aged receptionist, her reading glasses perched on her nose, looked up from her computer screen as they entered. She slipped off her glasses, and smiled.

"Can I help you?" she asked. Her voice was pleasant.

"Yes. We'd like to speak with Mario Correa," Eugene said. "I'm his cousin."

A disappointed look crossed her face. "I'm sorry, but Mr. Correa is not in Miami today."

Landry took over. "We called earlier," he said. His voice was anything but pleasant. "We were told Mr. Correa would be in all day."

"He was supposed to be here, but he got called away to an emergency meeting in West Palm Beach. He has another, smaller dealership up there."

"When will he be back?" Landry asked, obviously perturbed.

The receptionist shrugged. "I'm not sure. He said he might take a couple of days and play some golf. He prefers the courses north of Miami. He says they're not as crowded."

"Could you get him on the phone, please?" Landry asked.

She hesitated. "As I mentioned, sir, he's in West Palm Beach for an important meeting. He specifically asked not to be disturbed." She looked at Eugene. "I'll let him know that his cousin was here," she said. "I can take your name and phone number, if you wish."

Eugene glanced at Landry, and stepped forward to give his cell phone number. "Sure," he said, and gave her his name and number. If Mario knew anything about Pablo, he'd get in touch with him first. And, well, it was one edge he'd have on the team, which just might come in handy. And, unlike Pedro's situation, an incoming call wouldn't put him in harm's way. He joined Alexander Landry, who was leaning over checking out the sticker price on a Vel Satis, the flagship of the Renault luxury line. He looked puzzled.

"Holy shit," he said. "Look at the price they want for this thing. I could buy four Crown Vics for that."

Eugene laughed and shook his head. "Americans. The engineering in this car is phenomenal. It's on the same level with top of the line BMW and Mercedes. You're paying for European technology and engineering."

"I'll still buy American," Landry said, giving the sheet one last look and heading for the door. They broke out into the late-afternoon Florida sunshine, and Landry flipped open his phone. He dialed long distance and when it connected, he said, "Hi, Cathy, it's Alexander."

"How are things?" his CIA counterpart asked.

"Not so good," Landry said, resting against the metal railing and running his free hand along the painted surface. "Correa was gone when we got here, called away to an emergency meeting in West Palm Beach."

There was a marked silence, then Cathy Maxwell said, "What's going on, Alexander? First the banker, now Correa. Something isn't right."

Alexander Landry continued running his hand gently back and forth on the railing, his face a mask. Eugene was watching him closely and on the other end of the line, in El Paso, Cathy Maxwell waited for his response. Finally, he said, "Maybe, after all these years, we still have a leak."

Chapter Twenty-nine

They took the Florida Turnpike north from Miami to West Palm Beach. Traffic was moving well and Alexander Landry wound out the rental, topping a hundred miles an hour a few times, and reducing the hourlong drive to less than forty minutes. Eugene called ahead and got the address to the dealership. It was on the narrow spit of land across the Intracoastal Waterway from the main body of the city. He had Landry exit the turnpike at Okeechobee Boulevard and follow it straight though until they crossed the water and entered the high-rent district. Massive Royal palms lined the wide road, their fronds barely moving in the light afternoon breeze. About halfway to the ocean they spotted the Renault dealership on the right side of the road. Landry pulled into the parking lot and switched off the ignition.

"Want to bet whether he's here or not?" Landry asked.

"Only if I can bet that he's nowhere near West Palm Beach," Eugene said.

"No bet."

They walked into the air-conditioned showroom. At sixty feet by forty, it was about half the size of Correa's flagship enterprise in Miami. Land values flanking either side of Royal Palm Way were through the roof, but from the glittering glass and chrome look of the ultra-modern dealership, Correa appeared to be covering the rent with no problems. Alexander Landry crossed the exposed aggregate floor, his soft soled shoes squeaking slightly on the polished surface.

"Mario Correa, please," he said in a polite, but firm, voice.

"I'm sorry, sir, but Mr. Correa is in a meeting and cannot be disturbed." She smiled as she spoke, but her tone was equally firm.

Landry flashed his DEA creds at her. "Get him out here now, miss, or I'll have a SWAT team here in ten minutes to drag him out."

Her tough veneer cracked immediately. "He's not here," she said, her voice wavering. "Mr. Correa phoned from Miami earlier today and told me that if anyone came looking for him he was in a meeting and was not to be disturbed."

"How do you know he was in Miami?" Landry asked, leaning over the reception desk and using his size to get close to her. "And don't lie to me, miss, or I'll have you up on obstruction charges."

"We have call display. He was in his office in Miami Beach when he called."

"What time?"

"Around ten o'clock."

Landry fished a card from his shirt pocket and handed it to her. She took it with shaking hands. "If he calls or walks through that door, you call me. And if I find out you've seen him or spoken with him and haven't called me, I'll personally travel back here and throw you in jail."

He spun on his heels and marched out of the showroom, Eugene trailing behind him.

"You were a little rough on her," Eugene said. "She was just doing what she was told."

"Eugene, get something straight here. Someone lies to you, that makes them a dishonest person. Someone lies to me, that puts them in jail for obstruction. It's one of the perks of having the badge." He stopped next to their rental car and continued in a less aggravated voice. "I've been lied to so many times I can't remember a tenth of them. Sometimes I have to swallow it and sometimes I don't. When it's a car lot receptionist, I don't."

"Got it," Eugene said. He paused, his hand on the door handle. "What now?"

"Back to EPIC. This is going nowhere right now. We need time to find Mario Correa, and time is one thing we don't have."

Traffic was heavier heading south toward Miami and Landry had to settle for cruising at eighty miles an hour. It pissed him off, and turned a bad mood into a downright foul one. They were on the south tip of Fort Lauderdale when his cell phone rang. He answered it with a gruff, "Hello." A moment later he said, "Hello, Senator. What can I do for you?"

"Cathy phoned me, Alexander. She filled me in on the result of Bud's trip to Zurich and your wild goose chase to Miami. Did you find him in West Palm Beach?"

"No, sir. It was a lie. He was in Miami the whole time."

"Shit." A pause, then, "Are we all thinking the same thing here, Alexander?"

"I think so, Senator. We've got a leak."

"I agree. I'm leaving Kentucky inside the hour for El Paso. I've booked off the next few days and will be working side-by-side with you and Cathy for the duration of this problem. This is getting out of hand, and I want it reeled in right now. If Escobar is alive, I want him."

"We all do, sir."

"We'll see about that. I'll talk to you in Texas."

Landry dropped the phone on the front seat and shook his head. "What the hell is going on, Eugene?"

Eugene didn't answer, just stared out the window at the passing buildings. But he was wondering the same thing.

Chapter Thirty

Senator Irwin Crandle stood amid the organized confusion of their EPIC command center and made it perfectly clear who was in charge. This was his covert op. Cathy Maxwell and Alexander Landry were simply representing their respective agencies. Eduardo Garcia was an afterthought, and Eugene Escobar was a private citizen connected to the search for Pablo only through blood. It was late in the evening when Bud Reid arrived, straight from the airport after eleven hours on planes, but Crandle still took the time to put him in his place.

"Bud," he said, as the man took a chair at the conference table, "you missed my little speech to the group, so let me sum it up. No one makes a move without my approval. Every lead is to be channeled through me. There is no independent action without my clearance. If the wheels come off and the public finds out that Pablo Escobar is still alive, and that I knew about it, I'm the one who will take the heat. And unless I've miscalculated the response to this hitting the nightly news, the heat will be un-believable. Since you guys are insulated and my head is ultimately on the block, I want control. Now, is there anyone in this room who doesn't understand the chain of command?"

Five heads shook in unison. No one spoke.

"All right. Now, before we go any further, we've got a small problem. Someone tipped off Mario Correa that we were on our way to Miami. And I think we all agree that Jorge Shweisser's death wasn't a coincidence. The man had his carotid artery sliced with a curved scalpel. He was professionally murdered. Since we don't have any support staff, I'm going to suggest that someone in this room is responsible. Anyone care to disagree?" He took a few short breaths, and continued. "We've got a rat. Whether it is the same person who kept the *narcos* informed of our movements while we searched for Pablo thirteen years ago remains to be seen. If it is, then Agent Garcia is in the clear. But then again, our informant might be new to the DEA and on someone else's payroll." He turned to Eduardo Garcia. "Were you on your regular shift when Mr. Escobar showed up?"

Garcia shook his head and nervously bit his bottom lip. "No, I was on overtime. Filling in for a buddy."

"Why?" Crandle asked, then added, "And don't give me any bullshit, Garcia, because I'll check your story to make sure it's true."

"Ben Smythe wanted some time off. I offered to take over his shift."

"He wanted to be relieved of that shift in particular?" Crandle asked harshly.

"No. He needed some time to find a new house. His wife is having another child and they need a bigger house. I offered to take that shift if he could arrange to see houses with his realtor."

Crandle looked mildly amused. "And what realtor

doesn't make the time to show his clients houses. You knew he'd say okay when you offered. Which means, Agent Garcia, that you could have known within a fairly narrow time frame when Eugene was going to arrive. And you made sure that you were working that day."

Garcia was flustered, his face flushed and his mouth dry. He took a drink of water, and rallied. "How could anyone have known which DEA office Eugene would head for? He could have gone directly to D.C. just as easily."

"Common sense says that he's going to head to an office where he can get results. That's Arlington or El Paso. And our *narcos* probably have a man in Washington as well, Eduardo." Crandle twisted his head slightly in Bud Reid's direction. "And you've known what's been going on since I have. We've both been about ten milliseconds behind Alexander and Cathy throughout this whole thing."

Bud leapt from his chair, shaking with rage. "That's ridiculous, Irwin. I traveled to Zurich to find out Jorge Shweisser's identity and interview him. I certainly didn't fly to Europe to talk to someone I knew would be dead."

"Why not?" Crandle snapped at him, pacing about the room. "What a great alibi. No one is going to suspect the guy who flies to Europe to talk with the target he just had Escobar order a hit on. Well, Bud, fuck that. I suspect you. Right now, the only person in this room I don't suspect is Eugene Escobar." He gazed at Cathy Maxwell and Alexander Landry for a few moments. "And you two. Both of you had Pablo's name flagged in your computer systems. How many dead-ends and red herrings were dropped on your desk before this happened? Has one of you been on Pablo's payroll all these years? Were you watching for something like this so you could warn Escobar?" He stopped and sat on the edge of a desk. "Well, by the looks of things, we've all hit the big-time. I'm getting the distinct feeling that Pablo is alive, and we're the only ones who know what's going on here. Whoever is feeding Escobar the information has earned their money this week."

Alexander Landry didn't like the accusations. He looked like he was going to come out of his chair and use his immense size to pulverize the senator. Veins stood out on his forehead and, by the look on his face, his blood pressure was peaking at a dangerously high level. Finally he said, "You're an asshole, Irwin."

Silence descended. The hum of tiny fans in the desktop computers was the only audible sound. Crandle scanned each face, taking in eye movements and body language. He backed off a bit. "The point I'm trying to make is that none of us is above suspicion. Not one of us."

"Including you?" Cathy asked hotly.

"Yes, Cathy," he shot back, "including me. Only I know if I'm clean. But to everyone else in this room, I must be considered as likely as anyone to be feeding Pablo information. We all know whether we're clean or dirty, but no one else does. So I expect you to suspect me, just as I suspect you."

"This is quite the situation we have here," Landry said disgustedly. "How are we supposed to share sensitive information if one of us is a sell-out?"

Crandle was thoughtful for a moment, then said, "We need to keep the avenues of communication open. We can't afford to shut them down by compartmentalizing data flow. We'll continue to work in groups so no one person is privy to information without someone else knowing. But I want to stress this: all information is still pooled and all six of us have access to it. I don't think we've got a crisis at this point, as we're still a long way from figuring out where Pablo is living. The closer we get to that, the more we'll look at isolating information."

"Who works with whom?" Bud Reid asked.

"We'll draw straws," Crandle said. "Agent Garcia, get six

straws and cut them into pairs of differing lengths. Whoever has the same length of straw is your partner."

"Works for me," Landry said. Maxwell and Reid just nodded, and Garcia left the room in search of some straws. He returned a couple of minutes later and showed the group the six straws. Two were fairly short, two medium length and two uncut. Crandle took the straws and arranged them in his hands so that no one could tell their lengths. He offered the first choice to Cathy Maxwell with the comment, "Ladies first." She drew a medium straw. Bud Reid pulled out a full-length one. Garcia followed with the second full-length straw, and Eugene selected a short one. With two straws left, Crandle gave Alexander Landry his choice. He drew a medium one, putting him with Cathy Maxwell. Crandle held up the second short straw.

"Okay, I'm with Eugene. Cathy, you and Alexander stay together, no change there. The final pairing is Bud and Eduardo. Anyone have a problem with their partner?" No one challenged the selection and Crandle continued. He looked to Eugene and asked, "Your friend in San Salvador, how is he doing?"

Eugene hesitated for a second, then decided that giving the group a vague idea of how Pedro was doing wouldn't endanger his friend. "He's in San Salvador now and he's looking for Julie and Shiara. I think he said he's concentrating his search in Colonia Escalón, one of the city's more upscale neighborhoods. He told me he's making progress, getting closer all the time. But that's all I know right now."

"Does he know the kidnapper's name?" Landry asked.

"Yes," Eugene replied.

"But we don't," Landry added sarcastically.

"No, you don't." Eugene looked him directly in the eyes. "And the way things are going, I'm glad of it."

Landry bristled at the comment, but Senator Crandle interjected. "Stop it right now. Cheap comments will not be tolerated. Not even from you, Eugene. Understood?"

"Understood," Eugene said.

Crandle addressed Bud Reid. "The disks from Jorge Shweisser's house in Zurich, where are they?"

Reid fished in his pocket and pulled out a CD-RW in a clear plastic case. He handed it to Crandle who in turn set it on the central table. "Cathy, you're probably the best in the group at computer work. Can you and Alexander have a look at the files on that disk and see if there's anything that might point to Escobar's location?"

"Sure," Cathy said, leaning over and picking up the CD. Her jaw was set, her teeth clenched, and everyone in the room knew she was biting her tongue to keep from exploding at Crandle.

"Bud, you and Eduardo get on those transit codes for the funds transfers. Contact Hyram Ockey at the National Security Agency and see if he can crack the encryption algorithms. We need to find out which bank handled the cash from the two recent withdrawals from Pablo's account."

They drifted back to their desks where stacks of paper awaited them, the mood more than a little tense. Six people brought together by a situation that would quickly become front-page news across every continent if it were to leak outside the thin walls that contained it.

Six people.

One of them a simple man, thrown into a complex web of cunning and violence by his blood relationship with a ruthless drug dealer.

Five others.

Professionals from the past and present who dealt with death and treachery on a daily basis. Four men and woman who had seen more atrocities and suffered more losses than any normal person would in ten lifetimes. Yet despite the scars the *narcos* left on them, one of the five was a traitor, an informant to the most dangerous drug lord who ever lived. And now, after a dozen years, the killing had started again. A banker in Zurich was on a slab of cold metal because CIA records had identified Pablo's account.

Who was next?

That was the question on every mind in the room.

Every mind but one.

Chapter Thirty-one

The sun poked over the mountains surrounding El Paso on Tuesday morning, five days from Javier Rastano's deadline. Eugene could feel the intense heat the moment he opened the sliding doors and leaned over the balcony railing, coffee mug in hand. He gazed at the city, seeing a jumble of buildings and houses but nothing in particular. It all melded together, a mixture of adobe and brick, asphalt and concrete and glass and steel. He thought of the group of five, also varied and unique. Five individuals who had chosen careers fighting the proliferation of drugs. Yet one of them was a traitor. That was the best word he could find to describe the informant.

A traitor.

A traitor to the DEA, to their country, to the small group tracking Pablo and, ultimately, a traitor to Julie and Shiara. The lives of his wife and daughter rested with the group of professionals who would be meeting at EPIC in a couple of hours, determined to find and eliminate Pablo Escobar. He needed them, that was without question, but how much damage would be done in the interim. Pablo would know their every move and would react as he always had. He would run. Leaning on the balcony, he realized the futility of the search. No matter how successful they were, Pablo would remain one step ahead of them.

Unless they could unearth the informant. That was the key. But how? If it was one of the three veteran *narco* chasers, their covers were so well established that it would be impossible to rip the façade off in five days. And if the leak was Eduardo Garcia, well, Crandle was probably right that Pablo had informants in other DEA offices as well. As much as their small group was trying to stay transparent, a computer expert could easily be watching their progress online. As sick as it made him feel, he wondered if the leak was one of the veterans. If that were the case and they could identify who it was and neutralize them, the connection to Pablo would be severed.

"Christ," Eugene whispered under his breath to himself. *Neutralize.* He was starting to think like Maxwell and Landry. His phone rang and he checked his watch. It was time for Pedro's call. He finished the last sip of coffee, and hit the send button. "You exercising again?" Eugene asked his friend.

"Yeah," Pedro said, slowing to a quick walk, his breath coming back quickly. "What's up?"

"We've got problems at this end," Eugene said, filling Pedro in on the latest subterfuge.

"Shit," Pedro said. "Have you told anyone at El Paso anything that Rastano could use to identify me?"

"No. Nothing other than the very basics. I told them that I've got a man on the inside in San Salvador. They don't even know who it is. You should be okay for now."

"That's good, because these guys would kill me in a minute if they knew who I was."

"Not to worry. I'll keep your identity safe. Any sign of Julie and Shiara?"

"No. But that's not to say they're not here. This place is huge. There are parts of the house I haven't been in yet. I'll keep looking."

"Okay. I'm counting on you. Things are unraveling fast on this end. With someone feeding Pablo information, even if we find him, he'll be gone before we get there. It looks like you're the only one who can keep Julie and Shiara alive."

"I'm doing the best I can, Eugene. Trust me."

"I trust you, my friend. *Ciao*."

"Talk to you soon." Pedro hung up and deleted the call from the phone's memory.

Eugene snapped the phone shut and stared at the city, now even more melded as heat waves rose from the buildings and distorted the view. He returned to his room and turned on the shower. He slipped under the cold water, appreciating the coolness, and a sudden thought occurred to him. Maybe he didn't need the covert team as much as he had initially thought. And once that idea had planted itself in his mind, he encouraged it to germinate and grow and spread into different courses of action. Leaving the group gave him options that he didn't have with them, and the more he thought about it, the more it made sense.

By the time he finished showering, the only question that remained was when he would leave.

A tiny parabolic microphone jutted out from the gap in the driver's side window. When Eugene Escobar closed his phone and disappeared into his hotel room, the microphone was retracted into the car and the window rolled up. The engine was started and the car pulled away from the curb. The lone occupant drove through the early morning streets with a glimmer of a smile. Javier

Rastano would be pleased with this information. Not pleased that someone had infiltrated his private residence, but relieved that the treachery was unveiled.

The driver checked the dashboard clock and decided it was too early to call Javier. Later in the day would be fine. Once Rastano knew he had a rat in the house, it wouldn't take long to eliminate the problem. And once again, Javier Rastano would be grateful and would forward the money. Always the money.

Such an excellent working relationship.

The driver pulled in to a nearby restaurant and ordered breakfast, asking the waitress to put a rush on the order. The group would be meeting at EPIC soon, and it wouldn't do to be late.

Chapter Thirty-two

Shiara inched forward through the duct, her hands feeling the way in the total blackness. She felt a sharp edge and yanked her hand back before the metal cut through the skin. She used one of the Band-aids her mother had given her to cover the sharp metal, then continued on through the narrow ductwork.

She had been in the duct for about fifteen minutes, having passed the three-pronged split in the cooling system about five minutes ago. Her mom had been emphatic—no more than thirty minutes total, including time to get back to the starting point. It was midafternoon and leaving the room to enter the duct was risky. But on her second trip through the series of rectangular metal, she had reached a grate that opened into another room. Unfortunately, she had been unable to see the interior of the room for lack of light. They had to risk a daytime excursion. Julie had determined the guard's schedule and found that they seldom visited between two and two-thirty in the afternoon. They decided that was their window of opportunity. At precisely two o'clock Shiara had crawled into the duct and heard her mother twist the screws back in, effectively sealing her inside the walls. She was close to the grate now, just around one more corner.

Hints of light cut through the darkness as she neared the corner. As she rounded the bend, muted light from the grill partially illuminated the metal shaft and Shiara felt less claustrophobic. She hurried now, knowing she would be lucky to make it back in the half hour her mom had allowed. But to come so close to seeing what was in the other room and turn back now was madness.

She inched ahead, her arms and fingers aching from the exertion. She finally reached the grate and peered through. She was suspended above the center of a large utility room.

The construction of the walls and floor was entirely cement, with two boilers hooked in tandem against the far wall, some twenty feet distant. Numerous dials and valves peppered the input and output lines. A strange-looking machine was tucked in the corner next to one of the boilers, round and over six feet high. Shiara guessed it was the air-conditioning unit, as a number of tin ducts led from it to the series of ducts which took the cold air throughout the house. One of the input lines came in right around where her feet were, and when the fan started on the large, round machine, she felt the cool air entering the duct near her ankles.

She pushed her face against the grate and scanned the outer walls. There. She thought she saw the edge of a window. She pushed harder and was rewarded with a glimpse of sunlight. There was definitely a window to the outside world.

She pulled back slightly and focused on how the grate was attached to the duct. It was difficult to see, but after a minute or two she was sure that the grill was held on by four screws. And the slats were far enough apart that she could probably get her mother's home-made screwdriver at the screw heads.

She pushed back, feeling the sting of the cold air as she passed over the intake shaft. She kept moving, knowing that her mother would be frantic. But the important thing was, she had found a possible way out of their prison.

Javier Rastano took the phone call in his study on the main floor. He waited until the servant closed the door, then said, "Hello."

"Javier, it's me," the distant voice said. "I've got some news for you."

"What?" Rastano asked, knowing his contact was edgy about spending too much time on the phone.

"The person that Eugene Escobar has looking for you is inside your house."

Rastano stopped breathing. "What?" he finally said. "What do you mean, inside my house?"

"I don't know who it is, just that somehow they've made it inside your house. They're staying at your place."

"One of the boxers," Javier said aloud, but to himself. "Anything else?"

"Whoever it was has a cell phone and was exercising early this morning. About five-thirty El Salvador time."

"Okay," Javier said. "Thanks."

The line went dead and Rastano replaced the telephone receiver in its cradle. He leaned on the edge of his polished teak desk and fingered his Rolodex. Both Luis and Pedro were strangers to him, referrals from friends in San Salvador. He leaned over and checked his calendar. Luis had first been introduced to him at the club on March 14, three days after he spoke with Eugene Escobar on Isla de Margarita. It was tight, but possible. Pedro had first shown up at the club on March 18. More probable, but he was still unsure. Both men had cell phones, he had noticed that as they worked out or strolled about the grounds. And both fighters were up early, working out. Pedro liked to jog through the streets surrounding the house while Luis preferred the stationary cardio machines in the gym. Still, at that time of the morning, either man could have taken an incoming call or made an outgoing call without arousing any suspicions.

What to do? He could kill both men and rid himself of the problem, but that held a certain degree of risk. Even in El Salvador, cold-blooded murder was still a crime. Javier kicked around the idea of arranging a double murder; it would appear that Luis and Pedro had shot each other. But even that was tempting fate. He suspected the police would make a perfunctory examination of the murder scene and come to whatever conclusions he wanted them to, but there was still an element of risk he didn't like. The other option was to watch the two men over the next day or two and monitor the conversations on their cell phones. If he could determine which man was tied in with Eugene Escobar, he could kill him and report it to the police as a suicide. The more he thought about it, the better that option appeared. When he left his office ten minutes later, he was convinced that taking his time to remove the rat was the way to go.

Javier cut through the foyer and down the curved staircase to the basement. He nodded to a couple of off-duty guards who were playing pool in the games room and continued down the long hallway to where Escobar's wife and daughter were held captive. He pointed at the door and the armed guard twisted the key and opened the lock. He entered the room and stood face-to-face with Julie Escobar.

"Good afternoon," he said pleasantly. "How are you?"

"As well as can be expected," Julie said. "Considering."

"Ah, yes. Considering that you're being held against

your will." He pushed his hair behind his ears with his index fingers and glanced about the room. "Where is your daughter?"

"She's sleeping," Julie replied evenly.

"Sleeping? It's two-thirty in the afternoon."

Julie gave him a look of frustration. "You stick us in a room without windows and expect us to keep the same schedule we did when we had access to the sun. Other than that clock on the wall, we have no idea what time it is. What does it matter when she sleeps?"

"Get her up," Javier said.

"No," Julie snapped back.

"What?" Javier was taken aback by her defiance.

"I said no. She's having trouble sleeping and when she gets tired I want her to sleep. She's only been lying down for about an hour. She needs a good stretch of sleep, not just a nap." Julie's eyes were fiery with determination.

Javier considered slapping her out of the way and barging into the girl's room. Then decided against it. There was no reason to alienate the women any further. Saturday was fast approaching and he might need them in a final negotiation with Eugene. He smiled and waved one hand in her direction. "As you say," he said politely. "Let the girl sleep."

"Thank you."

"Is there anything else you need? How are your hands healing?"

"We're fine, thank you. And other than missing a finger, our hands are healing well."

"The guards are polite?"

"Yes. They treat us okay, I guess. It wouldn't be so bad if we could get outside occasionally."

"I'm sorry, but taking you outside is quite impossible at this time. Maybe later."

Javier retreated to the door and knocked. The guard unlatched the locking mechanism and the door swung open. He moved into the hallway without looking back and the door quickly closed behind him. Julie waited a couple of seconds, then turned and hurried to the air-conditioning duct. She had just reached the wall when she heard the sound of the key in the lock. She spun back toward the door as it opened. Javier Rastano stood in the opening. He didn't speak, just stared at her for a few seconds, then slowly walked into the room.

"You never asked me how your husband is doing," he said in a hushed voice. "That strikes me as a bit odd. Don't you think so?"

"No," Julie said, taking a glass of day-old water off the small bric-a-brac table against the wall. She took a sip and said, "Eugene is doing what he can. I figured if he had made any kind of progress you'd tell me. I hardly need to ask a question and be disappointed by the answer. It's difficult enough in this room."

Javier thoughtfully stroked his chin, then nodded and backed up toward the door. "Until tomorrow, then."

"Until tomorrow."

He left and the guard locked the door securely behind him. This time Julie waited at least a minute before reaching up and loosening the screws to the air-conditioning duct. She pulled it off and Shiara's feet appeared, followed by her legs and torso. Julie caught her around the waist and set her quietly on the carpet. Her daughter was scared and dehydrated, her breath coming in short gasps.

"Here," Julie said, handing her the stale water. "Drink this." The moment Shiara had the glass in her hands, Julie grabbed the grate from the floor and slid it back in place over the vent. She quickly screwed it solidly to the wall and hid her makeshift screwdriver, then swept up any dust that had fallen from the duct when Shiara exited. She refilled her daughter's glass with fresh water. "Are you okay?"

"I'm fine," Shiara said. "I thought he was going to go in my bedroom."

"For a minute, so did I."

Shiara brightened. "I may have found a way out. The duct leads to a utility room, with a window. I'm sure the window is large enough for us to get through."

"The duct doesn't just end at the air-conditioning unit?" Julie asked. That had been one of her fears, that when Shiara did find the end of the shaft it would run directly into the unit, negating any chance of escape.

"No, the cool air is pumped into the shaft about six feet from the end via another duct. From where I was I think we could drop down to the floor of the utility room. It's about seven or eight feet down, to a concrete floor."

"Straight onto concrete?" Julie asked, and Shiara nodded. "Head first." She shook her head. "That's a long fall, Shiara. I don't know."

"I'll go first, Mom. I'm not as heavy and my bones aren't brittle. I won't break anything. I'm sure."

Julie was skeptical. "What about getting the screws off the grate on the other end?" she asked.

"There are only four, and I'm sure I can get at them." She looked imploringly at her mother. "We can do it. I know we can."

Julie stroked her daughter's hair, and smiled. "Okay, but as a last resort. If your father hasn't got what they want by Friday, we give it a try. That's a little over three days, not too long to wait."

"Excellent," Shiara said. "I think I should make another trip to the other grate before Friday to see if I can get the screws started. That way you won't get stuck in the ducts if we have to back up."

"All right," Julie said reluctantly. "One more trip into the duct. Then we go on Friday."

They spent the rest of the afternoon and evening watching movies and talking. By nine o'clock they were both spent. Julie gave Shiara a kiss on her forehead and closed the teenager's bedroom door. She was immensely proud of her daughter's courage, but she knew that once they moved into that duct with escape on their minds, there was no turning back. They would succeed or fail. And failure could only have one outcome when dealing with Colombian drug dealers.

Death.

Chapter Thirty-three

Pablo Escobar clicked on the banking icon and his balances, both domestic and international, jumped onto the computer screen. He surveyed them coolly, calculating in his mind how much he could withdraw on short notice without attracting too much attention. Some of the international accounts were probably safe and would survive a forensic DEA audit, but others were iffy. He calculated that if he had to yank up his now well-established roots and make a run for it, he would lose approximately twenty million dollars. Not an excessive amount, but a loss that he hadn't envisioned a few months ago.

He rose from the desk and walked across his office to the bank of windows overlooking the lake. God, he missed his homeland. This barren land offered little to stimulate the senses, except perhaps during the peak summer periods when the vegetation was lush and green. Immersed in the forests he sometimes imagined the spruce and fir were actually eucalyptus and banana trees, and that he was wandering the vast expanse of his Nápoles estate in his beloved Colombia. But reality always brought him crashing back to earth.

He had made mistakes, and now he was paying for it.

He had been a dangerous and sadistic man when he floated at the top of the jetsam that was the Colombian cocaine scene. He had indulged in excesses beyond belief. And he'd enjoyed freedom for the first few years, when he controlled the Medellín cartel with the Ochoa brothers. But the good life had come to an end because he had believed he was above the law. And by his excesses. But his two biggest mistakes had been killing Rodrigo Lara and bringing down the Avianca airliner. How could he have been so arrogant as to believe that killing 107 innocent Colombian people would be overlooked just because he was Pablo Escobar? But back then he had believed he was indestructible.

He padded across to the bar in his slippers and poured himself a whiskey. He liked Crown Royal on the rocks; it was his drug of choice now. He seldom smoked any kind of pot or hash, and never touched cocaine. His physical condition was excellent and he carried very little extra weight on his frame. Quite a difference from the '80s, when he did everything to excess, including eating. They'd been wild years, great years. But now he was paying for them.

He'd had almost twelve years of relative isolation to think about it all. He'd probably started his own downfall in August 1989, when he ordered Luis Galán killed because the son-of-a-bitch refused to allow his own wife to give their daughter a bottle of milk. God, how stupid that was. Then President Virgilio Barco had called in the United States, and President Bush had jumped at the chance of removing the *narcos* from Colombia. He'd earmarked $250 million dollars to fight the cartels. And once the Americans were involved, it was the beginning of the end.

His life sentence was hell in a cold and distant land, without his wife and children. Although he spoke with Juan Pablo on a secure satellite phone every month, it was a distant second to talking with flesh and blood.

A rap on the door cut through his thoughts. "Come," he said.

Miguel entered and closed the door behind him. He had aged since the glory days at Nápoles, but he was fit and looked good for thirty-one, his face still showing some youthfulness. "You wanted to see me, sir?"

Pablo motioned to one of the leather couches and Miguel sat. "We may be moving soon."

Miguel's face remained impassive. "Any idea when?"

Pablo shrugged. "Eugenio is pushing hard to find me. He's proving more resilient than I thought. But today is Tuesday and he only has until Saturday. He's running out of time. Can he honestly think that Javier Rastano is going to release his wife and daughter if he finds me? If he does, he's a fool." He poured two fingers of Crown Royal in a crystal glass, handed it to Miguel, then said, "Talk about fools, I may be the biggest one on the face of the earth. Withdrawing that money was a mistake."

"You waited twelve years. You couldn't know Mario Rastano was monitoring the account."

"I should have known he'd be watching," Pablo said softly. "When you're waiting to get your hands on the better part of a billion dollars, you watch. I know I would. I didn't need the money. I did it because of boredom. I wanted to test the waters."

Miguel made a bit of a face and shrugged. *"C'est la vie."*

"Yeah," Pablo said. *"C'est la vie."* He finished his drink and poured another. "How long will it take you to pack?"

"A couple of days to prepare properly. But we could be out of here in two hours if necessary." Miguel was silent for a moment, then said, "Pablo, why don't you just call Mario or Javier and give them the access code to the account. If you do, they'll back off. The money's a write-off. More withdrawals will only help them locate you."

Pablo vigorously shook his head. "No, *amigo.* I don't think so. The Rastano family does not deserve that money."

"But Eugenio's wife and daughter . . ."

"I hardly know Eugenio, Miguel. And I have never given in to extortion. We never capitulated when they kidnapped Marta. I'm not eager to start now." Pablo was upset.

"Marta Nieves was Jorge and Fabio Ochoa's sister, Pablo, and the cartel was at the peak of its power when she was kidnapped. You don't have such resources now."

"True," Pablo said, settling down a bit. Miguel was not the enemy. "But I have the power to keep Mario Rastano from getting that money. Even if I gave them the number, Javier would kill Julie and Shiara. The man is a sadistic bastard. As I was, years ago."

"The years have mellowed you, Pablo."

"It wasn't just the years, Miguel. Isolation and boredom and eating healthy have mellowed me. But you know what? I'm enjoying being hunted again. It's brought life back into what has been merely existence. Mario and Javier Rastano have never beaten Pablo Escobar, and they won't beat me now. I'll play them all like big fish." Pablo Escobar laughed.

And Miguel laughed with him.

Escobar nodded and looked out over the lake. Canada geese were arriving back from their southern migration, flying in V-shaped formations across the water. They banked and landed on the calm waters, not far from the dock that served as a loading and unloading platform for boats and small planes equipped with pontoons. Three buildings were tucked against the water's edge, one of

them housing a twin engine Otter, and the other a ski-
boat. The third was empty, a place to protect visitors'
planes or boats. It was seldom used.

He ran his finger around the rim of his glass. The ice
cubes clinked together as they floated in the liquor, and
the sound echoed softly through the room. "It's quite the
team that's hunting for us," he said. "Who would have
thought that Eugene could dig up so many of my old
nemesis: Senator Irwin Crandle, Alexander Landry, Cathy
Maxwell and Bud Reid. It's a veritable who's who of the
old DEA-Centra Spike team. Trust me, Miguel, these four
are a potentially dangerous combination. They're no
fools. They might actually get lucky and find me."

"You'll know in advance," Miguel said. "Your contact
has never failed you."

"That's true," Pablo said. "You see, like Javier Rastano, I
am also a very patient man. Patient and prepared for any
contingency. I've always been amazed by what money can
buy. Goods and services are one thing, but someone's
soul, now that's another thing entirely." He leaned on the
bar and looked at Miguel. "How many people's souls have
I bought, Miguel?" It was a rhetorical question and
Miguel sipped his drink and didn't answer. "How many? A
hundred? A thousand? More? Judges, district attorneys,
lawyers, politicians, police, army officers; they took my
money and sold themselves."

"*Plata o plomo* may have had something to do with their
decision, Pablo."

"Ah, yes, silver or lead. That little technique worked
quite well, didn't it? It's surprising how many men and
women abandon their ideologies when faced with that
choice. It's actually a pity they didn't all acquiesce; but
then if they had, no one would have died and they
wouldn't have taken the offer seriously. Things were as
they had to be, given the situation."

"What about *this* situation, Pablo? What if Eugenio won't stop? What if he manages to find you? Will you kill him?"

Pablo stared at Miguel, his dark eyes introspective. "I don't know the answer to that question. If Eugene pushes the limits, I may have to kill him." Both men watched the returning geese waddle about the gardens close to the house, in search of food.

Finally Pablo said, "I will see which fish is the most fun to play."

Chapter Thirty-four

The team was just getting ready to close up shop for the day when an e-mail from Hyram Ockey at NSA popped up on Bud Reid's computer. Half of Ockey's e-mail was a bitch letter at the complexity of decrypting the transit codes and identifying the bank that had initiated the withdrawals from Banque Suisse de Zurich. Whoever had encrypted the files had also bounced the signal off two satellites and through a handful of offshore banks before coming back to the origin. The bank was the Canadian Imperial Bank of Commerce, and the branch was in Freeport, Bahamas. Bud tried the phone number included in the e-mail, but the bank was closed and a recording came on giving the bank's address, fax number and hours of operation. They wouldn't be able to contact anyone at the offshore Canadian bank until Wednesday morning.

"What do you think they'll do when we call?" Crandle asked Reid.

"We might be okay," Bud replied. "The Canadian banks are more cooperative than most. CIBC is probably the best, while Royal Bank is the worst. I won't know until tomorrow when we talk with them."

"Would it help to have someone from one of the government agencies on their doorstep when they open?" Crandle asked.

"Which agency?"

"CIA, NSA, DEA. Maybe ATF."

"Alcohol, Tobacco and Firearms is under the Department of Justice jurisdiction. We could lose control of this real quick with them in the know," Cathy Maxwell said.

Crandle thought about that, then nodded. "You're right. I don't have the ins at ATF that I have at the other agencies. But I could definitely have someone on their front door tomorrow morning."

"I could go myself," Reid said.

Crandle shook his head. "No way. This group stays together, Bud. You and Eduardo are Siamese twins until we find Pablo or break up the team. That's not negotiable."

"Okay."

Cathy said, "I've got a friend at Langley who could help us. He's damn good at scaring the shit out of people."

"Who is it?" Crandle asked.

"Chris Bisiker."

Crandle snapped his fingers. "I know him. You're right, he's a tough son-of-a-bitch. We worked together in Peru for a couple of months, chasing down some Shining Path assholes. You think he'll head over to Freeport on the QT?"

"If I ask him, he will. He owes me."

Crandle smiled. "Then ask him."

Cathy worked the phone and in less than an hour she had a commitment from Bisiker that he would be waiting outside the CIBC bank in Freeport when it opened Wednesday morning. And more important than his cooperation, she also had his promise that the trip to the Bahamas was completely off the radar. No one at Langley would be in the loop. He would speak with the branch manager and report back to EPIC immediately. Cathy was adamant; get the name and address of the owner of the account. She hung up and grinned at Crandle.

"Done," she said. "Chris will be persuasive."

"I have no doubt about that," Crandle said. He turned to the rest of the group. "That's it for tonight. Shut it down. We'll see you back here at seven tomorrow morning."

"Another wonderful night in a hotel," Cathy said, stretching her arms above her head. "I hate the pillows."

Landry gave her a disgusted look. "Missing your multi-million dollar house, Cathy?"

"I like my house, Alexander. And, yes, I am missing my bed and my family."

"Well, if it's any consolation, my pillow sucks, too," Eugene said.

Eduardo Garcia was assigned to driving Eugene to and from his hotel, and they talked about El Paso on the drive. Garcia's parents were originally from Juarez, just across the Mexican border. They had crossed the border legally when he was only six, and his father had supported the family of six, five boys and one girl, by cleaning swimming pools for the more affluent Texans living in the scorching valley. Eduardo was the oldest boy, and the only one so far to earn a college degree. Then, his parents could only afford to send one child to post-secondary school. Eduardo was grateful for the sacrifice.

"But two of my younger brothers are in college now," he said as they waited at a red light. "Both in Dallas. One's majoring in environmental sciences, while the other is enrolled in geology, of all things."

"I'm not surprised," Eugene said. "The Texas economy relies on oil and gas, and geologists and geophysicists are in demand." He added, "Your dad still cleaning pools?"

"Yeah, he's thinking about retiring and passing the business along to one of us, but when my brothers are finished with college we'll all be educated, and I don't think any of us will want to clean pools for a living."

"What about your sister?" Eugene asked.

"She's already married. Her husband's a nice enough guy, but he's a backyard mechanic and doesn't earn much. He doesn't think she should work, and his people skills are lacking. He's too rough around the edges to deal with the pool clientele. So it looks like the business will probably just die when my father's finished."

"Too bad," Eugene said as they pulled up in front of his hotel. "Thanks for the lift. See you at quarter to seven."

"Have a good night."

Eugene shut the door and waved at the young DEA agent as he hoofed it across the hot asphalt to the lobby. He checked for messages, but there was nothing in his slot. He reached his room, turned on the shower and stepped in. It was warm, so he turned the cold handle slowly to the right until the water ran cool. It felt good after the southern Texas heat. He thought of the Garcia family as he stood under the water, wondering what change had allowed the two younger brothers to attend college. The pool business surely hadn't picked up enough to afford two college tuitions and a place for the kids to live in Dallas. Eduardo was working, but the DEA didn't pay enough to cover those kinds of expenses. Something wasn't adding up in the Garcia household.

Eugene turned the handles and the water flow stopped. He listened for a second, then jumped from the tub and made a wild dash for his cell phone. It was still ringing when he picked it up and flipped it open. "Hello."

"Eugenio?"

"Yes."

"It's Mario Correa, Eugenio. Are you alone? Can you talk?"

"Yes, Mario, I'm okay to talk. I'm in a hotel room by myself."

"Good. I understand you stopped by my dealership in Miami yesterday."

"Yeah, I wanted to talk with you, but you disappeared."

"I'll disappear every time a DEA agent comes knocking, Eugenio." His cousin sounded pissed off.

"There's nothing I could do about that, Mario. Trust me when I say that the last thing I wanted to do was bring the heat down on you. I just need information."

"I've got a damn good idea what you want, Eugenio. I'll meet with you, but only you, no DEA. Understand?"

"I understand. Where?"

"Rochester, New York. How quickly can you get there?"

"Tomorrow sometime, depending on flights. I'm in El Paso right now."

"There's a shoe repair shop west of the river on the corner of State and Andrews. Four Corners Shoe Repair. I'll be there on the hour from eleven in the morning onward. Meet me at the top of the hour as soon as you get to Rochester."

"Okay, Mario. Can you answer one question for me?"

"If it's the question I think it is, no." The line clicked back to a dial tone.

Eugene closed the phone and finished drying off from the shower, glad that he had left his cell phone number with Mario's receptionist in Miami. Rochester, New York. That made absolutely no sense. Rochester was hardly a major center, and not all that easy to access from either Miami or El Paso. Why not just meet in Miami?

He picked up the phone book and called the airlines from his cell phone until he found a flight leaving in two hours for Pittsburgh. He booked his seat and quickly packed his small suitcase. He called downstairs and had the concierge order a cab, insisting it pick him up at the loading dock at the rear of the hotel.

He waited in the shipping-receiving area for about five minutes, and when the cab arrived he directed the driver to stop at a couple of banks with ATM machines, then to head for the airport. He withdrew cash against his credit card at the automated tellers, two thousand at each, until he had six thousand dollars. He tipped the driver well and checked in for his flight, with plenty of time to spare. He figured that once he reached Pittsburgh he could find a seat on a regional airline making the short trip north to Rochester from the Steel City.

His mind was racing an hour later when the plane departed El Paso. Eduardo Garcia and his brothers attending college. An informant hidden somewhere in the group of five. Mario Correa calling and setting up a clandestine meeting in Rochester. Things were happening, but where was it all leading? Then another bombshell dropped into the vortex inside his skull, a thought that closed down every other thought.

Four days. He had only four days to find Pablo. Or Julie and Shiara were dead.

Chapter Thirty-five

Javier Rastano had never prided himself on his patience. In fact, if there was one attribute he was sorely lacking, it was patience. He wanted to know which of the two men the snitch was, and he wanted to know now. He had one of his men monitor the gym area where Luis worked out in the morning, and a team of two follow Pedro, at a distance, as he ran through the pampered streets of Colonia Escalón. His instructions to the three men were simple. If either boxer's phone rang they were to listen to the conversation, if possible, then get their hands on the phone before either man could clear the number from the phone's memory. Whoever was feeding Eugenio Escobar the information was using his cell phone, and the incoming or outgoing number would be traceable. There was no possible way that Eugenio or his informant could know he was on to them, and therefore no reason to cut the lines of communication. Eugene would call, or one of the boxers would call him, of that he was certain.

He wanted the rat, and he would get him.

Javier stood at his bedroom window at the center of the house overlooking the rear gardens, and watched Pedro stretch prior to his run. Javier glanced at his watch, just after five-thirty in the morning. Was it Pedro? Neither man had shown any signs of skulking about, although Luis did like to let himself into the kitchen late at night to fix a snack. But none of the guards had seen him do anything but fix some food and head back up to his room. It was quite the puzzle.

The whole thing incensed him. How dare someone come inside his house under false pretenses? One thing was certain: that person was looking for an opportunity to snatch the women. But that was not going to happen. Actually, there was another certainty. One of the boxers was a dead man. Javier just needed to know which one.

Pedro finished stretching and jogged around the corner of the house toward the front gate. Out of sight, but not out of mind. Javier hit five on his speed-dial and one of his guards answered. "Pedro's on his way to the front gate," he said. The other man acknowledged and terminated the call. Javier smiled.

It was show time.

Eugene used the restroom in the Rochester airport to freshen up. He splashed water on his face, brushed his teeth and changed his shirt. It had taken him the entire night to get from El Paso to the city on the shores of Lake Ontario. The airline staff in Pittsburgh had insisted on seeing his passport when he bought the ticket to Rochester, which he had expected, but when the gate attendant scanned the bar code through her machine he knew it was only a matter of time before Irwin Crandle and his team located him. Her reaction to his ire was to smile and tell him to have a nice day. He felt like killing her.

He stepped into the brisk northern air and hailed a

cab. He checked his watch and did the math to convert to Pedro's time zone in San Salvador. Five-forty-three in the morning. Pedro would be calling soon.

"Where are you going, sir?" the Pakistani driver asked cheerfully in lilting English.

Eugene glanced up. He replied in English, although after consistently speaking Spanish ever since arriving in the United States, it felt kind of strange. "Do you know a good place for breakfast?"

"Of course," the driver said. "I know many. What kind of breakfast would you like?"

"Coffee and anything edible."

The driver grinned. "I know the place with the best coffee in all of Rochester. Twenty minutes and we're there."

"Sounds good."

Pedro had completed about one-quarter of his usual route through Colonia Escalón when he dialed and hit the send button, initiating a call to Eugene. The connection was poor, almost entirely static, and after fifteen or twenty seconds he hit the end button. Before he could dial again, a black Maserati accelerated around a bend in the road and came racing toward him. It stopped a few inches from where he stood and two men jumped out. Pedro recognized one of the men from Javier Rastano's estate.

Both men approached quickly and one of them said, "Could I have the phone, please?" He held his hand in front of him. Under his suit jacket Pedro could see a handgun in a holster.

"Sure," Pedro said, holding out the phone. The guard took it, punched something on the keypad and the hint of a smile appeared on his lips.

"I'll need to keep this for right now," he said.

"That's my phone," Pedro protested. He reached out to take it back, but the phone disappeared into the man's inside suit pocket.

"Mr. Rastano has asked us to bring your cell phone to him."

"What for?" Pedro asked. "Mr. Rastano has his own phone. He certainly doesn't need mine."

But he was talking to their backs. The two guards returned to their car and Pedro watched the high-end sports car turn around and head back to the Rastano estate. It didn't take a Mensa member to figure out what was going on. Rastano was suspicious and checking up on him. But why? And what did he hope to gain by taking the cell phone? Pedro started jogging again, sorting the disjointed facets of what had just happened into a logical sequence. First, the car hadn't appeared until seconds after he had placed the call. That would suggest that the men were following him and somehow listening. One of those spy microphones, perhaps. That wasn't much of a stretch, given Javier Rastano's wealth. Whatever toys he wanted, he could buy. So Rastano had instructed his boys to listen in on any incoming or outgoing calls, then grab the phone. And one of the goons had checked the phone and smiled. Then it hit him; he hadn't cleared the outgoing number. Rastano wanted to know who he was calling.

Rastano knew Eugene had someone on the inside.

But how? The last contact he'd had with Eugene was yesterday morning, almost twenty-four hours ago to the minute. No one had been watching him then, at least, not that he knew. Perhaps the problem was at Eugene's end. Maybe the person feeding Pablo information was playing both sides of the fence.

He kept his pace up in case they were still watching from some unseen location. Sweat formed on his forehead and dripped down on his shirt. He ignored it and kept pumping his legs, his Nikes gliding over the smooth asphalt. That might be the answer. If so, Eugene was in danger. Everything he did would immediately be conveyed to both Javier Rastano and Pablo. It would be childishly simple for both men to adjust their strategies to compensate for any gains the DEA-CIA team made. The efforts of five people were being undermined by one.

Pedro recognized his problems as two-fold. Straight off the top, he was now in harm's way. At some point Javier Rastano was going to rip off his flimsy cover and expose him. And that meant torture and imminent death. But leaving now was unthinkable. Julie and Shiara wouldn't survive through the upcoming weekend, and Eugene wasn't closing in on Pablo's location quickly enough to find him and get the ten-digit code. As Eugene had put it, he had problems on his end.

Getting word to Eugene was now imperative; he had to let him know that someone was feeding information to both Rastano and Escobar. It was risky, but not impossible. Rastano would probably keep the cell phone, which meant he would have to dial out on a land line. He made his decision as the gates to the Rastano estate came into view. He would find a phone somewhere in the mansion and make the call. Perhaps the one in the gardener's shed. The benefits outweighed the risks.

Pedro turned into the estate and doubled his speed up the driveway. He reached the house and ground to a halt, taking his pulse and keeping his legs moving to burn off the lactic acid. He walked around the south edge of the house to the backyard, wiping the sweat from his face on his shirt. As he rounded the corner, one of Rastano's men appeared at the back door and motioned to him.

"Mr. Rastano wants to see you," he said.

Pedro nodded. This was it. He was either okay or he was a dead man. The next five minutes would tell which.

Chapter Thirty-six

"What do you mean, he's gone?" Senator Irwin Crandle yelled at Eduardo Garcia. Crandle locked his upper and lower teeth together. There was a distinct grinding sound as his lower jaw moved back and forth.

"Eugene Escobar is not at the hotel, sir," Garcia repeated. "I checked with the night desk clerk. She said the concierge ordered him a cab last night, and that he instructed her to ask the driver to pull up at the back entrance. He didn't return."

"You assigned men to watch the hotel, Agent Garcia. You didn't think to station one of those men behind the building?"

"There are four entrances to the hotel, sir. I only had two men. They watched the main entrance."

"Shit," Crandle said, slamming his fist on the desk. The sound echoed through the small command center at EPIC. Landry and Maxwell sat at their desks, watching. Reid leaned against the far wall, coffee in hand. "The one person I wanted close at hand in case we found Pablo is gone." He pointed at Reid. "Get on the phone. Check on his credit cards, see if he's used one in the past twelve hours." He pointed at Cathy Maxwell. "Check every airline that flies out of El Paso. See if he flew out last night. And Alexander, you pull the taxi logs for last night and find out where the driver dropped him. Also, check the bus depot. Eduardo, check any incoming and outgoing calls Eugene made last night."

It took less than ten minutes to find out what they needed. Eugene had taken a United Airlines flight to Pittsburgh after stopping at three different ATM machines. At each of the banks, his credit card had been used to secure a cash advance for two thousand dollars. He was on the run. But why Pittsburgh?

"Have we got anything in this mess that points to Pittsburgh?" Crandle asked, waving his arms over the piles of paper burying the desks.

"Nothing that I've seen," Cathy responded.

Alexander shrugged his broad shoulders. "Nada."

"Not even close," Bud Reid said.

Garcia shook his head.

"Well, we know he was in Pittsburgh at eleven o'clock last night. Someone's got to head up to Pennsylvania. Any takers?"

No one raised a hand. Crandle didn't waste a breath on indecision. "Cathy, you and Alexander get up to Pittsburgh. My plane's at the airport. I'll have the pilot file a flight plan and be ready to fly within the hour." He addressed the entire room. "It's Wednesday morning, which means Eugene's only got three days before the deadline. He didn't waste his time flying to Pittsburgh for nothing. I'm starting to think that if we find Eugene, we might find Pablo."

Eduardo's phone rang and he answered it. He thanked the caller and hung up after just a few seconds. "Eugene took a phone call on his cell last night just before he disappeared. It originated in Miami."

"Mario Correa called him," Crandle said quietly. He pushed some files aside and sat on the edge of Landry's desk. "Correa ducks us in Miami, waits for a time when Eugene would be alone, then calls him. What for?"

"He knows where Pablo is," Bud Reid said.

"Maybe," Crandle replied. "Maybe not." He stopped pacing the room and sat on the corner of Landry's desk. "He knows something of value, that's for sure." He glanced down at the desk, looked up, then quickly looked down again. He read for a minute, then slowly picked up a sheet of paper. It was a fax. But what had caught his eye was that the correspondence had originated in El Salvador. "What's this?" he asked Alexander Landry.

"I just received that this morning," he said. "I was going to share it, but we've been concentrating on what happened to Eugene."

"You've been talking with covert DEA agents in Panama and El Salvador," Crandle said.

"I thought it might help things if we knew who had Eugene's wife and daughter," Landry said, feeling guilty when he had no reason to feel that way. "I've got a few friends down south. One of them narrowed it down to two possible people. Antoine Alzate or Javier Rastano. But another source eliminated Alzate. He's in Europe right now, left four days ago."

Crandle glared at him. "So you knew Javier Rastano was holding Julie and Shiara Escobar but said nothing."

"I told you, I was going to bring it up. I just didn't have time," Landry said, defensively.

"That's not proper procedure, Alexander," Crandle said. "Don't do it again. You find out something that's relevant to our case, you tell us."

"Yes, sir," Landry said.

Eduardo Garcia said, "I know this guy, Javier Rastano."

That turned every head in the room. Garcia expanded on his statement. "I don't mean I know him personally, but the El Paso division has seen his name on a few of our reports. Not nice stuff. The guy may be a psychopath; he likes to see people suffer. We've got three files where he brutally tortured and then murdered informants in Colombia. We suspect him of at least five killings in El Salvador. He runs a tight ship. His men are extremely well paid and very loyal. Most of them have military experience and know how to use their weapons. No rent-a-cops here. And we think he's moving some serious quantities of coke."

"Why is he still operating?" Crandle asked.

Garcia shrugged. "He's untouchable. Never goes near the drugs himself. We don't have a clue where he ships it from. We know it's not Colombia. The coke is going overland and being loaded on freighters in Central America somewhere, but we can't seem to get a handle on it."

Irwin Crandle took a few deep breaths, digested the information, then said, "Nothing's changed. Alexander, you and Cathy get to the airport and take the Lear up to Pittsburgh. Find Eugene Escobar. The three of us will divide our time between taking a serious look at Javier Rastano and using EPIC's resources to continue tracking possible places where Pablo may be living."

Cathy was already up and moving, glad to be out of there. "We'll call in the moment we have something, Senator."

Chapter Thirty-seven

Javier Rastano was relaxing on a padded chaise lounge when Pedro entered the great room from the patio. His running shoes squeaked on the tile floor and the sound echoed off the high ceiling. Luis was already there, sitting on a wrought-iron chair with a small cushion on the seat. Rastano waved at the chair next to Luis, and Pedro sat. The room was bright and airy, one side all windows. The metal chair was hot from the sun and the ornate design was pushing into his back. But somehow he didn't think being slightly uncomfortable was the worst of his problems. It was difficult to miss the two cell phones sitting on the table beside the Colombian.

"Finished your daily run?" Javier asked pleasantly, sipping his coffee.

"Yes," Pedro replied, wiping his brow with the towel he had draped around his neck. "The hills are good for my legs."

"That's the most important point in boxing, isn't it? Your legs."

Both men nodded, and Luis said, "You don't move your feet, you're dead in the water."

"Interesting analogy," Javier said under his breath. "Either of you gentlemen want coffee?"

"Please," Pedro said. Luis shook his head.

Javier waited until Pedro's cup was filled and the right amounts of sugar and cream added, then continued. "Any idea why I wanted to speak with you two?" he asked. Both men shrugged. "I've got a small problem. That's why I had my men confiscate your cell phones this morning. Both of you made an early morning call, and I wanted to see who it was you would speak with at this ungodly hour. Luis made a call to a friend of his in Panama City. Pedro's call was local, to a number registered to a house in El Centro."

Pedro kept his breathing normal. Jesus Christ, it was a wrong number. His fingers must have slipped on the keys while he was jogging and he had dialed a wrong number. Pedro couldn't believe his luck.

Rastano was talking again. "So the calls didn't tell me what I wanted to know."

"What's that?" Pedro asked.

"Which one of you is a spy for Eugenio Escobar." Javier Rastano's eyes were busy, pivoting between the two men, looking for a sign of recognition at the mention of the name. Pedro kept his eyes on Rastano; he didn't glance at Luis to see how the other man was handling the accusation.

"Who?" Pedro said.

"Eugenio Escobar."

"Who's that?" Luis asked.

Pedro took the opportunity to glance at him quickly. The boxer looked genuinely confused. Which, of course, he was. Pedro hoped his acting looked as genuine.

"Eugenio Escobar is a business associate of mine," Rastano said, still scanning the two men. "We're working on a mutually beneficial deal right now. He is in the United States at present, but I've been informed that he managed to insert a spy inside my house. The time frames are such that the only new arrivals since Eugenio and I have been involved are you two. So one of you is Eugenio's man." He paused and lit a cigarette. "Either one of you wish to tell me who it is?"

"It's not me," Luis said emphatically. "I don't know any Eugenio Escobar."

Pedro shook his head. "No idea who he is." The coffee cup in his hand was absolutely steady. He noticed that Javier was staring at it.

"I thought so. It would have surprised me if one of you admitted your involvement. So we'll have to take care of this problem as diplomatically as possible." He motioned to one of his men. The guard stepped forward and dropped a coin in Rastano's open palm. "You two can flip a coin," he said.

"What?" Pedro said. "That's insane."

"Perhaps," Javier said, his eyes locked on Pedro. "But what else can we do. One of you must be held accountable, and other than me guessing at which one, right now I have no other way of determining who is the guilty party. So we'll let luck take its course."

Luis was looking a little less confident now, scared even. "What happens to the loser?" he asked.

"He dies."

Luis started to jump from his chair, but the guards leveled automatic weapons at him, and he returned to his seat. "I didn't sign on for none of this shit," he said. He was sweating now, the beads forming on his forehead and wet stains appearing under his arms. "This is bullshit."

"You're kidding, right?" Pedro said.

"I never kid about such things," Javier said. He

glanced back and forth between the two men. "Who wants to call it?"

Neither man responded and he pointed to Luis. "Call it in the air. If you call heads and heads is showing when the coin lands on the floor, you win. Tails, you lose. Pretty simple, actually." He buried the tip of his thumb under his index finger and set the coin over the visible portion of his thumb. "Call it," he said, flipping it in the air. There was no mistaking the authority in his voice.

"Heads?" Luis said hesitantly.

The coin landed on the tile and spun for a second, then lay flat. Rastano leaned over and took a good look at which side was face up. He turned to Luis and said, "Heads. It's your lucky day, Luis."

Every gun in the room was immediately pointing at Pedro, who just sat staring at Rastano. The Colombian rose from his chair and pulled a pistol from under his shirt. He slowly lowered it and pointed the barrel at Pedro's head. He advanced to within a few feet and stopped. "Anything you want to say?" he asked.

Pedro shook his head. "This is stupid," he muttered.

Javier's finger tightened on the trigger, then in a flash so quick that no one in the room could react, he swung the barrel about and pulled the trigger. The bullet smashed into Luis's head and sent the man flying backward onto the floor. Blood and brain matter poured out the gaping hole in the rear of his skull and after a couple of involuntary twitches, the body lay still in a growing pool of blood.

"What the fuck?" Pedro said.

Javier smiled and sat down. He picked up his smoldering cigarette and took a long drag, then crushed out the butt. "It's my game, I can play it however I see fit," he said, leaning forward and staring into Pedro's eyes. "I still don't know if it's you or him, Pedro. But I do know this. If I want to promote a fighter, I want to promote the best I have. Even though you lost the coin toss, I'd much rather have your talent and good looks in the ring than that acne-scarred piece of shit. It's all an image thing, you know." He lit another cigarette, still staring into Pedro's eyes. "I just hope I killed the right guy."

Chapter Thirty-eight

Eugene sipped the coffee and cut into his over-easy eggs.
They were a little too runny for his liking, but he didn't
feel like causing a scene by complaining. The waitress already had it tough enough, working in a run-down diner
that served breakfast twenty-four hours a day. He finished
his meal and left a twenty-dollar tip on a seven-dollar tab.
Hell, it was Rastano's money.

There was a stiff breeze from the north, off the lake,
and he buttoned his coat against the chilly air. He darted
across the almost empty street, amazed at the cold. He
had seen television shows on the Arctic, and Rochester in
the spring reminded him of those shows. He jumped in
the cab and, after the dry heat of El Paso, appreciated the
warmth of the back seat. He had time to kill, so he asked
the driver to give him a tour, promising a good tip if he
kept things interesting. He wasn't let down. The man was
Robin Williams with a good tan and a Pakistani accent.

At ten to eleven the car pulled up a block from the in-

tersection of State and Andrews. Eugene waited until
three minutes to the hour, paid the driver, then walked
briskly along State until he reached number 125. He
pulled open the door and slipped inside, out of the wind.
The shop was long and narrow, with rows of shoes against
both walls, each one with a white tag tied to it. The odor
of adhesives and thinners was strong, and it tickled his
nostrils. It reminded him of the shoemaker who lived a
few blocks from his parents' house in Venezuela, and for
a moment he felt an intense longing to be with his family.
He shook off the feeling and approached the small
wooden counter. A dark-skinned man in his late fifties or
early sixties was writing a number on one of the white
tags. His stubby fingers had trouble grasping the pencil,
and he carefully formed each number before looking up.

"Can I help you?" he asked, his voice heavily Italian.

"I was supposed to meet my cousin at your shop," Eugene replied. "His name is Mario."

"He's here," the shoemaker said. "In the back." He motioned to the door behind him. "He's waiting for you."

"Thanks," Eugene said. He walked around the counter
and through the door into the rear of the shop. A row of
machines—insole and outsole stitchers and a Sutton 2000
finisher—were crowded into a small space on the right of
the long, narrow bay. The smell of acetone and contact
cement mingled with the burnt odor of rubber and
leather. A small, stained table covered with dyes and pre-
parer sat next to the finisher. On the other side of the
work area was a desk covered with receipts and bills. An
adding machine, a telephone and a desk lamp were half
buried by the paper avalanche. Mario Correa was sitting
in a ratty chair. The casters squeaked when he rolled it
back from the desk.

"Hello, Eugene," he said. He did not look great. Dark
circles rimmed his eyes and his lips were drawn tight
across his teeth, revealing age lines. Mario was older than

Eugene by a few years, but his hair was still dark, with no signs of gray. He was well dressed, in Armani dress pants and alligator loafers.

"Mario," Eugene replied, wondering why the man had worn such nonfunctional shoes to northern New York State.

"Let's take a walk, shall we," Mario said, moving toward the back of the shop. Eugene followed him into the alley. It was narrow, sheltered on both sides by multi-story brick buildings, and garbage was overflowing from the Dumpster a few feet from the door. Mario turned to his right and set a quick pace. They exited the alley, then branched off the sidewalk onto a path that ran parallel to the river, only a few yards from the water's edge. Naked trees, with tiny buds that had yet to open, lined the path. The only sign that heralded spring was a hint of green in the narrow band of grass between the path and the water. Eugene was surprised to find that there was even more of a chill to the air close to the water.

"What do you need, Eugene?" Mario asked.

"I need to find Pablo."

Mario took a quick stutter-step. Then his pace returned to normal. He looked sideways at Eugene as he walked. "You sound pretty sure that Pablo is alive, Eugene."

"Let's not play that game, Mario. We both know he's alive. My wife and daughter have been kidnapped. The guy who has them says he'll kill them this weekend if I don't deliver Pablo or the code to a Swiss bank account. The person holding my family is Colombian. He moves a lot of cocaine to the States, so I don't think he's bluffing."

"Probably not. Who is it?"

"Javier Rastano."

There was a noticeable hesitation in Mario's stride at the mention of the name. "Definitely not," he said.

"You know Javier Rastano?"

"Yes, I know him." They reached a bench by the water's

edge and Mario sat down. The translucent water was shallow at this point and it rushed over the rocks, creating a wall of background noise. Eugene realized that Mario had chosen the spot in case anyone was trying to listen. "Everything we talk about today stays confidential, Eugene. You agree to that on your family honor?"

Eugene nodded. "Of course."

Mario looked at the water rushing past, heading for the Great Lake just to the north. "Pablo and I were a lot tighter than anyone ever knew," he said quietly. He looked back at Eugene. "Not so much in the earlier days when he was getting established, but later, in '89, when the cartel started to run into problems. When Pablo called me for help, our government didn't even know who was running the cartel. They thought the number one man was José Rodríguez Gacha, but when he got killed the cartel didn't even blink. Col. Martinez caught on real quick after that, that Pablo was the man. And once they'd pegged him, his days were numbered. That's when he called me."

Mario paused, then asked, "This team you're working with. Who's in it?"

"Mainly American agents who were chasing Pablo in Colombia, in the '80s and '90s. Alexander Landry, Bud Reid, Cathy Maxwell, Irwin Crandle."

"Eugene, these guys, along with a handful of others, were responsible for *destroying* the cartel. There were lots of soldiers running around with guns, but not many chiefs. The group you've assembled were the chiefs."

"And one of them is in bed with Pablo. Otherwise how could you have known we were on our way to Miami to visit you? Unless they called Pablo and he called you."

Mario did not dispute Eugene's remark. "He's got a source all right. And whoever it is, their information is extremely accurate." He paused as a woman pushing a baby carriage walked by. She smiled at the two men and said good morning. They both returned the salutation, then waited until she was well out of earshot before continuing. "Is there anyone else in your little team?"

Eugene shrugged. "A junior DEA agent I met when I arrived from Venezuela to ask for help. Eduardo Garcia is his name."

"He works out of EPIC in El Paso," Mario said matter-of-factly.

Eugene just stared. "Yes. How did you know that?"

"You're talking about the DEA here, Eugene. I've been sitting on the fact that Pablo Escobar is alive for the last twelve years. I know who the opposition is."

"But Garcia is just a kid. He's too young to have been involved with the DEA in the early '90s."

"He is, but his uncle isn't."

"Garcia has an uncle who was in Colombia with Landry and the others twelve years ago?"

"Yes, he does. Fernando Garcia. Just ask any of your team about Fernando and you'll get a response."

"What does that mean?"

"Garcia had little respect for laws or statutes. He did what he wanted, when he wanted. I'm sure the others would describe him as a loose cannon. It's unfortunate he died while on the job."

"So Eduardo Garcia isn't as lily white as he appears," Eugene said under his breath.

Mario ignored the comment and continued describing his involvement with Pablo. "I was his ears and eyes for the year and a half he was in hiding, before he surrendered and moved into La Catedral prison in June '91. I kept him in the loop as best I could, but the cartel was reeling from his absence. Finally, he decided to broker a deal with the Colombian government and turn himself in. He thought that living inside a prison would be safer and more comfortable than living on the lam. He was right. All the guards were on Pablo's payroll, and he had a huge cache of guns buried on the grounds. La Catedral provided Pablo a safe haven from which to run his business. Once he was inside La Catedral, he was back on top. Gacha was dead, the Ochoa brothers in custody, Carlos Lehder extradited to the United States, and the Galeano and Moncada families were working with him. The long list of people who wanted him dead were out of luck. It was a brilliant move."

"Did you still help him after he moved into the prison?" Eugene asked, buttoning his coat tight to his throat against the cool wind.

"A bit, but not much. He knew that he could trust me and he would ask me to do things or get things on occasion. But mostly, he left me and my family alone. And he would have been fine if he hadn't killed Fernando Galeano and Gerardo Moncada. But he couldn't leave well enough alone. And the Galeano and Moncada families were some kind of pissed at Pablo. And so was the government. He had made them look stupid by killing two people who were in visiting him."

"He had another visitor about that time," Eugene said. "Cathy Maxwell went to see him about the death of her parents."

"That was before he killed Galeano and Moncada. But yeah, she saw him while he was in prison. Anyway," Mario said, continuing his story, "after he killed Moncada and Galeano he had to get out of La Catedral. When he made his getaway from the prison, he began to rely on me again. I arranged for safe places where he could hide and supplied him with the latest communication technology so he could stay in touch with his cartel buddies and his family. Like I said, he trusted me."

Eugene sat back on the bench, watching Mario closely. "Why are you telling me all this?"

Mario was quick to answer. "If not you, Eugene, I'll be in front of a grand jury with a subpoena in my hand. I want you to find Pablo. But I don't want you to have the DEA or the CIA with you when you do. They'll get the press involved, and I'll be up the creek. Get the code to the bank account and give it to Rastano. Maybe he'll give you back your family. I hope so."

"Where is he, Mario?" Eugene asked.

Mario shrugged. "I honestly don't know. This is where I always met him. Rochester, New York. That's why I wanted you to meet me here. This is the closest I've been to where he lives."

"Where did you meet him in Rochester? At the shoe repair shop?"

"Christ, no. That's just someone I pay to use his shop as a meeting place. Pablo always stayed at the Clarion Hotel Riverside."

"What name did he register under?"

"No idea. We met in the lobby. He was always waiting for me in the chairs by the restaurant. I never had any reason to ask for him at the front desk."

"When was the last time you saw him?"

Mario was thoughtful. "About four months ago. He called me and dragged me out of Miami into this snow-encrusted hole because he wanted a new Renault. I could have killed him. I had someone else drive the car up a couple of weeks later."

"How is he?" Eugene asked.

"He's okay, Eugene, but he misses Colombia more than you could ever imagine. And he's changed a lot, both physically and mentally. You wouldn't recognize him if you walked past him on the street. He exercises every day, eats smart and doesn't touch drugs. I think he drinks a bit, but not to excess. He's lost a lot of the arrogance and ego. He's even a little bit likeable."

"But he still kills people," Eugene said, thinking of Jorge Shweisser, the Zurich banker with no carotid artery.

"He's a survivor, Eugene. And if and when you do find

him, don't expect him to welcome you with open arms."
Mario stood to indicate the meeting was over.

"Hardly," Eugene said, also standing. "Thanks, Mario. I appreciate the help."

"Not a problem. Just remember, no DEA on my doorstep."

"Got it," Eugene said. He watched Mario walk back along the same path by the river, and disappear around a corner. Eugene was now alone in Rochester with precious little information, and little time to make something out of it. One thing was certain, though. He was close to Pablo now.

Very close.

Chapter Thirty-nine

NSA was having a devil of a time with the encrypted files on Jorge Schweisser's computer. The problem was that they couldn't identify the language the data was written in. It wasn't English, German, Swiss or any of the other modern languages that used the Roman alphabet. They tried the Cyrillic alphabet, but again nothing. Then Mandarin, Cantonese and Japanese with no success.

Irwin Crandle set the fax from his contact at the National Security Agency on his desk and rubbed his eyes. He glanced at his watch. Eleven o'clock, Wednesday morning. Maxwell and Landry would be arriving in Pittsburgh right about now. The team was disintegrating: Eugene on the run, two agents in Pennsylvania and three of them still at EPIC. And time was running out. Saturday was less than seventy-two hours away, and they weren't exactly knocking on Pablo's door. He stopped rubbing his already-red eyes and swiveled around in his chair to face Bud Reid.

"What was in Shweisser's apartment?" He was on a fishing expedition. "His selection of music, furniture, books, that sort of stuff."

Reid leaned back in his chair, coffee in one hand, the other scratching his bald dome. "His furniture was leather, the kind with studs in the arms, and the tables were heavy wood with glass tops. He had mostly classical music. Bach, some Beethoven and an extensive collection of Chopin: mazurkas, sonatas and both concertos, if I remember correctly. Lots of books on art, especially the Impressionists. He had a few really good framed prints on the walls: Pissarro, Monet, Degas and Caillebotte. One entire row on his bookshelf was computer programming texts, a few hard covers on anatomy and some pulp fiction paperbacks. He had a lot of DVDs, all English . . ."

"Whoa," Crandle said, stopping him in mid-sentence. "The books on anatomy. Were they written for the medical professional?"

Reid thought for a moment. "The one I glanced in was highly technical, if that's what you mean. Written by doctors, for doctors."

"That's exactly what I mean," Crandle said, grabbing the phone and dialing Hyram Ockey's direct line at NSA. It rang twice, and the computer expert picked up. "Hyram, this is Crandle. That disk you're working on, try Latin."

His other incoming line started blinking. He cut the connection to NSA after he secured a promise from Hyram to run the programs with a Latin-based language and call the results back to EPIC immediately. He answered the other line. "Hi, Chris, what have you got?"

Chris Bisiker, the CIA agent Cathy Maxwell had brought in to check the Freeport connection, was on the line, long distance from the Bahamas. "Irwin, what's going on?"

"What do you mean?" Crandle asked.

"Whoever owns this account has the branch manager in fear of his life. At first the guy refused to say a word, just told me to get out of his office."

"But you persuaded him?"

"Subtly, yes. There's a restaurant on the tip of the island where they throw food over the balcony to the sharks. I took him to lunch, and we sat at a table next to the railing."

"The view must have been spectacular," Crandle said, a smile creeping across his face as he envisioned Chris Bisiker casually telling the banker that he was going over the edge if he didn't cough up some information.

"Wonderful. Anyway, about halfway through our main course the guy decides to tell me what's going on. It seems that the money in the account has ties to Colombia."

"Why do you say that?" Crandle asked, gripping the phone hard.

"This manager has been at the Freeport branch for years. When the account was first opened, he had a visit from none other than Carlos Lehder."

"What?" Crandle said, sitting upright in his chair. "Lehder himself was in the bank?"

"Yeah. Lehder opened a different account, but he made it perfectly clear that if any questions were raised about either of the two new accounts the manager's family would disappear. The manager cooked the books, then sent the doctored ledgers to the head office in Canada and made the deposits look like clean money. Lehder's account has languished since he was imprisoned in the U.S., but the other account has remained quite active. Irwin, this looks like money from the old days when the Medellín and Cali cartels were operating." He was silent for a few moments, but Crandle didn't respond, and he continued. "I got a printout of the deposits and withdrawals over the past few years. I'll fax it to you."

"Please do." Crandle gave Bisiker the dedicated fax number that would direct the document to their small command center. "Thanks a million, Chris. I appreciate it."

"All right. But this little jaunt had better not count against my holidays."

"I'll talk to someone over at Langley," Crandle said, and hung up.

Eduardo Garcia and Bud Reid were watching him, having caught the name Carlos Lehder. Crandle sipped his coffee, and shrugged. "Bisiker might be on to something. He's sending a fax through. We'll see."

The Learjet was given priority in the landing queue, and once they were on the ground in Pittsburgh, Alexander Landry and Cathy Maxwell headed directly for the main terminal, creds in hand. Their plan was to hit the regional airlines first and then the taxi and limo services. Eugene had to leave the airport somehow. They hit pay dirt at the seventh counter, U.S. Airways, a local airline with its head office on Commerce Drive in Pittsburgh.

"One of our gate agents scanned his passport when he boarded," the counter person said, looking at her screen. "He flew to Rochester on our early morning flight. It departed Pittsburgh at six-seventeen and arrived in Rochester at seven-ten."

"That's quick," Cathy said.

The woman smiled. "We use a Boeing 737 for that flight, even though it's only about two hundred miles. It's really popular with business people who want to be in Rochester for an eight o'clock meeting at Eastman Kodak or Xerox. Bausch and Lomb has its head office in Rochester as well. It's a great route for our airline."

"Thanks," Landry said. They returned to the Learjet, asked the pilot to file a flight plan for Rochester, then called Crandle at EPIC to give him the news.

"What the hell is he doing in Rochester?" Crandle asked.

"Meeting Mario Correa, I bet," Landry replied.

"Well, it's better than New York City. What's Rochester's population, maybe a quarter million? Not a bad size center for a search."

"We'll find him," Landry said. They finished the conversation. Landry hung up just as the Learjet 45 got clearance from the tower. He paced the cabin, his six-four frame hunched over, pausing occasionally to drink some fruit juice and munch on the muffins laid out in the front refreshment center. They were less than twelve hours behind Eugene Escobar; his trail would still be warm. The airport staff would probably have gone through a shift change, and they would have to wait until the evening to show Eugene's picture around and see if anyone recognized him. But in the interim, they would work the taxi and car rental companies to see if he was careless enough to rent a car under his own name, or take a cab to some strange destination. Most of the business travelers arriving in Rochester on the early flight would be downtown fares. He and Maxwell would look for something out of the ordinary. Then the hotels and motels, bars and restaurants, nightclubs and dives until they found Eugene and followed him to Pablo. At least, that was the plan.

Crandle's jet cruised at almost six hundred miles an hour at 33,000 feet, and soon Rochester came into view out the starboard windows. Somewhere in that maze of buildings and houses was Eugene Escobar—their key to Pablo.

Find Eugene. And then they would find Pablo.

And this time, they would end the job properly.

Chapter Forty

Eugene steered clear of the major hotels and checked into a Super 8 south of Rochester on Lehigh Station Road in Henrietta. He knew that someone from Crandle's team would already be en route to Rochester, courtesy of the gate attendant who scanned his passport. But he had no intention of letting them find him easily. He was where they thought he was—but he didn't have to be visible. He placed a five hundred-dollar cash deposit on the counter, and the Super 8 accepted it. His cab driver, whose name was Bulbinder, had agreed to book off the next three days at a flat rate of five hundred dollars a day, payable each evening at five.

He had a regular driver, a safe hotel room and cash. Now all he had to do was use his brain to figure out where his cousin was living. Common sense told him that the Clarion Hotel Riverside would never divulge information about a guest—unless the request was accompanied by a federal subpoena. So walking up to the front counter and asking for a list of guests who had stayed in the hotel back in mid-November of the previous year would be pretty stupid. The only other way Eugene could think of to get the information was to access the hotel's computer files. And that was something about which he had no experience or expertise. He had one other avenue of inquiry, but that also required hacking into a database. Mario had sold Pablo a Renault and delivered it around the beginning of December. The DMV would have records of the car being registered.

He wandered over to the window and glanced out into the parking lot. Bulbinder saw him, smiled and waved. Eugene waved back and let the curtain fall in place. At least his coming to Rochester had made one person happy. Sunday was Bulbinder's oldest son's birthday, and the money was going toward his college fund. It wasn't anything world-shattering, but somehow that made Eugene feel good; a tiny sliver of the drug money Rastano had given him was going to a good cause. He put one foot slowly ahead of the other until he reached the bed, and flopped down. He needed to channel his efforts, now more than ever. But he was awash in listlessness, winds calm, sails sagging. He closed his eyes, and Julie's smiling and beautiful face filled the darkness.

"God, don't take her from me," he whispered. He could feel tears gathering, but he refused to open his eyes and release them. "It's all in your hands, Eugene." Then he realized he had the answer to what he needed, elusive, but close at hand. Something someone had said recently. But what?

He opened his eyes and stared at the ceiling. The gate attendant at the airport? The hotel desk clerk? Bulbinder? He stopped at the taxi driver, his mind churning as it regurgitated every word the cab driver had said since they met. Then it hit him. The money was for his son's college fund. He sat bolt upright, breathing shallow and fast.

That was it. Hacking into the hotel and DMV computers. Who knew computers better than college students enrolled in computer sciences courses? He leaped up, slipped on his shoes and bolted from the room, locking the door behind him.

At the cab, he asked the driver, "Bulbinder, you said your son is taking computer science courses?"

"Yes. But please call me Bill. Everyone does. It sounds more American than Bulbinder."

"Sure," Eugene said. "Bill it is. Where does he go to college?"

"At Finger Lakes Community College."

"Is it close by?" Eugene asked.

"It's just south of here on Canandaigua Lake."

"Drive," Eugene said, jumping into the backseat. "I'll explain on the way."

As they drove through Henrietta, Eugene explained to Bill what he needed and a little bit about why he needed it. At first the cabbie was unsure; it would mean asking his son to take a risk. But he decided to let his son make the decision. He drove, quiet now, his mind on what Eugene had proposed.

To Eugene, the landscape held a stark beauty. Not the lush beauty of his homeland, but the outline of naked deciduous trees against virgin countryside was breathtaking. The rolling, grass-covered hills were just greening up, and the scent of spring was heavy in the air. They passed quaint villages of traditional two-story clapboard homes. American flags flapped lazily in the afternoon breeze on front lawns and outside single-story municipal buildings. This was John Mellencamp's America, Eugene thought, "Pink Houses" running through his mind.

They reached Canandaigua, the town named after the lake, and continued south until Bill turned onto a well-paved access road bordered with barren trees. The road wove through a few acres of intermittent meadows and forests, until suddenly breaking out into the Finger Lakes Community College campus. They headed toward a central four-story building.

"The computer sciences department is on the third floor," Bill said. "Ben, that's my son's name, is a teaching assistant in one of the labs. I'll get him for you." He parked the car, got out and headed up the stairs to the main door.

Eugene got out of the cab and leaned against it. He watched Bill walk quickly into the building and disappear through the glass doors. Several minutes later, he reappeared, with two young men in their early twenties. One was dark skinned, athletic looking, with neatly trimmed hair, wearing blue jeans and a T-shirt. The other looked Scandinavian, with blond hair and a wiry frame, wearing khakis and a polo shirt. Bill introduced them. Ben and Andrew. Ben shook Eugene's hand. Andrew just nodded.

"As your dad's just told you, I need someone good with computers, Ben," Eugene said. "It would be a paying job, only a day or two, but good dollars."

Ben leaned on the car and asked, "What sort of work?"

"Getting information that I can't get."

Ben's eyes narrowed. "And that information would be in someone else's computer?"

"Yes."

"That might be illegal, Eugene."

"It might be. But I've got a very good reason for why I need it."

"I know. Dad filled me in. Sorry about your wife and daughter."

"Thanks. So I need someone who can hack into two secure sites: a hotel in Rochester and the DMV."

"What do you need from the databases?" Andrew asked, finally breaking his silence.

"I need a list of the hotel guests who stayed at the Clarion Hotel Riverside last November, and a list of the Renaults registered by the local DMV last December. I need to know who registered it and where that person lives."

"That's totally illegal," Ben said, and looked at his father.

Bill shrugged. "I wouldn't have asked you if Eugene's wife and daughter weren't in danger. He doesn't want classified missile technology. It's routine stuff. He just wants to save his family."

"Okay, okay. I'm cool with that, Dad," He turned to Eugene. "I brought Andrew with me because he and I are buddies. If we do this, we do it together. You okay with that?" Eugene nodded, and Ben continued, "I need a clean computer and a location the police can never trace back to me."

Andrew piped up. "Old lady Quigley's place in Seneca Falls. She's got a revved-up Pentium system with high-speed Internet access. She's taking a sabbatical from teaching this semester. She's in New York City until the end of the month."

"How do we get in?"

"That's easy," Andrew said. "I've got a key. I'm watering her plants while she's gone."

"Just for the record," Ben said, "how much did you say this job paid?"

Eugene quickly calculated what was left of the six thousand dollars after he paid Bill. "A thousand dollars," he said.

"Okay," Ben said, shaking Eugene's hand. "You just hired yourself a couple of hackers."

Chapter Forty-one

Senator Irwin Crandle sat in an uncomfortable office chair reading the e-mail for the second time. Unbelievable was the only word he could think of to describe what he was reading.

The decrypted files from Jorge Shweisser's computer were a daily diary that dated back to the year the numbered account was opened. Shweisser had suspected something illegal from the start and kept a detailed record of the early transactions, both deposits and withdrawals. He had also keyed in his personal feelings, in Latin, stored them on the disk, and then encrypted them. Crandle figured him to be somewhere between cautious and paranoid. But the amazing thing about Shweisser's personal take on the situation was that his ramblings were basically correct.

Shweisser mentioned Pablo Escobar's name no less than twenty-three times. Shweisser was being paid to ensure that the account remained in good standing and that no one in the bank hierarchy questioned where the money was coming from. In one paragraph he noted that he was being paid by "an unknown Colombian," but in the very next entry he admitted he suspected the Colombian to be Pablo Escobar. But the really shocking thing about the use of Pablo's name was that it didn't stop after December 2, 1993. Shweisser was never fooled by the apparent death of the Colombian drug lord.

Crandle finished reading the contents of the disk and leaned back in the chair. Shweisser could have sold his suspicions on the open market for countless millions of dollars. But then he would have been a target for Escobar's *sicarios* and his life would have been shorter than the already abbreviated version.

Shweisser had played his cards in the best fashion he could. He'd survived years longer than many who found themselves involved with the Colombian cartels. He'd been mute, but all the while he'd been making careful notations on an encrypted disk. It was Shweisser's decision to work both sides of the fence that had cost him his life. Once he started channeling information to the Rastano clan, his days were numbered. But Crandle was impressed by the man's patience and cunning. And coming from someone like Irwin Crandle, that was quite a compliment.

Crandle bundled the papers together and placed them in a file folder. It was late Wednesday night, and Bud Reid and Eduardo Garcia had left for the day. Crandle called their hotel and told them to check out and be at the airport in half an hour. Their usefulness in Texas was at an end. It was time to join Cathy Maxwell and Alexander Landry as they honed in on Eugene and Pablo. He called his pilot and told him to file a flight plan for Rochester. Then he shut off the computer and the lights. He locked the door behind him, and signed out at the front desk.

He set the list of withdrawals and deposits from Pablo's account in the Bahamas on the passenger seat in the car as he drove to the airport. At a red light he picked it up and perused it again. Money was moving all over the globe from this account, but over the years the balance had stayed rather static at twelve million dollars. There were credits and debits to banks in the United States, Canada, Switzerland, Caymans, Peru, Great Britain, Morocco, France and Germany. But with the influx of money from the numbered Swiss account, the balance was now almost twenty-three million dollars. One thing was certain; Pablo wasn't in need of cash. But despite the wealth of information on the six-page report, it was not much help. Too many banks in too many countries were involved. Some may have been legitimate transfers to help with Pablo's living expenses, others simply red herrings. It was impossible to tell which might lead to the man without a full forensic audit.

He glanced down at the passenger side of the car. A small calendar he had been using to mark the approaching deadline sat open on the seat. Each day up until Wednesday, March 23 had a cross through it. He picked up a red pencil and drew two diagonal lines through the number 23. One more day was over. They were one day closer to Javier Rastano's deadline.

And right now, it didn't look like they were going to make it.

Chapter Forty-two

The estate was dark, the only illumination from ground-level lights that delineated the pathways from the orchid beds. The moon was almost full, but obscured by low-lying cumulous clouds, and only a scattering of light penetrated through to the secluded grounds. An occasional toucan cawed, and monkeys skittered through the upper branches of the eucalyptus and mango trees. Armed guards patrolled the perimeter, both inside and outside the twelve-foot walls.

A solitary figure stole across the grass, moving quickly and with great stealth. Dressed in black and invisible against the dense foliage, Pedro reached the gardener's shed at the far edge of the property. He waited for the patrol to pass, then slipped inside the small building and closed the door behind him. The smell of freshly cut grass was strong inside the shed. He felt his way through the darkness until he reached the workbench covered with lawnmower blades and oily rags. He was extremely cautious; a cut on his hand from one of the blades would require an explanation the next morning at breakfast. An explanation that could never stand up to close scrutiny. Any mistake now would be fatal. He knew it, and sweat started to bead on his face. Finally, his hand closed on the object he was searching for. He lifted the receiver and dialed.

Eugene answered on the third ring, and Pedro whispered into the phone. "I can only talk for a minute."

"Is everything okay?" Eugene asked.

"Things are tense here, Eugene. Don't call me, no matter what. Rastano has the phone. He's watching the incoming numbers. And he's already killed Luis, the other boxer."

"Christ. You okay?"

"I'm all right, but calling out is next to impossible. The only phone line I trust is in the gardener's shed at the far end of the property, and there are guards everywhere."

"Any sign of Julie and Shiara?"

"No, but I'm going to have a better look around tomorrow. I can only see so much at once or Rastano will get suspicious. How are you doing?"

"I'm in Rochester, New York. Pablo lives near here somewhere. I'm getting close, Pedro."

"Good news. I've got to go. Don't call, Eugene, or I'm a dead man."

"Don't worry, Pedro. We'll get together, you, me and the women, in a couple of days."

"You got it, my friend." Pedro quietly slipped the phone into its cradle and moved carefully to the door. He started to open it, but stopped when he heard a noise just outside. He crouched down fast, then raised his head and brought his eyes just over the frame holding the window in place. As quickly as he had raised his head, he lowered it. Outside the door, only inches from where he knelt, was one of Rastano's guards. The odor of cigarette smoke drifted on the still night air and tickled his nostrils. He gently rubbed his nose to keep from sneezing. If the guard was sneaking a cigarette, he would be five minutes or more and Pedro knew his muscles would be cramping by that time if he wasn't in a more comfortable position. He lowered himself to the floor, then concentrated on keeping his heart rate low and his breathing deep and silent.

Five minutes passed with only a modicum of activity or noise from the other side of the door. Pedro began to wonder what was happening. Was the man simply smoking a cigarette, or was he waiting for additional personnel? Maybe they had passed the shed, heard him talking and one of the team had gone for backup. If that was the case, his only chance was to whip open the door, snap the man's neck, dump the body and get back to the house. But Rastano would immediately suspect him. Then there was a slight noise from the other side of the door and the sound of receding footsteps, almost imperceptible on the soft earth.

Pedro waited a couple of long minutes, then chanced a glance out the window. Nothing. The man was gone. He pushed open the door and glanced down at the crushed cigarette butt on the edge of the path. Pedro sucked in the fresh night air and crossed himself. That had been close. Too close. He weaved back to the house using the patches of vegetation as cover. Two sets of armed guards were standing near the entrance, and he had to wait for almost twenty minutes until they moved off and the last fifty yards was clear. He sprinted across the open grass and into the house. It was deathly quiet inside the mansion. He slipped off his shoes, and crossed the tile floor in his socks. It took almost three heart-pounding minutes to reach his room. He checked around the room and was satisfied that no one had come in while he was out.

He lay on his bed, breathing deeply. Two days and counting. Julie and Shiara were on the estate grounds somewhere. He just needed to find out where.

But time was running short, and the danger was growing.

Chapter Forty-three

Eugene flipped the phone shut and let out a long breath. Rastano had the cell phone. That was the end of their communication, unless Pedro called him. He didn't like it, but there was nothing he could do. And from what Pedro had said, calling out from Rastano's estate wasn't easy. Eugene slipped the phone into his pocket and glanced back to where Ben and Andrew were hunched over the Quigley woman's computer. He glanced at his watch. Three-thirty in the morning. He watched the two young men for another minute, then took a stroll about the house.

It was a pale yellow two-story Victorian with elaborate lattice work and trim around the doors, windows and portico. A wraparound front porch, enclosed by ornate white spindles, sported wicker chairs and a tarnished brass table, despite the cool weather. The house was set back from the road on a large, well-treed lot that Eugene guessed was close to an acre. There was little to no traffic, the road a cul-de-sac with the Quigley house sharing the end of the street with two other large homes.

Eugene paused at a recent picture of the owner. "Old Lady" Quigley was not so old. She appeared to be in her forties and damn good looking. Three different degrees hung on one wall, a BSc, MSc, and PhD. An accomplished woman. He returned to the computer room and asked how things were going.

"Here's the list of registered guests during November and December of last year," Andrew said, handing him three sheets of paper from the printer. "Ben's just working on the DMV right now."

"How's it going?" Eugene asked.

"I need a coffee," Ben said, looking up with bloodshot eyes.

"I'll make some," Eugene said. He retreated to the kitchen, found the coffeemaker and filters and brewed a full pot. When it had stopped dripping, he took two cups back to the boys. "Coffee. What do you take in it?"

"Black," Ben said. "Oh, God, thank you." He sipped on the dark roast, and smiled. "Next to beer and water, this stuff's the best."

Andrew accepted his cup without the fanfare, and they both watched as Ben worked at hacking into the Department of Motor Vehicles. There was a firewall, which was expected, but whoever had built the primary firewall had installed a secondary firewall of a sort that was giving Ben trouble. He worked at it until almost five in the morning, then threw his hands up in despair. "Can't get through it without some help."

"What sort of help?" Eugene asked.

"I've got some programs at school that could probably break this, but that means coming back tomorrow night. There's no way I can get them from FLCC, get back here and hack into the DMV before the whole neighborhood is up. In fact, we'd better go now or some early riser is going to see us leaving."

They left through the back door and walked the two blocks to where Bill was parked and waiting. "How was the hacking?" he asked, a hint of a smile on his face. He was enjoying the departure from his daily routine.

"Great, but we have to go back tomorrow night," Eugene said.

"At five hundred a day, I'm still your man," he said.

They dropped Ben and Andrew off at their residence with the promise that the boys would be waiting for Eugene in the park just down from the dorms at one in the morning. Bill headed back to Henrietta to drop Eugene off at his motel. Eugene told him to go home, get some sleep and be back at two in the afternoon. He paid Bill the daily rate, got a thank you and a smile in return, then headed for bed. The last thought he had before crashing into a dreamless sleep was how lucky he had been so far in his search for Pablo.

Luck. At least *that* seemed to be on his side right now.

Chapter Forty-four

They rose early, ate breakfast and were reading when the guards poked their heads in for the morning check. Julie glanced up, then looked back to her text. One of the men, an automatic weapon slung over his shoulder, took a quick tour of their apartment, then left without saying a word. The moment the door closed the two women were in motion.

"Just see if you can get the screws started," Julie said, as Shiara prepared to enter the air duct. Once you've got them turning, we'll be able to get them out."

"Okay," Shiara said, taking a deep breath and starting into the dark and narrow hole. "I'll be as quick as possible."

"All right, honey. Just don't cut yourself on the metal."

Shiara nodded, and was gone. She slithered into the duct and disappeared after a few feet, the darkness swallowing up the white soles on her running shoes. Julie replaced the grill, tightened one screw to keep it flush to the wall and went back to her reading. She stared at the page, but the words didn't register. They melded together into a backdrop of black on white, meaningless and irrelevant. She was amazed at how few things in life were really important when the cards were on the table. If Javier Rastano was serious, and she had no doubt he was, she and Shiara had forty-eight hours to live. And faced with imminent death, she saw the whole picture more clearly than ever before in her life.

Shiara and Miguel were everything in her life. Her children were the heart and soul of her very being, and without them she doubted she could continue. For certain, if either were taken from her, her life would never be the same. She would protect Shiara with her life, of that she had no doubt. And Eugene, her husband, her lover, her best friend. She knew he was working nonstop to satisfy Javier Rastano's demands. Julie was aware of her husband's abilities under pressure and had confidence that he could do the impossible. He wouldn't fail them; he couldn't.

She focused on the text, and one passage jumped off the page at her. She read it again and again, finding strength in the simplicity of the words.

"Dark moments are short corridors leading to sunlit rooms," she spoke the words aloud. And in that moment, she knew that if they did go down, they would go down fighting.

Javier walked briskly to the phone, and answered with a simple, "Yes?"

"The team has fractured," the voice said. "Some are still in El Paso, some in Rochester. Eugene has disappeared."

"How?" Rastano asked.

"He left El Paso sometime Tuesday night. He's in Rochester, New York."

"What's he doing there?" Javier asked.

"He met with Mario Correa. We don't know where or

when or what they talked about. And we don't know where he is right now."

"Where are you?" Rastano asked.

"It doesn't matter where I am," the voice snapped back. "It's enough that I call and keep you in the loop."

"Okay, okay. Anything else?"

"Sure, lots. But none of it's of any concern to you. Except, perhaps, that your name came up in passing. It's now common knowledge that you have Eugene's wife and daughter."

"That's irrelevant," Javier said. "They can't touch me."

"I've got to go. I'll call you when the team finds Eugene." The line went dead.

Javier replaced the receiver and walked back through the house to the patio. Pedro was just leaving the house on his way to the pool and they exchanged greetings. The boxer was talented, and he hoped that Luis had been the rat and that he wouldn't have to kill Pedro. For a fighter, he was good looking and articulate, two things the American media honed in on. And if the American public liked Pedro, then the chances of a title match at some point were a real possibility. Pedro had the moves in the ring; his footwork, his punches and his cerebral approach to the bout. But none of that would matter if he was in league with Eugenio Escobar. Pedro would simply be another corpse littering the streets of San Salvador.

Javier sat at the table and toyed with a glass of lemonade. A few new orchids had sprouted, but that brought him no pleasure today. The deadline for Eugenio to dig Pablo out of the woodwork was fast approaching with no success to date. He would have to kill the women, that was certain. If he failed to follow through on his threat, his reputation as a man true to his word would be destroyed. And that image was one that he had carefully nurtured his entire adult life. He decided on six o'clock Saturday evening as the time for their execution if the account number wasn't in his hand. He glanced at his watch and did the math.

Fifty-five hours. Time was running out on Eugenio.

Chapter Forty-five

Landry and Maxwell ate lunch at Braddock Bay Restaurant, which was actually on the banks of Salmon Creek, not Braddock Bay. The fare was beef and seafood and their table had an excellent view of the narrow waterway leading to Lake Ontario. They hit the restaurant at quarter to twelve and by the time their meals were being served every table was full, and it was noisy. That suited them just fine, in case someone was trying to listen in.

Alexander Landry cut into his steak, and said, "I can't believe we didn't get one hit from the rental cars or taxis. How did he get out of the airport?"

"He may have taken a cab to the city center and the driver just didn't recognize him. Eugene doesn't exactly stand out in a crowd. His skin is white for a Colombian, and his English is perfect."

"I suppose. There is that one cabbie who's taking a couple of days off. We haven't talked to him yet."

Cathy studied her notes. "Bulbinder Chadi. He lives in

Hilton, close to here. We could pay him a visit after lunch if you want."

"If nothing else turns up, we'll stop by," Landry sipped on his Pepsi, and glanced around the crowded restaurant. It was decorated with historical pieces and pictures and had a warm, rustic feel to it. He liked it, and the food was good. "How close do you think Eugene is to finding Pablo?"

Cathy shrugged. "God only knows. But I'm willing to bet Mario Correa wanted to meet Eugene in Rochester because Pablo is nearby. That's what my gut is saying."

"When do you want to call Crandle?" Landry asked.

"After lunch," Cathy said. She fiddled with her food for a minute, then set her fork on the side of her plate. "If we're closing in, he knows we're here."

Landry finished chewing his steak and nodded. "I would think so."

"And he'll know who is after him. He'll know it's us, Alexander."

"Probably. Why?"

Cathy Maxwell was silent for a minute, gazing over Salmon Creek and the wetlands beyond. Finally she pulled her cell phone from her pocket and dialed a number. When the other party answered, she said, "Darren, get yourself and the kids out of the house. Go somewhere safe. I don't care where, and I don't want to know. Just do it. And do it now."

Landry could hear a muffled response but couldn't make out the words.

"No, Darren. I mean right now. Within the hour." Again, there was a response, but this time she simply said, "Bye," and hung up.

She locked eyes with the DEA agent across the table. "It's not going to happen again, Alexander. My parents are dead. I'll do what's necessary to keep my family safe."

Chapter Forty-six

Eugene spent Thursday's daylight hours jotting down ideas and making notes on each EPIC team member. Pablo was close by. That was a given. But close didn't count; he needed to get face-to-face with his cousin. And that wasn't going to happen without some good deductive reasoning. The facts were in front of him but he just had to sort them out.

Someone was informing both Javier Rastano and Pablo of the team's progress. One person was undoing all the investigative work of the team and eliminating any chance of taking Pablo by surprise. But who? There was precious little to go on.

Alexander Landry had withheld Rastano's name, but according to him, he was about to tell the group when Senator Crandle had noticed the fax. Maybe Landry knew all along it was Rastano holding Julie and Shiara. Then there was the financial drain of having all those kids in college, yet he didn't seem bothered by it. And, of course, Landry had spent time in Colombia in the wild days when the cartel was throwing money every which way. Maybe Landry had been on the payroll since the hunt for Pablo. Maybe.

Cathy Maxwell appeared innocent, but Eugene had noted one telling bit of information on Tuesday at EPIC. When she had complained about her hotel room and the pillows, Landry had accused her of missing her multi-million dollar home. Multi-million, not just million. What kind of civil servant makes enough money to live in that kind of luxury? And Maxwell was as entrenched in Colombia as anyone on the team. Then she had visited Pablo during his incarceration at La Catedral. But Pablo had struck back at her for stemming the flow of chemicals to the cocaine labs by sending his *sicarios* to Boston. No one questioned the sacrifice she had made to the cause, losing her parents in a brutal execution. Perhaps, Eugene thought, the money from her parents' estate explained the dream house she and her family lived in. Perhaps.

Senator Irwin Crandle was an enigma. Eugene saw him as shadowy, almost untrustworthy. But the ability to lie at will and manipulate people had taken him far, especially in his political life. He certainly didn't hurt for money, jetting about in his own private Lear. His political connections in Washington were with some of the most powerful people on the Hill, including the president. If Crandle was dirty, toppling him would be a monumental task. He was insulated from any sort of attack, unless concrete proof could be laid on the table. If the senator *was* the informant, he hadn't likely left any incriminating evidence lying about.

Bud Reid was just as shadowy as the senator, but without the trappings of success and power. He had run roughshod over the *narcos* during the late '80s and early '90s, and his allegiance was to the field troops. He brought his men back from the sorties, busted the labs, took apart the jungle airstrips and brought down Cessnas filled with processed cocaine with greater skill than any other DEA man. He was revered by both Delta and Centra Spike, and that respect had to be earned. Still, Reid could have led successful raids on a few of the cartel's labs and airstrips as a cover, while allowing the majority to thrive. Every DEA agent who spent time in Colombia agreed that they only managed to bust the tip of the iceberg. Tons of cocaine still made it through to the States.

And that left Eduardo Garcia. He was most inconspicuous of the five, having no prior DEA experience in Colombia, and thus no opportunity to cement ties with the former drug lords. But the sudden appearance of his uncle, Fernando Garcia, was a wrinkle. Did the veteran Garcia have a deal in place with Pablo and the Rastano clan prior to his death? Perhaps Eduardo was continuing the Garcia tradition. Mario Correa had described Fernando Garcia as a loose cannon, the kind of person who sometimes stepped over the line. And the Garcia brothers were in college in Dallas, even though their father was still cleaning swimming pools. What had changed there that the money was now available for tuition and living expenses in a major city like Dallas? That took money. Serious money.

Eugene rubbed his hands across his eyes. He was tired from thinking, but something was telling him that the answer was right in front of him, in black and white. He reviewed his notes, but nothing jumped out at him. There was a light knock on the door and he checked the time. Two o'clock. That would be Bill. And the cab arriving meant he could get out of the dingy hotel room and get some lunch.

Tonight was key. He was picking up Andrew and Ben outside their residence at one in the morning and they were heading back to Sarah Quigley's house. Maybe the key he needed to put everything together was in a database out there somewhere. And maybe Ben would find it.

Maybe.

Chapter Forty-seven

Nadeem Chadi looked like she was about to keel over. She grabbed the door jamb and leaned against it, staring at Alexander Landry's credentials.

"What happened to my husband? He's been in an accident?"

"No, Mrs. Chadi. Nothing like that. We just want to know where he is."

"He's in trouble?" she asked, pulling herself off the jamb, a stern look crossing her face. She smoothed her sari and said, "I told him he was probably doing something illegal. Nobody pays a taxi driver five hundred dollars a day to chauffer him around. People who want a car for the entire day rent one. But no, he insists that this is just a nice man with lots of money."

"So he's taken a few days off to drive one person around Rochester. At five hundred a day?"

Nadeem Chadi bit the end of her tongue. "Did I say five hundred? Maybe that was high."

"Mrs. Chadi, we're not from the IRS, and we don't care if your husband is pocketing some cash on the side. But if you don't cooperate, I can have the IRS here in under an hour. Now, where is your husband?"

"He said something about picking up his fare in Henrietta. They were going somewhere after dark. I don't know where."

"Does he carry a cell phone?" Alexander asked.

"Usually. But it needed repairs, and when he got this job he decided he wouldn't need the phone for a day or two, and took it in to get fixed."

"Well, he'll be on dispatch," Cathy said, turning away and starting down the steps toward their rental car. "We can have the cab company call him and get his location."

"That won't work," Bulbinder's wife said, stopping both Alexander and Cathy in their tracks. "If he's not working he turns off the radio. The dispatch calls bother him."

"All right," Alexander said with resignation. "Thanks for your time."

"One more thing," Cathy said. "When do you expect him to get home?"

Mrs. Chadi shrugged. "I don't know. Tomorrow morning sometime."

The two agents left the tiny bungalow and trudged back to their car. They drove to the local police station and asked the sergeant on duty to put out an APB for the taxi. They recited the plate and taxi numbers that the dispatcher had given them, thanked the officer for his cooperation and left after jotting down both their cell phone numbers. It was just a matter of time before one of the police cruisers spotted the cab and called it in.

"What now?" Alexander asked.

"We can canvass the motels and hotels in Henrietta," Cathy said. "And when we get the call we'll decide what to do with Eugene Escobar."

* * *

As they exited the restaurant, both Bill and Eugene noticed the police at the same time. Two officers were scrutinizing the cab, which was parked in the stall next to the handicapped parking, and they were jotting down the license plate number. Neither cop glanced up, and Eugene pulled the cab driver back into the restaurant.

"Am I in some sort of trouble?" Bill asked.

"No, but I might be. I'd better get out of here. Give me a couple of minutes and then go to your car. You've done nothing wrong." Eugene counted out five hundred dollars and handed it across. To his surprise, the man didn't take it.

"I haven't earned the money," he said. "But I can, if you want me to."

"What do you mean?"

"I've got a brother who lives a couple of blocks from here. We could borrow one of his cars for the day."

"You're sure?" Eugene asked. "You don't mind?"

"No, it's okay. Follow me. It's not far." They left the diner through a side door and walked down the street at a brisk pace.

An hour later they were driving a four-door, dark blue Saturn with six thousand miles on the odometer. Eugene suggested they get out of Rochester, especially Henrietta, as quickly as possible. If the cops knew about the cab, they knew about the room at the Super 8. Eugene didn't care. The only items left in the room were his toiletries and a change of clothes, and he could pick up replacement items easily enough. He still had some cash left, although it was dwindling quickly.

He sat next to Bill as they drove toward FLCC. The EPIC team was in Rochester—one or two of them, anyway—as he had known they would be. The cops weren't singling out parked taxi cabs and scrutinizing them without a reason. And that reason would be a request from the DEA or the CIA. Either organization had plenty of clout and would have the local cops jumping when they suggested a height. It was still midafternoon, and hours to go before meeting with Andrew and Ben. But without the information from the DMV database to cross-correlate against the hotel records, none of the names meant anything. What he needed was for one name to appear on both the hotel guest list and on the registration for a new Renault.

Eugene pulled out the list Ben had given him last night, and scanned it again for the eighth time. Nothing. Not one of the names was familiar, and there were no easy-to-spot aliases. He'd read that most people chose an alias with the same initials as his or her real name. But there wasn't even one guest with the initials PE.

Bill steered into Naples, a hamlet at the southernmost tip of Canandaigua Lake, and parked the car. They walked the streets, looking through the shops, killing time. It seemed so strange to Eugene that with so little time left to track down Pablo, he was walking aimlessly down the main street of a tiny community, looking through crafts stores. One of them, alive with replicas of brewery paraphernalia from the days when over fifty breweries operated out of Syracuse, had a table in the rear with a computer connected to the Internet. Eugene bought a coffee and thirty minutes on the machine. He accessed the DEA homepage, at www.dea.gov, and scrolled down to the Wall of Honor. One click took him into the list of DEA agents and staff killed accidentally or in the line of duty. He found the file on Fernando Garcia, and read the script.

Garcia was stationed in Bogotá in February of 1993, assigned to the logistics sector, a specialist in aviation routes in and out of Colombia. In late February, Agent Garcia was transferred to Medellín, taken off the desk and put to work in the field. He scouted airfields and labs by helicopter with technical assistance from Centra Spike. Few details were given of his exact function while in the field, and the communiqué ended by stating that Agent Garcia had been shot while conducting a raid on a suspected laboratory. The article failed to mention which drug lord owned the lab or who Garcia was working with when he died. Eugene printed the page, folded it and stuck it in his back pocket. It was food for thought. He signed off the computer, and checked his time to ensure he hadn't gone over his half hour.

As he left the shop, he realized that he had only one avenue of attack on the go, and that if the foray into the DMV database didn't yield something conclusive tonight, he was sunk. As the afternoon dragged on and evening arrived, his mood grew more somber. After supper, he picked up some information that gave him a shred of hope. He purchased a pie for the boys to eat, when the woman manning the till asked them where they were from.

"Venezuela," Eugene said, not seeing any reason to be dishonest. "It's lovely there in the spring, just as it is here," he added.

"This is nothing," she responded cheerfully. "You should see it in the summer. Absolutely stunning. In fact, Canandaigua is Iroquois for "the Chosen Place."

Eugene wondered if the name had influenced Pablo's decision to live there.

And with that small shot of encouragement came hope.

Chapter Forty-eight

"He's closing in on you," the voice said. "And he's showing no sign of slowing down."

Pablo didn't respond for a few seconds, then asked, "Where is Eugene now?"

"Last we heard from him he was in Henrietta, a suburb of Rochester, earlier today. But we haven't managed to get our hands on him. The police found the cab, abandoned, but no driver. Eugene's no fool."

"No, Eugene is no fool. Has he managed to uncover your identity yet?"

"No. I don't think so. And I'm not worried. He's concentrating on finding you, not me."

"He may surprise you," Pablo said.

"Any surprise like that will result in him dying very quickly," the voice had turned icy.

"I'm beginning to prefer that my cousin live through this. But if the situation gets out of hand, either you or I may have to kill him."

"What are you going to do?"

"I'm ready to move if I have to. Javier's deadline is approaching quickly, and if he follows through with his threat and kills Julie and Shiara, Eugene will be heading straight to El Salvador to kill Rastano. So I may not have to do anything. It's all a matter of timing now."

"You think Javier Rastano will kill the women?"

"I know he will. If Eugene can't uncover me in the next forty hours or so, his family is going to be a lot smaller."

"All right. I've got to go. Just be warned, he's getting close."

"I can take care of myself," Pablo said viciously, and hung up the phone.

He appreciated being kept abreast of the situation, but he didn't need to be told the same thing more than once. The Crown Royal bottle on the bar was almost empty, and he poured the final couple of ounces in a glass and added ice. He sipped the drink, thinking about Eugene. He hardly knew him. The man had avoided him, and never asked for anything. Unlike many of his other relatives. He had never met Julie or Eugene's daughter, but he suspected they were good people. Sometimes good people died. It was a fact of life.

He shook his head at Eugene's tenacity. He had progressed much further in the hunt than anyone had expected, had succeeded where law agencies, armed with the latest technology and specially trained agents, had failed. Not that anyone had been seriously hunting him since December of 1993, but in the two years prior to his apparent death even Centra Spike couldn't catch him. And that was partially thanks to the informant he had just spoken with. What a relationship. Fourteen years and counting. It had been exceptionally useful then, and was proving equally valuable now. And this allegiance to him was based on one small favor. Amazing.

He punched the intercom, and a few moments later

Miguel entered the room. He had aged since the days when he worked as one of the guards at Nápoles, but his allegiance was without question, just as it had been the day he took Eugene into the jungle on the dirt bikes. Miguel reached the desk, and waited.

"I want you to run into town and get a few things. If we have to leave I want at least a couple of bottles of Crown Royal." He pointed to the empty bottle. "And that was the last one." Pablo handed Miguel a handwritten list. "Get the stuff on this list and pack it in the Lincoln."

Miguel checked his watch. "Too late to go today. The shops will be closed. I'll have to go tomorrow."

"Not a problem."

Miguel pocketed the list, and asked, "Anything else?"

"Back up the computers tonight. Get all the current bank balances and make sure you have all the account numbers and transit codes. I don't want to be scrambling if we have to leave quickly."

Miguel nodded and left. Pablo glanced at the empty whiskey bottle, and wished it were full. Then he shook his head at the futility of wishing for things. It was always a waste of time. Reality always told another story. He wondered briefly if Eugene was wishing for things right now; his wife back in his arms, his daughter safely at his side.

"Just wishes, Eugene, that's all they are," he said quietly, to no one.

Chapter Forty-nine

The Learjet touched down in Rochester at just before midnight Thursday. Cathy Maxwell and Alexander Landry were on the tarmac to meet Crandle and the rest of the team. They rode together in a rented Infiniti Q45 SUV, their scant luggage thrown in through the back hatch.

"What have you got?" Crandle asked, as Landry steered the vehicle off the access road and onto the expressway.

"Nothing new. We've asked the local cops to watch the cab driver's house in case he comes home. But his wife says he's gone until tomorrow morning, at the earliest."

"But you've got the cab," Crandle said. "They don't have wheels."

"Maybe they jacked a car." Landry entered the fast lane and accelerated to eighty miles an hour.

"Maybe this cab driver has relatives or friends with a car," Crandle said. "Have you checked out the people he knows who live near where the cab was found?"

"No,"

"Do it," Crandle snapped. "They had to get their hands on another vehicle somewhere. I want to know what they're driving."

"Okay. We'll get on it right away."

Crandle stared out the window at the passing scenery. Gas stations with neon signs that cut through the blackness popped up at irregular intervals along the road. An occasional late-night restaurant awash in light flashed by. But most of the buildings were dark and shuttered for the night. Rochester, New York. In a million years, who would have dreamed that Pablo Escobar would live in such a cold climate. Perhaps that was just another of the drug lord's crafty moves that always kept him several steps ahead of his pursuers.

"Tomorrow is Friday," Crandle said, breaking the silence. "Our last full day to find Eugene and Pablo. After that, the wife and kid die, and everything changes. One day, people. That's it. Let's be at our best tomorrow."

Chapter Fifty

The Saturn glided into Sarah Quigley's driveway at six minutes before two. The adjacent properties were dark, and no dogs barked as the four men piled out of the car and made their way to the house. Andrew had the key in his hand and had opened the door by the time Eugene and Bill reached it. They entered and made their way to the rear of the house to the computer. Ben fired up the machine. The other three sat, and waited.

"Okay," Ben said, inserting a CD and watching as the hacking program loaded onto the hard drive. "You want me to find all the Renaults registered between November fifteenth and December fifteenth last year. Right?"

"Right," Eugene said, shoulder-surfing.

Numbers were scrolling down the screen and Ben explained. "My program is breaking down the secondary firewall. It shouldn't take too long."

"Excellent," Eugene said.

A few minutes passed, and then the screen flashed and

the logo for the New York State DMV appeared. "I'm in," Ben said, keying in the request for Renaults registered inside the time frame Eugene had given him. He got nine hits on the request.

"Print them, please," Eugene said anxiously. He watched as the paper rolled out of the LaserJet, then picked it up and glanced down the list. He didn't immediately recognize any of the names. He took the list from the hotel registry and compared it to the DMV list. Checking the two against each other took almost a half hour, and when he was done he sat back with a discouraged look on his face. "No matches."

No one spoke for a minute. Finally Eugene said, "Ben, could you try to get into one more database?"

"Depends. Which one?"

"DEA."

Ben grinned. "You've got to be shitting me. The Drug Enforcement Agency?"

"That's the one."

"That's a far cry from the DMV, Eugene," he said. "Those guys play hardball."

"Trust me, I know how they operate. I need one file. Just one."

Ben was uncertain. "I don't know, Eugene. I've got a cloaking program with me, but their firewalls and software are going to be state-of-the-art. We could get pinged."

"What?"

"Pinged. They could trace our hack back to this system."

"That's a chance I'm willing to take. And I'll put my money where my mouth is. Five thousand dollars. I'll have to get the money from the bank tomorrow, but my word is good."

Ben perked up. "Five thousand dollars." He glanced at Andrew and Bill. "How would we split it?"

"Five hundred each for your dad and me, the other

four thousand in your pocket?" Andrew offered, and Bill nodded.

"Done," Ben said. "What file do you need?"

"I want to find out what really happened to an agent named Fernando Garcia. It's in the DEA database somewhere."

"If it's there, I'll find it," Ben said. "This may take a while, gentlemen. Please, make yourselves at home."

Eugene wandered around the house. After about fifteen minutes, a thought struck him and he searched out the master bedroom. A single lady in a large house on a dark cul-de-sac may keep a gun close to where she sleeps. He tried the night tables, under her pillow, the closet, the bureau drawers and her en suite bath. Nothing. He stood in the darkness, staring at the bed. It was a four-poster, high off the floor, with a thick mattress and box spring. He lifted the mattress and slid his arm between it and the box spring. His hand felt cold metal, and he pulled out a Glock pistol. Good old Sarah Quigley. He checked the breach, which was empty, and the clip, which was full. He made sure the safety was on, then tucked the gun in his pants, against the small of his back. He returned to the computer room to find Ben navigating his way through DEA personnel records.

"I've found two files on Fernando Garcia," he said, handing Eugene a couple of printed pages, "but I don't think I've got what you want yet."

Eugene read the material and shook his head. "No. There's more in the system somewhere. These are his personnel file and the press release on his death."

"I've got another hit," Ben said, "but I can't find the file. It's hidden, way back in the computer's hard drive. Someone went to a lot of effort to protect this file."

"Can you get it?" Eugene asked.

Ben gave him an admonishing glance. "Of course I can

get it. It takes time and patience to cut through all the lay-
ers of security. Time and patience."

"Great," Eugene said. "The two things I don't have."

Ben glanced at him through his hair. "I'm doing the
best I can, Eugene. This is the DEA, not the Girl Scouts.
And whoever buried this file knew what they were doing."

Eugene walked to the living room and sat in the darkness, feeling time slip by. Seconds turned into minutes,
minutes into an hour. He fought sleep, thinking of his
wife and daughter, imagining them safe at home in Playa
El Tirano. Nice thoughts, but not reality.

Eugene heard Ben calling his name and hurried to the
computer room. Ben had a file up on the screen and was
reading the text. "It's a field report from May 1993, of a
raid on some cocaine laboratory. That's when this Fernando Garcia fellow was killed." He hit the print button,
and the LaserJet spit out two pages. Eugene read the hard
copy twice and sat on a chair beside Ben. The content was
unbelievable. Intelligence reports prior to the raid had
indicated Mario Rastano was the intended target, and that
he would be at the lab. But the actual report, filed by the
second agent, who was only identified by a code word,
told a different story. Rastano was nowhere to be seen, he
reported, but there was significant resistance and during
the melée Fernando Garcia was fatally wounded. He died
at the scene.

"Does this read like I think it does?" he asked the college student.

Ben nodded. "The autopsy showed that it was the second agent's gun that fired the bullet that killed Garcia. It
doesn't come right out and say for sure it was friendly fire,
but the report sure implies it."

"That's what I'm getting out of it," Eugene agreed. "No
wonder someone wanted this buried." He was pensive for a
minute, then added, "Why didn't they just erase the file?"

Ben shook his head. "They couldn't. The file is permanently protected with an anti-erase code in its header. It's impossible to erase it, but hidden well enough, it's almost as good."

"Almost," Eugene said. "But you found it."

"I am good," Ben smiled as he said it. "Do you know the *narco* they mention in the file, this Rastano guy?"

Eugene's face hardened. "Oh, yeah, I know the guy. Mario Rastano. His son is holding my wife and daughter in El Salvador. This is all starting to add up."

"But they don't mention the other agent by name, just a code word. *Dragonfly.*"

Eugene was trying to piece things together. Whoever went into that lab with Fernando Garcia was already on Mario Rastano's payroll. The advance reports were probably correct; Rastano was most likely at the lab when the raid went down. The two agents busted in, and while Garcia was in the process of arresting Rastano, the second agent shot him. Rastano escaped, but had the dirt on the agent. But there was no name associated, just the code word *Dragonfly.* He needed that name.

"Ben, scan the DEA database and see what you find under Dragonfly. I need to know who it is."

The student bent over the keyboard and keyed furiously. Occasionally, he would stop and load another of his hacking or cloaking programs, designed to open doors while keeping the intruder invisible to the DEA security programs. At every turn, he carefully noted the path he was weaving through the database so they could find their way back, if necessary. It took over an hour before he got a hit.

"Eugene," he said excitedly. "I've got something."

Eugene stared at the screen over Ben's shoulder.

"Give me one second, I just need to open the file." He keyed in a couple more commands, and then a personnel file appeared for a split second. It vanished, and the screen went blank. "Oh, shit," Ben said, his voice scared. "Oh, Christ. We've got problems."

"What?" Eugene asked, as Bill and Andrew spilled in from the living room. "What's wrong?"

"We've been traced. They've got us. That file had some sort of a protection program written inside it, if the person accessing it didn't use a password. We never entered the password. And I'll guarantee it traced us and fed our location back to the DEA command center. They know we're here. It's just a matter of time before someone's at the front door."

"Shut it down," Eugene said. "Wipe your fingerprints off the keyboard, the monitor and the door handles. Then let's get the hell out of here."

"I touched lots of stuff in here," Andrew said, panicked.

Ben nodded. "Me too." He had the presence of mind to note the final path to the personnel file on a slip of paper, and hand the paper to Eugene.

"Doesn't matter. The team that will respond to this is going to be small. One of them won't want anyone else to know what's going on. Trust me. Wipe your prints off the obvious stuff, and let's go. We drive the speed limit and don't panic and we're okay." Three pairs of eyes stared at him in the darkness. "Trust me, guys. There will never be a report filed on this."

They cleaned up, locked the house and piled into the Saturn. The street was deserted, and they didn't pass a car on the main road leading back to FLCC. Everyone was far more relaxed when they finally pulled up in front of the dorm.

"Not a word," Eugene said. "Not a word to anyone." He looked at Ben and Andrew. "I owe you that money, Ben, and I'll get it to you. Trust me. The only way I won't be back is if I don't live through this."

"You're involved in some serious shit, Eugene," Andrew said. He stuck out his hand. "Good luck."

"I hope you make it, man," Ben said, also shaking Eugene's hand. "And I'm not just saying that because you owe me money."

Eugene laughed. It felt good. "Thanks," he said.

Bill pulled the car away from the curb, and drove slowly down the twisting road. "Where to?" he asked.

Eugene glanced at his watch. Four-ten in the morning. "Just find a parking lot with a few cars, Bill. We'll catch a few Z's in the car, if that's okay with you."

"Fine with me," Bill said. "I hope you got something useful out of that, because it was kind of scary having to run out of the house like that."

"Yeah," Eugene said. "Yeah, Bill, I got something very useful from our night out. Very useful indeed." The personnel file for the agent codenamed Dragonfly had only been on the screen for a split second, but it was long enough for Eugene to recognize the face. A face he had gotten to know very well over the past few days.

He had failed to find a link to Pablo, but he now knew who the informant was.

Chapter Fifty-one

The call was patched through to the hotel switchboard at five-eighteen Friday morning. The caller asked for the guest by name and, although the switchboard operator cautioned him about the early hour, the man was adamant. The call went through.

"Hello." The voice was sleepy, a person just awakened.

"This is Mel Jacobs in Arlington. There's been a security breach. Could I verify your identity, please."

"Certainly." The correct identification procedure and codes were exchanged, and the caller continued.

"At three-fifty-four this morning there was an unauthorized entry into two files on the mainframe. The one where we managed to flag the intruder was your personnel file."

"What was the other one?"

"A classified document dealing with a raid on a Colombian drug lab back in May of 1993. I can send you a copy of the file if you wish."

"No. I know what's in the file. Did you trace where they hacked in from?"

"Yes. I have an address in Seneca Falls, New York. It's a residence owned by a Ms. Sarah Quigley." He recited the municipal address of the house.

"Thank you. We're close by and will take care of it. Please delete this from your records. It never happened."

"Yes, sir."

Senator Irwin Crandle hung up, and stared in the mirror. So this was it. Eugene Escobar had uncovered what no person or group in the entire United States security community had been able to. Eugene had connected the dots back to the raid on Mario Rastano's lab. The raid where he had been forced to kill another DEA agent to keep Rastano from being arrested.

He dressed quietly, thinking about his sordid association with Mario Rastano. There was no other course of action he could have taken in the Colombian jungle, all those years ago. The intel prior to the raid was dead-on, but he and Fernando Garcia weren't given all the facts before going in. They weren't told Mario Rastano would be there. If someone had told him, he would simply have called and warned the man. Instead, they had busted in the doors only to find one of the cartel heavyweights standing in the center of the room, surrounded by processed cocaine. Garcia was on top of the world. They had a big fish in their net, and he wasn't about to let Rastano get away. He'd had no choice other than to shoot Garcia in the back.

He was already taking money from Rastano. Christ, the money flowing through Colombia in those days was unfathomable. The cocaine business drove the country's economy. What was the harm in taking a few million dollars in return for an insider's voice on where and when the Americans would strike? Rastano didn't care about the Colombian government, but Centra Spike and Delta sure scared the shit out of him and Pablo and the Ochoa brothers. With Crandle on the inside, the cartel chiefs could sacrifice just the right number of labs and planes to keep anyone from suspecting the rat in the pack. But the *narcos* moved too quickly a few times, and suspicion grew that someone inside was dirty. But nothing was ever proven. He had remained a faceless ghost. Until today.

Damn Eugene Escobar to hell. This should never have happened. When Javier Rastano had contacted him and told him about the Swiss account, the plan appeared simple. They were going to get Eugene to find Pablo and get the code to the account. His cut was to be fifty million dollars—despite his healthy financial status, fifty million tax free was a lot of money. What could go wrong? Eugene was just some dumb hick who took tourists scuba diving for chump change. They figured that the motivation to save his wife and daughter would be enough to drive Eugene to find Pablo. But they had not foreseen how far this motivation would take him.

He glanced at the address. Seneca Falls. He spread a map of the greater Rochester area on the table and found the town. It was on the west side of Canandaigua Lake, about twenty-five miles south of the city. It was just past five-thirty and traffic would be light. He could make it to Sarah Quigley's house and back before eight. He phoned down and left a message for Alexander Landry that he had gone for a morning drive and jog along the river, and would meet them at eight in the restaurant. Then he slipped on a windbreaker and tucked his gun in the pocket.

One thing was for sure. Eugene Escobar had signed his own death warrant.

Chapter Fifty-two

Friday morning.

The last full day before Javier Rastano's deadline.

Eugene woke early, stiff from sleeping in the cab. He walked through the parking lot and down to a small stream trickling under a stone footbridge. He splashed the cold water on his face, and felt his senses sharpen from the shock to his system. He sat on the grass by the stream for a few minutes, collecting his thoughts and deciding on a course of action for this final day.

Irwin Crandle. The Kentucky senator was nothing more than a spy for a Colombian drug dealer. By now Crandle would know that his association with the Rastano family had been compromised. The evidence to charge him with murder was in the DEA computers, buried but retrievable. And Eugene was keenly aware that his possession of that evidence meant that Crandle couldn't afford to have him walking around telling what he knew. The senator was now coming after him with one intention. To kill him.

Eugene returned to the cab to find Bill just waking up. They drove to a nearby restaurant for breakfast and coffee. After his third cup of the life-sustaining liquid, Eugene announced to Bill that he had made a decision.

"First thing we do," he said, "is to head north of the city and stop at a couple of banks. I don't know how all this is going to play out, and I won't leave without first paying Andrew and Ben."

"If you get the money, I'll deliver it," Bill said.

Eugene nodded. "We'll see, Bill," he said, as they left the coffee shop and got in the car. "But I don't mind driving with you back down to the college after we get the money. I think best in a moving car."

"Okay, boss. Whatever you want."

Eugene settled back in the passenger seat and watched the countryside rush by. Perhaps he could cultivate an ally. He figured that Eduardo Garcia's interest in this whole thing ran deeper than just finding Pablo. Garcia might have suspected the death of his uncle was something other than an act of violence by a cornered *narco*. If Eduardo wanted retribution for Fernando's death, why not give him the target. With Eduardo Garcia after Irwin Crandle, Eugene could breathe a little easier. But how to alert Garcia without the rest of the team knowing? That was a problem. The team would be staying at a Rochester hotel. But which one? He didn't have the time or resources to start canvassing the hotels and asking for information that they may not divulge.

Then he had an idea. Not many people flew into medium-size cities in a Learjet. He asked Bill to pull over at a pay phone. He dialed the number to the executive terminal at the Rochester airport and spoke with the receptionist. She told him the pilot for Senator Crandle's jet was already in and having coffee with some of the maintenance staff. She put him on hold for a couple of minutes, then a voice came over the line.

"This is Captain Archer. Who am I speaking with?"

"Captain Archer, it's Eugene Escobar. I don't know if you remember, but you flew me from El Paso to Kentucky to meet with the senator."

"I remember. What can I do for you, Mr. Escobar?"

"I'd like to speak with the team. But by phone, not in person. I need to know where they're staying."

"They're at the Hyatt Regency Rochester on Main Street."

"Thanks," Eugene said. He dropped the phone back in its cradle. He got out the phone book, looked through the yellow pages for the number, then dialed and asked the switchboard operator for Eduardo Garcia. She put the call through. It rang a few times, then went back to the operator.

"Mr. Garcia is not answering right now," she said. "Would you like to leave a message?"

"Yes. But not on his voice mail. I'd like the message I leave to be personally delivered to Mr. Garcia when is alone. This is extremely important."

"Yes, sir. What is the message?"

"Tell him to call Eugene Escobar." He gave her the cell phone number. "But make sure Mr. Garcia knows that he is not to say a word to anyone until he's spoken with me."

"I understand."

"Thank you."

Eugene returned to the cab and had Bill drop him at three different banks, in quick succession. He withdrew the daily maximum of two thousand dollars from each bank, pocketed the six grand, and they headed for Finger Lakes Community College. He had a debt that needed paying.

Chapter Fifty-three

Irwin Crandle powered up the computer system and waited. He initiated the Internet and checked the history to see which sites had been accessed recently. The hackers had not taken the time to clear the files from the memory, and he followed the path Eugene had used the previous evening. When he reached the highly classified file that detailed the raid on Rastano's lab, he closed the files and deleted the path from the memory. Then he took the second path, the one Eugene had traveled just a few hours ago. Crandle's personnel file flashed on the screen, then quickly disappeared. He swore under his breath, and deleted that path from the memory. Then he shut the machine off, wiped the keyboard clean and left the house.

His suspicions were confirmed. Eugene Escobar had pieced together his involvement with Mario and Javier Rastano. Time was now the enemy. The longer Eugene was on the streets with this knowledge, the greater the chance that he would pass it along to someone else. What would Eugene do with the information? Go to the DEA? He doubted that. Try to contact someone at Langley or in the FBI? Again, doubtful. The truth was, he had no idea what the son-of-a-bitch might do. Eugene was proving to be a far more resourceful person than he'd thought. Go figure. A dive master from Venezuela with information that could bring down one of the richest and most powerful men in the United States. What a crazy world.

His phone rang. He answered it as he started his car.

"Senator Crandle, this is Bobby Akins at the Rochester City Police. I think we've got a hit on the car your suspect is driving."

"Really?" Crandle said. "What kind?"

"This Bulbinder Chadi has a relative who lives near where we found the cab who admits that he loaned Bulbinder a blue, 2005, two-door Saturn coupe." He recited the license number. Crandle jotted it down.

"Thanks, Bobby," he said. "Listen, when one of your squads spot this car could you do me a favor? I want them to back off and call in the location. When you get the call, please forward the information along to me. Just me. On this line. I'll have this cell phone with me all day."

"Yes, sir. Of course. I'll instruct the officers not to approach the car if they spot it."

"Thanks, Bobby."

Crandle jammed the rental into gear and pulled out of Sarah Quigley's driveway. It wouldn't take the police long to spot a blue Saturn. Eugene's hours to live were dwindling quickly.

Chapter Fifty-four

Bill pulled over at a quaint, mom-and-pop restaurant in Bloomfield, a five-mile jaunt from the northern edge of Canandaigua Lake. It was almost lunchtime, and both men were hungry. They ordered homemade dishes from a thick menu. Eugene jotted down some notes while Bill perused a local newspaper.

The first question on Eugene's mind was why was there no match between the names on the hotel registry and the new Renault owners? What was he missing? When Pablo wanted to talk with Mario, he had Correa fly up from Miami and meet him in Rochester. Eugene presumed that Pablo wanted the meeting in the city because it was convenient for him. And convenience meant that Pablo must live nearby. That was the assumption that he had been basing everything on. That Pablo was living somewhere close to Rochester. But if that were true and Pablo had a house close by, then why would he stay at the Clarion?

Christ, that was it. Pablo drove into Rochester for the

meetings. He didn't stay at the hotel, he simply used it as a meeting place. That's why his name wasn't on the hotel registry. Eugene kicked himself for making that wrong assumption; the mistake had cost him time when he should have been looking elsewhere for corroboration of Pablo's new name. So the hotel registry was out. But the much shorter list of new Renault owners was in. That was good; it would be much easier to deal with a list of nine individuals than page after page of names and addresses, most of them from out-of-state.

He jotted that down. *Pablo not registered at hotel, need another source for his name.* Without some sort of corroboration on Pablo's new name, he was left with chasing down all nine Renault owners and hoping he found Pablo first, rather than last. Too much risk that he would run out of time. He needed something more definitive. But what?

Think. Why did Pablo choose the Canadian Imperial Bank of Commerce in the Bahamas? Why not some other bank? A local bank with the head office in the Bahamas or the Caymans. Why a Canadian bank? He pulled out the map and stared at it. Rochester was as far north as you could go and still be in the United States. The southern border of Canada was just across Lake Ontario. Was there a connection? Is that why Pablo had chosen to live in such a cold climate; because he needed access to Canada? But if that were the case, then why not just live in Canada? He had no answer to that question. But maybe that explained why Pablo had chosen Rochester. He needed to be close to the border.

Okay, now he was getting somewhere. Pablo needed to be near the Canadian border. But why? Did he have family in Canada? No, that didn't make sense. Juan Pablo and the rest of his immediate family were in the Caribbean. What about a business? Was Pablo running some sort of legitimate business based in Canada? That would explain the transfers from the offshore CIBC branch in the Bahamas. Maybe. But why? Pablo probably didn't need money, or he'd have withdrawn funds from the Swiss account years ago. Maybe he'd been reluctant to withdraw money from the Swiss account because the activity could raise red flags, which was exactly what had happened. But maybe he *did* have a thriving business, and he didn't need money. Maybe he was living off the profits of his latest venture. Pablo may have figured Mario and Javier Rastano would finally lose interest in monitoring the account. If that were the reason for finally transferring some of the money, his judgment had been very poor. The Rastanos had not forgotten the billion-dollar account.

Their very efficient waitress, a smiling woman in her mid-thirties, set the check on the table, and asked, "Anything else?"

"No, thank you," Eugene said, laying down forty dollars and telling her to keep the change—more of Rastano's money going to a nice person, he thought. "Let's go," he said to Bill, "I want to get the money to Ben and Andrew."

"No problem," Bill said, smiling. He had fifteen hundred dollars in his pocket and was one very happy man.

The drive to Finger Lakes gave Eugene more time to think. But this time it wasn't about Pablo. Irwin Crandle occupied his mind. The senator was a disgrace, and he needed to be toppled. It wouldn't be easy. But with the evidence on the DEA computers, all he needed to do was get the truth rolling and it would find its way out. Crandle's connection to the Rastano family would destroy him, just as a murder conviction would see him rot in jail. And the rat was gone. If Eduardo Garcia could take care of Crandle, then Rastano's eyes and ears inside the team were silenced. Then Eugene had another thought, one that made his stomach bile rise.

Jorge Shweisser, the banker murdered in the picturesque city of Zurich. Murdered because he had succumbed to the lure of working for both Pablo and Rastano. But it was not in Rastano's best interest to kill the

banker. The only person who would have wanted
Shweisser dead was Pablo. But how could Pablo have
known that the team was sending someone to visit
Shweisser unless Pablo was being kept in the loop. And
one thing was for certain: Irwin Crandle was not playing
both sides of this mess, or he would have brokered a deal
for the ten-digit code without involving Eugene Escobar,
Cathy Maxwell, Alexander Landry and Bud Reid. And the
last thing Crandle needed was to have Fernando Garcia's
nephew hanging around. No, it wasn't Crandle who was
feeding Pablo his intel. Which could only mean one thing.

There was another snitch in the group. If Crandle wasn't
working both sides, then someone else was Pablo's spy.

Eugene rubbed his temples and tried to clear the cob-
webs. Christ, he had just figured out the identity of one informant and now he had another. His brain ached as he
tried to keep the neural pathways from shorting out under
the stress. Three people were left in the running: Maxwell,
Landry and Reid. One of them was dirty. He placed Cathy
Maxwell extremely low on the list because Pablo was responsible for her parents' deaths. Landry and Reid were
about even. They were both involved in the search for Pablo
after his escape from La Catedral prison, and either one
could have been on Pablo's payroll all along. Pablo had had
many miraculous escapes from the American forces under
Centra Spike and the Colombian army. Too many. And this
explained why. One of the major players had been taking
his *plata* and feeding him information. He closed his eyes
and wished the whole mess would just go away.

It didn't happen.

They skirted the village of Canandaigua and pulled
onto the campus grounds at one-thirty. Eugene went to
the Registrar's Office and persuaded them to tell him
which class Ben Chadi was in. Computer Sciences, third
floor, room 312. He took the stairs and found the class-
room without any trouble. When he poked his head in

the door, Ben saw him, spoke to the teacher, and joined Eugene in the hallway.

"Hi," Ben said. "Good to see you. Everything okay?"

"Fine," Eugene said, handing him a pre-counted stack of bills. "All even. Thanks a million, Ben."

"My pleasure." His face was glowing at the sight of the cash. "Any problems with using Quigley's house?"

"None that I know of." He looked up and down the empty hallway. "Do you know where Andrew is right now?"

"Yeah, he's in a chemistry lab. I'll show you, if you want."

"Sure. That would be great." They started walking, and Eugene said, "Andrew and I were talking while you were in Sarah Quigley's computer. I thought he was a biology major."

Ben steered Eugene down the stairs onto the second floor. "He is, but the two overlap. He takes chem, biology, zoology, and a lot of math." They reached a door on the lower floor, and Ben rapped sharply. A teacher opened the door.

"Can I help you?" she asked.

"Andrew Livingston, please," Ben said. "His uncle's in from out of town."

She smiled at Eugene, and said, "He's almost finished. If you can wait a minute, I'll get him."

Eugene and Ben stood at the door looking in at the rows of lab tables that were covered with beakers, test tubes and burners. The twenty or so students were all busy with experiments, and paid no attention to the diversion at the door. Andrew's head was down and he was writing something in a log book. The teacher tapped him on the shoulder and pointed at the door. She said something to him, and he smiled, removed his safety glasses, gathered his books and approached the door.

"Hi, Eugene," he said. "How are things?"

Eugene didn't answer. He was staring into the lab room. Something was in the recesses of his mind, trying

to get out. Something important. He stared at the assortment of lab equipment for a moment longer, then answered Andrew. "Everything's great. I've got your money."

"Hey, a man of his word."

"Yeah," Ben said, exposing the tip of the wad Eugene
had given him. "Check this out."

"Holy shit," Andrew said. "The freakin' mother lode."
He accepted the cash from Eugene. "Thanks, buddy."

"You guys helped me out. It's the least I can do. Thanks
again."

They shook, and he left them, two very happy students
with no worries about where their weekend beer money
would come from. He exited the building, but glanced
back. The chemistry lab was bugging him; some bit of information was locked away in his brain but he didn't have
the key. Why would a college chemistry lab create a spark
somewhere in his memory banks? He thought back to the
ill-fated day at Pablo's Nápoles estate. The cocaine lab in
the jungle, the realization that Pablo was indeed a *narco*.
They weren't pretty memories.

But how were the two related? Cocaine couldn't be processed without certain chemicals. Along with being the
enforcer, one of Pablo's main functions for the Medellín
cartel had been to procure the hydrochloric acid, acetone
and ether for the labs. Centra Spike and DEA had gone
after the chemicals, attempting to stop the shipments before they reached Colombia. Without the chemicals there
would be no processed cocaine.

Then, like a blast of water from a high-pressure sprayer,
it hit him. The chemicals. Pablo had not only been an expert on violence and moving cocaine into America, he
was also an expert on the chemicals used to process the
raw coca leaf. Eugene was shaking with anticipation when
he got back to the car.

"Bill," he said, barely able to breathe. "Get me to an Internet café. I need to go online."

Chapter Fifty-five

Eduardo Garcia took the stairs two at a time. Since he wasn't able to get to the gym and keep up his regular workout, the stairs helped keep him in shape. He reached the fire door on five and yanked the handle. He walked briskly down the hall, fished his room key from a pocket, swiped it through the reader and opened the door. Moments after he closed the door, there was a soft knock. Garcia opened the door and found the woman from the front desk in the hall.

"Mr. Garcia, I have a message for you. But I must ask, are you alone?"

"Yes. Why?"

The receptionist fished a piece of paper from her pocket. "Could you please tell me the last eight digits of the credit card you used when you checked in?"

"What the hell is going on?" Eduardo asked, getting angry.

"Mr. Garcia, I have a message for you. But it is only for you, no one else. I must make sure it is you."

"All right," Garcia said, pulling out his wallet. Palming the credit card, he read, "6493 9018."

"Thank you. The message is from Eugene Escobar. Please call him at this number." She handed him the piece of paper. On it were written his credit card number, and Eugene's phone number, including the area code. "And Mr. Garcia, Señor Escobar was adamant. Only you must know about this."

"Thank you." He closed the door and sat down on the edge of the bed, fingering the tiny piece of paper. Eugene Escobar, the very man they were hunting, had called and left a message for him. Why him? He plucked the receiver from its cradle and dialed the number. The connection was filled with static, but he recognized Eugene's voice at the other end of the line.

"Eugene, it's Eduardo Garcia. What can I do for you?"

"Thanks for calling. Anyone else with you right now?" Eugene pressed his back into the hard, wooden slats on the chair and looked away from the computer to concentrate on the phone call. The small Internet café was quiet, and despite a bit of static, he was able to hear Garcia quite clearly.

"No. I'm alone in my hotel room."

"I've got some information which you may find rather unsettling. But I think you deserve to hear it."

"Go ahead."

"Your uncle, Fernando, he was a logistics expert with the DEA and stationed in Bogotá back in '93. Correct?"

"Yes."

"Then they moved him to Medellín?"

"Yes. They wanted him closer to the labs and airstrips."

"Well, the storyline the DEA was fed by the agent in the field about how your uncle died is a lie. He was killed by another agent, not drug traffickers. But I think you suspected that, didn't you?"

There was silence for a minute, then Eduardo said, "It

was his sister, my aunt, who suspected they were covering up something. She tried to dig into it, but she got stonewalled. The agency was hesitant to give her any information; everything was always deemed classified. She finally gave up about three years ago."

"But you've continued to look around, in a covert sort of way?"

"Sort of," Eduardo said. "Listen, Eugene, I like my job and I don't want to say anything to jeopardize it. If the agency finds out I'm digging around in an old file, I could get fired."

Eugene almost laughed at the absurdity of it. Him going to Alexander Landry and tattling on one of his agents. "Eduardo, I'm going to tell you what happened to your uncle. And who has been passing information back to Javier Rastano."

Eugene spent the next five minutes detailing out his findings and giving Eduardo the file names in the DEA database for confirmation. He gave the young agent Crandle's code name and explained how he had cross-correlated the two files and discovered it was Crandle who was working for Rastano. He had Garcia copy the path Ben had taken through the DEA computer to the two files. It would be much easier for Garcia to find the elusive files with the pathway.

"Now you know," Eugene said when he was finished.

"Christ, Eugene, this guy is a United States senator. Who is going to believe me over him?"

"He's also a traitor and a murderer, Eduardo. And the proof is on the DEA database. And from what I've been told, it's protected with some sort of anti-erase software. The evidence to convict Crandle is there, you just have to be ready to use it."

"Why me?" he asked.

"Two reasons, Eduardo. First, the guy killed your uncle. Shot him in the back. And payback is always nice. And second, there is still one more mole in your little group. And this person is feeding Pablo information: Cathy Maxwell, Alexander Landry or Bud Reid. You're the only person I can trust."

"What are you talking about, another mole in the group?"

Eugene explained his logic. "Crandle is Rastano's boy. But we know someone is keeping Pablo abreast of our progress, too. And that Pablo knows we're after him. That's part of the reason I left El Paso, Eduardo. You guys can't make a move without both Pablo and Rastano knowing, and I doubt we'll ever find Pablo if he knows we're coming."

There was a moment of silence, then Eduardo said, "Okay. I understand. And thanks for the info on my uncle. Maybe we'll see each other soon."

"Maybe."

"And, Eugene, the police know you're driving a blue Saturn. You should get rid of it."

"Thank you."

Before Eugene returned to the Internet connection, he walked out into the late afternoon sun and spoke to Bill, telling him to take off and ditch the car. He thanked the driver for his time, paid him for the final day and returned to the computer screen. He desperately needed to find some kind of corroboration of one of the nine names on the DMV list.

And he was feeling confident that he knew how to do it.

Chapter Fifty-six

The guards performed their perfunctory evening check, picked up the supper dishes and let themselves out, locking the door behind them. Julie threw Shiara a nervous glance and wet her lips.

"You ready?" Julie asked.

"I guess so," Shiara replied. She was shaking with fear.

Julie hugged her daughter and held the trembling girl close. "It's going to be okay, honey. You father has until tomorrow. He may get what Mr. Rastano wants."

"But once we're in the air duct, that's it," Shiara said. "There's no turning back."

"We can't wait until daylight. We need the darkness so we can move once we're outside the house. We have to go tonight."

"Okay." Shiara was settling down, her breathing more regular, the shaking almost subsided. She would need to be relaxed in the duct or she could hyperventilate, and that would be dangerous in the confined space. "I think I'm ready," she said calmly.

"Excellent," Julie said, smoothing her daughter's hair. "Then let's go."

They removed the screws from the grate, but this time Julie put four of the screws back in, almost flush with the wall, two at the bottom corners and two at the top. She gave them a couple of twists. Then she hooked the grate on the protruding bottom screws and let it hang down, just below the hole in the wall. Julie went first. Shiara then got on top of the dresser and, with great difficulty, entered the duct feet first. When she was completely in—her running shoes touching the soles of Julie's running shoes—she lifted the grate up and secured it on the top screws. The procedure took just a few minutes, but the grate was almost flush with the wall and disguised the entrance to their escape route. They had decided that if the guards did come in while they were still in the ducts, that they would still stand a better chance of escaping if the avenue they had used to get out of the locked room wasn't immediately clear.

The downside to the plan was that Julie was leading, and this was her first time in the ducts. Being smaller, Shiara had to be the one who went backwards, and carried the screwdriver. Shiara could guide her when they came to the forks, and could keep up with her mother, even moving backward. But when they came to the grate on the other end, the older woman would have to drop through onto the concrete floor. Both Julie and Shiara were intensely worried about the possibility of broken bones.

"I've reached the first fork," Julie said quietly, as her hands felt the main shaft split into three different ducts.

"Take the left one," Shiara said, her voice traveling easily through the metal tunnel.

They continued through the darkness. Julie had been

warned by Shiara to watch for the sharp metal edges, and she felt every inch with quivering fingertips. She reached a second junction and Shiara again gave directions. Julie was feeling the effects of being in such a claustrophobic environment for almost an hour, and felt a newfound respect for her daughter's bravery in searching out their route, alone and in such an unforgiving place. Finally, a glimmer of light reflected off the metal ductwork. The end was in sight. They kept moving, Shiara pushing herself backwards through the ducts, keeping her shoes in contact with her mother's. When Julie reached the grate at the end of the duct, Shiara placed the screwdriver beside her in the duct, then they both backed up until Julie's groping hand found it. Even moving back ten feet had been almost impossible, and she realized that if they couldn't get out the opening, they were trapped.

"Don't drop the screwdriver," Shiara cautioned her mother, "or that grate isn't coming off."

"I'll be careful," Julie said. She pressed her face against the grill until she could see the heads of the screws. Then she gripped the screwdriver between her index and middle finger and slid it though the grate. It took almost fifteen minutes per screw, turning them an eighth of a turn each time, before she had loosened all four screws. When the last one fell to the floor, she grabbed the grate and pushed. It swung off its moldings and hung suspended in the air, cluched tightly in her right hand. She pulled herself forward until her head and shoulders were out of the duct and hanging over the concrete floor. A pile of boxes sat against the wall. Holding her breath, she carefully tossed the grate on top of the boxes. It landed safely without much noise. A solitary emergency beacon provided enough light to see about the room. She looked down.

The floor was at least eight feet, probably closer to nine feet, below her. There was nothing to break her fall; she was going to go head-first onto the concrete. Their escape depended on her ability to hit with her hands first and roll with the impact. If she was badly injured, hope was gone. She pushed herself farther out into thin air, until just her hips and legs were left in the shaft. The muscles in the small of her back and her abs were burning from the exertion of holding the upper half her body rigid. She gripped the edge of the shaft with both hands and pushed with every bit of strength she had.

Her legs cleared the edge of the duct and then she was falling. Falling fast and slightly off balance. The floor came up too fast and her hands were unable to break the fall. She felt the back of her head hit the concrete, and she rolled as best she could with the impact. Excruciating pain shot through her body, down her spine, through her arms and legs. Her brain felt like it was going to explode. Then there was blackness.

When Julie came to, she could hear Shiara quietly calling to her. She tried to move her right arm, but nothing happened. Then her left. She saw that hand rise, and was relieved that she wasn't paralyzed. She tried moving her right arm again, and this time felt pressure near the small of her back. She rolled slightly to the left and tried again. She realized she had been lying on her arm, and pulled it out from under her. She raised both hands and twisted them in the air. Neither arm was broken, and her wrists seemed fine too. She heard Shiara call again, and glanced up. Shiara's feet were sticking out of the duct. She was waiting for Julie to help her.

"I'm okay, Shiara," Julie said quietly, now moving her legs and wiggling her toes about. She arched her back, then rolled over. The motion sent a wave of pain through her skull that almost made her scream. She moved slower, but managed to get to her feet. She was dizzy, and felt like she was going to pass out, but somehow she stayed on her feet. "Can you wait another minute, sweetheart?" she asked. "I need a little time to get my senses back."

"Sure," Shiara said. "Take as long as you need. I'm not going anywhere."

"Thanks," Julie said. She sat down again, feeling less dizzy. A couple of minutes later, she got up and stood beneath Shiara. "Anytime you're ready."

"On three?"

"On three. One, two, three."

Shiara came out of the duct quickly. She pushed off hard to avoid catching her upper body on the sharp edges. Julie broke her fall, grabbing her legs and letting her daughter slide through her arms, then tightening her grip just before Shiara hit the floor. The impact sent Julie off balance, and she went down to the concrete again, hard on her back. Her head snapped back and hit the floor, and she was out cold for the second time in ten minutes. When she revived, her head was resting in her daughter's lap.

"You okay?" Shiara asked, her face gray with worry.

Julie tried to move but the pain in her skull was too much. "I've got one hell of a headache," she said. "But other than that, I think I'm all right."

"Excellent," Shiara said. She looked for and found the small window she had seen from the duct. "There's our next challenge," she said.

Chapter Fifty-seven

Eduardo Garcia flipped open his laptop and connected to the Internet. He went directly to the files that Eugene Escobar had given him, reading the text on the lab raid that had claimed the life of his uncle. There wasn't much doubt about it; the author of the report considered the death to be a result of friendly fire. And Dragonfly was the shooter. He pulled up the classified file on Senator Irwin Crandle. His code name during his tenure in Colombia was Dragonfly. Eugene had been telling the truth. Somehow, for all these years, Crandle had managed to suppress the incriminating files.

He shook his head in disbelief. Crandle had been along for the ride, feeding Javier and Mario Rastano the team's progress as they tracked Pablo. The son-of-a-bitch. Eduardo checked the clip on his government-issue revolver, and slid it into his shoulder holster. He slipped his jacket on and headed for Irwin Crandle's hotel room. He knocked, and the senator called for him to enter. Eduardo turned the handle, and pushed open the door.

"Come in, Eduardo," he said, turning to face the young DEA agent, a glass of whiskey in his hand. "Where's Bud? We've got to get going. It's already dark out." He faced the muzzle of Eduardo's .38. "What are you doing, Garcia?"

"What am *I* doing? What the hell are *you* doing? *Dragonfly*. I'm not sure which is worse, you selling out to Mario and Javier Rastano or killing my uncle. No matter, you're going down for what you've done."

Crandle didn't move. Then he shrugged and sat down slowly on the edge of the bed. He took a small sip from the glass and let out a deep breath. "You have no idea what it was like," he said. "Locked up in a windowless room, driven to and from work in cars with tinted windows, always moving to keep ahead of the *narcos*. They were all-powerful, Eduardo. *Plata o plomo*, Eduardo. Silver or lead. If you went up against them, you died. It was that simple. You could have every good intention, but that didn't mean shit if you were dead. Do you have any idea how many good agents we lost in Colombia between 1987 and 1993? Hundreds. Hundreds of agents just like your uncle. When I linked up with Mario Rastano, it was for a good reason. It wasn't just the money. It was for the promise that they would stop killing our men, and that they would give us a reasonable number of busts each month. It was a negotiated settlement, Eduardo. It was the best we could do at the time."

"It didn't work out very well for my uncle."

"That should never have happened. You've got to believe me, Eduardo. I didn't go to that lab that day to kill your uncle. Centra Spike had a couple of green guys working the surveillance gear and they failed to notify the advance team that Rastano was at the lab. One simple phone call and it never would have happened."

"But they didn't make that call, did they, Senator?" Garcia's use of Crandle's title dripped with sarcasm. "And you shot my uncle in the back."

Crandle shrugged. "What could I do?"

Garcia reached behind his back and pulled his cuffs from their leather pouch. He threw them to Crandle. "Put them on. You're going in."

"We're trying to find Pablo Escobar, you stupid shit," Crandle hissed. "We only have a few hours."

"What? Or your bonus from Javier Rastano disappears. Tough shit. Put the handcuffs on."

They heard the sound of the handle twisting as someone opened the door. Garcia kept the gun leveled at Crandle, but looked over his shoulder toward the sound. Bud Reid was there, a stunned expression on his face. Garcia glanced back at Crandle just in time to see the silenced pistol, but not in time to react. The bullet caught him in the center of the forehead, crushing his frontal lobe and killing him instantly. He dropped to the carpet without a sound, blood streaming from the round hole just above his unseeing eyes. Crandle turned the gun on Reid and fired twice more, both killing shots. Reid slumped to the floor just inside the door.

"Shit," Crandle cursed under his breath. "God damn you all to hell, Garcia. Now look at the fucking mess I've got to clean up."

Chapter Fifty-eight

The streetlights were on, their soft lights casting a pale yellow glow on the stores and businesses in rural Bloomfield. A few shoppers were out, but the streets were quiet. A light still burned in The Arabian Nights, the Internet café where Eugene was ensconced in a far corner, his fingers busy on the keyboard. A stack of papers littered the table next to him, and the counter on the LaserJet printer was much higher than when he first signed on. The clerk working the front counter didn't care; he had three hundred dollars in his pocket with which to settle up the tab. And the generous customer had told him that anything extra was his to keep.

The clerk stopped by to see how Eugene was faring, and brought a fresh coffee with him. "Everything okay?" he asked Eugene, as he set the coffee down on the table next to the monitor.

"Thanks," Eugene said when he saw the coffee. "Yeah,

everything's fine. Just can't seem to find what I'm looking for."

"What's that?" the kid asked.

"You wouldn't believe me if I told you."

"Try me."

"I'm searching out all the chemicals necessary to process cocaine."

"Now that's not something you hear every day," the
young man said. He shrugged. "Good luck."

"Thanks."

Eugene hunkered down on the computer again, re-
newed with fresh caffeine in his system. But this time the
answer did not elude him for long. He had started his
search of the Internet with 'Pablo Escobar', then tried
'cocaine,' then 'refining cocaine,' until he had hit on
some of the necessary chemicals in the procedure. Once
he had some of the chemical names, he had pulled up
webpage after webpage, and read time and time again
about acetone, ether and hydrochloric acid. But now a
different chemical popped up as he opened a new webpage. Potassium permanganate. The articles inside the
webpage described it as a precursor chemical for the production of cocaine hydrochloride. Eugene pushed on,
uncovering more on the chemical. Once he had its name,
he searched the Internet using 'potassium permanganate,' and got a slew of relevant hits. One thing became
very clear, very quickly.

Potassium permanganate was the key to producing re-
fined cocaine. Without it, there would be no cocaine. Ten
kilos of cocaine can be produced by one kilo of potassium
permanganate, and the cost per kilo for the chemical was
astronomical. It was a natural money-maker for Pablo. He
already had the Colombian connections; getting into the
business of supplying expensive chemicals to the cocaine
industry was just working another part of the process.
And, since potassium permanganate was not found or

manufactured in Colombia, it had to be imported. Once Eugene started looking at where the chemical was made, the Canadian connection became obvious. Most of the companies marketing potassium permanganate were Canadian. Eugene scanned through the hits, jotting down the names of the producers, then opened a path to a registry office, gave them his credit card number and began profiling the directors and owners of the major producers. It took forty minutes and sixteen companies before one of the names scrolling across the screen jarred his memory. Eugene froze the screen and grabbed the list of new Renault owners.

Roland Arnett.

The name was on the list of Renault owners, and the name was on the list of directors for Okomono Chemicals Inc., a Canadian-based, top-level producer of potassium permanganate. Eugene delved into the history of the fantastically successful company. It had a head office in Toronto and subsidiary offices in seven other countries. Colombia was one of the seven. The company regularly shipped the precursor chemical to South America, under the guise of providing a necessary ingredient for the production of computer chip boards. And when Eugene saw the chemical formula for potassium permanganate, he knew he had found Pablo. KM_nO_4—Okomono was an anagram of the chemical formula. Eugene cleaned up the mess around the computer and strode up to the front counter. The clerk was just putting the finishing touches on a mocha that smelled like warm chocolate. He waited until the man had exchanged the specialty coffee for cash.

"I just need a couple more things," he said.

"Sure. Anything."

"A set of white pages for the area, and a taxi."

"I've got the white pages right here," he said, reaching under the counter and lifting out a Rochester and Area telephone book. And you can get a cab two blocks down

at the post office. There are three cabs in town, but one of
them is always parked there waiting." He glanced at the
top page in the pile that Eugene had printed. "Hey, Pablo
Escobar. What a guy. The most notorious gangster in the
history of the world."

Eugene glanced down at the picture. Pablo was lounging comfortably on a leather couch, smoking a cigarette.
The caption under the picture read, "Pablo Escobar, at
home in La Catedral." Eugene flipped open the white
pages and scanned down to where the name Roland Arnett appeared. He copied the address on the paper showing Pablo in La Catedral, and handed the clerk the
remaining pages.

"Recycling," he said. "And thanks for everything."

"No. Thank *you*."

Eugene exited The Arabian Nights and headed in the
direction the clerk had indicated. He walked the two
blocks to the post office, but no cab was at the curb. He
glanced around. A handwritten note was attached to a
telephone post that was beside a bench. It read, "Had to
take Mrs. Murphy home. Will be back in five minutes."
Eugene laughed at the simplicity of small-town life. He sat
on the bench and looked up and down the street. Nothing happening. Most stores were now closed, and there
was no foot traffic. He stared at the piece of paper in his
hand, at the name and address he had written at the top
of page, at the picture of Pablo and then, because he had
nothing better to do, read the text. About halfway
through the article, he sat bolt upright. He read it again
and again. That couldn't be right. The date Pablo left the
prison, the date the Galeano and Moncada brothers were
murdered. No, something was wrong. Something was very
wrong. Unless . . .

Then it all snapped into place, and for the first time he
saw the whole picture. What had been a murky quagmire
of deception and lies was now painfully clear. He knew

who was in tight with Pablo. And he knew why. It was all so simple once the veneer of lies was stripped away. He spotted a phone booth just across the street, and walked over to it. He dialed the number of the hotel and asked for a guest by name. The receptionist put the call through and a voice answered. The voice he knew would answer.

"It took a while," he said, "but now it all makes sense. I know why you're Pablo's accomplice, and I can prove it." Then he hung up.

The figure calmly set the phone in the cradle, then picked it up and dialed another number. Pablo Escobar answered.

"He's figured it out. And I suspect he's on his way to see you."

"When?"

"Now."

"Thank you," Pablo said and hung up.

Chapter Fifty-nine

An hour after her tumble from the duct to the concrete floor, Julie Escobar's head was feeling better. She suspected she had suffered a minor concussion, but definitely had broken no bones. She'd been very lucky, considering the drop. Shiara had helped her drag a bin used for storing glycol directly beneath the window. Standing on the hard plastic container, they could look out the window into the rear garden. A grove of bushes was planted close to the window, and they figured getting out the window without being noticed would be fairly easy. Although the low bushes were an asset in one way, they were a liability in another. They blocked the view. Julie and Shiara had no idea of what lay beyond them.

The window itself wasn't barred, but a padlock secured the sliding portion. Julie found a real screwdriver in a tool kit on one of the shelves, and spent fifteen minutes gouging out the wood from around the lock. When she had weakened the wood base in which the screws were embedded, she levered the metal with the tip of the screw-driver until it gave way. She set the lock on the far side of the jamb and slid open the window. It was her first breath of fresh air in two weeks, and the sweet taste and fra-grance almost floored her. She drank in the air, then hoisted herself up and out the window. Staying low, she crawled to the edge of the bushes and peered out. In front of her was an expanse of open grass, perhaps fifty feet across. Beyond that was a small hump-backed bridge and then a grove of mango trees. If they could make it to the trees, they would have some cover. Julie helped Shiara through the open window. They waited in silence, listen-ing for passing guards or dogs. After twenty minutes, Julie had made her decision.

"We'll try for the trees. Once we're there, we'll have a good view of the back of the house, and maybe an idea how far it is to the property line."

"We don't even know if we're in the country or in a city," Shiara said. "We could get out of here only to find ourselves in some sort of jungle."

"We'll deal with whatever we have to, as it happens. Let's not get off on a tangent."

"Sorry."

Julie clasped her daughter's hand. She could feel the stump where Javier Rastano had sliced off her finger. It re-minded her what kind of person she was dealing with. "It's okay. I think we should go together. Run fast and straight. Keep low. Got it?"

"Got it."

They braced themselves at the edge of the bushes, then when Julie gave the word, they sprinted toward the trees. Fifty feet seemed like a mile, but they made it over the bridge and into the trees. Concealed by the mature man-gos, they remained motionless until their breathing had returned to normal. They could see the back of the house now, a hulking monster of glass and stucco. Only a couple of lights were on, and everything seemed quiet. From their new vantage point they could see a curving walk running between the expansive patio and a swimming pool. The water looked calm and inviting.

The first sign of trouble was a pair of guards moving quickly out the back door and into the garden. Their guns weren't hanging loosely by their sides, but were tucked up close to their ribcages, and their fingers were on the triggers. Lights started to go on in the house, until the entire back of the mansion was lit. They could see shadowy figures moving about in the rooms, but couldn't make out who they were or what they were doing. Another few guards spilled out into the garden, and began looking around.

"They've discovered we're missing," Julie said.

"What do we do?" Shiara asked, scared.

"I don't know, Shiara. I honestly don't know."

Javier Rastano's face turned six shades of red, then one of purple. "What do you mean, the women are gone?"

"Their suite is empty, sir," the guard said. "And there's no sign of how they got out."

"Jesus Christ. Get someone upstairs and check on the boxer. If he's not in his room, I want to know. And scour the house. Turn the lights on and check every room, every closet. Get at least six more men in the garden."

"Yes, sir."

Javier ran down the stairs, through the games room and down the hallway. A couple of guards stood at the door, but he pushed them aside and barged into the suite where Julie and Shiara had been captive for the past two weeks. Everything appeared normal. He moved around the room quickly, into the bedrooms and the bathroom. Once he had ascertained that the women were gone, he slowed down and looked the living room over carefully. Once, twice, then three times, until his eyes finally rested on the air-conditioning grate. Every room in the house had one and, because it was so commonplace, he had even never noticed it before. He looked more closely, and saw that the grate was almost tight against the wall. Almost. And that no screws showed.

He jumped on the dresser under the duct and grabbed the grate in his hands, then gave it a good pull. He looked inside the duct. There was some dust, but only near the edges. He slammed the grate on the floor.

"Get me a schematic of the ductwork on this floor," he yelled.

Pedro noticed the increased activity levels immediately. One of the guards came running in, gave Pedro a curt nod, and searched the room. Pedro asked him what was up, but the man didn't answer. He finished the search and returned to the hall. Pedro could hear as the guard called in on his radio, reporting back that the boxer was in his room, and all was clear.

Pedro clued in on what was going on. Julie and Shiara had escaped.

Pedro jumped off the bed, and dimmed the lights. Then he stood at the window and watched the scene playing out in the back garden. A handful of guards were searching, but it was going to take them hours to cover the entire estate. He watched and waited. If Julie and Shiara had made it out of the house and were still on the grounds, they would be somewhere in the garden. And with all the guards out, they wouldn't be moving. He watched for the slightest motion; a sign that someone was trying to remain motionless, but cramping up. It took almost twenty minutes, but he finally saw a tiny glint of light from the grove of mangos close to the pool. Something or someone had moved. He kept his eyes on the location and, about ten minutes later, he saw a definite movement. Once he had the exact spot, he could make out the dim shape of a person, hunched over and immobile. It had to be Julie or Shiara.

What to do? Leaving them in their current predicament was impossible, they'd never make it to the morning. Their position was too close to the pool, and the guards would be methodical in their search. They'd be discovered in another hour or two. He had to do something.

The gardener's shed was the best option. The guards would have checked it first thing, and probably wouldn't bother to check it again. And his guns were hidden there. If the worst case scenario came to pass, at least he'd have something to defend himself with. He made his decision. He slipped on a dark shirt and pants, checked the hall and ran to the back staircase. If he was careful enough, he should be able to reach the women without the guards seeing. Then they could try for the gardener's shed or go over the far wall. Either option was better than leaving Julie and Shiara to the mercy of the guards.

Chapter Sixty

Alexander Landry was just pulling the Infiniti Q45 out of the above-ground parking lot when there was a rap on the passenger's window. He jerked around, his hand automatically going for his service revolver. Cathy Maxwell's face was looking through the glass at him. He rolled down the window.

"Christ. You scared me," he said.

"Sorry," she said casually. "Where are you going?"

"Just going for a drive to clear my head," he said. "Want to come?" His shooting hand relaxed and rested on the gear shift.

"Why not," Cathy said, waiting at the door, and when Landry hit the automatic door locks, she jumped into the passenger seat and snapped her seat belt in place.

They drove through greater Rochester without speaking. When they reached the southern edge of the city, Landry took the secondary road leading to the hamlet of Honeoye Falls. The road was narrow, without shoulders or lights, and twisted dangerously through the undulating hills. An occasional farm slipped past, but mostly the road was a deserted band of asphalt connecting unknown points. Other than the vehicle's headlights, the faint points of stars and a full moon provided the only light. Landry kept the SUV at just over the posted speed limit.

They drove on. A road sign indicating a side road was briefly illuminated in the headlights and Landry slowed the vehicle. He turned sharply to the right onto the gravel road, the deep grooves in the tires throwing rocks against the undercarriage. He drove a hundred feet or so, then stopped and turned off the engine.

"What's going on, Alexander?" Cathy asked.

"I've got to take a leak," he said, pocketing the keys and sliding out of the driver's seat. "Be right back." He disappeared into the thick underbrush.

Landry was just zipping up when he heard a twig snap behind him. He spun, his hand going for his gun. "Who's there?" he asked the darkness.

"Who do you think?" Cathy Maxwell answered, moving closer, so she was visible. Her pistol was leveled at his chest. "Take your gun out with two fingers and throw it to your right," she said. Her tone of voice left no doubt that she would pull the trigger if he did anything but what she said.

"What the hell are you doing, Cathy? What's going on?" He complied with her demand as he spoke.

"You really are thick, Alexander," she answered, moving to within ten feet of her partner. Enough distance that he couldn't reach her before she fired, and close enough that he stood no chance of escaping into the maze of trees and shrubs.

He glanced at the gun. The safety was off, and her finger was wrapped tightly around the trigger. "You?" he asked incredulously. "You of all people, Cathy? He killed your parents."

She laughed, her icy bark cutting through the cool

night air like a razor. "You know what amazes me, Alexander? That no one, not one person, took the time to have a close look at the whole thing. If they had, what really happened would have been obvious."

"Why don't you tell me, Cathy. I'm genuinely interested."

She smiled. He was buying time, but it didn't matter. The outcome of this confrontation was without doubt. "Pablo was in La Catedral prison when my parents were murdered. Everyone assumed he was responsible, that he had sent his *sicarios* to Boston to do it. But that's the beautiful thing about assumptions, they're often wrong."

"What actually happened?" Alexander asked.

"Fernando Galeano and Gerardo Moncada ordered the hit, and their brothers, Mario Galeano and William Moncada were the killers. They couldn't get to me so they butchered my parents." Her face was contorted with rage. "The bastards were going to get away with murder, Alexander. They were too well insulated by the cartel for us to get to them. I needed another way."

"So you went to Pablo."

"I saw it as my only option. Pablo or the Ochoa brothers were the only ones who could get close enough to the Moncada and Galeano families to exact revenge. I did what I had to."

"But you killed one of his men in front of thirty onlookers."

"He didn't care. In fact, when I snapped that guy's neck, it told him what kind of person I was. For some reason, he took a liking to me. It's what happened after that that no one knows about. Pablo cleared the room. He and I were alone. He knew why I was there. He offered me Moncada's and Galeano's heads in return for my allegiance. I didn't even think twice. I wanted the bastards who had killed my parents more than anything in the world. Cementing a pact with Pablo seemed a fair price to pay."

"Was it?" Alexander asked, his voice filled with disgust.

"Yes. Pablo is a murderer and a drug dealer. But he keeps his word. He's kept up his end of our business arrangement over the past thirteen years. And in all that time he never asked me to give up a single DEA or CIA agent. In return, I've kept quiet about his new life."

"You knew all along that Pablo was still alive?" Alexander asked.

"Of course. I helped him escape from Centra Spike more times than you could possibly imagine. Centra Spike and Delta would have had him numerous times if he hadn't been warned in advance. It was part of the deal. Then he came to me in the summer of 1993 and told me he wanted to disappear. I told him the only way he could hope to get the Americans off his ass was to die. He and I set it up. It went off without a hitch. But you already know all that. Pablo was dead and the cartel finally collapsed. We all went home. I hitched up with Darren and got on with my life. Of course, it wasn't Pablo who died in that tiny courtyard."

Landry was truly puzzled. "But you called Darren from the restaurant and told him to get out of the house, that you were worried about Pablo coming for your kids."

She laughed again, a sinister sound that carried through the chilly night air. "For a high-ranking DEA agent, you really are stupid, Alexander. Darren moved the kids in case Eugene actually got to Pablo and my involvement in this somehow leaked out. We have a house in a country without an extradition treaty with the States. He took the kids there. I can run if I have to."

"You sick bitch," Landry said.

Her body trembled with rage. "You brought this on yourself, Alexander. All I needed was the vehicle to get to Pablo's house. But you had to pick just that time to go for a drive. Now look at the mess we're in."

"How does it end?" he asked quietly.

"You die," she said, pulling the trigger. The first bullet smashed into his breastbone and deflected enough to miss his heart, but the second and third bullets found their mark. They bored through flesh and muscle and tore his heart apart. Landry dropped to the forest floor, blood pouring from the gaping wounds.

"I noticed you didn't wear your Kevlar vest tonight," Cathy whispered, as she watched him bleed out on the ground. She waited ten minutes, until the blood was beginning to congeal. Then she left.

It was time to visit Pablo.

Chapter Sixty-one

Pedro stole through the house in his socks, holding his shoes. He reached one of the side doors leading to the garden and slipped on his Nikes. Using the ornamental shrubs and eucalyptus as cover, he ran from tree to tree until he reached the cover of the mango grove, fifty feet from the house. He waited for a minute, listening for the guards, then whispered.

"Julie, it's Pedro. I'm coming to you. Don't say a word."

He moved through the trees to where he had spotted the women from the window. Julie and Shiara were crouched behind the shrubs, amazement painted on both their faces. He put his finger up to his mouth, and shook his head.

"Follow me. We'll try to make the gardener's shed." He sliced through the trees with a natural agility, the women close behind. They were forced to wait quietly a few times as groups of guards marched past, intent on checking another part of the estate. They were getting close to the shed when Pedro moved out from his cover just as a guard rounded the corner.

"What the hell are you doing out here?" he asked, as he recognized Pedro.

"Javier wants everyone looking for the women," Pedro said. "Me included."

The guard relaxed his grip on his weapon. "You see anything?"

"Nope. I was just looking through those trees, but all I saw was a couple of toucans."

"Okay." The man continued down the path, and Pedro motioned for the women to follow. They were close to the shed, just one more open expanse of grass near the rear wall. The guards patrolling the perimeter and searching for the escaped women were scarcer here, and Pedro figured their chances were good. He waited until the moon disappeared behind a cloud and then whispered, "Let's go." The three of them sprinted the eighty feet to the trees that delineated the shed area. They reached the thicket safely. Pedro pointed to the small building tucked against the wall.

They dashed inside. "Oh my God, Pedro," Julie cried, hugging her friend close. "How on earth . . . ?"

"I've been in the house for a few days," He swept Shiara into his arms too, and held them both close. "But I didn't know where Rastano was keeping you."

"We were in a room in the basement," Shiara said.

"How did you escape?" Pedro asked, grinning at the teenager. He was overcome with happiness to see them alive and well.

"Through an air-conditioning duct. It wasn't easy."

"I'm sure it wasn't," Pedro said. He steered them to the back of the shed and rigged up the tools and machines so they could hide behind them. Then he retrieved his guns.

He checked the breach in the H & K and took off the safety. He tucked the pistol in his belt. "How are your hands?"

"Okay. No infection," Julie said. "Pedro, where is Eugene?"

"Last time I spoke with him he was in Rochester, New York. He said he was close to finding Pablo."

"Well, maybe he won't have to. We may be able to get out of here on our own." Julie wiped her brow and asked, "Where are we, Pedro?"

"At Rastano's estate in San Salvador."

"We're in the city? If we get over the walls we should be safe."

"Maybe," Pedro said. "But he's got cameras covering the entire fence line. If we go over someone will see us and they'll know exactly where we are. I think we're better to stay here for a while. Collect our thoughts. Let the guards finish their search."

Tears formed in Shiara's eyes. "They were going to kill us tomorrow, Pedro," she said.

"Yes, I know. So does Eugene. He knows he's on a tight schedule."

"Do you think he'll find Pablo and get what they want?"

Pedro nodded. "I think so. I know he's close."

Chapter Sixty-two

Roland Arnett.

Eugene stared at the name and the address. If the truth were known about Mr. Arnett, it would make the front page of almost every newspaper in the world.

Pablo Escobar. Alive.

He studied the tourist map the taxi driver had given him. Pablo lived on a quiet cul-de-sac fronting onto Conesus Lake, a popular location for second homes for some of Rochester's more elite families. According to the blurb on the map, Conesus Lake was an excellent place to spend a million dollars on a getaway house. Eugene was sure Pablo's house would fit right in. He looked out into the blackness beyond the car window, and thought back to a couple of weeks ago when he'd lived simply on the shores of Margarita with Julie and Shiara, safe and happy. So much had happened, so many twists and turns. He shifted slightly and felt the cold metal of the Glock pushing into his back. And here was yet another twist. Now Eugene was hunting the killer.

Cathy Maxwell's involvement had come as complete surprise. A total shock. She had been Pablo's eyes and ears inside the DEA for all these years. Pablo hadn't killed her parents, Moncada and Galeano had. She had gone to La Catedral to enlist Pablo's help in tracking down the killers and exacting justice. The date that she visited the prison confirmed it. He knew that she would be coming after him now. She had to. Her secret was compromised.

How the evening would play out he had no idea. But one thing was certain: he had to secure the release of Julie and Shiara. Ultimately whether his women lived or died was up to Pablo. But he had done his part; he had set out to find Pablo and he had succeeded. He knew in his heart that Roland Arnett was the supposedly dead Colombian, and that soon they would meet face to face. The cab began to slow. The time had arrived. His driver pulled into a paved access road and crept up to the gate, which opened as he approached. The trees thinned, then opened up to reveal a single-story house with a steeply pitched roof and gables. The house was awash in light that flooded from the windows and exterior globes. His driver slowed to a gentle stop by the front door. Eugene paid him, got out, and watched the car disappear down the drive. He looked up and saw a man standing in the door. As he came to within a few feet, he recognized the face as one he knew from when he was young.

"Hello, Miguel," he said, extending his hand.

The other man accepted the hand, and said, "You remember my name after all these years, Eugenio. I'm surprised."

"Same name as my son," Eugene said. "And that afternoon we spent on the dirt bikes at Nápoles is still a vivid memory."

"You're here to see Mr. Arnett."

"Please."

"Any weapons?"

Eugene smiled. Some things never changed. He reached behind his back, and extracted the Glock from his belt. He handed it to Miguel, who slipped it under his coat. Miguel pointed to the interior of the house, then led him through a grand foyer to a massive room overlooking the lake. A fire crackled in the hearth. One other person was in the room. He sat on the couch, near the roaring fire.

"Hello, Eugenio," Pablo said. He did not move from his place or offer his hand.

"Pablo," Eugene said, amazed by the change in the man whose pictures he had seen back in the early '90s. Here was a trim and clean-shaven man. His skin was pale, and he looked just like an American who lived in the northern states.

"Come in, please, and sit down. Near the fire is good. It is so cold, even in the spring." Pablo spoke unaccented English.

Eugene sat on the end of the couch, opposite Pablo, and facing him. Miguel sat in a leather chair, a few yards away. Now that he was here, Eugene did not know what to do or say, and he spent a few moments looking around the room. It was very American with open-beam ceilings and cream-colored walls. The fireplace was river rock and burned real wood, not gas and fire logs like so many of the new ones. The furniture was all light beige leather and the tables were maple with glass tops.

Pablo broke the silence. "So you were given an impossible task by Javier Rastano, yet you managed to succeed. I'm impressed, Eugenio. But I have to pay a price for your success." Pablo motioned to Miguel, who poured two glasses of Crown Royal. "I won't be safe here any longer. I will have to move."

Eugene didn't care that this man was impressed, or

whether Pablo had to move. He hadn't arrived at this point in his journey to hear praise or to give sympathy.

"Your success is unfortunate for me. You've found me and now others will find me. I will have to leave this place, Eugenio. I don't like the climate, but I've had a satisfying life here for a lot of years. It's not my choice to go into hiding, to make a whole new life for myself somewhere else. You've forced this on me."

Eugene was incensed by Pablo's indifference to his plight. "I haven't forced anything on you. You and the Rastanos have forced this on me. I'm just a pawn, Pablo. As are my wife and daughter in this terrible game you play with other people's lives."

"You're in my house now, Eugenio. You're not in a position to get angry."

Eugene mellowed in his tone of voice, but not his choice of words. "I don't know you, Pablo. But I do know that what happens to my family is entirely up to you. We live or die on what you decide. But I will not kiss your ass, Pablo. So let's just finish this game. You've got a number Javier Rastano wants. I need that number."

"I know all this, Eugenio. And the game, as you call it, is almost finished. I've done what I had to do to stop the news of my survival from going any further. The team you were working with, they're all dead. You and Cathy Maxwell are the only ones left."

"Dead? What are you talking about? What's happened to them?"

Miguel answered. "Senator Crandle killed them."

"How do you know this?" Eugene asked.

Pablo waved his hand as if brushing off an inconsequential bug and said, "Crandle has been getting out of hand lately. The power he has in Washington has gone to his head. He was going to be caught sooner or later, and then he'd search out a deal to save his skin. Which wouldn't have been good for the Rastano family or for me." Pablo shook his head. "Miguel was at the hotel to re-move Senator Crandle. He just didn't get there quickly enough to save young Garcia. So Crandle's dead. I was go-ing to take care of him at some point anyway. This just happened to become an opportune time. The prick was Mario Rastano's boy, nothing more."

"Yeah, I figured that out. Crandle was feeding Mario Rastano information as far back as the early '80s. But it was the raid on the lab where Fernando Garcia was killed that really tied the two at the hip."

"You should go into the investigation business, Euge-nio. You've figured it all out."

"Not the ending, Pablo. The ending is up to you."

Except for the crackling fire, the room was quiet.

The doorbell rang. Miguel got up and left the room. They waited in silence, then Cathy Maxwell entered the room, Miguel right behind her. She saw Eugene. She stopped, reached her right hand inside her coat and came out with a pistol. She aimed it directly at Eugene.

"You son-of-a-bitch," she said. "You've ruined every-thing."

"Cathy. Put the gun away." Pablo spoke calmly.

She held the gun outstretched for another few seconds, then holstered it and sat down. No one disobeyed Pablo. "What are you going to do about him?" she asked Pablo.

"I haven't decided." Pablo let his eyes wander from Eu-gene to where she sat. "What happened to Landry?"

"I had to kill him. And that's going to bring a lot of heat down on me. I'm going to have to leave the country."

"Landry's dead. Reid, Garcia and Crandle are dead. There's going to be a lot of heat, a lot of questions. And not just for you."

Maxwell looked hard at Pablo. "What happened to the others?"

"Crandle killed Reid and Garcia, and Miguel killed Crandle. There are just too many people who know I'm alive and where I live. Christ, Eugenio, I wish you were a little dumber." He paused and took a sip of whiskey. "Miguel, take care of our problem."

Miguel rose, a gun in his hand. He walked toward Eugene until he was midway between him and a smug looking Cathy Maxwell. "Sorry," he said, then spun and fired one bullet into Cathy Maxwell's brain. The back of her skull exploded and brain and skull fragments spattered against the chair and the wall.

"What the hell . . ." Eugene's breath was coming in short gasps. He thought he was going to faint.

"Ordinarily, I wouldn't ruin a perfectly good chair," Pablo said to Eugene. "But we're leaving tonight, so it doesn't matter." He walked over to where Cathy Maxwell's body lay and stared at her dead eyes.

"I had to make a decision, Eugenio," Pablo said. "At first, I was going to kill you if you got close. But in the end, I suppose you can say that blood is thicker than water. But not in the way you think. I have no hold over Cathy Maxwell. Like the senator, she would have talked to save her skin. But you, Eugenio, you have a family. You won't talk." He paused and his face grew serious. "But you still have a problem, Eugenio."

"Julie and Shiara."

"Javier Rastano will kill them, you know that."

"Yes."

Pablo scratched the back of his neck. "What's the value of a life, Eugenio? Is it a billion dollars? That seems a little steep."

"I suppose it depends on the life. I think Julie and Shiara are worth it."

Pablo managed a small smile. "Of course you do. But you're being rather subjective here, Eugenio."

"This is a hell of an opportunity to get some serious karma on your side, Pablo. A billion dollars for two lives buys a lot of absolution."

Pablo was silent for the better part of a minute. Somewhere in the room, a clock ticked. The sound was deafening. "All right, cousin. You played the game well. You deserve a chance to save your wife and daughter." He picked up a pen from the desk and wrote something on a piece of paper. He handed it to Eugene. On the paper, in blue ink, were ten digits.

The numbers swam in front of Eugene's eyes. He couldn't focus. He and his family had gone through hell. For this. For a number. Finally, he pocketed it and said, "Thanks, Pablo."

"It's okay."

Eugene glanced about. "I need to use a telephone."

Pablo shook his head. "No way. Javier Rastano is a snake, Eugenio. He will take the code, verify it, then kill your family. You have to see him face-to-face and negotiate the release of Julie and Shiara."

Eugene stared at Pablo. "I'm in Rochester, for Christ's sake. There's no way to get to San Salvador in time. Crandle's plane is the only way I could possibly get there, and it'll be grounded once they find all the bodies at the hotel."

"But mine won't," Pablo said. "Okomono owns a corporate Gulfstream. It's useless to me now. You may as well use it. I'll call the airport and have the pilot file a flight plan for San Salvador. We have to leave tonight as well, but not by plane. That method leaves a trail."

"And now you disappear again?" Eugene asked.

"Yes. In fact," Pablo said, pouring another drink, "it will be nice to get back to some decent weather. But please, Eugenio, don't come looking for me again."

"Not a chance," he said, shaking Pablo's hand. Miguel fished Eugene's Glock from inside his suit jacket and handed it over, grip first.

Eugene took one last look at Cathy Maxwell's body, then left Pablo's house with a set of car keys, directions to the executive hangar at the Rochester airport, and a ten-digit code in his pocket. It was almost three in the morning in Rochester, making it after midnight in San Salvador. Saturday morning.

The deadline had arrived.

As he drove through the dark back roads toward Rochester, he had a final thought, an idea that might help his position when it came time to negotiate for the release of his family. He needed to make one more phone call, but he could do that from the plane.

Then it would be time to meet Javier Rastano.

Chapter Sixty-three

The first rays of sun filtered through the eucalyptus and mango trees, quickly heating the air inside the gardener's shed to an uncomfortable level. The night had been a series of close calls, with Javier's men roaming the estate and popping in and out of the shed with no regularity. Sleep was impossible and the constant threat of being discovered was wearing on already frayed nerves. Pedro had gone out a few times during the night, scouting possible escape routes, but the cameras mounted atop the estate walls covered every inch, and scaling the wall would have simply resulted in their capture. They were now relying entirely on Eugene to arrive in time.

Shiara was having trouble breathing, her asthma acting up in response to the heavy scent of cut grass and fertilizers that permeated the small shed. There was no water, and all three were quickly becoming dehydrated as the temperature inside and outside the building rose. Pedro recognized the signs of dehydration and scoured every corner of the shed for something to drink. He came up empty.

"We can't survive all day without water," he said to Julie. Shiara's head was in her mother's lap and the teenager's breathing was shallow.

"What if Eugene doesn't make it?" Julie asked quietly.

Pedro shrugged. "We're doing the best we can. Getting off the estate with all these armed guards is impossible. We've got to hope Eugene makes it in time."

Pedro heard a sound and glanced over the row of machinery. Inside the shed and only five feet from where they hid stood one of Rastano's men, his gun pointed at Pedro's head. Pedro ducked as a spray of automatic gunfire raked the air where he had been only a split second before. He leveled the pistol and pumped off four rounds through a gap between the ride-on mower and a fertilizer attachment. All four bullets hit the target and the man staggered backwards, hit the door and crashed into the garden, blood oozing from his mouth. Pedro ran forward to the shed door and pulled it closed, then smashed a small hole through the wood so he had a line of vision on anyone approaching. He took a breath and readied the automatic.

Rastano's men would be coming.

Chapter Sixty-four

The Gulfstream taxied to the executive terminal at San Salvador's airport and came to a halt. Customs and immigration officials boarded the plane immediately, partially out of a desire to see the inside of the thirty-five million dollar aircraft, and partly to check the incoming traveler's documentation. They gave Eugene a bit of a hard time, mostly because he was traveling with a Venezuelan passport on a jet registered in the United States, but after a few minutes they had seen the interior of the craft and they stamped his passport. Eugene hurried to the taxi queue, the Glock pressing against the small of his back.

He gave the driver Javier Rastano's address and sat back, impatient at the slow pace now that he was on the ground. The Gulfstream was a marvel, flying at forty-seven thousand feet at almost Mach 1. The jet had shaved two hours off the time a Boeing 757 would have required, plus the private jet had left the minute he arrived at the Rochester airport. Flying coach would be difficult after that.

The taxi driver perked up and stepped on the gas when Eugene dropped two American one hundred dollar bills on the front seat and promised two more if he could make record time to Colonia Escalón. They flew past the shopping center and onto the smoothly paved streets of the ritzy neighborhood, barely slowing for a woman with a baby carriage. He checked his map and drove at break-neck speeds through the winding, hilly streets until he came to a wrought-iron gate with two serious looking guards.

"We are here, señor," he said. "Is good?"

Eugene handed him another two hundreds and jumped from the cab. He ran to the gate, ignoring the guns which were pointed at him. In the background he could hear the distinct sound of gunfire.

"Tell Javier Rastano that Eugene Escobar is here," he yelled. "Now! Call him now!"

Chapter Sixty-five

Javier's men had the shed surrounded and were ready for a full-out assault. The only reason they had yet to overrun the single defender was Rastano's reluctance to have a barrage of gunfire on his estate during the middle of the morning. The boxer didn't care about the noise, and fired indiscriminately at the guards when one of them came into view. Pedro had hit three and the remaining men were giving him a wide berth. Javier took the call from the front gate and waved at his men to back off.

"Let him in," he said, turning from the shed and walking back toward the pool. "No more shooting unless I give the order," he screamed.

Eugene was already crossing the patio when Javier reached the tree line on the far side of the grass. They met about half way and stood a few feet apart.

"Did you get it?" Javier asked.

"Where are my wife and daughter?"

"Safe, but not for long if you don't have the account number."

"I have it," Eugene said, watching the man's eyes glitter at the prospect of finally laying his hands on the billion dollar account.

Javier spoke softly and without any inkling of a threatening tone. "What is it?"

Eugene shook his head. "No way. Not until I see my family."

"And Pedro?" Javier asked.

Eugene studied the man's face and saw that he knew. "And Pedro."

Javier waved at one of his men. "Tell the boxer and the women that Eugenio is here. They are to come out and meet with us."

The man scurried off with the message and a minute later Eugene heard Pedro's voice yelling for him. He yelled back and a couple of minutes later Pedro, Julie and Shiara appeared from behind some trees. Pedro had the H & K at the ready and the women behind him. Julie and Shiara started running to Eugene when they saw him but Javier yelled for them to stop.

"No one moves until I get the code," he said when everyone had stopped moving and there was silence.

"What guarantee do we have that you'll let us go once you have the code?" Eugene asked.

"You have my word," Javier said.

"What's that worth?" Eugene said, staring at his wife and daughter; fifty feet away, but not yet out of harm's way. The Glock weighed heavy in his waistband and his hand itched to go for it and put two or three well placed slugs in Rastano before the guards could react.

"I told you I wouldn't hurt them and I didn't. Ask them."

Eugene looked their way and Julie nodded. "They treated us fine, Eugene."

Eugene stood on the grass, surrounded by armed guards with automatic weapons pointed at him, his wife and daughter and his friend. Finally he nodded and said, "All right, Javier, you win." He dug in his pocket and retrieved the paper that Pablo had written on. He handed it to Javier.

"Watch them," Javier said. "I'm going to make sure this is correct."

He disappeared into the house for the better part of ten minutes, then returned a blistering shade of red. "Nine hundred million dollars was transferred out to another account four hours ago. What would you know about that?"

"Let's call it my insurance policy. You get one hundred million dollars today. Two years from this date, you get another one hundred million. Another two years, another one hundred million until the entire nine hundred million has been repaid. If anything happens to me or any of my family, the transfers stop." Eugene stared at the Colombian. "You didn't think that I would just give you the entire amount on the spot, did you?"

Rastano had calmed, calculating the length of time to recover all the money, and the rate at which it was coming back in. A hundred million every two years was almost a million a week, and that was hard to argue with. He took a couple of deep breaths and asked, "How do I know you'll release the hundred million every second year?"

Eugene returned his stare, his blue eyes unblinking. "You have my word," he said.

A toucan cawed, but every other living creature in the garden held their collective breaths. There could be acceptance, or there could be a bloodbath. Javier finally cracked a smile and held out his hand. "All right, Eugenio Escobar, you have a deal."

They shook and Julie and Shiara ran across the grass and fell into Eugene's arms. He held them tighter than he'd ever held anything in his life. Teams streamed down his face as he kissed Julie and ran his hands through Shiara's hair. Pedro dropped his gun and walked calmly over to his friend. Eugene, with his arms still wrapped around both women, just shook his head at the sight of his friend and smiled.

Even one word would have been overkill.

SHELL GAME

JEFF BUICK

When NewPro Stock collapses, Taylor and her husband Alan lose millions, forcing them to sell their home and business. But they're not going down without a fight. They're determined to track down the elusive Edward Brand, the mastermind behind the enormous fraud….

Taylor and Alan are about to learn two hard facts: A man who doesn't want to be found can be extremely dangerous…and in the world of high-level scams absolutely nothing is what it seems. If they're going to pin Brand down and recover their money, they're going to need an ingenious—and very risky—plan of their own.

Dorchester Publishing Co., Inc.
P.O. Box 6640
Wayne, PA 19087-8640

___5846-4
$7.99 US/$9.99 CAN

Please add $2.50 for shipping and handling for the first book and $.75 for each additional book. NY and PA residents, add appropriate sales tax. No cash, stamps, or CODs. Canadian orders require an extra $2.00 for shipping and handling and must be paid in U.S. dollars. Prices and availability subject to change. **Payment must accompany all orders.**

Name: _____

Address: _____

City: _____ State: _____ Zip: _____

E-mail: _____

I have enclosed $_____ in payment for the checked book(s).

CHECK OUT OUR WEBSITE! www.dorchesterpub.com
_____ Please send me a free catalog.

PRETTY GIRL GONE

DAVID HOUSEWRIGHT

Mac McKenzie has had a lot of girlfriends. But only one went on to marry the governor of Minnesota. So how can Mac refuse when First Lady Lindsay Barrett tells him that someone has sent her an anonymous e-mail claiming to have evidence that Governor Jack Barrett killed his high school sweetheart.

As soon as Mac starts poking into Jack Barrett's past, he riles up a wide array of goons—including some political insiders who have big plans for Barrett and aren't above using kidnapping and murder to get their way. Mac has no choice but to keep digging for the facts…and hope he isn't digging his own grave.

Dorchester Publishing Co., Inc.
P.O. Box 6640 ___5847-2
Wayne, PA 19087-8640 $6.99 US/$8.99 CAN

Please add $2.50 for shipping and handling for the first book and $.75 for each additional book. NY and PA residents, add appropriate sales tax. No cash, stamps, or CODs. Canadian orders require $2.00 for shipping and handling and must be paid in U.S. dollars. Prices and availability subject to change. **Payment must accompany all orders.**

Name: _____

Address: _____

City: _____ State: _____ Zip: _____

E-mail: _____

I have enclosed $_____ in payment for the checked book(s).

CHECK OUT OUR WEBSITE! www.dorchesterpub.com
_____ Please send me a free catalog.

SUBSCRIBE NOW!

SAVE 50% OFF THE
NEWSSTAND PRICE

Celebrating 20 years as America's #1 hard rock music monthly, *Metal Edge* celebrates the hottest and coolest bands with bold photography, exclusive interviews and sizzling concert coverage.

☐ Start my 12-issue subscription to Metal Edge... Enclosed is my payment of $30.00.

SEETHER
POWERMAN 5000
BLACK STONE CHERRY
H.I.M. (HIM)
SILENT CIVILIAN
RISE AGAINST

HEAVY METAL MECCAS

CINDERELLA
POISON
BORO PESCH
DIRTY RIG
DEREK SHERINIAN

GIANT POSTERS!
SLAYER
STONE SOUR

EVANESSENCE

Name _____ (Please print)

Address _____ Apt. #

City _____ State _____ Zip _____ J6MOS.

PAYMENT ENCLOSED ☐   BILL ME ☐   Charge my VISA ☐ MASTERCARD ☐ DISCOVER ☐ AMERICAN EXPRESS ☐
(Check Or Money Order)

Make checks payable to Dorchester Media. Add $10.00 for Canadian & Foreign postage. (US Funds Only)

ACCT.# _____

Signature _____

Expiration _____

For Credit Card Orders Call 1-800-666-8783

PLEASE NOTE: Credit card payments for your subscription will appear on your statement as *Dorchester Media*, *not* as the magazine name.

Mail this coupon with check or credit card information to this address:

**Metal Edge
P.O. Box 5623
HARLAN, IOWA 51593-3123**

ATTENTION
BOOK LOVERS!

Can't get enough
of your favorite **HORROR**?

Call **1-800-481-9191** to:

— order books —
— receive a **FREE** catalog —
— join our book clubs to **SAVE 20%**! —

Open Mon.-Fri. 10 AM-9 PM EST

Visit
www.dorchesterpub.com
for special offers and inside
information on the authors you love.

 We accept Visa, MasterCard or Discover®.